THE HONEY TRAP

THE
HONEY TRAP

Clive Egleton

St. Martin's Minotaur
New York

THE HONEY TRAP. Copyright © 2000 by Clive Egleton. All rights reserved. Printed in the United States of America. No part of this book may be used or reproduced in any manner whatsoever without written permission except in the case of brief quotations embodied in critical articles or reviews. For information, address St. Martin's Press, 175 Fifth Avenue, New York, N.Y. 10010.

www.minotaurbooks.com

ISBN 0-312-26924-2

First published in Great Britain by Hodder and Stoughton, a division of Hodder Headline

First St. Martin's Minotaur Edition: March 2001

10 9 8 7 6 5 4 3 2 1

This book is for Bernard and Mary Lambert.

Chapter One

All Adam Zawadzki wanted was to be left in peace but the woman refused to listen to him and kept squeezing his right shoulder until he finally capitulated and opened both eyes. Still half asleep he gazed blankly at the illuminated sign four rows to his front before it dawned on him that everybody else in the business class had adjusted their seats and were now sitting bolt upright. After removing the blanket from around his legs and right shoulder, Zawadzki did the same, then fastened his seat belt.

His day had started at six o'clock, when he'd left the house in Putney to drive down to Gatwick where he had caught the British Airways flight to Dallas-Fort Worth. Because BA didn't fly to Costa Rica, he had cooled his heels in Dallas for over two hours waiting for American Airlines flight AA2165 to San José. It occurred to Zawadzki that by the time the plane landed at Juan Santamaria International Airport and he went on to his final destination, people back home would be getting up to face another working day.

He had never been to Costa Rica before and there had been no time to get a travel guide out of the library. As was not unusual in his line of business, he'd received scant warning that he was off to Central America. What he had been told about Costa Rica wouldn't have filled a page in a pocket diary. The most striking thing about the country was the fact that successive

I

governments had never found it necessary to maintain a standing army, largely because there had been no instances of civil unrest since 1949. Bananas and coffee were the two biggest earners for the economy, with tourism a close third. Instead of spring, summer, autumn and winter there were just two seasons, the wet and the dry, the latter normally starting in late December and lasting until April. On this night the weather was unusual for early March; after descending through the overcast, the plane's arrival at Juan Santamaria Airport was heralded with a tropical downpour.

The baggage of premier- and business-class travellers was always unloaded first but Zawadzki didn't need to wait for his at all. This was a short trip, four days at the outside, three if the Nicaraguan rep joined him in San José from Managua. Zawadzki calculated two shirts, a change of underwear, spare pairs of socks, pyjamas, a pair of cotton slacks and shaving tackle would be sufficient, and had packed the lot into his 'carry on' baggage.

As soon as the plane was positioned at its designated gate, Zawadzki undid the seat belt and retrieved his bag and executive briefcase from the overhead bin. Provided they didn't spend more than ninety days in the country, UK passport holders didn't need a visa to enter Costa Rica. Consequently the Immigration official barely glanced at Zawadzki's passport before waving him on. The same applied to the Customs officer, whose only concern was to make sure he had filled in the standard declaration form correctly.

Although Zawadzki knew the embassy had made a reservation for him at the Hotel Villa Tournon, he hadn't expected to be met at the airport. It had been arranged that he would telephone the First Secretary and Head of Chancery at home after he had checked into the hotel but apparently there had been a last-minute change of plan. While his name, printed on a piece of cardboard which the Costa Rican was holding across his chest, was incorrectly spelled, he had reason to assume the man was waiting for him. Underneath his own name was the legend, 'Luis, administrative assistant, British Embassy'.

'I believe you're looking for me,' Zawadzki said, approaching Luis.

The Costa Rican turned to face him. He was a small man, standing no more than five feet six, and slender with it. In appearance he was the epitome of Hollywood's image of the Latin American, dark, handsome, fine-boned, suave and a touch menacing, but not so threatening that women would pick up their skirts and run a mile from him.

'You are Mr Swatski?' Luis enquired politely.

'Yes. Actually it's Zawadzki but we won't make a fuss about it.'

'I don't understand what you are saying. My English . . . Please, my English is not so good.'

'My fault. Sometimes I speak much too quickly.' Zawadzki smiled. 'Do you know the way to the Hotel Villa Tournon?'

'The driver does, he is ready to leave now.'

The Costa Rican turned about and walked off. Momentarily taken aback by his brusque manner, Zawadzki was slow to follow Luis out of the arrivals hall. By the time he neared the automatic doors, the Costa Rican was waiting at the kerbside, one arm raised as if to hail a cab while sheltering from the rain under a small retractable umbrella. The crimson saloon which pulled up outside the entrance to the terminal had obviously rolled off a production line in Detroit not so very long ago. The car was, Zawadzki thought, a singularly inappropriate vehicle for the British Embassy. It certainly wasn't going to do anything for the export sales of Rover and Jaguar.

'A Cadillac Seville,' Luis told him. 'The embassy hires it from a limousine company in town,' he added as if reading Zawadzki's mind. 'Saves on maintenance and servicing.'

The chauffeur opened the boot from inside the Cadillac, the lid rearing up like a startled horse. Zawadzki dropped his travelling bag into the boot, but decided to hold on to his executive briefcase. 'I'm not supposed to let this out of my sight,' he said almost apologetically.

'It's a sensible precaution; you can't be too careful in San José.'

3

Luis closed the rear nearside door, then, instead of joining the driver in front, he walked round the back of the Cadillac and got in beside Adam Zawadzki. A split second before they moved off there was an audible click which suggested that the automatic transmission was acting up and needed looking at. Zawadzki knew different when he noticed the release catches had been retracted, thereby locking all four doors.

'We also take precautions,' Luis said casually. 'At night, the downtown area is not very nice. There are gangs of thieves on the prowl. A favourite trick is to wait at an intersection for a car like this Cadillac to be caught by the lights when they then wrench the doors open and rob the occupants at knifepoint.'

Zawadzki frowned. What Luis had just told him painted a far grimmer picture than the one formed from the briefing at the Foreign and Commonwealth Office. True, he had been advised to avoid Avenida 2 and the Parque Central after dark because of pickpockets, but nothing had been said about gangs of violent criminals operating in the area. In fact he had been led to believe that Costa Rica was one of the safest countries in Latin America. The chauffeur, however, had acted as if they were in imminent danger even though Juan Santamaria Airport was a good ten miles from the centre of town. Zawadzki couldn't explain why the action taken by the driver should have made him feel nervous but it had.

'How far is the hotel from the British Embassy?' he asked, trying to sound casual.

'No more than three kilometres.'

Say a couple of miles to be on the safe side plus ten more from the airport. Unable to see the speedometer from where he was sitting, Zawadzki estimated they were doing between thirty-five and forty miles an hour and had been on the move for approximately five minutes. That meant the journey would take about half an hour, allowing for speed restrictions in San José itself.

'I reckon we should be there by nine fifty,' Zawadzki said, voicing his thoughts.

'Where?'

'The hotel, Luis. Where else?'

'There are roadworks on the Avenida Central. We have to go the long way round.'

The rain suddenly stopped as if somebody upstairs had turned off the tap. Way over in the distance, lightning cleaved the black night sky, heralding the approach of another storm.

As in a good many capital cities, the outskirts of San José were pretty uninspiring. There were no buildings higher than one storey in the residential area, and many of the bungalows, sitting back from the road in small isolated and haphazard groups among the trees, had roofs of corrugated iron. The side streets were badly lit and unnamed as far as Zawadzki could tell.

'I'm curious, Luis,' he said. 'Just how does a stranger find his way around San José?'

'It's not difficult. The city is laid out on a grid like Manhattan in New York.'

As Luis explained it, the streets running east to west were avenidas whilst those from north to south were called calles. North of Central Avenue the avenidas were odd numbered while those to the south were even. The north-south Calle Central ran through the heart of the downtown area. Working on the same principle as the avenidas, those calles to the east were numbered 1, 3, 5, and on up to 23 whereas to the west the even numbers ran from 2 to 20.

'Whenever you ask for directions,' Luis continued, 'you will be told to go so many blocks east or west followed by so many north or south. Most times the direction will be linked to a landmark like the Opera House.'

Zawadzki didn't get the chance to see the Opera House or any other well-known landmark. Before he knew what was happening, the driver had turned off the main road into a dark, narrow side street.

'What's going on, Luis? Why have we left the highway?' Zawadzki asked.

'We have to cross the river. The Villa Tournon is the other side of the Rio Torres.'

'I thought you said the hotel was near the centre of town?'

'It is.'

'Well, it seems to me we're still in the outskirts of San José.'

'There are roadworks ahead.'

'I haven't seen any warning signs.'

'No matter,' Luis told him. 'We know where we are.'

The road they were on was not only badly lit, it was also chock-full of potholes. Furthermore it was obvious to Zawadzki that they were leaving the city behind them to head out into the country.

'Pull up,' Zawadzki said forcefully.

'I no understand what you say.'

Luis was mocking him. There had been nothing wrong with his command of English before; now he was acting as if he was incapable of stringing more than three words together. Zawadzki leaned over the seat and punched the driver on the shoulder.

'Stop the damned car,' he roared.

'You will sit down,' Luis told him.

'Who the bloody hell do you think you're talking to?'

'A fool,' the Costa Rican said, and produced a .22 calibre revolver.

Zawadzki stared at the handgun in disbelief. This couldn't be happening to him. For God's sake he was a Queen's Messenger and entitled to diplomatic protection.

But it was. He felt the pain at first, then heard the gunshot and finally caught a whiff of burned cordite. Falling back into his seat, he looked down at his left foot and saw blood oozing from the shoe. He tried to wiggle his toes and cried out in agony; moments later he was in deep shock, chilled to the bone and trembling like an autumn leaf in the wind. A grey mist swirled in front of his eyes and there was this curious and frightening sensation of floating weightless in space.

By the time he recovered consciousness the road had become an earthen track that ran arrow straight through open grassland. There was no sign of habitation, or so Zawadzki believed until the headlights of the Cadillac picked out a large timbered shed with a corrugated iron roof.

The track ended at a parking area directly in front of the shed where a Range Rover was drawn up facing the way they had come. The headlights also revealed that the building was in a bad state of repair, which led Zawadzki to conclude that it had been abandoned some time ago.

The Costa Rican driver parked alongside the Range Rover and switched off the engine and main beams. As he did so, a figure emerged from the barn-like structure and moved purposefully towards the Cadillac. Broad across the shoulders, he had a barrel for a chest and was bow-legged as if he had had rickets when a child. Zawadzki thought the newcomer was about as prepossessing as an orang-utan.

'Get out of the car, Mr Zawadzki. The Colonel is anxious to meet you,' Luis said, and jabbed him in the ribs with the revolver.

The driver tripped the central locking. Urged on by Luis, Zawadzki opened the nearside door, stretched out his right leg and, putting his full weight on the one limb, he eased himself out of the Cadillac and straightened up. He could only move forward by hopping on his right foot, which didn't suit his kidnappers. He had taken the equivalent of three paces when the orang-utan made his displeasure known by sinking a fist into his stomach hard enough to dump him on the ground. The dizziness returned but this time the Costa Ricans didn't give him a chance to recover. While he was still winded and barely conscious, he was yanked to his feet and marched into the shed on the double. The top of his head felt as if it was lifting off every time his wounded foot touched the ground.

The shed was illuminated by a single pressure lamp, suspended from one of the rafters. Beyond the pool of light from the lamp, Zawadzki could see a wood-burning stove with a metal chimney stack that was red hot at the base. The Colonel was watching him from the shadows. He was sitting on some

7

sort of chair, his legs outstretched and crossed at the ankles, the only part of him that was clearly visible.

'Good evening, Mr Zawadzki,' he said in a wheezy voice which suggested he was a heavy smoker. 'I am Colonel Herrara. I hope you will be sensible and not give us any trouble.'

'He already has,' Luis told him. 'Mr Zawadzki attempted to escape and I had to shoot him in the foot.'

'Well, that was very foolish of him but it's too late now for regrets. Let's see the contents of his dispatch case.'

'The key,' Luis demanded, and nudged Zawadzki in the ribs.

'I'm a Queen's Messenger—' Zawadzki began.

'Of course you are,' Herrara said. 'That's why I arranged for Luis and his friend to meet you at the airport. Unless you want to be shot in the other foot, I suggest you give him the key.'

Zawadzki didn't hesitate. When the odds against him were four to one there could only be one outcome and he had no desire to become a dead hero. Loosening his tie, he undid the top button of the shirt, then reached inside the collar and fished out the long thin chain to which the key was attached. Before he could take it off, Luis grabbed hold of the chain and yanked it over his head.

Zawadzki hadn't the faintest idea what the Costa Ricans expected to find in the briefcase but their disappointment and anger was only too evident. It showed in the way the driver unzipped his overnight bag and emptied the contents on to the earthen floor before slashing the lining with a flick knife.

'All right, Major,' Herrara said, 'where have you hidden it?'

Zawadzki clenched both hands, digging the fingernails into the palms. How the hell did this man in the shadows know that he had been an army officer? Back home you could get a copy of Whitaker's Almanack out of the public library, look up the Foreign and Commonwealth Office in the index and you'd find the names and the former service ranks of all thirty-three Queen's Messengers. But in Costa Rica? He didn't think so, and concluded that somebody must have betrayed him.

'Loyalty and devotion to duty are two fine qualities,' Herrara said philosophically. 'No doubt you learned that as a young officer in the Duke of Wellington's Regiment but no one would expect you to lay down your life for a scrap of paper.'

'What scrap of paper?'

'Now you're being stupid, Adam.'

Adam. Was there anything the Costa Rican didn't know about him? His date and place of birth, for instance?

'Well, Adam?'

'The only documents I have were in that briefcase,' he said, and wished his voice were steadier.

Herrara rattled off something in Spanish too swiftly for Zawadzki to catch more than one word in three. It didn't matter, he found out soon enough what the Costa Rican had in mind for him. Before Zawadzki could raise a hand to defend himself, the orang-utan had handcuffed both wrists behind his back. While the other two held him, the driver pulled off his shoes, then removed his clothing with the aid of a switch blade until he was stark naked but for the socks. They then lashed his ankles together with a length of rope, threw the loose end over one of the transverse beams and hung him upside down, his head only a few inches clear of the ground.

They began to beat him systematically about the legs, buttocks and thighs with bamboo canes an inch or more in diameter – or so Herrara informed him. And always the same question repeated over and over again. What had he done with the memorandum?

They were going to kill him because he couldn't answer the question and they refused to believe he didn't know what the Colonel was talking about. His only hope of surviving the ordeal lay in stringing them along in the hope that the Embassy would alert the police when the First Secretary discovered he hadn't arrived at the Hotel Villa Tournon.

It wasn't difficult to persuade the Costa Ricans that they had broken him; the many abrasions on his body and the way he screamed every time the skin was broken was enough to still any

9

doubts that he was faking it. His story, however, was not so readily accepted.

'Let me understand this,' Herrara said. 'You gave the paper to the senior member of the cabin staff and asked him to leave it with the American Airlines desk where it would be collected later tonight by Mr Paul Younghusband, the First Secretary at the British Embassy?'

'Yes.'

'Liar.'

Zawadzki heard the swish of the bamboo cane, then screamed in agony as it flayed his back and opened yet another cut.

'Why wasn't the paper in the diplomatic bag?'

'It wasn't an accountable document,' Zawadzki told him, improvising. 'At least Whitehall didn't want it accounted for.'

'Liar.' Herrara spat it out and the cane drew more blood, this time from the fleshy part of the right arm above the elbow.

'You asked me what I had done with the paper,' Zawadzki groaned, 'and I have just told you.'

'And I tell you we won't find it at the American Airlines desk.'

'You're so right, Colonel. Mr Younghusband will have beaten you to it unless your people get a move on.'

There was an agonising silence which seemed to last for all eternity before Herrara finally took the bait and sent Luis plus the driver hurrying towards the vehicles parked outside the shed. A few minutes later Zawadzki heard them drive away. Given a huge slice of luck, Luis might make such a nuisance of himself that the staff on the American Airlines desk sent for the police. It was, he had to admit, one hell of a long shot.

A ribbon of blood from the bullet wound in his left foot ran down the leg, meandered across his stomach and chest to drip on to the earthen floor. Time had little meaning for Zawadzki as he drifted in and out of consciousness. He was dimly aware of the orang-utan raking ash from the wood burning stove before stoking it up again with more logs. All too soon he heard the

Cadillac return; then the screaming and shouting began and he prayed when the end came it would not be unbearably painful. But he knew God wasn't listening when they mutilated his buttocks with a red-hot branding iron.

Chapter Two

Except for his socks the dead man had been stripped naked before he had been suspended from a beam by the ankles. The colour photographs showed that his calves, thighs, buttocks, and lumbar region had been severely beaten, almost certainly with the inch-thick bamboo canes lying on the earthen floor directly below his head. The men who'd killed him had then inflicted third-degree burns on the upper arms, chest, stomach and feet with what appeared to be a steel poker. This, or something very similar, had subsequently been inserted in his rectum and driven home until it was buried deep in his intestines.

Ashton wasn't squeamish. During the Falklands campaign and earlier on the streets of Belfast while serving with the army's Special Patrol Unit, he had seen things which could turn a man's stomach inside out but this was something else. The injuries and manner of the victim's death sickened Ashton.

'Who was this man?' he asked, looking up from the colour photographs at Roger Benton, the Assistant Director in charge of the Pacific Basin and Rest of the World Department.

'Adam Zawadzki.' Benton cleared his throat. 'He was a Queen's Messenger, joined the Foreign and Commonwealth Office after retiring from the regular army where he had been a major in the Duke of Wellington's Regiment. Zawadzki was on his way to see Paul Younghusband at the British Embassy in San José.'

'So why is the Secret Intelligence Service interested, Roger? We don't have a Head of Station in Costa Rica.'

'Give him a chance and he'll tell you, Peter. You're so impatient.'

Ashton turned to face Jill Sheridan at the head of the table.

'That's rich coming from you,' he said.

No one had been more impatient for success then Jill. Seven years ago she and Ashton had been sharing a flat in Surbiton and planning to spend the rest of their lives together. Then Jill, who was in the fast lane, had been chosen to run intelligence operations in the Arab Emirates and she had decided she was not ready to give up a promising career for a life of domesticity. In making her choice, she had in fact done Ashton a favour; had they still been engaged, he would never have taken up with Harriet and that would have been his misfortune.

'Let's get on with the business in hand,' Jill said coldly. 'We've got better things to do than bandy words with one another.'

'Quite so.' Benton cleared his throat for the second time, then said, 'We're interested in Adam Zawadzki because he was carrying a Top Secret memorandum from our Director General. The secure briefcase he had signed for was found at the scene of the crime; needless to say the memorandum and certain Foreign Office papers were missing.'

'Am I allowed to know the subject of our memorandum?' Ashton enquired.

'It was Codeword material,' Benton told him.

Allocating a codeword to a classified document was a means of ensuring that only those intelligence officers with a 'need to know' could see it. This meant that although cleared for constant access to Top Secret, Ashton couldn't even send for the relevant file since his name did not appear on the approved list.

14

'Tell him,' Jill said tersely. 'There's no need for secrecy now that the document has obviously been compromised.'

'We are exploring the possibility of establishing an operational base for an SAS detachment on the west coast of Costa Rica in the area of Punta Banco near the Panamanian border. The task of the SAS is to wage war on the Colombian drug barons.'

'I wouldn't have thought Costa Rica would make an ideal jumping-off point. I mean, it must be all of six hundred miles from Colombia, which is well beyond the range of our helicopters.'

'I didn't say we were planning to insert the SAS by chopper.'

'That's all water under the bridge now,' Jill said. 'The SAS won't be going anywhere near Costa Rica. We need to focus on what happened to Adam Zawadzki. He was a last-minute substitute for Martin Edmunds, who had suddenly gone down with the flu. Adam had less than eighteen hours' notice, yet according to the local police the opposition were waiting for him at the airport. One of the plainclothes security men on duty in the arrival/departure hall recalled seeing a man resembling Adam's description approach a Costa Rican who was holding up some sort of notice for all to see. They had a brief conversation, then left the terminal building more or less together.'

That had been the last time anybody had seen Zawadzki alive. When he still hadn't checked into the Hotel Villa Tournon a good two hours after American Airlines flight AA2165 from Dallas-Fort Worth had landed at Juan Santamaria International Airport, Younghusband had notified the appropriate Costa Rican authorities. The police had found Zawadzki's body forty-eight hours later in an abandoned packing shed that had originally belonged to the Caldera Banana Corporation.

'They're American-owned,' Benton said, piping up, and got a withering look from Jill Sheridan for interrupting her.

'I doubt the Americans kidnapped Zawadzki, Roger,' she

told him bitingly, rubbing salt into the wound. 'And I'm equally sure the men who murdered him were not interested in the memorandum you'd written.'

Ashton looked at the photographs again and decided Jill was probably right. The lock on the security briefcase hadn't been forced and in the desperate situation Zawadzki had been confronted with, Ashton knew that he personally would have surrendered the key long before they started to burn him. No, the killers had been after something which Zawadzki didn't have and they had refused to believe him. That was why they had tortured and then murdered him in a blind rage.

'Your job is to investigate Adam Zawadzki and Martin Edmunds.'

Ashton suddenly realised that Jill's instructions were directed at him.

'Me?' he said blankly.

'Yes. Why are you so surprised, Peter? I'm not asking you to do something which doesn't fall within your remit as the Grade I Intelligence Officer, General Duties.'

'Oh yes? What about the Foreign and Commonwealth Office? The Corps of Queen's Messengers is very much under their umbrella.'

'Don't worry about the Foreign Office.'

Jill Sheridan hadn't got where she was today without taking chances and capitalising on her phenomenal luck. Who else but Jill could have prospered after asking to be relieved of her Intelligence appointment in Bahrain on the grounds that the Arabs refused to deal with a woman? Posted back to London she had been assigned to the Persian Desk, a sideways move which would have spelled the end of the road for anybody else. Victor Hazelwood's predecessor as Director General had, however, picked Jill to run the Mid East Department with the result that at the age of thirty-six she had become the newest, youngest, and easily the most attractive assistant director. She also happened to be the brightest. Like most chancers, Jill made the odd mistake now and again but somebody else always paid for the errors of judgement.

Ashton thought there would be no prizes for guessing who would be in the firing line on this occasion should anything go wrong.

'What about Victor?' he asked. 'Does he know about this investigation?'

'He's happy to leave the day-to-day running of The Firm to me in his absence.'

In common with thousands of others, Victor had been attacked by a particularly virulent strain of flu and had been forced to take to his bed. That he should be *hors de combat* at a time when Jill was still running the Mid East Department while waiting to be confirmed as the new Deputy DG hadn't thrown her one bit. According to Hazelwood's PA, Jill had chaired the daily meeting of Heads of Departments, commonly known as morning prayers, as if she had been doing it all her life.

'Happy now, Peter?'

'Ecstatic.'

'Good.' Jill pushed her chair back and stood up. She was wearing a black, single-button jacket over a matching singlet and a pencil-slim skirt with a hemline a couple of inches above the knee, an outfit which, like the rest of her wardrobe, was intended to draw attention to her figure.

'You'll find the files on Adam Zawadzki and Martin Edmunds waiting for you at Matthew Parker Street,' she added.

'The Foreign Office is willing to let me read them?'

'But of course. I'm not without influence,' Jill said, and started to leave the conference room.

It was well known that Jill had friends in high places, amongst whom was Robin Urquhart, the senior of four Deputy Under Secretaries at the Foreign and Commonwealth Office. Except that from what Ashton had heard, Urquhart was a good deal more than a friend.

17

'Oh, one last point.' Jill paused in the doorway and turned about. 'First, last and always, you report to me, not Victor. Is that clear, Peter?'

'Crystal,' he said.

'Lucky old you,' Benton drawled when he was satisfied Jill couldn't hear him.

The security department which was responsible for the positive vetting of Her Majesty's Diplomatic Corps was located in a four-storey Edwardian house fronted by an impressive wrought-iron gate and railings. The fact that the postal address was number 4 Central Buildings was something of a letdown. Matthew Parker Street itself was situated in a quiet backwater off Storey's Gate, a bare ten-minute walk from Downing Street.

Ashton showed his identity card to the clerk on duty in the reception office, then filled out a visitor's pass which required him to state his name, the department he represented, and the nature of his business. In the appropriate boxes Ashton indicated he was representing himself and that the nature of his visit was to liaise with the Chief Archivist. After comparing his signature with the one on the identity card, the clerk stamped the visitor's pass showing the date and time Ashton had entered 4 Central Buildings.

The Chief Archivist and his clerical officers occupied two large offices on the ground floor next to the post room. Ashton didn't go near them; instead he rode the ancient lift up to the second floor and reported to Mrs Shirley Isles, Head of the Foreign and Commonwealth Security Department.

'I don't think we've met before, have we?' she said, and shook hands with him.

'No, I haven't had the pleasure until now,' Ashton told her.

He did, however, know a great deal about Shirley Isles. She had joined the department from MI5, the Security Service, where she had been responsible for the physical protection of government buildings nationwide. Aged fifty-two, she was the complete antithesis of Jill Sheridan. Designer labels didn't interest her − she bought her clothes at Marks & Spencer − but then if your husband was a victim of Alzheimer's and you were the only breadwinner and your daughter was still at medical school, an outfit by Calvin Klein didn't figure on your list of priorities. Shirley Isles didn't have an influential friend who could give her a helping hand; she had climbed the ladder on her own merit. Furthermore, according to Ashton's source, she was liked and respected by her peers and subordinates, which couldn't be said of Jill Sheridan.

'I have the papers your Deputy DG called for,' Isles told him. 'However, I'm afraid you can't take them away; the files have to be read on the premises.'

'That's understood.'

'My secretary is off sick so I thought you could use her office.'

'Thank you.'

'My pleasure,' Isles said, and handed him the relevant files before opening the communicating door. 'I hope you find whatever it is you're looking for,' she added.

The security file pertaining to Adam Zawadzki included the one that had been opened on him by the army when he had been positively vetted for the first time prior to attending the Staff College, Camberley. He was born in Richmond, York-shire, on 8 January 1942. His father, who had married a local girl, had been a pilot in 197 Polish Squadron of RAF Bomber Command stationed at Dishforth. After the war the family had moved to York where his father had found employment as a booking clerk with British Rail while attempting to qualify as a solicitor in his spare time. There was nothing in the subject interview to indicate whether or not he had succeeded but Adam had attended St Peter's as a day boy and even in the 1950s the fees would have been beyond the means of most working people.

A moderately bright pupil, Adam Zawadzki had collected three respectable A level grades in English, History and Politics.

His housemaster had told the interviewing officer that in his final two years at school he had captained the hockey First XI and had played in a variety of positions for the Second XV but had never been quite good enough to be selected for the first team. He had also been an enthusiastic member of the Combined Cadet Force which, in fact, had influenced him in his choice of a career. As soon as the A level results were published he had attended the Regular Commissions Board at Westbury and passed a series of tests designed to assess his qualities of leadership. After two years at Sandhurst, he had been commissioned into the Duke of Wellington's Regiment

As he worked through the file, Ashton made a note of all the referees and senior officers who had reported on Zawadzki's fitness to have constant access to Top Secret material. Not one had said anything detrimental about him. He had displayed no homosexual inclinations, or any other adverse character traits. He was a non-smoker, drank only in moderation, and lived within his means. That such a paragon of virtue should have been married and divorced twice seemed an aberration, except that in both cases he had been the innocent party.

Martin Edmunds was born in 1934, eight years before Adam Zawadzki. As an eighteen-year-old National Serviceman in the Royal Navy he had been on active service with the light fleet carrier HMS *Glory* off North Korea. Following his release, he had joined the Surrey Constabulary and pounded a beat in Woking for the next three years when he had then transferred to the colonial police. Edmunds had arrived in Kenya in time to take part in the final stages of the campaign against the Mau Mau.

Eighteen months after Kenya had become an independent republic, a niche had been found for him within the ranks of the Hong Kong Police Force. In 1989 Edmunds had retired in the rank of chief superintendent and had immediately been accepted by the Queen's Messenger Service on the strong recommendation of His Excellency the Governor of Hong Kong. He was still married to the same woman he'd wed back in 1962.

Ashton slipped the notes he'd made into the inside pocket of his jacket, packed up the files and returned them to Shirley Isles.

'Were they of any help?' she asked.

'Well, Edmunds comes across as whiter than white and two failed marriages is the only grey area in Zawadzki's profile, at least on paper.'

'Are you saying his file is incomplete?'

'I'm a little uneasy about the clearance the army gave him before he went to the staff college in 1971. According to Adam his father had no relatives living in Poland. Unfortunately Jan Zawadzki was killed in 1969 when his car was involved in a head-on collision with a motor coach so he couldn't be inter-viewed.'

However, Mrs Zawadzki had been adamant that in all the years they had been married her husband had never received so much as a postcard from anyone in Poland. She had also told the investigating officer that her husband's family had lived in Warsaw and had been killed in an air raid on either the first or second of September 1939. Jan Zawadzki, who had been an NCO pilot in the Polish Air Force, had been mobilised on 29 August and sent to join his squadron at Łódź.

'Jan Zawadzki wasn't taken prisoner,' Ashton continued. 'He and a bunch of other pilots escaped to Romania. They were interned for a couple of months, then released and helped on their way to France by the Romanian authorities.'

'I think you've lost me.'

'I'm just wondering how Jan learned that his parents and sister had been killed on the outbreak of war. By all accounts things had been pretty chaotic with telephone lines down all over the place.'

'Tell me something, Mr Ashton. If Jan Zawadzki had lied about his family, would that have any bearing on what happened to his son in Costa Rica?'

'No, it wouldn't. On the other hand we've only got Adam Zawadzki's word for what happened to his grandparents and aunt.'

'And if he had been less than honest about his Polish connections, you think he may have lied about other aspects of his life?'

'It's possible.'

'Adam's mother supported his story.'

'Well, she would, wouldn't she? I think Adam was smart enough to realise he might be denied a PV clearance if the full story came out. This was 1971, the height of the Cold War, and he badly wanted to go to the staff college.'

'Well, you will have a hard time proving it. Mrs Zawadzki died eighteen months ago.'

'I don't remember seeing that in the file.'

'I read the file and came to pretty much the same conclusion as you. So I had a word with the Superintendent Officer in charge of the Queen's Messenger Service. That's how I learned about the mother.' Shirley Isles wrote something on a memo pad, then ripped off the top sheet and handed it to Ashton. 'Here's something else that isn't on the file and should have been. Adam Zawadzki was cohabiting with a Ms Laura Greenwood.'

Bernard H. Backhouse was forty-six, thin as a rake and had to duck his head every time he entered a room. His feet were correspondingly large. Given these physical characteristics it was small wonder that he was one of the best-known American expats in San José. He had come south in 1974, a couple of months after getting out of the army. Most people visiting Central America found it quicker and cheaper to travel by air, others thought going by bus was more fun. Backhouse had chosen to drive himself and had set off from Brownsville, Texas in a reconditioned World War Two Jeep. On the Mexican border, Brownsville happened to be the nearest American town to San José some 2500 miles away but, at the time Backhouse had crossed the Rio Grande into Matomoros, Costa Rica hadn't been on his itinerary.

Anybody using the Carretera Interamericana or any of the major side roads soon learned that it was advisable not to drive at night. The highways were narrow, potholed, badly lit and you could look in vain for a white centre line painted on the asphalt surface. Although the American Automobile Association sold insurance for driving in Mexico, their brokers were not prepared to extend the cover to the Central American Republics. Consequently, Backhouse had had to take out a policy with a branch of Sandborn's in McAllen, fifty-six miles west of Brownsville.

Backhouse had driven through Mexico and then on to Guatemala, Honduras and Nicaragua. Although his papers and travel documents had been in order, there had been time-consuming bureaucratic delays at every crossing point. But, with no particular destination in mind, Backhouse hadn't been in a hurry and the unnecessary hold-ups hadn't bothered him one bit. If the guidebook to Central America indicated there was a spectacular ruin or an extinct volcano that was worth a diversion, he would travel miles out of his way to see it. To drive on down to the Panama Canal had been a typical spur-of-the-moment decision.

The extended vacation, however, had ended prematurely on the outskirts of San José when a banana truck had sideswiped him off the road. The Jeep had rolled over into a concrete storm drain with the result that the radiator had been driven into the engine, both front shock absorbers had been snapped off and the chassis had been bent hopelessly out of line. An unconscious Backhouse had been pulled out of the wreck with several cracked ribs, a broken leg and a fractured pelvis. When he'd woken up in the San Juan de Dios Hospital, one of the interns had told him he was lucky to be alive. When he got to know nurse Juanita Peralta, Backhouse figured the traffic accident was the best thing that had ever happened to him.

His American passport had allowed him to spend up to ninety days in Costa Rica. At the end of this time he had hopped a bus to Managua in Nicaragua, returning seventy-two hours later for another three months' stay, which was perfectly legal. To support himself while courting Juanita he'd taken a whole series of menial jobs from washing dishes to waiting on tables in restaurants and hotels around the town. To please her parents Backhouse had taken instruction to become a Catholic but even so he'd had a hard time persuading Juanita's father that he was a suitable match for his favourite daughter.

After they were married, Backhouse had twice gone back home, the first time in 1978 to attend the funeral of his father, who'd suffered a massive coronary, and again nine months later when his mother died of cancer. Using the money inherited from them, he had gone into business on his own account, leasing suitable premises to open a car and body repair shop. Over the next fifteen years, Backhouse had established the biggest self-drive rental agency in San José; with a great deal of help from certain friends back home in Virginia, he had also secured the Ford dealership for the whole of Costa Rica. That morning when he walked into his Ford showroom on the Avenida Central he found Jorge Ortego, airport manager at Juan Santamaria, waiting for him.

'Come to buy a new car, Jorge?' he asked cheerfully.

'I'm thinking about it,' Ortego told him. 'Depends how much you give me for my present model.'

'I think we can arrange something that will make us both happy. Let's talk about it in my office.'

When Ortego left the showroom twenty minutes later he was clutching glossy brochures for the Ford Contour and Crown Victoria. He also had thirty thousand more colones in his pocket than when he'd entered. This sum, equivalent to two hundred US dollars, was a reward for information concerning the movements of Osvaldo Herrara, a Cuban national who had departed from Juan Santamaria Airport on Aeronica flight 141 to Managua on Thursday, 7 March. Checking with Immigration, Ortego's suspicions had been aroused when he had learned that Herrara had arrived from Nicaragua by bus, crossing the border at Peñas Blancas.

Backhouse considered the thirty thousand colones had been money well spent, and knew there would be no comebacks from the CIA. Osvaldo Herrara was a full colonel and deputy chief of Fidel Castro's intelligence bureau.

Chapter Three

Jill Sheridan was busy conferring with the art curator from the Property Services Agency when Ashton returned to Vauxhall Cross. As the Director General, Hazelwood was the equivalent of a permanent under secretary and as such had been allowed to choose up to three paintings for his office from the list of original oils and watercolours held by the Property Services Agency. The same privilege was extended to the Deputy DG.

It was, Ashton thought, typical of Victor Hazelwood that instead of a Canaletto, Utrillo or Turner, he should have selected a signed print of Terence Cuneo's *The Bridge at Arnhem*. Victor, it had to be said, had a soft spot for the armed forces, and the other two services were represented by a picture showing a battered-looking corvette on a storm-tossed Atlantic entitled *Convoy Escort*, and *Enemy Coast Ahead*, which depicted a vic of three Wellington bombers on a moonlit night approaching a smudge of land on the horizon. With Jill there were grounds for thinking her taste was heavily influenced by the monetary value attached to the painting. It would explain why she had gone for an early L. S. Lowry before the matchstick people and northern industrial scenes had become all the rage. The same applied to the Jackson Pollock and Andy Warhol she had selected from the PSA catalogue.

'What do you think, Peter?' she asked after announcing her choice.

Privately Ashton thought she was being a little premature. Her promotion to Deputy DG was still awaiting confirmation but she never lacked confidence or self-belief.

'The paintings certainly make a statement,' he said drily.

'Good, I'm glad we agree.' Jill returned the catalogue to the art curator with the warmest of smiles that practically had him waggling his bottom like an excited puppy. 'Thank you, Edwin,' she said graciously. 'You've been a great help to me and I did so appreciate your advice.'

'It was a pleasure,' the art curator said, and moved towards the door. Jill's fixed smile died the moment he left the office.

'What a tiresome little man,' she muttered.

'Not your cup of tea.'

'Definitely not. What did the files tell you?'

'Martin Edmunds doesn't appear to have any skeletons in the closet. I'm not so sure about Zawadzki.'

Ashton told her about the two failed marriages and the latest girlfriend with whom Zawadzki had been cohabiting. He also conveyed his misgivings about the Polish side of the family.

'But apart from that he has led a blameless life,' Jill said, cutting him short.

'Yes.'

'So what's your recommendation, Peter?'

'We could call it a day and drop the whole thing or we could try digging a little deeper.'

'How?'

'I think we should see Zawadzki's annual confidential reports from the time he graduated from the Staff College to the date of his retirement. Ninety to ninety-five per cent of officers who go to Camberley end their careers a lot higher than major and I'd like to know why he didn't. The confidential reports will be held by the Military Secretary's Branch. All we have to do is ask the army's Directorate of Security to get them for us. Shouldn't take more than a couple of days or so.'

'Hold it a moment, Peter. Aren't those senior officers who

28

initiated the confidential reports going to be the same people who were interviewed when Zawadzki was being vetted?'

'Probably, but it's one thing to say there's no reason why he shouldn't have constant access to Top Secret, quite another to recommend him for promotion to lieutenant-colonel. Maybe he reckoned he'd been hard done by and was nursing a grudge.'

'When did he leave the army?'

'In 1989. He was then aged forty-seven and would have known that his last chance of promotion to lieutenant-colonel had passed him by.'

'And from the army, he went straight into the Corps of Queen's Messengers?'

'Yes.'

'His security status,' Jill said, 'how many times was it reviewed?'

'Three, following the initial clearance in 1971.'

A positive vetting clearance was reviewed every five years, which meant that Zawadzki had been looked at again in '76, '81, and '86. However, a subject interview was only conducted every ten years. As a result, Zawadzki hadn't been grilled since 1981, when he was still in the army. This was probably why the Security Department of the Foreign and Commonwealth Office had interviewed him at length in 1989, even though the '86 clearance was still good for another two years.

'Leaving the confidential reports aside,' Jill said quietly, 'what's your other proposal?'

'Anybody who is being vetted nominates his own referees, some of whom will be interviewed. The remainder will be asked to complete a standard pro forma.'

'So?'

'So I think we should look for some really neutral referees and see what they have to say about Adam Zawadzki.'

'Sounds a tall order to me, Peter. What exactly does it entail?'

Jill was right, it would be a time-consuming job. The Military Secretary would have little difficulty in listing the various staff appointments Zawadzki had held; discovering

29

the names and present whereabouts of those officers who had served alongside him would involve a great deal more work. Generally speaking, the bigger the headquarters or establishment, the greater the task. There was bound to be a number of overlaps too – officers who had completed their tours of duty on the staff and had been replaced during Zawadzki's time. The appropriate personnel branch would be faced with the same herculean task when called upon to provide a similar list to cover those periods when he had been serving with the 1st Battalion, the Duke of Wellington's Regiment.

Jill Sheridan had started to frown before Ashton was halfway through; by the time he was drawing to a close, her eyebrows met in a straight line.

'That's not the end of it,' he said. 'Most of Zawadzki's contemporaries will also have left the army by now. To discover their present whereabouts, we'd have to go to Paymaster Limited at Crawley, and that's assuming every man jack is in receipt of an Armed Forces pension.'

'Are you really sure of your facts?'

Ashton nodded. 'I was in charge of the Security Vetting and Technical Services Division for a time. Remember?'

'And are you still harbouring a grudge?' Jill asked with a knowing smile.

Back in the days when the SIS had occupied Century House Ashton had got very close to a certain lieutenant-colonel in Russian Military Intelligence, the Glavnoye Razvedyvatelnoye Upravleniye or GRU for short. Although the operation had been successful there were those, amongst them the DG himself, who thought Ashton had become slightly contaminated by the KGB in the process. He had therefore been transferred to Security Vetting and Technical Services at Benbow House over in Southwark where he did not have constant access to Top Secret and codeword material.

'At first I thought I had a raw deal,' Ashton told her. 'Then I met my new assistant and the chip on my shoulder disappeared.'

'Ah yes, the delectable Harriet Egan, as she was in those days.'

30

Ashton let it pass. Jill could have been referring to his wife's maiden name or else inferring that Harriet had lost some of her looks since marrying him. When it came to the barbed, double-edged comment, Jill was in a class on her own.

'I can't help feeling that everything we have done so far has been a complete waste of time.'

Ashton frowned. 'What prompted that thought?' he asked.

'Zawadzki had never been to Costa Rica before. Like I told you, he was a last-minute substitute for Edmunds.'

'Suppose he was involved in drug trafficking? A Queen's Messenger would make an ideal mule. Diplomatic privilege and all that; there's no way Customs would examine his baggage. And let's face it, Zawadzki could have phoned his contact to let him know the venue had been changed the night before he left.'

'You think he could have been working for one of the Colombian drug barons?'

'It's not impossible.'

'Oh yes it is. Zawadzki didn't work the Latin American beat; the Middle East and North Africa was his stamping ground.'

'When did you learn that?'

'I had a word with the Superintendent of the Queen's Messenger Service while you were at Matthew Parker Street.' The frown returned, deep enough this time to wrinkle her forehead. 'The truth is I'm reluctant to saddle the army with a monumental task on the strength of the information we've got. On the other hand I don't want to admit defeat.'

'I can understand that,' Ashton told her.

Jill didn't want to throw her hand in because she had persuaded Robin Urquhart that the SIS had an overriding interest in the Zawadzki affair and should conduct the investigation.

'I'm not looking for sympathy, Peter. I'm trying to work out where we go from here and I'd like to know if you have any bright ideas?'

'Afraid not.'

'I might have guessed,' Jill said bitterly.

'But I do have a suggestion. Why don't we restrict ourselves to the confidential reports? There's a chance they will have been backloaded to the Records Office at Hayes by now but it's not too much to ask the Military Secretary to obtain them. If we do get a few pointers after we've read the reports, we can always go back to the army for the rest.'

'And in the meantime we might hear something from the Costa Ricans,' Jill murmured.

Ashton thought that could well be the case. But the Costa Ricans would channel everything through the British Embassy in San José and the SIS wouldn't be kept informed unless Jill prevailed upon Urquhart to make sure the Latin and Central American Department passed the information on to Vauxhall Cross.

'Do you want me to call for the confidential reports?' he asked in the absence of any clear instructions.

'Of course I do,' Jill said tersely. 'I didn't realise you wanted me to spell it out for you.'

Requests for assistance from the army, navy and air force were channelled through the Armed Forces Desk, a small independent cell which used to consist of four clerks working under the direction of a higher executive officer. Three months ago, in yet another cost-cutting exercise such as never seemed to affect the Treasury or the Foreign and Commonwealth Office, the cell had been transferred to the Admin Wing and incorporated within the Security Vetting and Technical Services Division. As a result of this internal reorganisation, the higher executive officer and two clerks had been made redundant. The reduction had also saved Roy Kelso's appointment as Assistant Director, Administration, from being downsized to a Grade I Intelligence Officer with special responsibility pay.

There had been other changes since Christmas. Frank Warren, the former head of Security Vetting and Technical Services Division had taken early retirement. He had been succeeded by ex-Detective Chief Superintendent Brian Thomas, formerly of E District, the London Borough of Camden. In his heyday with the Met he had been noted for lighting a fire under the lower forms of life, rather than winning hearts and minds. When he had joined the SIS as a Grade III Interviewing Officer he had brought with him a reputation for being a real hard nose who believed in speaking his mind no matter whose toes he trod on. Kelso gave him a wide berth, which meant he was not subjected to the kind of interference Frank Warren had had to put up with.

Ashton had got to know him when he had been put out to grass at Benbow House. As a colleague Thomas was invaluable. In the Metropolitan Police alone, the Deputy Assistant Commissioner (Criminal Investigation), two commanders, the equivalent of assistant chief constables in any other force, and at least five superintendents had all served under him early on in their respective careers and were prepared to do him a favour any time he asked. But to Ashton he was first and foremost a good friend.

'What can I do for you, Peter?' Brian asked before Ashton had even reached the ever-open door to his office.

'Since when did you become second-sighted?'

'Since I received a phone call from her ladyship on the top floor.'

'Jill Sheridan hasn't changed her mind, has she?'

'Didn't sound like it to me.'

Brian Thomas had removed his jacket, loosened the knitted tie he was wearing in order to undo the top two buttons on the striped shirt, and had rolled up his sleeves. The office was like an oven and his face was brick red.

'Something's wrong with the heating,' he said. 'The air-conditioning unit has packed up, I can't open the bloody window and Housekeeping seems unable to get hold of a plumbing and heating engineer. If one doesn't appear in the next five minutes, I'm off home so let's make it snappy.'

'Fine by me. All I want is the confidential report book on

Major Adam Zawadzki, late of the Duke of Wellington's Regiment.' Ashton produced a slip of paper and pushed it across the desk. 'That's his army number.'

'He was the Queen's Messenger who was murdered in Costa Rica. Right?'

'Where did you hear that, Brian?'

'There was a brief report in the *Daily Mail* this morning. Reuters said he was a businessman. I actually knew about it yesterday after morning prayers when Kelso told me what a hard time Roger Benton had been given after he'd disclosed that a particularly sensitive document had ended up in the wrong hands following the death of a Foreign Office courier.'

'I didn't see anything in the *Telegraph*,' Ashton said.

'Well, there was probably only a small paragraph. You know what they say about yesterday's news, and the guy has been dead for six days now.'

'I was told the police found Zawadzki's body barely forty-eight hours after he was murdered?'

'That's right. He was killed some time on Wednesday evening the sixth of March. The police found him around mid-afternoon last Friday.'

The murder had been covered by a Reuters correspondent who had been referred to the British Embassy in San José by the Costa Rican authorities. Although Paul Younghusband, the First Secretary, had confirmed that the dead man was British, he had refused to disclose the identity of the victim until next of kin had been informed. Furthermore, Younghusband had made no effort to correct the correspondent's mistaken assumption that Zawadzki had been in Costa Rica on Business.

'That virtually killed the story,' Thomas said.

'You know more about this business than I do, Brian.' Ashton retrieved the slip of paper which Thomas had left on the desk and added two further names.

'Susan Mary Zawadzki née Honeyman, and Camilla Zawadzki née Smythe-Peters. Zawadzki divorced Susan Mary in 1973, two years after graduating from the Staff College, on the grounds of her adultery with a brother officer. He and Camilla parted company eighteen months ago, somewhat acrimoniously according to him.'

'Why are you telling me all this, Peter?'

'As if you couldn't guess.'

'You want me to call in a few markers?'

'Yeah. I'd like to know where to find his ex-wives should I need to have a word with them.'

'Where are you going with all this?' Thomas asked.

'I wish I knew. You got any bright ideas?'

'You've come to the wrong place; this isn't the bright ideas department.'

'Wait a minute.' Ashton snapped his fingers. 'Ms Laura Greenwood, St John's Avenue, Putney. Zawadzki moved in with her a few months ago.'

'What about it?'

'Well, how about getting one of your friends in British Telecom to find out whether she made any phone calls to Central America during the early hours of March the sixth?'

Thomas sighed. 'Better give me the address again,' he said wearily.

Ted Mullinder had lost count of the number of different jobs he'd done since leaving school eighteen years ago. Refuse collector, barman, minicab driver, security guard, ticket tout, bookmaker's assistant, forecourt attendant, nightclub bouncer, deck hand on a cross-channel ferry, window cleaner and debt enforcer to name but a few. Currently, and for one day only, he was a painter and decorator with a white van and an extending ladder on the roof rack. By trade, he was one of the best amateur locksmiths in the business.

From the lock-up garage in the Edgware Road where the van was kept by the real owner, he had driven across London to pick up the Fulham Road which would take him into the High Street and then over the river on Putney Bridge. He had called the house in St John's Avenue before setting off and he did so again now as heavy traffic ground to a virtual halt in Putney High Street. As had previously been the case, no one answered when the number rang out.

Caught at every light in the High Street it took him over ten minutes to crawl six hundred yards to the crossroads at the bottom of Putney Hill. The houses in St John's Avenue were all semi-detached and had been built around the time when the vast majority of the population didn't own a car but there the similarity between them ended. In more recent years the property-owning residents of the avenue had sought to make their homes look different from the neighbours'. Some had opted for double glazing, others for bow windows, while a number had had the attics converted into extra rooms. Only a few had had the small front garden concreted to make a hard standing for the car. Consequently there were very few parking spaces at the kerbside.

However, this didn't mean that at least one person in every household was at home. Properties in St John's Avenue didn't come cheap these days and a double income was needed to service the mortgage. Between eight in the morning and six at night the street was practically deserted.

Turning right into St John's Avenue, Mullinder was lucky enough to find a vacant space big enough for the van outside number 108, two doors away from the house where Laura Greenwood lived. Alighting from the van, Mullinder walked back to number 104. He was wearing a short V-neck sweater over a plaid shirt and a pair of jeans under dungarees that were covered with paint splashes. In the left hand he carried a colour chart, while tucked under his arm was a large book of wallpapers for the house owner to choose from.

Without a sideways glance to see if anybody was watching him, Mullinder opened the front gate and walked up the path. The porch shielded him from the upstairs room of the neighbouring houses; further cover was provided by the overgrown privet hedge at the front and both sides of the property. He

36

looked at the number of the Yale lock securing the front door and saw it fell within the bracket of a bunch of spare keys in his possession. It was, of course, an enormous stroke of luck but had it been necessary he would have forced the door with the jemmy concealed in the hollowed-out section of the sample book of wallpapers.

Despite the phone calls that had gone unanswered, he still rang the bell and rattled the letter box as a further precaution. 'Better safe than sorry,' he murmured, then fished out the bunch of keys in his right-hand pocket, inserted the appropriate one into the lock and, nudging the door with a shoulder, let himself into the house. Backing into the door to close it, he laid the colour chart and sample book on the hall table and pulled on a pair of cotton gloves.

The staircase was on the left, flush with the outside wall. Across the hall on the right there was a sizeable dining room and directly behind it, an equally large sitting room. The kitchen and utility room were at the back forming the short arm of an inverted letter L. In Mullinder's current line of work you started at the top of the house and made your way downwards as quickly as possible. Upstairs the lavatory and bathroom were above the kitchen with two double bedrooms along the dividing wall with the adjoining house and above the porch, a box room with just enough space to accommodate a single bed. Standing on an upright chair he'd taken from the nearest bedroom, Mullinder lifted the access board to the loft, placed it on one side and pulled down the stowaway stepladder. There were two switches on the landing; by trial and error he found the one which illuminated the loft.

In most of the houses Mullinder had burgled, the loft had been a glorified rubbish tip and not worth bothering with. He would have given this one a miss too but the client had specified a complete search. However, as it happened, he was pleasantly surprised to find that Laura Greenwood's was relatively tidy. Apart from a set of rusty golf clubs, a wooden press containing a tennis racket that needed restringing, there was only a wooden box packed to the brim with books which she evidently no longer wanted.

Mullinder abandoned the loft, retracted the stepladder, put the board back in place and returned the upright chair to the bedroom used by Laura and her boyfriend. He removed the drawers from the dressing table and emptied the contents on to the double bed, then did the same with the chest of drawers before going through the clothes in the wardrobe. Opening a silver jewel box, he pocketed a solitaire, a half-hoop of diamonds and sapphires, an emerald brooch and an aquamarine dress ring. There was, however, no sign of the document he was looking for.

Mullinder treated the guest and box rooms in the same cavalier fashion with the same negative result; then went downstairs to continue the search. He wasted little time on the kitchen and utility rooms where there were few hiding places that weren't blindingly obvious. The sitting room looked far more promising, especially the drop-leaf writing bureau. The fact that it was locked and the key conspicuous by its absence led him to believe there was no need to look elsewhere. Returning to the kitchen he found the steel belonging to a carving knife which he then used to force the drop leaf. The pigeon holes were stuffed with receipted bills, snapshots, and letters which apparently Ms Greenwood hadn't answered yet. He had almost cleared the desk when he heard a faint grating noise in the hall, then a woman called out and his stomach took a nosedive.

'Laura? Are you at home, Laura?'

The sample book and the colour chart were on the hall table and the bloody woman had seen them. He crossed the room swiftly and positioned himself behind the door, his back pressed against the wall.

'Laura?'

The footsteps came nearer, then the door opened wide and a young woman edged her way into the room. Mullinder didn't wait to see if she was going to look round; instead he came out of hiding and knocked her flat with a brutal shoulder charge.

'Don't look round,' he snarled. 'Keep you face buried in the carpet and you won't get hurt.'

'My little girl . . .' the woman said breathlessly.

'Shut up. Shut the fuck up and do as I tell you.' Mullinder removed her low-heeled shoes and raised the miniskirt above her hips. 'I ain't going to rape you,' he said, and ripped off her tights.

Pinning her down under one knee, he hacked the tights to pieces with a clasp knife and used the strips of nylon to bind her ankles, knees, wrists and elbows together. Wadding another piece into a ball he shoved the gag into her mouth and tied it in place.

'I'm going into the kitchen,' Mullinder told her. 'If you move so much as an inch while I'm out of the room, I'll cut your bloody throat from ear to ear.'

In the store cupboard where Laura Greenwood kept the cleaning materials he found a roll of plastic bin liners. Tearing one off, he returned to the sitting room and unfolded it.

'Keep your fucking eyes closed,' he growled. 'Keep them shut tight.'

Mullinder drew the bin liner over her head and pulled it down to her waist level, then passed another strip of nylon under her stomach and knotted it behind to ensure the bin liner stayed in place no matter how she thrashed about. He talked incessantly, assuring her time after time she was going to be all right because he'd cut a couple of air holes in the bag and if she just stayed calm there would be no need for all that wheezing.

But she wasn't the only one who was afraid. His stomach wouldn't stop churning, he kept breaking wind and any moment now he would have to drop his pants and relieve himself before his guts exploded. He grabbed hold of the woman's feet, and dragged her towards the hall and tied the ankles to the sitting-room door handle with the last strip of nylon. With her legs up in the air while the rest of her body was face down on the floor, he was satisfied there wasn't a damn thing she could do to raise the alarm.

Mullinder was halfway down the hall when the stomach cramps finally got to him. There was nothing for it but to squat down even though the street door was wide open and the little girl in the pushchair was in full view. The spasm was over as suddenly as it had begun, he tiptoed to the door and, trying not to wake the little girl, he wheeled the pushchair into the hall. Anxious to get the hell out of the neighbourhood before somebody missed the nosy bitch and came looking for her, he grabbed the sample book from the hall table, slammed the front door behind him and walked quickly down the path. As he reached the pavement Mullinder thought he could hear the little girl crying.

Chapter Four

From his office on the fourth floor Ashton enjoyed a commanding view of the railtracks from Vauxhall to Queenstown Road,
Battersea which was not the most enthralling vista in the world.
Assistant Directors, their deputies and a few privileged Grade I
Intelligence Officers occupied north-facing rooms with river
views from the National Westminster tower block to the Houses
of Parliament. Sixteen months ago Ashton had been numbered
amongst the privileged few but in one of those internal re-
organisations which all government ministries indulged in from
time to time, he had been moved across the corridor.

On Tuesday, 2 May, five months after the office swap
around had been completed, Clifford Peachey, the previous
Deputy DG had introduced IDAS, the Intelligence Data Access
System. This innovation had put paid to any inclination Ashton
might have had to admire the view from his window.

IDAS was a stand-alone computer-based information system
which meant that all terminals were located within Vauxhall
Cross. Unlike the version Roy Kelso had attempted to establish
for the Security Vetting and Technical Services Division with
such disastrous repercussions, IDAS was crypto-protected. No
outsider, and this included the SIS Training School at Amberley
Lodge, could either gain access or key in an input. As a further
safeguard a visual display unit had to be positioned well away
from any window. Ashton's VDU was tucked away in the near

corner of the room where it was screened by the door. However, following a major breach of security in the autumn of 1995, a Board of Inquiry presided over by Jill Sheridan had recommended that Venetian blinds should be fitted in all outward-facing offices where there was access to IDAS.

This latest measure was unnecessary. It was impossible for a snooper to see anything from the far side of the railtracks, but it would have been a bold man who turned the recommendation down on that basis, especially when Jill Sheridan had the ear of Robin Urquhart, the senior Deputy Under Secretary at the Foreign and Commonwealth.

Ashton rarely had occasion to log into IDAS and hadn't done so since the Venetian blind had been fitted. Although there was over an hour of daylight left, he rapidly discovered that without the overhead fluorescent, he couldn't see the keyboard properly and was misspelling the entry code. With nothing to go on Ashton trawled the Central America file, which was programmed in alphabetical order.

Belize was the first country to be featured, and he immediately moved the file on to Costa Rica. The available data contained a digest of the nation's history and not much else. Costa Rica, he learned, had remained politically stable throughout the twentieth century with the exception of two brief periods from 1917 to 1919 and again 1948. In January 1917, a Federico Tinoco had ousted the President, Alfredo Gonzalez, who had been elected by a very narrow margin. America had refused to recognise Tinoco's government, but a counter-revolution, which had resulted in a presidential election victory by Julio Acosta, had put matters right between the two countries.

There had been virtually a repeat performance in the presidential election campaign of 1948, which had been characterised by violent protests that had included a fifteen-day general strike. Following the defeat of its own candidate, the government of the day, with the support of the army, had declared the election result null and void. The counter-revolution in support of the rightful president elect had led to a new constitution which abolished the army in 1949.

There was, Ashton decided, nothing under Costa Rica that he couldn't have gleaned by taking the 1986 edition of *South America, Central America and the Caribbean*, produced by European Publications Limited, out of the library on the ground floor. The inputs for El Salvador, Guatemala, Honduras and Nicaragua were much more revealing. However, it was noticeable that all the intelligence data was attributable to US sources, proof, if ever it were needed, that Central and Latin America was the CIA's stamping ground. Furthermore, the existing material in no way suggested a reason why Zawadzki had been murdered.

Ashton signed off the file and tapped in the entry code for South America, then flipped through the menu until he had Colombia in the frame. His choice was based on the fact that the Firm had been exploring the possibility of establishing an operational base for the SAS in Costa Rica in order to go after the Colombian drug barons. He had just put up the information Roger Benton had garnered on the various drug cartels when the phone rang. Answering it, he gave the number of his extension and found he had Brian Thomas on the line.

'What have you got for me?' Ashton asked.

'Not a lot. Ms Greenwood didn't call San José on the sixth of March or anywhere else for that matter.'

'Maybe she has a mobile?'

'She has,' Thomas said, 'and the answer's still the same. BT checked. Incidentally, they told me Ms Greenwood has been living at that address in Putney since 1986. I don't know what story Foreign Office Security gave you but it looks as though Adam Zawadzki moved in with her and not the other way round.'

'Could be. What about—'

'The ex-wives?' Thomas anticipated the question. 'My friends haven't discovered the present whereabouts of either one yet but they're working on it. I'll let you know as soon as I hear anything.'

Ashton thanked him and put the phone down. He went back to the VDU and resumed the task of scanning the intelligence data on Colombia which Roger Benton had acquired from various sources, notably the CIA and Her Majesty's Diplomatic Service. It was, he discovered, a country with a long history of instability and political violence. Following the break-up of Simón Bolívar's 'Gran Colombia', which had led to the separation of Ecuador and Venezuela in 1830, there had been no less than eight civil wars between 1839 and 1901. On every occasion nineteenth-century dyed-in-the-wool Conservatism on the one hand and Liberalism on the other had been the political schism that had divided the country.

Forty-four years of peace had followed, then in 1945 the old sectarian blood-letting between Left and Right had started up again, with the result that by 1960 some 300,000 deaths had been recorded in rural areas. As of today, the traditional liberals and conservatives had spawned one right-wing, and six left-wing parties ranging from the Maoist Workers Movement to the Marxist Patriotic Union. There were as many guerrilla organisations as there were political parties and splinter groups. According to Roger Benton's South American Desk the most active were the Castroite Ejército de Liberación Nacional, and the Muerte a Secuestradores abbreviated to MAS, a right-wing paramilitary group funded by drug dealers.

The MAS also happened to be the largest and best-equipped guerrilla organisation. Apart from the usual small arms, their arsenal included 81mm mortars, 25mm Oerlikon antiaircraft cannons and Redeye, the man-portable surface-to-air guided missile system. They had the measure of the police, and the army wasn't exactly keen to go up against them either.

It occurred to Ashton that the brutal slaying of Adam Zawadzki made sense if it had been the work of the MAS. The manner of his death had been their way of warning the British Government of the sort of treatment an SAS soldier could expect to receive should he have the misfortune to fall into their hands. If that were true, it meant the MAS guerrillas had known what was in the diplomatic bag. Furthermore, even though Adam Zawadzki had been a last-minute substitute for Martin Edmunds they had been advised that he would be on American Airlines Flight AA2165 arriving San José at 21.20 hours. And that, Ashton thought, would make quite a few people in Whitehall reach for their worry beads.

Ashton switched off the computer, checked the safe to make sure it was locked, then left the office. For once he would arrive home at a reasonable hour and that, he thought, would shake Harriet to the core.

Mullinder left the Jubilee Line train at Kilburn, walked down the steps to the street below and, after surrendering his ticket at the barrier, turned right under the railway bridge and made his way to the Irish pub off the High Road. Mr Copeland had said to meet him in the saloon bar at ten minutes to seven on the dot, and when Charlie Copeland told you to do something you didn't argue the toss.

The evening trade hadn't really started when Mullinder walked into the bar. Two men were playing the fruit machines near the entrance, three more were propping up the bar and Copeland was in conversation with the landlord. The former detective inspector waved a hand at him, then pointed to a corner table before resuming his conversation with the publican. A few moments later, Copeland joined him at the table with a pint of Guinness for himself and a mild and bitter for Mullinder.

'So how did you make out, Ted?' he asked.

'So what's with you and the landlord?' Mullinder said, neatly sidestepping the question.

'I was making small talk, told him I was waiting for one of my salesmen.' Copeland grinned. 'That's you,' he added. 'Now suppose you answer my question.'

'I didn't find anything except a few pieces of jewellery.' Mullinder paused while he took out a packet of Embassy cigarettes and lit one. 'You want them?'

45

'No, of course I don't. Did you search the place from top to bottom?'

'I started with the loft and worked downwards like you told me to, Mr Copeland.'

'What happened?'

'What do you mean, what happened?'

'Don't try to bullshit me, I can tell something went wrong. You're on edge, tighter than an overwound spring.'

Mullinder picked up his glass and drank half the mild and bitter in one long draught, then set the glass down and used the back of his hand to wipe the froth from his lips. 'This burglary,' he said, 'it was an official job. Right? I mean the trinkets I took was a bit of window-dressing to make it look a regular burglary.'

'What happened?'

'Some bloody woman turned up while I was still in the house, let herself in with a key.' Mullinder drew on the cigarette, took the smoke on to his lungs and started coughing. 'That went down the wrong way,' he gasped.

'Did the woman see you?'

Charlie Copeland was extremely indifferent to the fact he had bloody nearly choked to death but that was typical of him. Whatever his physical appearance might suggest, he was not the cheerful, irrepressible East Ender who was easy-going and generous to a fault. He most certainly wasn't one of nature's gentlemen. Under that surface layer there was a nasty piece of work. If ever a copper deserved to do time it was ex-Detective Inspector Charles Copeland.

'Well, did she eyeball you?'

'No. I knocked her flying soon as she walked into the sitting room. Believe me she didn't get a chance to look round and after she went down she kept her nose buried in the carpet like I told her to do. Then while she lay still, I tied her up and used a plastic bin liner to make a blindfold.'

Mullinder swallowed the rest of the mild and bitter, and dumped what was left of his cigarette in the dregs at the bottom of the glass.

'It was all your fault, Charlie,' he said.

'Mr Copeland to you.'

'Yeah, sure. Fact is, Mr Copeland, you told me this Laura Greenwood was never home before six and some woman and her little girl show up in the middle of the afternoon.'

'Suddenly there's a little girl,' Copeland said in a low, menacing voice. 'How old was she, Mullinder? Three, going on four? Please don't tell me she's older.'

'I doubt she's even two years old.'

'She only knows a few words?'

'The little girl didn't say anything, she was fast asleep.'

'You knock the mother down and tie her up and she sleeps through it all?'

'The woman left her on the porch in her pushchair.'

Copeland wanted to know why the woman had done that and he could only presume she must have realised there was someone in the house. Other questions followed one after another. Where had he left the pattern book? Might the woman have seen it? Had he remembered to wear cotton gloves? Had any one of the residents seen him leave the house and drive off? Had he behaved in a manner liable to arouse suspicion or draw attention to himself?

'I didn't run,' Mullinder told him. 'I walked to the van and I didn't leave any particles of burning rubber behind when I pulled away from the kerb.'

'Where's the vehicle now?'

'Back in the lockup on the Edgware Road.' Mullinder produced a key from his fleece-lined bomber jacket and pushed it surreptitiously across the table to the former DI.

'A white van won't have gone unnoticed in a street like St John's Avenue,' Copeland said thoughtfully.

'I told you it wasn't a good idea at the time,' Mullinder said. 'You should have borrowed a Mini. Nobody looks twice at them.'

'Did you leave any fingerprints on the steering wheel?'

'I wiped it clean when I returned the van to the lockup. Did the same with the handbrake, gear shift, instrument panel, door handle and roof. You name it, I wiped it.'

'Even so, I'll tell George to give the van another manicure.'

George had to be the owner of the Ford van. Mullinder had never met him and didn't know his surname. There was, however, one thing they had in common: Copeland undoubtedly had something on George which made him come running anytime he crooked a finger.

'I can't do anything about the house. We'll have to assume you didn't leave any calling cards behind.'

'You've no worries there, Mr Copeland.'

'Oh, I'll be all right, you're the one who will do the worrying.'

'Meaning what?' Mullinder asked, his mouth suddenly dry as dust.

'I think you should lie low for a while, take a holiday. Spain's got a lot going for it at this time of the year.'

'Yeah? What I'll do for money?'

'You're not short of a bob or two,' Copeland told him. 'You were paid a grand to break into that house in St John's Avenue. Try dipping into that.'

'A grand won't last for ever, Mr Copeland. How will I know when it's safe to come home?'

'I'll put a quotation in the personal column of the *Daily Telegraph*. Something not too obvious, something which even you won't forget.' Copeland fingered his top lip. 'How about a quote from the Old Testament? Genesis 1: "Be fruitful, and multiply, and replenish the earth . . ." Think you can remember that?'

'You can depend on it.'

'Good. Now it's time you were leaving.'

Anybody observing Copeland who didn't know him would be taken in by his friendly smile. But sitting across the table from him it was a different story. There was no warmth in the smile and his cold, grey eyes looked right through you.

Mullinder pushed his chair back and stood up. 'I'll be seeing you then.'

As he walked towards the door, the man playing the fruit machine nearest the entrance scooped the jackpot and whooped in triumph when the coins filled his cupped hands and spilled over on to the floor.

'Some people have all the luck,' Mullinder muttered, and went out into the street.

Copeland had told him the burglary had been authorised at the highest level and he had believed the former DI because Ms Greenwood's house in St John's Avenue wasn't the first job he had done for the Government. Eleven months back he had broken into the head office of Universal Services, a firm of security consultants which was suspected of circumventing the arms embargo imposed on Mozambique by the United Nations. Using a set of master keys supplied by Copeland he'd unlocked their filing cabinets and photographed all the sales invoices that had been sent to various clients in the financial year ending 5 April 1994.

Although Copeland had never said so, Mullinder had got the impression that the DI had been acting on behalf of MI5. He had never doubted that he could rely on Copeland to see him right if, through sheer bad luck, he was apprehended on the premises. After their conversation this evening he knew Copeland wouldn't lift a finger to help him. Not that he was going to need any help because there was nothing, absolutely nothing, to connect him with the burglary at 104 St John's Avenue.

And then it hit him. He'd picked up the pattern book he'd left on the hall table all right but not the bloody colour chart. He hadn't put the cotton gloves on until he was inside the house, which meant his fingerprints were all over the chart. He had one previous conviction for breaking and entering when he was nineteen and had been sentenced to six months' imprisonment by a hard-nosed judge who'd claimed he'd taken Mullinder's youth into account. Five years later he had been done again, this time by Detective Sergeant Copeland who'd harboured a grudge ever since his brief had got Mullinder off on a technicality.

The National Identification Bureau would match his prints and get his present address from the Department of Social Security. For all he knew the police could be waiting for him on the doorstep right now. And they wouldn't believe a word of his story, not after they searched his one-bedroom flat and found a solitaire, a half-hoop of diamonds and sapphires, an emerald brooch and an aquamarine dress ring.

Home for Ashton was 84 Rylett Close in Ravenscourt Park. At one time the semi-detached house had belonged to the SIS, when it had resembled a fortress. The sentries had been the television cameras mounted under the eaves which had covered the front, back and east side of the property, while the shared wall with the other semi had been protected by audio sensors. The external line of defence had been an infrared intruder system which triggered a flashing light on the monitor screen in the basement should the invisible fence be broken. The innermost defence had been a sophisticated burglar alarm connected to Hammersmith Police Station.

With Perestroika came the so-called peace dividend, the Treasury's favourite love child. Among the cuts imposed across the board, the SIS had been ordered to sell off fifty per cent of their housing stock. Number 84 Rylett Close had been one of the houses offered up; thanks to Victor Hazelwood, Ashton had been able to buy it at a knock-down price before it was advertised by the Property Services Agency. The TV cameras, infrared intruder system and audio sensors had all been removed before contracts were exchanged. Finally, although the burglar alarm had been left in situ, the link to Hammersmith Police Station had been disconnected.

However, what goes around, comes around. Seven months ago, in response to a perceived threat from the IRA, Terry Hicks, the electronic whiz-kid of Vauxhall Cross, had turned up on Ashton's doorstep to install what appeared to be a satellite dish. In fact the dish threw an infrared fence around the Ashtons'

Ford Mondeo, always provided the car was parked right outside the house. The system not only sounded an audio alarm, it also presented an image on the monitor screen located in the basement and automatically photographed the intruder. Alerting the police was the one thing the system was not programmed to do.

It was still daylight when Ashton let himself into the house and announced he was home.

'Miracles will never cease,' Harriet said as he entered the kitchen and found her ironing a pile of laundry.

Ashton eyed the child-size dungarees, jumpers, underpants, vests and pyjamas, not to mention his own items which still awaited her attention.

'I thought most of Edward's things were drip-dry?' he said.

'You wish.'

'Well, leave my shirts, I'll do them.'

'No thanks, I've seen how cack-handed you are with an iron. We'll end up with a scorch mark on a shirtfront and that will be another thirty-five pounds down the drain.'

'I could give Edward his supper,' Ashton said, trying to be helpful.

Harriet laughed. 'You may be home earlier than usual, love, but he has already been fed and watered.'

'Where is—'

'Upstairs in his room, playing with bits of Lego,' Harriet told him before he could finish his question. 'And, yes, the gate on the landing is closed.'

The gate had been installed after a serious domestic accident which had ended in tragedy. Some nine months ago, when four months into her pregnancy, Harriet had trodden on a drumstick which Edward had left on the landing and had miscarried after falling downstairs. The fear that they could lose their only child in a similar accident was the reason the purpose-made gate had been fitted.

'Why don't you go upstairs and keep Edward amused while I finish the ironing?' Harriet suggested.

Ashton said he would do that and had got as far as the

staircase when the telephone rang. The unique tone of the Mozart secure-speech facility was instantly recognisable.

'You'd better take the call,' Harriet said in a resigned voice. 'It's got to be for you.'

The Mozart was the last word in communications technology. Built into an executive-style briefcase it was basically a crypto-protected radio telephone which could be operated from anywhere in the world, providing a power point was available. The plug itself could be instantly adapted to be compatible with the local voltage/amperage. The cryptographic material was sealed inside a cassette which was inserted into the machine. The tape contained twenty-eight variables which meant the cassette was changed every four weeks. The moment Ashton lifted the handset the crypto for the day was activated.

A woman said, 'Duty Officer here, Mr Ashton. You are advised that alert state Bikini Black has been raised to Bikini Amber with immediate effect.'

'Roger that. Time now is 19.13 hours.' Ashton put the phone down, then called to Harriet. 'It seems the IRA may be planning something. We've just been put on Bikini Amber.'

'Right.'

'Have you used the car today?'

'No. I walked to the shops for once.'

'OK, I'll check it out with the peeper,' Ashton told her.

The peeper was a stave some four feet in length with a mirror slotted into the tip at an angle of five degrees. By pushing the mirror under the Ford Mondeo and walking right round the car, Ashton was able to make sure that no foreign body had been attached to the chassis. That done, he went down into the basement and switched on the infrared fence. As he started upstairs, he heard their private phone ringing in the kitchen and assumed the caller must be some acquaintance of Harriet's when she lifted the receiver. He could not have been more wrong.

'Brian Thomas for you,' she said when Ashton walked into the kitchen. 'Says it's urgent.'

'When wasn't it?' Ashton took the phone from Harriet. 'What can I do for you, Brian?' he asked.

'It's what you can do for the police. They're looking to you for guidance.'

'Me?'

'Yes, they're aware of your interest in Ms Greenwood and they want to know why. Seems she returned home this evening to find her house had been burgled.'

'That's a coincidence.'

'It gets better,' Thomas said. 'She also found the dead body of one of her neighbours in the sitting room.'

Chapter Five

Mullinder turned off Charing Cross Road into Old Compton Street and walked on past establishments selling adult books, girlie magazines and porno movies, clip joints promising live sex shows and, on the opposite side of the road, a newsagent and tobacconist. His one-bedroom flat was in Pentonville but from Kilburn he'd stayed on the Jubilee Line as far as Green Park, then changed on to the Piccadilly and alighted at Leicester Square. There was always a purpose behind everything Mullinder did and in this instance he had come up west to see a girl who would do him a favour for a consideration.

A few yards ahead of Mullinder, a man in a grey-coloured belted raincoat suddenly wheeled to the left as though some item among the second-hand electrical goods displayed in a shop window had caught his eye. Nothing had; the whole performance was simply a subterfuge. The man in the raincoat wanted to make sure the coast was clear before he slipped through the open doorway a few paces to the right. No way, Mullinder thought, no way was he going to allow this fat-bellied punter to beat him to it. Striding out he drew abreast of the punter and spoke to him out of the corner of his mouth.

'You dirty old bugger,' he said in a voice loud enough for the punter to hear. 'We all know what you are looking for.'

When Mullinder looked back as he turned into the open

doorway, the man in the grey raincoat had taken fright and was hurrying towards Charing Cross Road.

The narrow hallway Mullinder entered was dark green to a height of roughly seven feet, above which the walls had been painted a pale cream that had now yellowed with age. It was the sort of décor Westminster Council, among other local authorities, had at one time chosen for their public lavatories. The flat on the first floor was rented by a working girl called Bettina. An arrow on the facing wall advised would-be punters that Maxine could be found upstairs. Maxine, he thought, sounded much more enticing than Ruth Potts, her real name.

Like a genie materialising out of a bottle, the maid appeared from her cubbyhole of a room before he could knock on Ruth's door. Although Mullinder had never been any good at guessing a person's age, he was pretty sure the maid had to be nudging fifty if she was a day. She was about five feet seven in low heels, had mousy hair, a sharp pointed face and was as thin as a rake. She was wearing tan-coloured slacks and a check shirt under an old cardigan.

'Maxine's busy entertaining a friend at the moment,' the harridan told him. 'But she won't be long if you'd like to wait.'

Mullinder said he would and followed her into the cubbyhole. A rug measuring nine by six left very little of the floorspace uncovered. There was just room for a kitchen table, two Windsor chairs, and a broom cupboard. There was also a kitchen sink with a worktop-cum-draining board, a 13 amp power point and a basket for a malevolent-looking Doberman pinscher. The crockery and kitchen utensils comprised a chipped teapot, two mugs and an electric kettle.

'How long have you been working for Ruth?' Mullinder asked out of curiosity.

'Who's Ruth?'

'Maxine then.'

'Five weeks,' the woman told him before hiding her face behind the *Mirror*. A muffled sound of voices reached him from the adjoining room. Presently there was a lot of gasping and cries

56

of pleasure, all of it faked by Ruth. The cries died away to order and there was a momentary silence before a door opened and closed.

'There goes another satisfied customer,' the harridan observed from behind her newspaper. 'You won't have to wait much longer. Any moment now Maxine will poke her head round the door.'

Ruth did no such thing, she merely opened the communicating door a fraction and announced she'd had one fruitcake too many and needed some time to herself.

'Haven't you got time to see an old friend then?' Mullinder asked.

The door opened wider. 'Ted?' Ruth appeared, looking ridiculous in a blouse, gymslip, white knee-length socks and sandals. 'Ted, what the hell are you doing here?'

'I need a favour.'

'You'll get no freebies from me.'

'It's not like that.'

Mullinder moved towards Ruth. Although he didn't threaten her in any way, she instinctively backed off and retreated before him into the bedroom. The Doberman got up from the basket and started growling, the hairs on his back forming a ridge. Glancing over his shoulder at the dog, Mullinder saw his lips curl to reveal razor-sharp fangs and knew the animal was about to attack him.

'For God's sake tell that mutt of yours to calm down,' he said nervously.

'Sit,' Ruth commanded, 'sit . . . good boy.'

Mullinder eased past her and sighed with relief when she closed the door.

'All right, Ted, what is it you want from me?'

'I'm in a spot of bother and I need to lie low until it blows over.'

'You're not thinking of hitting me for a loan, are you?'

'No, I've got over a grand stashed away in my flat.'

'Lucky old you.'

'The thing is I can't show my face round there. So I want you to collect the money and pack a bag for me. The sooner the better . . .'

'Forget it, I've got a living to earn.'

'I'll make it worth your while.'

'Yes?' Ruth skirted the bed, picked up the remote and switched off the porno video which had been running silently. 'How much do you have in mind?' she asked.

Mullinder hesitated, wondered how little he could get away with.

'A hundred?' he suggested.

'You've got to be joking. I'll earn more than that before I go home.'

'Two hundred then, plus a share of the jewellery.'

'What jewellery?'

'A solitaire diamond, half-hoop of sapphires and diamonds, an emerald brooch and an aquamarine dress ring – must be worth at least three thousand. Course, you'd have to hold on to them for a bit.'

'They're stolen property?'

'So what?' Mullinder said. 'It won't bother you none.'

Ruth sat down on the bed, undid the ankle straps on the sandals and kicked them off, then removed the white, knee-length socks. Her eyebrows were almost knitted together and he could damn nearly hear the tumblers clicking in her brain as she weighed the pros and cons. Right from the time he'd first met her at the William Wilberforce Secondary Modern at the age of twelve, Ruth Potts had been a grasping little minx. She had been the school bicycle from the outset of puberty and every boy who'd ridden her had had to pay through the nose for the pleasure.

'Where do I meet you with the stuff?' Ruth asked presently.

'Back here,' Mullinder told her. 'I'm staying the night.'

'That'll cost you another pony, Ted.'

'Don't push your luck. I'm being more than generous.'

Ruth shrugged her shoulders. 'It was worth a try.'

'Are you on?'

'Yeah, I'll do it.'

While she changed, Mullinder told her where the money and the jewellery was hidden, what to pack and where to find his passport. He told Ruth to keep her eyes peeled in case the police were watching the flat, waiting for his return and what to say to the Law, if by chance she was apprehended.

'I must be mad. Why am I doing this?' Ruth zipped up her skirt. 'I could find myself in real trouble.'

'You're doing it for the money. And you will be in and out of my flat before the police even think of applying for a search warrant.'

'Yeah, yeah.' Ruth wiped her mouth on a Kleenex, removed most of the eye shadow and did the same with the face powder. 'How do I look?' she asked presently.

'Respectable,' Mullinder said. 'Now get weaving.'

'I'm going.'

'And send that old bat home.'

'Are you going to look after the dog?'

'No way.'

'She stays then,' Ruth told him, and left, closing the door to the maid's room behind her.

Mullinder quietly turned the key on his side, then locked the other door which opened on to the landing. Charlie Copeland had suggested he take a holiday in Spain and in some ways that wasn't a bad idea because, as yet the extradition treaty between the two countries hadn't been ratified. The downside was that Copeland would know where to look for him. How far he could trust the former detective inspector was something he would need to think about while he waited for Ruth to return with his money.

Mullinder picked up the remote control, which was lying on the dressing table, aimed it at the TV, selected Channel 9 and set the video running. He then stretched out on the bed and watched a twosome become a threesome indulging in a variety of contortions that would have taxed an Olympic gymnast.

*   *   *

59

The ambulancemen were just bringing a body out of number 104 when Ashton turned into St John's Avenue. The house and the neighbouring houses on either side had been isolated by the usual blue and white plastic streamers, which also fenced off the pavement from numbers 104 and 108. Additional police warning signs had reduced the road to half its normal width. A constable on duty at the makeshift barrier waved Ashton down and asked him if he lived in the avenue or was just curious to see what was going on.

'No, I'm here at the request of DI Hughes,' Ashton told him.

'Well, that does make a difference, sir.'

The officer removed a couple of metal signs that were in the way and directed Ashton to park outside number 106. When he got out of the car, the PC steered him towards the investigating officer. The DI in turn led Ashton down a hallway smelling of lavender into the sitting room at the back of the house that looked as if it had got in the way of a hurricane.

Hughes verged on the minimum height for the Metropolitan Police. He was in his early forties, had wiry, dark hair flecked with grey, pale blue eyes and the kind of face that seemed vaguely familiar to strangers. At a guess Ashton reckoned the Detective Inspector weighed between 145 and 150 pounds which, in the absence of middle-age spread, suggested he had changed little over the years.

'Good to meet you, Mr Ashton,' he said, and sounded as though he meant it.

'Likewise.'

'I hear Brian Thomas is a colleague?'

'Yes. Do you know him too?'

'I'd never heard of him before this evening,' Hughes said. 'But it seems the Commander of W District had been a detective sergeant under Brian Thomas when he was a detective chief superintendent in the London Borough of Camden.'

And Brian Thomas had asked the Commander to have a word with British Telecom about Ms Laura Greenwood because Putney happened to be within the boundaries of W District. So

60

as soon as the great man learned what his officers had found at 104 St John's Avenue, he had telephoned ex-Detective Chief Superintendent Thomas and asked him what the hell was going on.

'Are you allowed to tell me why you're interested in Ms Greenwood?' Hughes asked. 'Our Commander must have some idea but he isn't letting on.'

'A man called Adam Zawadzki was living with her. He was a Queen's Messenger who got himself murdered in Costa Rica six days ago. It was his first trip to Central America and even though he was a last-minute substitute, a reception committee was waiting for him at the airport. We wanted to make sure that Laura Greenwood hadn't alerted the opposition. She hadn't, of course.'

'Miss Greenwood told me that she works in the Passport Office.'

Ashton suppressed a smile. Obviously Hughes was a little old-fashioned. A single woman was Miss to him not Ms.

'That's correct,' he said. 'She has spent the last ten years in Petty France.'

'Is there a connection between the murder of this Adam whatever his name is and the burglary?'

'You tell me, Inspector. I mean this woman who was murdered, what was she doing in the house?'

'Her name was Tracy Beckingham; she was twenty-three, divorced and the mother of a two-year-old girl. She was living on income support and a pittance from her ex which, more often than not, he omitted to pay.'

Laura Greenwood had got to know about Tracy's financial circumstances and had employed her as a cleaner for a couple of hours every weekday morning, which was why she had a key to the house. Knowing that her employer was never home before six thirty, Tracy Beckingham had got into the habit of doing the two hours when it suited her best. She had met her death because she had chosen to go to work fairly late in the afternoon.

'How was she killed?' Ashton asked.

'She suffocated. I don't think the burglar intended to murder her; he'd made two holes in the plastic bin liner to enable her to breathe. However, according to Miss Greenwood, Tracy was a chronic asthmatic. My guess is she had a panic attack, tried to get out of the bag and in so doing, moved her head away from the air holes. Of course we shan't know for sure how much asthma contributed to her demise until the pathologist completes his post mortem.' Hughes paused, then said, 'So I'm asking you again, Mr Ashton, do you see any connection between the two killings?'

'Was anything stolen?'

'A few pieces of jewellery worth about three and a half thousand.'

'What was Laura Greenwood's reaction to all this?'

'Well, naturally she was pretty upset. Who wouldn't be? I don't know too many people who would be delighted to find a pile of shit on their hall carpet when they opened the front door.'

Ashton had guessed what had happened the moment he'd entered the house and smelled the deodorant. He recalled Brian Thomas once telling him there were two reasons why an intruder excreted on the premises: either the act was an expression of rage at the affluent lifestyle of the victim or else something entirely unexpected had occurred and the burglar had been so unnerved that he had been unable to control his bowels.

'I don't see any security implications in the burglary,' Ashton said. 'At least not on the strength of what I know. Nevertheless I think we would like to be kept informed of developments.'

'Well, with any luck we might be able to put a name to this particular villain before very long. He left in such a hurry he forgot about the colour chart he'd brought with him. Ten to one he's got a record, evens we'll find his dabs all over the chart.'

When questioned, Laura Greenwood had been adamant that she had never seen the chart before and wasn't planning to have the house repainted. Furthermore, in the course of house-to-house enquiries in the immediate vicinity, two of the residents told the police they recalled seeing a white van belonging to a painter and decorator parked up the road from 104.

'One of them was able to give us part of the registration number.'

'What's happened to the little girl?'

'The grandparents have been contacted and they're on their way down from Darlington. Meantime she has been taken into care.'

'And Laura Greenwood?'

'One of the neighbours has offered her a bed for the night; she didn't fancy sleeping here. Can't say I blame her.'

Ashton glanced at his wristwatch and thought there must be something wrong with it until he checked with Hughes and learned it really was eight forty. Since there was no reason for him to stay on, he said good night to the DI, left the house and got into the Ford Mondeo. As a slightly jokey present for Christmas Harriet had given him a mobile phone. This would be the first occasion he had ever used it, and what better purpose than to let her know when to expect him? Opening the glove compartment, he took it out, erected the aerial and started to punch out their home number only to discover he'd omitted to load the batteries, which had been wrapped separately.

'Brilliant,' he said aloud, 'bloody brilliant.'

The *Nine o'clock News* on BBC 1 with Peter Sissons had been running for over ten minutes now and time was slipping away. Mullinder punched a clenched fist into the palm of his left hand. What the hell was Ruth playing at? If the silly bitch had taken a cab, as anyone with an ounce of common sense would have done, she would have made the round trip to his council flat in Collier Street in under an hour, instead of which she had been gone nearly seventy minutes. Two miles there, two miles back and that was going the long way round.

The train to Holyhead left Euston at 22.05 hours and arrived in time to connect with the 03.45 hours sailing to Dublin. He had friends there who would hide him until they knew the police weren't looking for him. The other thing to be said in favour of Ireland was the fact that Charlie Copeland would believe Mullinder had taken his advice and gone to Spain. But if Ruth didn't get a move on he was going to miss the sodding train, and when he'd phoned the National Rail Enquiry Service, the girl who'd taken the call had assured him that there wasn't a later service from London.

He heard footsteps on the landing and immediately put the television on standby with the remote. The bell rang, the maid went to the door and there was a brief exchange. The caller was the second punter who'd wanted to spend some quality time with Maxine since Ruth had left. However, this time the old bat next door didn't have to call on the Doberman to convince the caller that her employer wasn't available.

Mullinder switched on the TV again, saw the regional news had just started and let rip with a string of four-letter words. Forty minutes to go before the train departed and still no Ruth. Had the police nicked her or had she double-crossed him, taken his bundle and done a runner? He told himself that Ruth wouldn't risk her neck for a lousy grand but no matter how many times he repeated the assertion a nagging doubt persisted. It was only dispersed when he heard her voice in the adjoining room as the weather forecast began. He opened the communicating door, glared at the old bat and told Ruth to move her arse pdq.

'What's the hurry?' she demanded. 'I thought you were staying the night?'

'I've changed my mind. OK?'

'I should care.'

Mullinder wrenched the holdall from her grasp, dumped it on the bed and unzipped it. Several changes of underwear, half a dozen pairs of socks, three shirts, a towel and his passport. She'd even thought to pack his washing kit, something he'd omitted to tell her. But no loot.

'What have you done with my money?' he growled.

'Oh, that's nice. I put myself out for you and what do I get? A mouthful of abuse.'

'I'm not going to ask you again. Where's my fucking money?'

'Right here, pig.' Ruth opened up her cheap PVC handbag, took out a roll of twenty-pound notes done up with an elastic band and hurled the bundle at his face. Mullinder fielded the bundle one-handed, removed the elastic band and rippled through the banknotes, checking to make sure Ruth hadn't replaced some of them with blank sheets of paper cut to size.

'I've already taken my share.'

'I bet you have.'

'I'm just telling you. I don't want anyone accusing me of being light-fingered.'

'Sure.'

'A thank you wouldn't come amiss.'

Mullinder finished counting and looked up. 'There's only eight hundred here,' he said.

'And we agreed you'd pay me two hundred, all told that makes a grand in my book.'

'What about the rest?'

'The rest?' Ruth echoed in a voice which suggested she hadn't the faintest idea what he was talking about.

'The two hundred and eighty in fives and tens. They were in an envelope under the bundle of twenties.'

'I didn't see any envelope. You know how pitch-dark it is under the kitchen sink on your hands and knees. And after I'd lifted the linoleum and removed the trapdoor it was as black as the ace of spades. I had to reach down between the floorboards and feel for the money. I could have missed the envelope.'

On purpose, he thought. You deliberately left it behind, knowing I couldn't pick it up later.

'What have you done with the jewellery?' he asked quietly.

Ruth produced the rings and emerald brooch from her coat pocket and tossed them on to the bed.

'And my door key.'

'Give me a chance.' Ruth opened her handbag again and took out the small bunch of keys Mullinder had given her and put it down with the jewellery. 'Satisfied now?'

'Yes.'

'I'd like the half-hoop and the aquamarine, if that's all right with you?'

'Did you meet any of the neighbours?' Mullinder asked, ignoring her question.

'No.'

'What about the police? Any sign of plod.'

'No.'

'I'll take your word for it but God help you if my collar is felt when I walk out of here.'

'Why don't you piss off, Ted? You're beginning to bore me.'

Mullinder tucked the passport and cash into his jacket pocket along with the solitaire and the emerald brooch, then zipped up the holdall.

'Well, I guess I'll be on my way,' he said, smiling.

He was still smiling when he sank a punch into Ruth's stomach and completely winded her. Then he pocketed the other two rings, picked up the holdall and unlocked the door which opened on to the landing.

'I'll send you a postcard from Spain,' he added.

Mullinder was halfway down the stairs by the time Ruth managed to stagger out of the bedroom and lean over the banisters to mouth abuse at him. She hoped he caught a roaring dose of the clap and got poxed up to his eyebrows. Or better still, he contracted a particularly virulent strain of the Aids virus.

Mullinder emerged on to the street, turned right and set off towards Charing Cross Road. A hundred yards north of Cambridge Circus he flagged down a cab and told the driver to take him to Euston station. It was then nine forty-three and he had twenty minutes in hand. Barring a major traffic accident he would catch the Holyhead train with ease.

★   ★   ★

66

The bell was loud and insistent. Unable to ignore its summons any longer, Benton turned over in bed on to his right side and reached out to shut off the alarm. After flailing the air for some moments he eventually located the clock and depressed the appropriate button. The bell, however, continued to pulsate, which puzzled him no end, but not his wife, Iris, who thumped his back.

'For God's sake, Roger,' she said wearily, 'it's the damned Mozart. Please go downstairs to answer it.'

Benton lifted the bedclothes, swung his feet out on to the floor and sat up. Urged on by Iris, he shoved his feet into a pair of carpet slippers and unhitched his dressing gown from the hook on the back of the door. The luminous hands on the alarm clock indicated four twenty-seven.

'Middle of the bloody night,' Benton grumbled to himself.

The Mozart was located in the study. Since assistant directors were required to be on call during silent hours, Terry Hicks, the electronic whiz-kid of Vauxhall Cross, had installed a wake-up bell in the bedroom which was linked to the secure speech facility. Switching on the landing and hall lights, Benton went downstairs into the study and answered the phone.

A girl said, 'Nancy Wilkins here, sir, night-duty officer, Central Registry.'

'Good morning, Nancy. What have you got for me?' Benton tried to seem cheerful but even to his ears he sounded querulous.

'A priority signal from Head of Station, Washington.'

Benton gritted his teeth. He had been woken up in the middle of the night for a stupid priority signal that should have gone to the appropriate desk officer. Then he remembered that Nancy Wilkins had less than six months' service, three of which had been spent on the induction course at Amberley Lodge. All the same, she should have sought the advice of the senior watch-keeper.

'Are you ready, sir?' Nancy asked.

'As I ever will be.'

'Message reads: "Our friends report that Colonel Osvaldo

Herrara, Deputy Chief of the Cuban Intelligence Bureau, left Costa Rica on Aeronica Flight 141 to Managua on Thursday, 7 March. Immigration Officers state subject entered Costa Rica from Nicaragua by bus, crossing the border at Peñas Blancas on Tuesday, 5 March. On Saturday, March 9 Herrara was observed in Mexico City boarding the Air France flight to Paris. His present whereabouts is unknown . . ."'

'How much more is there?' Benton asked impatiently.

'Only two more paragraphs, sir.'

'Well, try paraphrasing them, Nancy.'

'Yes, sir.' She went silent for nearly thirty seconds, then said, 'Herrara is reported to have links with the Kurdish Workers party in Western Europe. This information was provided by a hitherto reliable source and could well be true, according to the Americans. They also suggest Herrara could have been responsible for the murder of Adam Zawadzki. Finally, Head of Station, Washington, is adamant that none of the foregoing should be disseminated outside Vauxhall Cross.'

'Well, he needn't worry about that,' Benton said forcefully. 'As far as I'm concerned this comes under the heading "file and forget".'

Chapter Six

The confidential reports on Major Adam Zawadzki appeared on Ashton's desk shortly after Heads of Departments had assembled in the conference room for morning prayers. Since the Armed Forces Desk at Vauxhall Cross had only submitted the request yesterday, the swift response could only mean the Ministry of Defence had anticipated that sooner or later somebody would want to see the confidential report book and had instructed the Military Secretary's branch to have it ready.

The book was accompanied by a typewritten note explaining the significance of the various gradings and how they would be interpreted by the Army Board when officers were being considered for promotion to lieutenant-colonel and above. An officer, Ashton learned, could not be graded 'outstanding' unless the first reporting officer was convinced his subordinate would undoubtedly reach the rank of major-general and would probably go on to become a lieutenant-general. For the vast majority, however, gradings ranged from 'Below the standard expected of an officer of his/her rank and service' to 'Well above the standard'. In between these two extremes, an officer could be either 'Up to the standard', or simply 'Above the standard'.

Until he was promoted to major, Adam Zawadzki had been regarded as a very promising young officer and his gradings had reflected this assessment. He had been recommended for 'Extra

Regimental Employment', and as a lieutenant had been a platoon commander in the Infantry Junior Leaders Battalion for two years, which Ashton gathered had been quite a feather in his cap. His star had ceased to be in the ascendant when he had graduated from the Staff College, Camberley, where instructors had found him to be pedantic and on some occasions, unable to see the wood for the trees. In fact Zawadzki had just scraped through the year-long course and had been assigned to a grade 3 appointment in logistics, which meant he had remained a captain instead of gaining temporary promotion to major.

After two years on the staff he had returned to regimental duty with the 1st Battalion, the Duke of Wellington's Regiment for a similar period of time, a career pattern that was common to all Staff College graduates. His star had shone a little brighter when he had been appointed Deputy Chief of Staff 24 (Air Mobile) Brigade in which post he had been responsible for logistics, the application of military law and all matters affecting morale.

Looking at Zawadzki's army career in its entirety there were three unusual aspects which caught Ashton's eye. The initiating officer had indicated that, when a junior major, Zawadzki wasn't suitable for an assistant military attaché's appointment. The next superior officer had put it more bluntly. He had written: 'On no account should this officer be considered for a diplomatic appointment; his wife drinks far too much and is openly promiscuous. The Foreign and Commonwealth Office would never accept her in one of Her Majesty's Embassies.'

Much later, when training major of the 9th Territorial Army Battalion of the regiment, he had been given an un-equivocal recommendation for command and promotion to lieutenant-colonel. However, Zawadzki had been acutely aware that the recommendation would have carried a lot more weight had he been serving in the regular battalion where he would have been subjected to much greater stress. After being passed over by three successive promotion boards he had submitted a Redress of Grievance, which had been rejected.

A Brigadier G. H. Johnstone had written: 'This officer is not as good as he thinks he is.'

The penultimate report before Zawadzki retired from the army had marked an all-time low. In it he had been graded 'Up to the standard required of his rank and service' which was probably the kiss of death. Even more telling was the observation: 'This officer has allowed his bitterness and sense of injustice to affect his everyday performance.'

Ashton put the confidential report book into the pending tray. The only thing he'd learned was the fact that Adam Zawadzki had finished his army career with a sizeable chip on his shoulder. However, nobody had ever questioned his loyalty, and from the nature of his death it was pretty evident that he hadn't been suborned by a foreign power or some criminal organisation. Ashton was tempted to return the confidential report book to the Ministry of Defence with a compliment slip, but he knew Jill Sheridan would want to peruse the document. What she would also want was a brief summary of Zawadzki's strengths and weaknesses. Ashton had got as far as writing the subject heading on a sheet of A4 when the telephone rang. Lifting the receiver he was greeted by an unusually ebullient Brian Thomas.

'Hope you're ready for this, Peter,' he said, and didn't wait for an answer before adding, 'I assume you're still interested in Zawadzki's former wives?'

The situation had changed and Ashton doubted if he needed the information now but he wasn't about to say so.

'What have you got for me?' he asked cheerfully.

'His first wife was a bit of a tart. After Zawadzki divorced her on the grounds of infidelity, Susan Mary Honeyman was cited in two other cases and took to the bottle with gusto. I don't know why she wasn't arrested for drink driving but one night in February 1979 her luck ran out. She was living in Leicester at the time and was batting along Charles Street doing a steady sixty when she lost control of her Ford Capri, mounted the pavement and ploughed into a lamppost. The lady didn't have her seat belt

71

on and went out through the windscreen. Smashed her skull like an eggshell on the pavement. Death was instantaneous according to the pathologist.'

Tracing the present whereabouts of Zawadzki's second wife, the former Camilla Smythe-Peters, had presented few difficulties for the friends of Brian Thomas. Armed with her personal details which Ashton had culled from the vetting papers held by the Foreign Office Security Department, they had gone straight to the Office of Population Censuses and Surveys at St Catherine's House. There, they had checked the registration of deaths and marriages under both her maiden and married names.

'Before she married Adam Zawadzki,' Thomas continued, 'Camilla used to be a school teacher. She took it up again after he left the army. When they split, she obtained a teaching post in Dedham. Six months ago, she married the local vet, a man called Steve Kirkpatrick. Their address is Steyne House, Priory Lane, Dedham, Essex.'

'Let me check that address.'

'That won't be necessary, Peter. It's on the way up to you.'

'Thanks.'

'All part of the service. Everybody's on their toes this morning.'

'Oh? Why's that?'

'Victor Hazelwood is back and champing at the bit,' Thomas said, and put the phone down.

There was nothing unusual about Hazelwood champing at the bit. He was a thruster, a man who liked to make things happen, a reputation he had established at the height of the Cold War when he had been in charge of the Russian Desk. His bullish approach to intelligence gathering had not endeared him to the Foreign and Commonwealth Office. Nevertheless, his rise to power had become meteoric after the Assistant Director of the Eastern Bloc, as it had been known in those days, had suffered a massive and fatal coronary in the office and Hazelwood had been promoted to run the department. Barely eighteen months later, Stuart Dunglass, who had spent most of his service in the Far East, had been appointed to the post of Director General and, much to his surprise, Hazelwood had been informed that he was to be Deputy DG. The onset of cancer of the prostate had forced Dunglass into early retirement and Hazelwood, who had been keeping the chair warm for him on and off while he was recovering from the effects of chemotherapy, had been confirmed in post by a reluctant Foreign Secretary.

Ashton heard somebody tap on the door to his office; then before he could look round to see who it was, Jill Sheridan announced her presence in a voice cold as the Arctic.

'A word with you, Peter,' she said.

'Sure.' Ashton stood up and turned to face her. 'What can I do for you?'

Jill closed the door so that they wouldn't be disturbed, then leaned against the wall, arms folded across her chest. Her eyes narrowed in anger.

'Perhaps you can explain why I had to learn your involvement in a murder investigation from Roy Kelso during morning prayers?'

'Brian Thomas must have told him and you know what Roy's like. He's always trying to impress Victor.'

'And that's all you have to say, is it?'

'Well, naturally I'm sorry—'

'That you didn't think to brief me last night or first thing this morning,' Jill said interrupting him.

'I didn't see any reason to do so,' he said coldly.

'In your judgement?'

'Yes.'

'Well, let's see if you made the right decision, Peter. Give me the whole story right from the beginning.'

In Ashton's opinion the whole story didn't amount to much and he said so unequivocally. The men who had murdered Adam Zawadzki had known exactly when he would arrive at Juan Santamaria Airport. Since Laura Greenwood was one of the very few who had been aware that her partner had been a last-minute replacement for Martin Edmunds, it was only sensible to

73

check whether she had made any international phone calls immediately prior to his departure.

'And had she?' Jill asked.

'No.'

'So you eliminated Laura Greenwood from your inquiries?'

'Yes. I told DI Hughes that she was of no interest to us.'

'Despite the fact that her house had been burgled and her daily murdered?'

'I believe the man who broke into her house was looking for something which neither Adam Zawadzki nor Laura Greenwood had ever seen or known about.'

'That's pure speculation.'

'You've seen the photographs of what they did to Adam,' Ashton reminded her. 'I've said it before and I'll say it again. If he'd known what they were after, don't you think he would have told them where to find it?'

'Zawadzki and the woman are all we've got.'

Ashton half turned away from Jill Sheridan and pointed to the pending tray.

'All the confidential reports that were ever written on Zawadzki while he was in the army are in that book. You should study them—'

'Later,' Jill told him. 'I'll look at the reports when I have a spare moment.'

'Yeah? Well, in the meantime we should start looking elsewhere. Martin Edmunds may appear whiter than white on paper but he wouldn't be the first man whose adverse character traits never came to light when he was being cleared for Top Secret and Codeword material. He could be in debt up to his eyebrows for all Foreign Office Security knows.'

Edmunds wasn't the only person Ashton wanted to put under the microscope. He was equally interested in those officials with whom Edmunds was in regular contact. But from the way Jill kept shaking her head it was clear she was not prepared to go down that particular road. Truth was they should have left it to the Foreign and Commonwealth Office to handle the Zawadzki business.

74

Maybe he was kidding himself but it seemed to him that Jill was beginning to wish she hadn't involved The Firm.

'What about Zawadzki's ex-wives,' Jill asked. 'Any word on their present whereabouts?'

'His first wife is dead. Camilla Zawadzki is now married to a vet called Steve Kirkpatrick. They live in Dedham.'

'When did Camilla divorce Zawadzki?'

'August 1994 and it was the other way round; Zawadzki initiated the proceedings and it was pretty acrimonious.'

'So when they split up he had already done five years with the Queen's Messenger Service. Right?'

'Yes.'

'OK, go and talk to Camilla, see what she has to say about her first husband. And do it today. This takes priority over whatever else you've got on your plate.'

'Have you any further instructions for me before I go down to the library?' Ashton asked, tight-lipped.

'What do you want from the library?'

'The appropriate phone book for Dedham. I'm not going anywhere until I know Camilla Kirkpatrick is at home.'

'Quite.' Jill straightened up, moved to her left and opened the door. 'Does the name Osvaldo Herrara ring a bell with you?'

Ashton shook his head. 'I've never heard of him.'

'Neither had I before Roger Benton mentioned him at morning prayers.'

Ashton waited for enlightenment but the seconds dragged by and Jill remained silent.

'Well, don't keep me in suspense,' he said. 'Who is he?'

'Colonel Herrara used to be the deputy chief of Fidel Castro's intelligence bureau until he went freelance. He was in Costa Rica from the fifth to the seventh of March. The Americans believe he murdered Adam Zawadzki. You might try bringing Herrara into the conversation when you meet Camilla Kirkpatrick.'

✱   ✱   ✱

The squat was on the Warlock Estate off West Green Road in North Harringay. In the Concise Oxford Dictionary, the noun 'warlock' was defined as a sorcerer or wizard but there had been nothing magical about the firm of architects who had designed Fabian House and similar housing units. Built in the 1960s and set in a concrete jungle, Fabian House had been a prime example of high-density living with 210 flats evenly distributed over seven floors. There was just one lift and that more often than not had been out of order, as had most of the washing machines and tumble dryers in the basement laundrette provided for the residents. The communal areas on every level had been poorly illuminated with the inevitable result that the staircase and gloomy passageways had eventually become a favourite stamping ground for drug pushers and muggers. Vandalism had been rife and the local authority slow to repair the damage. The good tenants had moved heaven and earth to get relocated and had been replaced by difficult families, a policy that had accelerated the downward spiral. The final nail in the coffin for Fabian House had been the discovery in 1989 that, as a fire precaution, the walls and ceiling in the boiler room had been insulated with asbestos. The gas, electricity and water had been cut off and the residents provided with alternative accommodation while the building was being refurbished. However, shortly after the fibrous silicate mineral had been ripped out, the government of the day had rate-capped council spending and work on Fabian House had been suspended. Eight months later, the council workmen had returned to board up most of the windows.

In 1993 Fabian House had been scheduled for demolition but to date that was still no more than a decision on a piece of paper. Although the building had been gutted it had become a playground for children by day and a haven for vagrants and meths drinkers at night

O'Meara and her two friends were camping out in a room on the fourth floor. In common with others living rough on the streets their clothes were crudely darned, shabby and in need of washing. They were, however, better equipped to face the rigours of life in Fabian House than all the other squatters. All three possessed a camp bed, sleeping bag and a foldaway canvas-bottom armchair. Between them they had two four-and-a-half-gallon jerricans full of drinking water, two Elsan chemical toilets and sufficient hexamine tablets to produce three hot meals a day as well as numerous cups of tea or coffee. They were also supplied with enough tinned rations to last them a week. Finally, there were two unusual items in their baggage, namely a tripod-mounted pair of binoculars and a Night Hawk surveillance system, which was essentially a second-generation image intensifier. Through an aperture made in the boarded-up window, these optics were trained on one of the lock-up garages opposite Fabian House.

Geraldine Dawn O'Meara was a detective sergeant in Special Branch. She was thirty-seven years old, going on thirty-eight, stood five feet nine in her stockinged feet and was as slim now as she had been when a weight-conscious teenager. Nursing a strong aversion to her first two names from childhood she had, on joining the Met, informed all and sundry that she would answer only to O'Meara.

The other woman on the surveillance detail was Francesca York, a former lieutenant in the army's Special Counter Intelligence Team, commonly known as SCIT. She had been taken on by MI5 at the end of her five-year short-service commission and was inclined to see herself as God's own gift to the Security Service. Technically, York was in charge of the surveillance operation. However, since officers of the Security Service had no greater powers of arrest than the ordinary citizen, the deployment of the mobile backup was vested in O'Meara.

The oldest and most junior member of the surveillance team was forty-five-year-old Detective Constable Kenny Browne, a sound, unambitious, but utterly dependable officer. If anybody was running the show it was Kenny Browne. It was he who organised the shifts, decided what they were going to eat, cooked every meal and kept the place tidy. Officially he had stood watch from 02.00 to 06.00 hours but he had allowed

O'Meara to have an extra thirty minutes in bed before waking her. Now, just over three hours later, he was up and about again, busily cooking breakfast for all three of them.

'Bacon and eggs in another five minutes,' he announced. 'You want some orange juice to start with?'

'I didn't know we had any,' O'Meara said.

'I brought a small carton with me, saved it for our last day on surveillance.'

'Well, thank you, Kenny.'

'My pleasure,' Browne said, and filled a polystyrene cup for her. 'Anything happening out there?'

'It's raining and nobody has been near the lockup.'

'It's early days yet. I mean, you think about it, the IRA didn't go near one of their arms dumps for months.'

'That was in Wales,' O'Meara told him, 'and they'd dug a deep cache in the middle of nowhere. This is a lock-up garage on a run-down housing estate in London. They can't afford to leave the stuff here for any length of time; it's too insecure. Of course I'm assuming we haven't been given a bum steer.'

'You have no worries on that score,' York said, suddenly wide awake. 'Our information is A1, the best you can have.'

'I'll take your word for it,' O'Meara said, and immediately regretted it, conscious of having sounded churlish.

Francesca York just smiled and told her she was an incorrigible pessimist, which made O'Meara feel even worse. This was the fourth day they had been living on top of one another, and she supposed it was small wonder that at times the atmosphere was definitely strained. She was tired and so dirty her skin felt as if it was crawling. The team was due to be relieved at 21.00 and the hours couldn't pass quickly enough for O'Meara. There was nothing like a good long soak in a hot bath to help you unwind. There was nothing like being a single parent with two difficult teenagers in the house to make you feel uptight again.

Two difficult teenagers? No, that was unfair on Wesley; at eighteen, he was now the same age as she had been when she'd married and the only grief he'd caused her was his determination to move out of the family home into a place of his own as soon as he could put enough money together. Common sense told O'Meara this was still a long way off but it didn't stop her worrying about how he would manage. The teenager who really stressed her out was fourteen-year-old daughter, Lisette, who had started being difficult when her dad had walked out on his family in 1989.

If there were two things O'Meara's children had in common it was hatred of the police and a strong aversion to all white people. They had reluctantly made an exception in her case and she had never had to put a personal relationship with whitey to the test. Six months ago she had begun an affair with Eric Daniels, a former sergeant in the Royal Military Police who was now employed as a full-time driver at Vauxhall Cross. In the few short weeks they had dated one another, O'Meara had lost count of the number of times she had resolved to end their relationship before it got too serious. In the end, the IRA had made things easy for her; one night in December 1995, when she had been dining with Eric at his place in Inkerman Road, two of their soldiers had paid him a visit. His front door had resembled a sieve after the two gunmen had put twenty-six rounds through it, which was the closest they had got to killing Eric. However, since it had been self-evident that the IRA had deliberately targeted him, the SIS had moved Daniels out of Inkerman Road, Camberwell to alternative accommodation in Worcester Park, far removed from where O'Meara lived in Islington.

She had visited Eric only once since he had moved house, and then just for an hour or so because Worcester Park wasn't too well served by public transport. No scenes with Lisette and Wesley over Eric Daniels and goodbye to a relationship that always worried her. But if things had worked out the way she wanted, O'Meara wondered why she felt down in the mouth most of the time.

'I think we are in business,' York said quietly. 'Small, dark blue van driving slowly past the lockups from right to left.'

O'Meara laid her plate of rapidly congealing eggs and bacon

to one side and joined Francesca York at the spyhole in the boarded-up window. Of the nine lockups, the one they were interested in was the sixth from the right. As they watched, the van continued on past the suspect garage then the driver put the wheel hard over to his left until the vehicle pointed towards Fabian House. Shifting into reverse, he backed up to number seven, stopping just short of the up-and-over door to allow his companion to get out and unlock it. As soon as the door was in the raised position, he engaged reverse gear again and closed up to the garage.

'Damn,' York said, then added, 'Relax everybody, it's a false alarm.'

Chapter Seven

It was almost inevitable that the man detailed to drive Ashton to Dedham should be Eric Daniels. An association which had begun quite by chance had become an established fact in the mind of the transport supervisor.

Daniels had joined the SIS in 1979 after completing twelve years' service in the Royal Military Police and rising to the rank of sergeant. The army had taught him the skills of defensive driving and he was one of the very few people who'd had occasion to put theory into practice. The SIS Head of Station, Athens, was alive today thanks to Daniels. In 1985, while he had been serving with the British Embassy as a specialist driver-cum-bodyguard, an active service unit of the Provisional IRA had tried to ambush the SIS man on the way to the international airport. The terrorists had opened fire much too soon and Daniels had been able to execute a hundred-and-eighty-degree-turn at speed. He had then rammed and killed the gunman whom the IRA had put out as a backstop.

At the age of forty-six, Daniels tipped the scales at a hundred and sixty-five pounds, which meant he'd gained only a couple of pounds during the seventeen years he'd been a civilian. He had, however, begun to acquire a double chin, but as yet there was no sign of grey in his light brown hair and there was hardly a line in his moon-shaped face. Nature had given him the sort of mouth that seemed permanently on the brink of a smile but not this morning or any other for quite some time. In fact Daniels had hardly said a word from the moment they had decided to head west on the M4 and join the orbital motorway at junction 15 rather than cross London to pick it up further north. He was still uncommunicative when they left the orbital to follow the A12 trunk road to Ipswich.

'How is O'Meara keeping these days?' Ashton enquired, broaching a subject he suspected was taboo.

'I wouldn't know,' Daniels told him. 'We've gradually stopped seeing each other since I moved to Worcester Park.'

'It's not an easy place to get to from where she lives.'

'I'll give you another of her excuses: a ninety-hour week is par for the course when you're in Special Branch.' Daniels sucked on his teeth. 'Truth is she couldn't handle this black and white syndrome and I didn't mean enough to O'Meara for her to try. End of story.'

'Pity.'

'I've no regrets,' Daniels said, trying too hard to sound as if he meant it. 'Anyway, what's with this Camilla Kirkpatrick?'

'She was Adam Zawadzki's second wife; he divorced her nineteen months ago. Since the split was pretty acrimonious our Deputy Director thinks Camilla might be a valuable source of information where her ex is concerned.'

'But you don't?'

'It'll be a complete waste of time.' He wasn't saying that because Jill Sheridan had told him to interview Camilla. It had everything to do with the fact that he'd had to phone her to make sure she would be in before he and Daniels set off for Dedham. As a result Camilla Kirkpatrick would be on her guard and careful what she said to him.

'Look at it this way,' Daniels said philosophically, 'it's all pensionable service.'

Seven miles beyond the A604 to Colchester they picked up the local sign for Dedham and turned off the A12 trunk road. The picturesque village was famed for its link with Constable and was a great tourist attraction, but on this grey, miserable-looking day there weren't too many visitors about. They stopped at the post office to ask directions to Priory Lane and were told to keep straight on past the church and take the next but one turning on the left beyond the almshouses.

Steyne House was not quite as impressive as its name suggested. Despite the leaded windows it was more early Victorian than Georgian. Outwardly a solid-looking box-shaped building with a portico, it was under siege from Virginia creeper, which had established an unshakable grip on the façade and was eating into the mortar. What had once been the stables had been converted into a veterinary clinic. The gravel drive, originally laid for a pony and trap, had been widened at the top end to provide parking spaces for up to a dozen vehicles. Daniels made a wide clockwise U–turn in front of the clinic and stopped outside the house a few feet beyond the portico.

Ashton got out of the car and walked back; before he could ring the bell Camilla Kirkpatrick opened the door to him. Since Brian Thomas had been unable to tell him much about the lady, Ashton had assumed that she would be roughly the same age as Adam Zawadzki, whose date of birth had been 8 January 1942. In fact far from being in her early fifties, he doubted if Camilla Kirkpatrick had turned forty yet. She was a couple of inches shorter than Harriet, which made her about five feet nine. She was wearing a pair of dark green slacks with matching waistcoat over a cream shirt with double cuffs. The colour of her hair, parted in the middle to frame a pert face, was burnished copper and had come out of a bottle.

'My name's Ashton,' he said.

'I'd already guessed as much,' she replied, amused. 'Do please come in.'

Ashton stepped inside, waited for Camilla to close the door behind him, then followed her down the hall and into the sitting room at the back. It seemed churlish to refuse her offer of coffee when she had already laid a tray in anticipation. All the same, Ashton was left with the uncomfortable feeling he was allowing Camilla to take charge.

'Your phone call was a bit of a bombshell,' Camilla told him. 'I didn't know Adam had been murdered.'

'That's understandable. It wasn't widely reported and by the time the Foreign and Commonwealth Office was prepared to release his name, the press had lost interest.'

'But not you people?' Camilla suggested.

'That's true. We're anxious to find out why he was murdered. In his official capacity he wasn't carrying anything that was worth killing for. So, to put it bluntly we are left wondering if he was up to no good. Both his colleagues and his superiors rated him highly but it wouldn't be the first time such character assessments proved wide of the mark.'

'And you'd like to know my opinion of Adam?'

'That's the general idea,' Ashton said.

'He divorced me, you know?'

'Yes.'

'So I could be prejudiced where he is concerned.'

'I'll chance it.'

Camilla said she wasn't sure where to begin but still made a pretty good fist of it. She had met Adam Zawadzki when she'd been teaching in Colchester and he had been on the staff of Headquarters Eastern District. This had been in 1982 when she was twenty-four. Two years later they had married and moved into army quarters.

'I thought Adam was very personable and good-looking but I was pretty naïve in those days and didn't realise he regularly dyed his hair.'

She had believed him when he had claimed that, at the very least, he would make brigadier, which Ashton thought was a prime example of self-delusion. Zawadzki would have entered the promotion zone to lieutenant-colonel at the age of thirty-seven and would have already been passed over on four separate occasions. Only a Walter Mitty character could have closed his eyes to the inescapable fact that for him to be selected thereafter would be nothing short of a miracle.

'It took me a long time to realise Adam couldn't deal with

life's disappointments. Whenever anything went wrong it was never his fault. The army board had a down on him because he was half-Polish and the Poles were on the wrong side in the Cold War, which was the most stupid thing I ever heard. I mean, if that had been their thinking why would they have backed his application to join the Queen's Messenger Service?'

After leaving the army Zawadzki had initially been in a much happier frame of mind. They had moved out of quarters in Colchester and bought a house in Dedham, using his terminal grant for the deposit. The building society had given them a mortgage of £150,000 on the strength of his army pension and their joint salaries. Over the next two years, soaring interest rates had put them in a financial bind. To reduce the mortgage payments Zawadzki had been allowed to commute sixty per cent of his pension, a solution which, though beneficial in the short term, did not allow for emergencies and restricted the amount of money available for living expenses.

'Instead of having the property independently surveyed, Adam cut a few corners and relied on the building society's valuation, which is a big mistake. Suddenly we discovered we had dry rot in the rafters and the whole damned roof needed to be replaced.'

Short of capital to effect the necessary repairs, they'd had to go to the building society and obtain a second mortgage. Faced with this setback Adam's old bitterness had returned and had rapidly become ugly.

'He started knocking me about, Mr Ashton; that's when I took up with Steven. Of course I wasn't the only target for his bitterness: Adam turned against his colleagues in the messenger service, whom he claimed were financially so much better off. They had to be up to something in his view, especially Martin Edmunds. He was always going on about him; wouldn't have it that the man might have a private income. I must say he certainly would have needed one if only half of what Adam told me was true . . .'

Suddenly Camilla had Ashton's undivided attention; suddenly he began to feel that driving up to Dedham hadn't been such a waste of time after all.

The weapon-training class was conducted in the flat above a Kurdish-owned dry goods store on Henning Road in Tottenham. The instructor, who was fluent in English, was Matias Inciarte, a Spanish citizen according to the passport in his possession. Since Matias Inciarte couldn't speak a word of Turkish, he was assisted by Mehmet Ozbek, who had collected the weapons from the Warlock estate earlier in the day.

The weapon was the RPG-7V rocket launcher, the standard man-portable short-range anti-tank weapon of the Red Army and their allies in the now defunct Warsaw Pact. It was also in general use throughout Asia, Africa and the Middle East. The three launchers now in the hands of the Kurdish dissidents had originally been supplied to the IRA by Colonel Gaddafi.

The RPG-7V was fitted with a range-finding optical sight for day use and an image intensifier for night firing. The 84mm grenade could penetrate 330mm of armour and had a maximum range of 300 metres against a moving target as opposed to 500 metres for a stationary one. The missile had large knifelike fins which sprang out when the missile emerged from the launcher tube. To improve stability in flight there were a number of small offset fins in the tail which gave the missile a slow rate of roll. Ten metres into the flight the rocket assistance kicked in to maintain the muzzle velocity at 120 metres a second.

The one drawback was the piezo-electric-type fuse. This produced a voltage when the nose of the grenade struck a wire mesh, which resulted in the fuse shorting out so that the high-explosive anti-tank warhead failed to function. However, the Kurdish dissidents were not planning to use the weapon against a vehicle fitted with a wire-mesh screen.

∗   ∗   ∗

86

With the relief watch due to take over from them at 21.00, Detective Constable Browne had reorganised the roster, reducing the hours spent on duty from four to two and a half with effect from 13.30. O'Meara had begun her last shift at 16.00 and had been on duty for exactly thirty-six minutes. By the time she finished her spell it would be close to last light, especially on such an overcast day as this. The more O'Meara thought about it the more she was convinced they should take a close look at the seventh lockup while there was still time to stand down the relief watch.

Unfortunately Francesca York was in charge of the operation and convincing her they should do this was not going to be easy. O'Meara had already questioned the validity of their information and had been firmly put in her place by the MI5 officer. If she was going to raise the issue again she would need to approach it from a different angle.

'Do we know the name of the person who is renting number seven?' O'Meara asked casually.

'Of course I do,' York said. 'Why do you ask?'

'Just interested.'

'It's rented by a Mr Hilak Ersoy, a Turkish gentleman who lived on the estate before moving to Woodlands Park two months ago. He's a plumbing and heating engineer and needed a lockup to keep the bits and bobs of his trade. Any other questions?'

O'Meara took a deep breath and let it out slowly, determined she wouldn't allow York's supercilious manner to rile her.

'Only one,' she said calmly. 'When did Mr Ersoy take possession of the lockup?'

York consulted her millboard again. 'November the sixth 1995, and he paid twelve months' rent in advance.'

'It's right next door to our suspect garage.'

'So is number five, and for your information, Sergeant, that one is rented by a Mr Jesson.'

O'Meara was observing the target through the spyhole, her

87

back to Francesca but it wasn't necessary to see the expression on her face to know how irritated she was.

'Mr Jesson has a flat in Beveridge House,' York continued, 'one of the few units on the estate which isn't scheduled for demolition. Since all the lockups over there were already taken before he moved in, he was allocated number five Fabian House to garage his Vauxhall Viva.' York paused, then said, 'I hope you're now convinced that our information is very good?'

'I keep thinking about the dark blue Ford van,' O'Meara said, sidestepping the question. 'The way the driver backed up to the garage.'

'What was unique about that?'

'He hardly left himself any room to get past the vehicle.'

To O'Meara it looked as if the van had been deliberately positioned to conceal the interior of the garage. It had been impossible to see what bits and bobs Mr Ersoy had kept inside the lockup, never mind what he and his workmate were loading into the vehicle.

'Did you notice that as soon as they had finished what they were doing, Mr Ersoy had pulled forward just far enough for his workmate to lower the up-and-over door?'

'That hadn't escaped me,' York said tartly. 'What I'd like to know is where all this is leading?'

'I think we're watching an empty stable.'

'You're talking about the target garage, are you?'

'Yes.'

'Dear God, how many times do you need telling—'

'They entered it from the one next door—'

'Oh, come on, Sergeant—'

'The dividing walls are undoubtedly constructed from breeze blocks. Wouldn't take much effort to chisel a few of those out and re-lay them after the mortar had been removed.'

'Well, granted that's not impossible but I'm not going near those lockups until you can come up with something more compelling than a mere hunch.'

'How old would you think that van was?' O'Meara asked. 'Eight years?'

'Ten,' York said.

'The number plate looked pretty new to me.'

'The original was either stolen or it fell off; in either event Mr Ersoy had to get another made up.'

'I should have made a note of the registration number,' O'Meara said.

'Don't fret yourself, I took it down,' York glanced at her millboard a third time. 'The number is C154XYY.'

'A London index,' Browne said. 'You want me to call it in?'

'We're going to need some quick answers, Kenny. I think I'd better speak to our Chief Super.'

Browne switched on his mobile, tapped out the number, then asked for extension 6784 before handing the instrument over to O'Meara. Her request was simple enough: what she wanted from the Driver and Vehicle Licensing Authority, Swansea, was the name of the registered owner and a description of the vehicle. She also explained why the information was required urgently and gave the number of Browne's mobile phone.

Seventy minutes later O'Meara learned that the name of the registered owner was Mr R. J. Dyer. The registration number she had quoted belonged to a 1.5 litre Nissan Cherry which had not been taxed since 1993.

'It's decision time,' O'Meara informed Francesca York. 'The dark blue Ford van had false number plates. That's reason enough to search those garages.'

'And if we don't find anything, what then? We'll have blown the whole operation.'

'I can open whatever garage you like,' Browne said, 'and nobody will ever know we've been inside. Picking the lock on an up-and-over door is child's play.'

'Kenny isn't boasting,' O'Meara assured York. 'Believe me, breaking and entering is his speciality.'

York still hesitated, seemingly unable to make up her mind

one way or the other. 'What time is last light?' she asked eventually.

'Sunset is 18.13 hours,' Browne told her.

'We'll wait until dark.'

'We don't have to give it that long,' O'Meara told her. 'The sky has been murky and overcast since eleven a.m.'

York moved up to the window and took O'Meara's place at the spyhole. 'You're right,' she said, 'it is pretty gloomy out there. Nevertheless we'll give it another half-hour to be on the safe side.'

The signal from Head of Station, Washington, was classified Secret and had been accorded an Op Immediate precedence. It read: 'Subject is Colonel Osvaldo Herrara. Further to my Int 25/ CA date and time group 13 March 0249Z hours. Friends now report that subject boarded Air France flight to Paris on 09 March travelling under the name of Matias Incirte and presented a Spanish passport to airline officials.'

The incoming signal was marked up for the attention of the Central America Desk of the Pacific Basin and Rest of the World Department by the Chief Archivist. It reached Roger Benton at 17.18 hours. Mindful of the roasting he had received from Hazelwood at morning prayers for failing to take positive action on the previous signal from Washington, he immediately had three photocopies made, sending the first to MI5, the second to the DG and the third to the acting Deputy DG. To Hazelwood's copy he attached a brief memo explaining that he had decided to keep the Security Service informed in case Herrara visited the UK, using the Spanish passport to go through Immigration on the nod as a citizen of the European Union. As very much an afterthought, Benton decided it would do no harm to make one more copy for Ashton's attention.

O'Meara peered at the luminous face of her wristwatch for the umpteenth time. Half an hour could seem an eternity when you were just waiting for it to pass. To keep herself occupied she had tried to calculate how much of her working life had been spent like this, watching and waiting.

'Three minutes to go,' York murmured.

Three minutes? O'Meara couldn't believe it. Francesca's watch must have stopped. Anyway, what possible difference could three minutes make? They should go in now.

'I think we've got a problem,' York said. 'One Rover 400 passing our position . . . turning right and parking next to the end garage . . . engine and lights switched off . . .'

O'Meara joined the MI5 officer at the spyhole and crouched beside her. The courtesy light came on inside the Rover as both front doors were opened simultaneously. The man who got out on the driver's side was wearing a dark suit which was almost *de rigueur* for the white-collar office worker. The girl with him was less inhibited: she was dressed in a hip-length jacket over a sweater, a short skirt and high-heeled leather boots.

'Well, what do you think?' York asked after the couple had got into the back of the car. 'Are we looking at an office affair or is he a kerb crawler who's picked up a tart?'

'If she's doing the business they'll be gone in five minutes.' O'Meara shrugged her shoulders. 'Otherwise who knows how long we may have to wait. Fact is the man won't give us any trouble regardless of whether he's getting it for free or putting money into her hot little hand. Same goes for the woman.'

'I hear what you say,' York told her, 'but it won't hurt to wait another five minutes.'

'Yes it will. The vagrants who have been away all day begging for hand-outs will be returning before long.'

York refused to change her mind. She just sat there, eyes glued to the Night Hawk image intensifier. The minutes dragged by, light rain began to fall again and the couple in the back of the Rover 400 stayed put.

'All right, let's do it,' York said in a resigned voice. 'Keep your personal radio on low volume. I'll beep you at the first sign of trouble.'

'Sure.' O'Meara picked up the pocket-sized radio, switched on the power supply and, having selected the correct channel, tucked the transceiver into her jacket. Followed by Browne she then left the room and felt her way down the staircase. Approaching the second-floor landing, she almost bumped into a bag lady who was taking up residence for the night, but at the last moment the woman turned off into the passageway to her left.

They reached the ground floor, walked along the corridor and left the building by the emergency exit, which the squatters had lifted off its hinges long before Special Branch had moved in. The Rover was still parked by the end garage but there was no sign of the occupants, not even the blurred outline of a head and shoulders in the rear window.

When Kenny Browne had claimed that springing the lock of an up-and-over door was child's play he hadn't been joking. Using a skeleton key which he had confiscated from a small-time car thief when he was in the uniformed branch, he effected an entry in under ten seconds. However, even with the aid of a pencil type flashlight, it took him considerably longer to find the loose breeze blocks in the side wall. He looked round for something flat to prise the first block loose and noticed that, amongst all the empty plywood boxes and assorted items of rubbish, a garden spade had been propped against the wall in the opposite corner. The blade was thin enough to slide between the blocks; levering the spade up and down, he succeeded in inching the topmost one far enough out from the others for him to get his fingers under the rim and remove it from the wall. Thereafter the task became progressively easier.

The irregular-shaped hole into the adjoining garage was roughly three feet by two at its highest and widest points. Ducking his head and right shoulder under the lintel, Browne swept the interior of the lockup with his flashlight.

'Looks as though you were right, Sergeant,' he said quietly. 'If there was an arms cache here, those two guys in the dark blue van cleared it out. Of course the cache could be hidden under the foundations.'

'Can you see any sign that part of the floor has been picked out and replaced with a wooden trapdoor painted to resemble concrete?'

'Not from here I can't. I'll take a closer look.'

'No, you wait until I've had a word with Ms York.' O'Meara took out her pocket radio, pressed the transmit button and called up Francesca York. Getting no response, she tried again and still failed to raise her.

'Either this set is on the blink,' she told Browne, 'or else the garage is screening the signal. I'm going outside to give it another shot. Meantime you stay where you are.'

'Better tell her ladyship it looks as if the Provos have put in a false ceiling. I reckon it's about a foot below the flat roof.'

'We'll check it out.'

'Gotcha.'

O'Meara walked out of the garage and found a spot in the shadows which offered a clear line of sight to their OP on the fourth floor. Before she could establish communications, York came up on the air to report that her signals were intermittent.

'Roger that,' O'Meara said. 'How do you hear me now?'

'Loud and clear.'

'OK. The cupboard appears to be bare.'

Above the background mush of her radio, O'Meara heard Browne scream, then a freak tornado hit her in the back.

York saw a slab of concrete from the flat roof of the suspect garage lift off into the air, saw the closed up-and-over door burst out of the frame, saw a body being swept along the ground, then heard the loud whoompf of an explosion. The kinetic energy also travelled sideways blasting a section out of the end wall of the garage block into the Rover 400. There followed a series of minor explosions as the windscreen, rear and side windows imploded.

There was a standard operating procedure for just such an incident, but totally shocked by what she had witnessed, York was incapable of putting theory into practice. Her hands wouldn't stop trembling and her heart went into overdrive so that she had to fight for every breath. She was vaguely aware that one of the police mobiles on the surveillance net was asking for a sitrep. Then suddenly the paralysis receded and she started to function again.

'Unknown X-ray station,' she said with a slight quiver. 'This is zero. Bombrep, I say again, bombrep Fabian House, Warlock Estate. All emergency services required soonest. Acknowledge. Over.'

A crisp, decisive voice said, 'X-ray one. Wilco.'

The first paramedic team arrived on the scene exactly four minutes later and were followed by a fire engine and two more ambulances. By then Francesca York was sufficiently composed to call her superior officer, report what had happened and ask for further instructions.

Chapter Eight

Ashton alighted from the District Line train at Ravenscourt Park, walked down the staircase to the booking hall below and out on to the street. The quick cut to Rylett Close was through the park and on down the side of the Royal Masonic Hospital. The park gates, however, were always locked at sunset, which meant that until the evenings started to draw out, he was obliged to go the long way round via King Street and Goldhawk Road. Tonight was no exception.

He could not recall a single occasion when he had arrived home and hadn't found Harriet doing something – ironing, preparing the evening meal or effecting some minor house repair which he had neglected to do in spite of umpteen reminders. And sometimes when he was home early enough, which was not very often, he would find her upstairs bathing Edward or reading him a story. Tonight, however, Harriet met him in the hallway, an empty glass in one hand, anger showing in her narrowed eyes and tight-lipped expression.

'Why the hell didn't you phone me?' she said with barely suppressed fury. 'I can't tell you how many times I tried your mobile number.'

'When was this?'

'From six fifteen onwards.'

'Oh, well, that explains it. I was on my way home, so I switched it off.'

'You idiot, you might have guessed I would be worried sick.'

'I'm not with you,' Ashton said quietly. 'You mind telling me what this is all about?'

'You mean you haven't heard? There was a terrorist incident on a housing estate in Harringay. At least two people were killed.'

'I wasn't anywhere near the place.'

'That isn't what the duty officer led me to believe.'

Harriet had telephoned Vauxhall Cross and had asked the switchboard operator to put her through to the duty clerk of the Admin Wing. Had Ashton been killed or injured somebody in Roy Kelso's department would have broken the news to her, as she was only too well aware. It had been Frank Warren who had called on her after a man called Gillespie had put a bullet through Ashton's left shoulder immediately below the collarbone with a 6.35mm Walther PPK semiautomatic pistol.

From what Ashton could gather, it looked as though there had been an unfortunate misunderstanding between the duty clerk and Harriet. She had referred to the news flash on BBC1, had told the duty clerk she couldn't raise her husband on his mobile and had then asked if the Admin Wing had heard anything. The clerk had evidently assumed Harriet knew for a fact that Ashton had been present when the bomb had detonated and had therefore told her that at present she knew no more than Harriet did.

'I was overwrought,' Harriet said, 'and I wasn't thinking very clearly.'

Ashton slipped an arm around Harriet's waist and steered her into the sitting room. He didn't have to tax his brain for a reason to explain why she had felt distraught. Since July last year Harriet had suffered one personal tragedy after another. First the miscarriage after falling downstairs. Then, Margaret Egan, her mother, had committed suicide. The discovery that she had cancer of the breast had come too late for surgery; instead the specialist had decided to kill the growth with chemotherapy but eventually the cancer had spread and there had been nothing more the doctors could do for her except ease the pain. A singularly determined woman, Margaret Egan had made up her mind that she would choose when to die. To facilitate this she had obtained a large plastic bag and one morning, soon after her husband had gone downstairs to make a pot of tea, she had found the strength to put her head inside the bag and suffocate herself.

The news of Margaret Egan's death had been a double blow for Harriet because she hadn't known her mother had cancer. If that hadn't been bad enough, the general tenor of the coroner's questions at the inquest had created the impression he believed Frederick Egan had assisted his wife to commit suicide. Now, six months later, Harriet was having to cope with the gradual physical and mental deterioration of her father. Only that morning she had received a letter from Frederick Egan's house-keeper giving notice of her intention to leave his employment a week this coming Friday. Her reasons were twofold: she was not prepared to put up with his foul language a moment longer and she was tired of being groped. She would be the second housekeeper to give notice since Margaret Egan had died and the problem of finding somebody to look after her father would fall on Harriet, rather than her brother and sister-in-law who lived in the same city.

'I think you could do with another drink,' Ashton said. 'What'll you have?'

'I'd better stick to whisky and soda.'

Ashton took the empty glass from Harriet and poured her a single from the bottle of Teacher's on top of the drinks cabinet, then almost drowned it in soda water.

'With my background in MI5 I shouldn't have panicked. It's the Security Service which is responsible for countering the threat posed by the Provisional IRA and its various factions.' Harriet accepted the tumbler from him and drank some of the diluted whisky, then said, 'Logically I knew you couldn't have been involved but wherever and whenever there is trouble you seem to be involved. Memory and imagination did the rest.'

She could not forget how emaciated he had looked when he'd been released from Moscow's Lefortovo prison after spending seventy-eight days in solitary confinement. And how long ago was it since he had returned from California with a hole in his shoulder and had had to spend two mornings a week working out in the gym belonging to Lincoln City Football Club to get himself fit for the next time he was sent in harm's way?

'Soon as I learned that Victor Hazelwood was back, I was convinced you were somehow involved in the Harringay incident.'

Ashton didn't say anything. He had ceased to remonstrate with Harriet when she had a go at Victor. She had never understood the bond which existed between them and was never likely to. Harriet believed that Hazelwood simply used him. To her way of thinking loyalty extended in both directions – down as well as up – but with Victor it was, in her opinion, strictly one way.

'Anyway, what sort of day have you had?'

'Not bad.'

Ashton followed her out of the sitting room into the kitchen. 'Eric Daniels and I took a run up to Dedham.'

'Whose idea was that?'

'Jill Sheridan's.'

'Really!'

'She is my boss. Remember?'

'And a great improvement on Victor.' Harriet opened the door of the fan-assisted oven and looked inside, then closed the door and pushed the regulator up to 190 degrees centigrade. 'Why Dedham?' she asked, and turned away from the cooker.

'To see a lady named Camilla Kirkpatrick who used to be married to Adam Zawadski.'

Ashton told her why he had thought the journey would be a complete waste of time and how he'd changed his mind when Camilla Kirkpatrick repeated what Adam had told her about Martin Edmunds. He did not have to tell Harriet the

98

adverse character traits that might indicate a mole; he merely gave her the facts such as they were and let her draw her own conclusions.

'According to Camilla Kirkpatrick, Edmunds is a gambling man. He has an account with William Hill, the bookmakers, and will bet on anything – horses, dogs, prizefighters, snooker, pool, golf. And he never had a gentle flutter either. Zawadzki claimed he had seen a fair number of his betting slips and the smallest was a round hundred. Edmunds is also into roulette, blackjack and poker. Plays the tables at Annabel's and elsewhere until the sun comes up.'

'Does he have private means?' Harriet asked.

'There is nothing in his security file to indicate he has. Same applies to his wife.'

'Perhaps he's a percentage gambler, bets heavily on the favourite?'

'He'd need to be to wear Armani suits.'

'All right, what did Edmunds do before he became a Queen's Messenger?'

'He was a chief superintendent in the Hong Kong Police Force.' Ashton clucked his tongue. 'Could be he made his money out there – one way or another.'

'Was there no detailed assessment of his finances in the security file?'

'No, but Edmunds is portrayed as whiter than white.'

'Then something isn't right,' Harriet said. 'If it were up to me I would want to interview him in depth.'

Me too, Ashton thought, but it wasn't going to happen. Jill Sheridan had already indicated that she wasn't prepared to look at Edmunds.

'Dinner will be another half-hour,' Harriet announced.

'Good. What are we having?'

'Ragout of lamb. You can open a bottle of Merlot . . .' She paused, head cocked. 'After you've answered the damned Mozart,' she added.

It wasn't every day of the week that the DG rang Ashton at

home and he couldn't recall a single occasion when Hazelwood had done so for social reasons.

He could tell Victor was enjoying one of his favourite Burma cheroots by the throaty sound of his voice and that meant he was calling from his study, the only room in the house where smoking was permitted. The fact that he seemed in a hurry to get off the phone led Ashton to conclude that his wife, Alice, was giving one of her dinner parties and he had been given strict instructions to keep it short and sweet. Hazelwood was brief all right, but only because he knew little more than Ashton did and what few details he was able to pass on were far from pleasant.

Ashton hung up, then lifted the phone again and rang the duty clerk of the Admin Wing. On learning that Daniels' home number in Worcester Park wasn't available, he asked the duty officer to ring him back on the open line as soon as she had the information. By the time he returned to the kitchen, Harriet had already uncorked the wine.

'So who was that on the phone?' she asked.

'Victor Hazelwood. He told me O'Meara was caught in that bombing on the Warlock Estate. She was rushed to St Ann's General Hospital, which fortunately is practically on the door-step because her injuries are said to be severe.'

'I'm sorry to hear that, Peter.'

'I'm trying to contact Eric Daniels.'

'Yes, of course, he'd want to know. Did Victor tell you how it happened?'

'Only that O'Meara and a Detective Constable Browne were searching one of the lockups on the estate when the bomb went off.'

'It had to be a trip wire,' Harriet said.

'Probably.' Ashton shrugged his shoulders. 'Maybe we'll know better when MI5 conduct their in-house inquiry at the training centre. Anyway, that's where I'll be tomorrow; Victor has arranged for me to sit in on the proceedings.'

'What has it got to do with the SIS?'

'Everything and nothing,' Ashton told her. 'Victor has got it into his head that some terrorist group besides the Provos were involved.'

The powerful are lamps were still burning one hour after what should have been sunrise had the sky not been hidden by a thick overcast. The effects of the blast were, however, clearly visible in the harsh white light which made the tiny fragments of glass from the shattered windscreen of the Rover glitter like diamonds. The driver's side of the vehicle had been bombarded with bricks and lumps of concrete that had punched great holes in the bodywork. A jagged piece of metal had ruptured the fuel tank and the escaping petrol had formed an ever-widening pool under the vehicle. Like flood water seeping over a river bank the fuel had meandered across the asphalt towards the end garage where several sacks of cotton waste had been set alight.

The fuel had ignited with a hollow whoomph and a tongue of flame had raced towards the Rover. A split second later the tank had exploded, creating a ball of fire that had incinerated the two people in the back of the car. In response to a 999 call more ambulances had arrived on the scene than there had been casualties to deal with. A couple of fire engines from the station on Sperling Road had extinguished the burning waste and damped down the wreckage of the neighbouring lockups. By far and away the biggest task had been the evacuation of Fabian House and the temporary rehousing of the squatters in the Harringay Community Centre. Officers of the Anti-Terrorist Squad had then searched the derelict building to make sure the IRA hadn't planted a second bomb. Finally the whole garage area had been taped off and left under guard.

At 08.00 hours scene of crime officers together with the bomb squad would literally sift through the rubble looking for traces of explosive which might enable them to identify the bombmaker.

★　　★　　★

The training centre run by MI5 was located in Bruton Place off New Bond Street. It was situated directly above a picture gallery and shared a common entrance. Since the Security Service did not advertise its presence the uninitiated frequently blundered into the picture gallery whose attendants cheerfully redirected the lost and strays to the Spooks Department on the floor above. This description was inaccurate; the centre existed purely to train those civil servants from government ministries who had been designated as branch security officers in addition to their normal work. Officers of MI5 were in fact trained elsewhere.

Ashton was no stranger to the centre; he had gone there almost three years ago to pick the brains of Clifford Peachey who had then been head of K1, the Kremlin watchers. He had heard of Richard Neagle, the MI5 officer who had been in charge of the surveillance operation on the Warlock Estate, but although he knew a great deal about the man, he had never met him. On the other hand, Francesca York wasn't even a name.

Neagle had passed the landmark age of forty but you would never think it to look at him. Something in his genes had given him the round puckish face of a mischievous child which time was unlikely to ravage. The same could not be said for his wispy fair hair, which he had carefully brushed across the scalp to disguise the number of bald patches.

Francesca York was in her mid-twenties and had blonde hair which she wore shoulder-length, possibly in an attempt to soften her face. Her voice was too precise to be natural which suggested she had had elocution lessons when very young. She exuded an innate air of superiority which Ashton thought would not have gone down too well with O'Meara.

'I was going to hold the inquiry in the chief instructor's office,' Neagle said after he'd introduced Ashton to Francesca York, 'but I'm afraid we would have found it a bit cramped. So I moved us into the syndicate room next door.'

The syndicate room was roughly eighteen feet by nine, which meant there was just enough space for a table and half a dozen tubular steel chairs. The solitary window was shoulder high and offered no view whatsoever. Neagle sat at the head of the table with Francesca York on his immediate right opposite Ashton. There was no shorthand writer to record the proceedings and no means of taking notes either.

'I thought we would keep this pretty informal,' Neagle told him.

Informal was not the word Ashton would have chosen; downright cosy would have been a more accurate description of the manner in which Neagle intended to conduct the inquiry. He wondered if in fact they were simply rehearsing their stories prior to a full-blown investigation.

'If you would like to begin, Fran . . .' Neagle said, smiling at York.

'Where should I start, Richard? With the briefing?'

'From dawn yesterday will do.'

'Right. Well, we had been on watch for over three days and were due for relief at 21.00 hours last night.'

There had been several close calls with individual squatters who had taken up residence in Fabian House. One drunk had kicked in the door to the room they were using and had been ejected by Kenny Browne. The detective constable had given the man a good kicking to convince him that paying them another visit would not be a sound idea. Between the hours of five to midnight, the condemned section of the estate was a favourite haunt for kerb crawlers and the Toms they had picked up. None of them had ventured inside Fabian House; when it came to fornicating, the back seat of a car or the interior of a van was infinitely preferable to a condemned building that stank of urine.

'Their presence was a formidable deterrent,' York continued. 'I couldn't see the IRA going near the cache while that sort of activity persisted. If we were right, the critical period when we really needed to be on our toes was the seven and a half hours of darkness between midnight and dawn.'

All nine lockups were rented out, and from observation they knew which tenants used them daily. The arrival of the dark blue Ford van was, however, unusual.

'I thought we were in business but the driver went past the garage we were watching. Naturally I made a note of the registration number but otherwise I took no action. Our information was very precise and I was satisfied the van was not making a pick-up.'

Ashton didn't like the way the inquiry was being conducted; it was all too laid back and lacked penetration. There were questions that needed to be raised and Neagle was giving a pretty good impression of a Trappist monk.

'When exactly did you check the registration number with Swansea?' he asked, butting in.

'Sergeant O'Meara called the number in at 16.40.'

'In other words more than six hours after you saw the vehicle?'

'I wasn't sitting there with my mind in neutral,' York said angrily. 'The registration mark was appropriate for a ten-year-old vehicle.'

'So why did you eventually check it out?'

'It had a lot to do with Sergeant O'Meara. Patience is not one of her strong suits; it took less than twenty-four hours to conclude that the source had given us a bum steer. She went on and on about it, said we should open the garage and see what, if anything, we were keeping under surveillance. Finally I asked her to give me one good reason why we should jeopardise the whole operation and of course she couldn't. Not long after that O'Meara fastened on to the registration mark of the Ford van. She said the plates looked brand new and therefore had to be false.' York turned away from Ashton, gazed instead at Neagle and smiled warmly. 'I pointed out that the original plates could have been stolen or one of them could have been lost but Sergeant O'Meara wouldn't have it.'

O'Meara was impatient, pig-headed, arrogant and contemptuous of anybody whose opinions ran contrary to her own. Maybe York hadn't said so outright but it was certainly the general thrust of her observations. What annoyed Ashton was the fact that O'Meara wasn't there to defend herself.

'Funny she managed to get it right and you didn't,' Ashton said in a voice loaded with sarcasm. 'Perhaps it was sheer luck.'

'That's uncalled for,' Neagle told him.

'When did you learn that the van had false plates?' Ashton said, ignoring him.

'Approximately seventy-five minutes after O'Meara phoned the Yard.'

'And that was when you decided to break into the lockup?'

'No, I waited until it was dark. Although DC Browne had a skeleton key which would open all nine garages and had assured me nobody would ever know he had been inside the place, I was concerned to keep the surveillance operation in being. There was less chance of being seen at night, that's why I refused to countenance a break-in while it was still light.'

'What about the dark blue van? Did you do anything about it?'

'No I didn't, Mr Ashton. While the operation was in the planning stage, the police had warned us that petty crime was rampant on the estate. Half the vehicles we saw running about were untaxed and uninsured.'

To Francesca York the Ford van had been just one more dodgy vehicle and she certainly hadn't wanted the local boys in blue clodhopping all over the place. In her view too much had been at stake to prejudice the operation because two petty criminals were up to no good.

'But in the end you did,' Ashton said quietly.

'Because O'Meara kept dripping away and I allowed her to cloud my judgement.'

Ashton scowled. She made it sound as if O'Meara was solely responsible for what had happened; that there wouldn't have been an incident had she not been so headstrong. He thought of O'Meara lying in a coma, her life hanging by a thread. He had phoned St Ann's General Hospital every hour on the hour only to be told that she was doing as well as could be expected. It wasn't until gone midnight that he had learned the full extent of her injuries. Fractured skull, flash burns from neck to waist, both legs fractured, the right in two places, pelvis broken, left elbow shattered, nose and jaw broken. If that wasn't enough, it had been necessary to perform an emergency operation on the brain to remove a blood clot. Had she not moved towards the Rover, death would have been instantaneous; even so the neurosurgeon was only prepared to give her a fifty-fifty chance and doubted if she would ever walk again.

Deep in thought, Ashton didn't catch what Neagle had just asked him.

'I'm sorry,' he said, 'would you mind repeating that?'

'I wanted to know if there was anything else we could tell you?'

'Yeah, there is.' Ashton turned to Francesca York. 'The two men in the dark blue van – did you take a photo of them?'

'The co-ax failed,' Neagle told him.

'Come again?'

'It's a new surveillance device. Briefly, the binoculars incorporate a miniature camera which is automatically focused on to whatever object you are observing. Unfortunately the film jammed in the cartridge and none of the exposures came out.'

'But I was able to describe the driver to the police,' York said eagerly.

'Could you describe him again for my benefit?'

'I don't see why not. He's medium height and build, say five feet eight to five nine, a hundred and fifty to one fifty-five pounds evenly distributed. His hair is very dark and there are pockmarks on the right cheek. Despite this blemish and the suggestion of a cleft chin, he is not bad-looking.'

'How far was your OP from the lockups?'

'Thirty yards line of sight. And, yes, the binoculars I had were extremely powerful.'

'They'd need to be,' Ashton said drily. 'What else can you tell me about him?'

'I think he's of Mid East origin. And there could be a Turkish connection.'

'Why's that?'

York smiled and looked even more pleased with herself, if that were possible.

'Because the garage is rented by a Mr Hilak Ersoy, who was born in Ankara.'

'Does he live on the estate?'

'Ersoy did until he moved to Woodland Park Road a couple of months ago,' Neagle said, then added, 'And yes, we will be present when the Turkish gentleman is questioned by Special Branch.'

'I guess that's it then,' Ashton told him. 'I'm sorry to have taken up so much of your time but it has been very illuminating.'

'What, no pearls of wisdom to offer?' Neagle said in a mocking voice.

'Well, since you ask, in your shoes I'd dump the source.'

There was, Ashton decided, no need to give his reasons. Neagle was smart enough to see that either his source was working both sides of the street or the IRA had sussed he was a tout and had used him to sucker MI5 into an ambush.

'Any other snippets you'd care to pass on?'

'Yes. I wouldn't count on finding Mr Hilak Ersoy at home when you call on him.'

Ashton left the syndicate room, went down the staircase and walked out into the street. It was a typical day in March with a persistent drizzle falling from a murky sky and a wind strong enough to drive the rain into his face.

Chapter Nine

Measured in a straight line Vauxhall Cross was a mile and three-quarters from New Bond Street. It seemed to be considerably further by public transport. By the time Ashton walked through the door it was seven minutes after eleven and morning prayers had finished long ago. Undoing the top button of his raincoat, Ashton fished out the plastic ID card which was attached to a thin chain around his neck and showed it to the MoD policeman on duty in the lobby, then went over to the bank of lifts. A faint hope that he might escape the eagle eye of Enid Sly, the senior clerical officer on the reception desk, was doomed when she called out to inform him that she had been instructed to let the DG know the moment he arrived.

'You haven't seen me,' Ashton told her, and pressed the call button to summon one of the lifts.

'Oh, but I have, sir.'

'Well, give me ten minutes before you phone his personal assistant.'

'That would be more than my job is worth, Mr Ashton.'

'OK, tell Mr Hazelwood's PA that I've gone for a morning constitutional but he's welcome to join me in the gents' lavatory on the fourth floor.'

A car arrived from the second floor and, stepping into it, Ashton pressed the button for the fourth. There was, he thought, a good chance that Ms Enid Sly would convey his message word for word and enjoy doing it because she couldn't stand Victor's PA. Alighting from the lift, he bought himself a cup of what passed for coffee from the vending machine, then dropped by the clerks' office to let the Chief Archivist know he was in.

As the Grade I Intelligence Officer (General Duties) his responsibilities were ill defined and puzzled many people. Those who didn't want to be caught out, like Henry Orchard of the Asian Department and Roger Benton, Head of the Pacific Basin and Rest of the World, bombarded him with files and detached folios marked 'For information only'.

'There are a couple here from Mr Benton which arrived after you'd left the office yesterday evening,' the Chief Archivist said gloomily, and proceeded to load the in-tray with files until the stack was a good eighteen inches above the rim and in danger of toppling over. 'The initial-and-forget stuff is at the bottom of the pile,' he added.

'What about the loose-leaf memo I wrote to the Deputy Director before I went home? Has she seen it yet?'

'First thing this morning, Mr Ashton, and she's returned it with a note. You'll find it right on top.'

Ashton thanked the Chief Archivist, picked up the phone and rang the MT Section. From the transport supervisor he learned that Eric Daniels had phoned from St Ann's General Hospital to report that O'Meara's condition was unchanged, and could he please take the rest of the day off to be with her?

'He didn't really give me any option, Mr Ashton.'

'Quite right too,' Ashton said, and hung up.

The note from Jill Sheridan was brevity itself; in her forward-sloping hand she had written, 'Please speak'. The same message was also attached to the army's confidential report book on Major Adam Zawadzki, which he had marked up for Jill's information yesterday before leaving for Dedham. Ashton transferred the document to the pending tray and plucked a slim, brown-coloured folder from the top of the pile awaiting his attention. The folder contained photocopies of two further communications relating to Colonel Osvaldo Herrara plus a query from the Chief Archivist, who wanted to know if they should open a branch memorandum on the Cuban. The signal from Head of Station, Washington, drew attention to the fact Osvaldo Herrara had travelled to Paris on a Spanish passport under the name of Matias Inciarte. Of even more interest was a photograph of Herrara, which had been faxed by the CIA at Langley in response to a request from the SIS Head of Station.

The face Ashton was looking at resembled the driver of the Ford van whom Francesca York had described. Unfortunately the repro quality was not good and he couldn't tell whether there were pockmarks on the right cheek, nor was there any sign of a cleft chin. On the other hand he was not bad-looking and according to the addendum below the picture he was about the right height and weight. He held the fax out at arm's length and studied the face from all angles, then reached to answer the phone as it started ringing. The prim voice of Hazelwood's PA asked him if he was now ready to face the DG.

'I'll be right up,' Ashton told her and put the phone down.

He left the filing trays on the desk, locked the door to his office and pocketed the key. Rather than wait for a lift, he used the staircase under the delusion that the exercise would be good for him.

Anybody who wanted to see Victor Hazelwood had to go through his PA, which did a lot for her self-esteem. There were a couple of light bulbs above the communicating door between the two offices. The red meant the DG was engaged while the green indicated he was free. For at least half the time neither light was switched on. The moment Ashton walked into the office, the PA pressed a button on the underside of her desk and the green lit up.

'Please go through, Mr Ashton,' she said with a smile that was entirely saccharine.

Officially, smoking had been banned in all government ministries while the SIS was still occupying Century House. Never one to comply meekly with a regulation he regarded as an infringement on his personal liberty, Hazelwood had had an extractor fan installed in his new office before the Firm had actually moved to Vauxhall Cross. When a few months later Hazelwood had replaced the ailing Sir Stuart Dunglass as DG, Roy Kelso had found himself landed with a bill for another extractor fan which had to be met from the contingency fund. Despite the extractor fan, the office was impregnated with the aroma of countless Burma cheroots. Although the cut-down shellcase that served as an ashtray was emptied every night it already contained five stubs. The number would shortly be increased to six as Hazelwood selected another cheroot from the ornately carved wooden box which he had bought on a field trip to India long before Ashton had joined the SIS in 1982.

'Sit down and tell me about the inquiry,' he said, and struck a match.

'It was more like a dress rehearsal,' Ashton told him. 'Neagle seemed to be coaching Francesca York, the junior officer in charge of the surveillance team.'

'Is she attractive?'

'If your taste runs to snooty blondes who fancy themselves. Anyway, the operation was a cockup and she did her best to lay the blame on O'Meara.'

As briefly as he could, Ashton related the sequence of events from the time the Ford van had arrived on the scene to the detonation of the bomb some hours later. 'The only positive thing to emerge from the inquiry was York's description of the van driver. If he isn't Colonel Herrara he could certainly pass as his double.'

'You're referring to this fax Roger Benton received from Washington?'

'Yes.' Ashton wondered how to put the next bit tactfully since what he was about to suggest was akin to teaching his mother to suck eggs. 'It might be an idea to send a copy to Five,' he said diffidently.

'Roger has already done that. Wouldn't do any harm to have a friendly word with Neagle and point him in the right direction.' Hazelwood contemplated the cheroot he was smoking for a moment or two. 'That's a job for you,' he said eventually.

'I don't think Neagle will take it kindly coming from me. I've only met him the once and we've already crossed swords.'

'Then you'll have to uncross them. If Miss York is satisfied the man she saw was Colonel Herrara it will be your job to hunt him down.'

Ashton resisted the temptation to ask if he was expected to do this all by himself. There had been a time when he could gently take the mickey out of Hazelwood but that was long before Victor became Head of the Eastern Bloc Department and he, Ashton, had been the number-two man on the Russian Desk, occupying the next door but one office to him. Those were the days, he thought, and felt a twinge of regret at their passing.

'Naturally you will be given adequate resources,' Hazelwood continued.

'That's nice,' Ashton said vaguely.

'You seem preoccupied, Peter. What's on your mind?'

'To be honest, I don't know who I'm working for. You tell me to do one thing, Jill gives me a different task.'

'I'll have a word with her.'

Briefing over, Ashton told himself, a supposition which proved correct when somewhat pointedly Hazelwood drew his attention to the in-tray and the solitary file it contained.

The door to the Deputy DG's office was wide open but there was no Jill Sheridan and all the filing trays had been removed from the desk. From her PA he learned that Jill was wearing her other hat and was spending the morning working in the Mid East Department.

On the principle that no good ever came from putting things off, he rang Gower Street and asked for Richard Neagle. In accordance with MI5 standing orders, the switchboard operator pretended she didn't recognise the name and asked what extension he wanted. Faced with this impasse, Ashton told the girl to ring Vauxhall Cross and asked for 0028. Once his identity had been established to her satisfaction he was put through to Neagle. Cool was the word that came to mind when Neagle learned who was calling him on the Mozart link. Thereafter both parties wanted to finish their conversation as quickly as possible. Neagle said he had never heard of Herrara and wasn't aware that Benton had sent a number of faxes about him to the Security Service. He thanked Ashton for putting him wise and undertook to return his call after he had obtained the likeness and shown it to Francesca York.

Brian Thomas glanced at the notes he'd made on a piece of scrap paper and left the office, locking the door behind him. It would have been easier to pick up the phone and tap out 0028 but he was glad of any excuse to go walkabout. Life had become very dull since he had been promoted to Head the Security Vetting and Technical Services Division. He hated being cooped up in an office all day and missed the investigative work of a vetting officer. He liked meeting people and was good at striking a rapport with the person he was required to interview. More often than not this was done at the workplace. Occasionally, however, it was conducted in the privacy of the individual's house, and it was truly amazing what some people would tell you when their guard was down. Thomas recalled a man in his late thirties who'd shot himself well and truly in the foot when his current vetting status was being enhanced before he was offered the post of Chief Archivist in what was then the Eastern Bloc Department. When asked towards the end of his subject interview if there was anything else he thought Brian Thomas should know, the man had suddenly disclosed that he was being blackmailed.

It had started at Christmas in 1986 with the amateur theatrical production of *Cinderella*. His wife had been the principal boy in the pantomime and he had been cast as one of the ugly sisters with the twist that he had looked far from ugly. He had told Thomas that after the production he and his wife had discovered a taste for cross dressing. It had seemed harmless enough to them when they had indulged in this fetish at home. Unfortunately they had become more and more adventurous and had taken to frequenting clubs and singles bars where they had flirted with members of their own sex. For two years both partners had got away with the deception but as they had become even bolder, the inevitable had happened and he had been photographed in a compromising situation. From then on he had been paying hush money at the rate of five hundred a month.

Thomas had turned him down for constant access to Top Secret and Codeword material; his name had been deleted from the list of candidates for the appointment and the DG had informed his opposite number in the Home Office, where he was employed as a senior executive officer in the Police National Computer Unit at Horseferry House. Thomas had heard later that the man had been dismissed by the Home Office and had taken to alcohol and drug abuse. Eventually the couple had split up and gone their separate ways. The convulsions in the lives of the two people as a result of his investigation hadn't bothered Thomas at the time and still didn't. He could sympathise with the man but there was not the slightest doubt in his own mind that he had done the right thing. Had the man become the Chief Archivist of the Eastern Bloc Department, there was every possibility he would have done irreparable damage to the UK.

Thomas reached the fourth floor, turned left at the head of the stairs and went on down the corridor to Ashton's office. He tapped on the door and walked into the room before he was invited to come in.

'Well, well,' Ashton said, 'this is a pleasant surprise, Brian. What brings you here?'

'Ted Mullinder.'

'Who's he?'

'The man who broke into Laura Greenwood's house in St John's Avenue. Of course I know you told the police that you didn't see any security implications in the burglary but I thought you would be interested to hear CID has been able to identify the intruder.'

'Has Mullinder any previous form?'

'One conviction in 1981 when he was nineteen,' Thomas said. 'Got six months for breaking and entering. Mullinder had his collar felt again five years later but he had a sharp East End brief who got him off on a technicality.'

'I bet that went down well with the arresting officer.'

'Yeah, it's said DI Charlie Copeland has nurtured a grudge against him ever since. But the failure to get a conviction couldn't have done Copeland any harm. He was a detective sergeant in those days.'

'Is he still serving?'

Thomas shook his head. 'No, he took early retirement a few years back. Had a bypass operation after a heart attack. He finished his service in Special Branch; some people reckon he couldn't take the stress that went with the job. Wouldn't be surprised if he didn't have another heart attack when he hears Mullinder—'

Thomas broke off and kept quiet while Ashton, with a murmured 'Excuse me' answered the phone. Anxious not to give the impression he was eavesdropping, Thomas ended up gazing at the photograph of Harriet which Ashton kept on the desk next to the Visual Display Unit. He had been present in Kelso's office the day she had reported for duty at Benbow House on secondment from MI5. One of the girls on reception had escorted her up to the Assistant Director's office and Kelso had started drooling the moment he had laid eyes on her. Thomas didn't blame him; Harriet Egan, as she had been then, was a truly beautiful woman. Although she had a good figure, it was the perfect symmetry of her face that claimed most people's attention and remained firmly imprinted in their minds ever afterwards. Of course he couldn't answer for Roy Kelso but that had certainly been the case with him.

'What were you going to tell me about Mullinder?' Ashton said, after he had put the phone down.

'Only that he appears to have done a runner. He hasn't been near his council flat in Pentonville since he burgled the house in St John's Avenue on Tuesday afternoon.'

'Well, I'm not going to lose any sleep over him. Mullinder is just a tadpole in a very large pond.'

Ashton's mind was up and running on another track. Brian Thomas knew that, even before he started talking about a Colonel Herrara, one-time deputy chief of Castro's Intelligence Service, who was now travelling on a Spanish passport as Matias Inciarte. Herrara, it transpired, had just been identified as the driver of the dark blue Ford van by Francesca York, the MI5 officer in charge of the surveillance operation on the Warlock Estate.

'We've got an unusual situation,' Ashton continued. 'Since the present troubles in Northern Ireland began twenty-seven years ago, individual members of the Provos have attended training camps in East Germany, Libya and the Lebanon. However, this is the first time there has been a Cuban involvement. Furthermore, so far as I'm aware no foreign instructor has ever taken part in an IRA operation before. Also I would have thought the days when the IRA needed somebody to show them how to make a bomb are long gone. Matter of fact it's they who can teach the rest of the world a thing or two. So the question is, just who was helping who last night?'

'Search me.'

'It was purely a rhetorical question,' Ashton told him.

'The answer's still the same.'

'You're a fount of knowledge, Brian . . .'

Now we're getting to it, Thomas thought. Ashton wanted him to call in a few markers; he seemed to regard Thomas's many contacts in the Met as members of some sort of Masonic order, which in a way they were.

'Every bombmaker has a signature,' Ashton said. 'No two people make them exactly alike. They use different means of initiation: some prefer a trembler, others a time pencil, a few still prefer an alarm clock. The composition of the explosive device, the way the charge is shaped, and the type of remote control are other indicators.'

'All right, Peter,' Thomas said wearily, 'what is it you want from me?'

'Neagle at MI5 has promised to let me have everything the bomb squad and scene of crime officers find but they may not be enough.'

If they were incredibly lucky they might be able to name the bombmaker. In reality the most they could hope for was to recover sufficient evidence for the bomb disposal experts to recognise the handiwork.

'In that event,' Ashton told him, 'I want the names of the possible suspects, plus the addresses of their next of kin.'

'That could mean going to the Royal Ulster Constabulary for the information.'

'So what?'

'I'd like to know how you propose to use the information.'

'I aim to use the next of kin to contact the bombmaker.'

'I don't like the sound of that. In fact it stinks.' Thomas shook his head in disbelief. 'I gave you credit for more sense. When word gets out, as it will, you'll have every politico on both sides of the Irish Sea after your hide.'

'You let me worry about that, Brian.'

'Listen, you won't be the only one whose head will be on the chopping block.'

'You keep your head down, say nothing and you'll be all right. I'm not going to divulge my source of information and you can bet your contact will keep his mouth shut.'

'If push comes to shove, Peter, Hazelwood won't stand by you.'

'I'm not asking him to.'

Thomas closed his eyes. Maybe Harriet could talk some sense into him but he sure as hell couldn't.

'Suppose I refuse to help you?' he said. 'What will you do then?'

'You want to know how Colonel Herrara and his gorillas

killed Adam Zawadzki? They fired up a poker until it was red hot, then rammed it up his anus and incinerated the colon, the small intestine and the stomach. He must have died in agony.'

Thomas was not a squeamish man but the bile rose in his throat and he damn near vomited.

'Now I mean to find out exactly what goodies the IRA gave that murderous bastard and I'm not too fussy how I go about it.'

'You're taking a leaf out of Herrara's book, is that it?' Thomas demanded.

'No, but I feel sure I can persuade the bombmaker that, he or she, would be well advised to assist us in our inquiries.'

Thomas knew some people who liked to think they could be ruthless when the occasion demanded but Ashton was the only person he'd met who had the necessary steel in him.

'OK, you win,' he said reluctantly. 'I'll pull a few strings.'

'Cheer up,' Ashton told him, 'you never know, maybe you won't have to. Maybe Bomb Disposal will get lucky.'

Copeland alighted from the Northern Line train at Waterloo and rode the escalator up to the main line station. At a quarter to six the evening rush hour was at its peak and the concourse resembled an ants nest that had been disturbed. Newspaper folded in three and tucked under his left arm, Copeland weaved through the homeward-bound commuters to make his way to the departures information board beyond the W. H. Smith bookshop. Although the rendezvous had not been his choice, he had to admit the concourse was a damned sight more anonymous than any West End pub where he and his client were likely to be the only drinkers.

The client was Alistair Downward, who was supposedly one of the legal counsellors at the Foreign and Commonwealth Office. Copeland had been introduced to him some eighteen months before he, Copeland, had retired in 1993, on the grounds of ill health following a heart attack which had necessitated a bypass operation. Back in the days when he was in Special Branch he had been the link man with both MI5 and the SIS, in which capacity he'd performed various tasks for Downward's predecessor.

Downward, however, had made little use of Copeland's services during his final eighteen months in the Met and he had assumed all contact with the SIS would automatically be severed with effect from the date of his retirement. The day you walked out the door was the day your PV clearance was cancelled, which meant you were dead so far as the intelligence services were concerned. Copeland had therefore been completely taken aback when Downward had got in touch shortly after he had set himself up in business providing tailor-made alarm systems. The work Downward put his way was unlawful but it was no worse than what MI5 had done during the Cold War on those occasions when the Home Office had refused to authorise a phone tap.

Copeland had been standing there reading the *Evening Standard* for roughly five minutes when somebody tapped him on the shoulder. He turned slowly about to see who it was.

'Hello, Charles. Fancy meeting you here,' Downward said, as if they were old friends who hadn't seen one another for quite some time. 'How are you keeping?'

'Pretty well,' Copeland told him. 'Can't say the same for my business.'

'Cash-flow problems?'

'That and staff trouble.'

'Why don't we have a drink and drown our sorrows?' Downward suggested.

'Good idea.' Copeland dropped the *Standard* into the nearest trash bin and followed Downward as he drifted away from the small crowd watching the departures board.

'You've got five minutes, Charlie,' he said when they were safely out of earshot.

'I need another cash input.'

'You can forget that.'

'I told Mullinder to take a holiday and lie low for a while.

120

Thing is, he did a runner. Neither of us knew he'd accidentally croaked the daily. Now Mullinder will have to stay abroad a whole lot longer than we had anticipated and he's going to run out of money.'

'What figure do you have in mind?' Downward asked.

'Five thousand should keep the wolf from the door.'

'Don't be ridiculous.'

'The Government's popularity rating keeps on dipping; you think it won't fall off the graph paper if word of this latest scandal gets out? I mean, you may think you're safe enough but the burglary was done at the behest of the Foreign and Commonwealth and there's a lot of circumstantial evidence to—'

'Where is Mullinder now?' Downward asked, interrupting him.

'I don't know but I can contact him through the personal columns of the *Daily Telegraph*.'

'You can have three thousand in cash on Monday,' Downward said after thinking about it, '19.45 hours, same rv as before.'

'It's not enough,' Copeland told him.

'You don't understand. There's a limit to the amount of cash I can draw from the secret fund at any one time without arousing suspicion.'

'I'll believe you, thousands wouldn't.'

'This is where we part company,' Downward said coldly. 'I'm going to take a cab, you go back to the Underground where you belong.'

Copeland ignored the jibe, his mind already busy composing the announcement to go in the *Daily Telegraph*. 'Be fruitful, and multiply, and replenish the earth . . .' was the message Mullinder was expecting to see. To this biblical quotation he would add, 'But check with Head Office first.'

Chapter Ten

Ever since they had gone their separate ways, Ashton had never sought out Jill Sheridan. There was, however, a first time for everything and this Friday morning happened to be it. When you worked for two superiors who didn't keep each other fully informed, things had a habit of going awry and he needed to catch Jill before morning prayers. To this end he left the house an hour earlier than usual and arrived at Vauxhall Cross at seven forty-five. Although there was a new armed guard on duty at the entrance to the underground garage, Ashton knew he would have a list of those vehicles whose owners had been allocated parking spaces. Without bothering to consult the list of vehicle numbers, the MoD policeman told him Sheridan hadn't arrived yet.

'Are you sure?'

'Absolutely. She's the only senior Intelligence Officer who rides around in a top-of-the-range Porsche 928 GTS, Mr Ashton. You can't help noticing a car like that.'

Although her marriage had only lasted eighteen months, Jill had done pretty well for herself. Apart from the car, which had been the pride and joy of her ex, she had also kept the four-bedroom house overlooking Waterlow Park at the top of Highgate Hill.

Ashton thanked the guard, walked up the service road to street level and entered the building. Enid Sly, who was on early

123

shift again, wished him good morning before observing how such a fine morning made her feel that spring was just around the corner, which was practically an invitation for a tropical downpour.

Ashton took the first available lift up to the top floor and walked along the corridor to Jill's office. In accordance with the security instructions dealing with procedures to be observed at the end of each working day, the door had been left open, there were no filing trays on the desk, and the hanging card suspended from the combination dial had been reversed to show the safe had been locked. The art curator from the Property Services Agency had done his stuff, producing, with unusual alacrity, the early L. S. Lowry as well as the Jackson Pollock and Andy Warhol originals that Jill had chosen. They didn't sit well together but that was beside the point. The paintings made a statement: they said Ms Sheridan was influential enough to command an art gallery worth several hundred thousand to brighten up her office.

'Admiring my taste, Peter?'

Ashton turned round. 'Just cashing them up,' he said.

'So how much do you think they're worth?'

'Half a million,' he said, hazarding a blind guess.

'Try doubling it.'

Jill moved past him, removed her dark green swagger coat and hung it up on the government-issue hatstand. A double-breasted hip-length jacket and skirt completed the outfit that looked expensive and probably was.

'What made you come in this early?' she asked.

'I needed to brief you about Herrara.'

'Really?'

With a slight inflection of her voice Jill gave a whole new meaning to the word. She wasn't expressing surprise or confirming a fact; her suggestive tone inferred that he had an ulterior motive for wanting to see her.

'Have you heard the latest about Herrara?' Ashton asked tersely.

'I think you'd better tell me. I'm not in the mood for guessing games.'

'He was involved in the IRA bombing on Wednesday evening. He was positively identified by MI5.'

'When did you learn this?'

'Yesterday afternoon. Unfortunately your PA didn't know where you had gone after leaving the Mid East Department.'

'That silly woman will have to go. I told her that I might have to confer with the Near East Desk of the Foreign Office.'

'Yeah. Well, I withheld the information from Victor for as long as I could but he had seen the latest fax from Washington and in the end I had to tell him. I thought you should be aware of this development before morning prayers.'

'Quite. I'm sure it would have given Victor a lot of pleasure to catch me out.'

'You should also know that Victor has tasked me to run down Herrara. Apparently I'm to be given adequate resources to do this, and I understand Victor is going to sort out the chain of command with you.'

'Oh, is he?' Jill said, her face white with anger. 'Well, we'll have to see about that. You will get the necessary resources, all right, but I fancy you will still be working for me.'

'I don't mind who I work for,' Ashton told her. 'Just get it sorted. And while we are sorting things out, you attached a memo to Zawadzki's confidential report book asking me to speak.'

'There's no need to make a song and dance about it, Peter. I merely wondered if you had anything to add to the note you wrote summarising his strengths and weaknesses. Don't tell me his second wife didn't shed any fresh light on his character?'

Camilla Kirkpatrick most certainly had and it was all there in the memo he'd written to Jill on his return from Dedham. However, there was nothing to be gained from pointing this out to her. It would only make things worse between them and he would sound too bloody clever for words.

'You already know Adam was an embittered man from

reading his confidential reports. Camilla Kirkpatrick told me his bitterness towards the army spilled over and was directed against her. That was the reason why she found herself another partner. She also said he tried to do everything on the cheap and frequently got himself into financial trouble as a result. Seems he bought a house without having it independently surveyed and subsequently discovered it was infested with dry rot, which cost him a fortune to eradicate.'

'In other words he had all the character defects of a man who was prepared to sell his country short,' Jill said crisply.

'You're right, but when you recall how he was killed it's clear he did no such thing. You can't say the same for Martin Edmunds.'

Ashton repeated everything Camilla Kirkpatrick had told him about Edmunds' lifestyle, the expensive suits he wore and his addiction to gambling. Throughout, he was constantly interrupted by Jill, who had anticipated what he was going to recommend and wanted no part of it.

'It's all hearsay, Peter.' Jill began to pace the width of the office, arms folded across her chest. 'You've just spent a good ten minutes reminding me what an envious and bitter man Zawadzki had been. He was insanely jealous of Edmunds; that's why he made these slanderous allegations.'

'Are you saying Edmunds is off limits?'

'We've been through all this once before; I'm glad you've got the message at last.'

'Zawadzki is a last-minute substitute for Edmunds who has gone down with flu. Six days after his brutal murder, the house belonging to the woman he was living with is burgled—'

'Oh, for God's sake, a few days ago you told me Laura Greenwood was of no interest to us. Furthermore you assured DI Hughes that you didn't see any security implications in the burglary.'

'I'm not denying that. At the time, I thought it was just a coincidence.'

'And now you have changed your mind,' Jill said scathingly.

'Yes, because of Herrara. The CIA suggests he could have been responsible for the murder of Zawadzki. Then we hear that barely seventy-two hours after the killing he travelled to Paris under an assumed name using a Spanish passport. On Wednesday he's over here, playing a key role in the IRA bombing on the Warlock Estate. OK, the links are tenuous but they're there and we shouldn't close our eyes to them.'

Jill stopped dead and turned to face him. 'What damned links?' she demanded.

It was a clear invitation to go over the same ground again but Ms Sheridan wasn't stupid or dense. Even her worst enemies had to admit she was highly intelligent. Even when they had shared the same bed, Ashton had known that Jill never did anything without a definite purpose in mind. In this instance, he guessed she wanted to hear him repeat the argument for putting Edmunds under the microscope before coming to a decision.

The case as he saw it was simple enough. 'Had Edmunds not fallen sick, he would have flown to San José, met Herrara and handed over some package that would have been put into the diplomatic bag among the Foreign Office papers. Whoever had warned Herrara that Edmunds was unfit to travel and Zawadzki was therefore taking his place, must have unintentionally led the Cuban to believe that nothing else had changed. When Herrara discovered the cupboard was bare he rightly concluded that somebody had removed the package from the diplomatic bag.'

'Laura Greenwood,' Jill said emphatically.

'It's not impossible,' Ashton conceded, 'but I think Edmunds had the package. I'm betting it was always in his possession. All being well it would have found its way into the bag somewhere between Heathrow and Juan Santamaria International Airport.'

'Does he still have it, Peter?'

'No, I believe Herrara collected it soon after he arrived in this country.'

Jill didn't say anything; she just stood there gazing at him, her face expressionless. Bridge had been her game when they had been engaged. Ashton used to think she could have made them a fortune in Vegas had she been introduced to stud poker.

'Take a good look at Laura Greenwood,' Jill told him, breaking a lengthy silence.

'What about Edmunds?'

'Be very discreet — nothing official.'

'What does that mean, Jill?'

'It means this conversation never took place,' she said, and busied herself with the Manufoil combination lock on the safe.

Before World War Two passport control offices had provided cover for SIS station chiefs abroad, particularly in Poland, Germany, Austria and the Low Countries. Whether in London SW1, Liverpool, Glasgow, Newport Gwent, Peterborough or Belfast, the Passport Office was an adjunct of the Foreign and Commonwealth Office. It followed that the vetting papers relating to personnel who worked at Clive House in Petty France would be held by the Foreign Office Security Department at Number 4 Central Buildings. Lifting the phone, Ashton rang Shirley Isles, head of the vetting organisation, and asked her if she would do him a favour and verify the current security status of Laura Greenwood. In a matter of a few minutes he learned that she had been cleared by normal vetting.

An NV clearance meant that Laura Greenwood was only allowed occasional access to Top Secret material. It also meant that she had not been interviewed in depth nor had she been required to nominate any referees to character. On the other hand, her personal details, as well as those of her parents and, where applicable, the spouse, had been sent to the National Identification Bureau and MI5.

The National Identification Bureau would say whether or not she or any member of the immediate family had a criminal record. Meanwhile MI5 would screen her to see if she had ever been a member of the Socialist Workers Party or some other subversive organisation. Although Laura Greenwood was unlikely to see a document graded higher than Confidential in her job, for obvious reasons the Passport Office didn't want to employ anybody who was either politically disaffected or had criminal tendencies. The NV clearance therefore gave her a clean bill of health: it would be immediately withdrawn if subsequently she came to the notice of MI5 or committed an offence. So far as Ashton was concerned, the NV clearance was part of the process of taking a good look at Laura Greenwood. Just what the next step should be was something he still had to figure out.

Ashton went through the pending tray, and took out the notes he'd made on Martin Edmunds. According to his security file, the Queen's Messenger was 'Persil White'. To the late Adam Zawadzki he was a compulsive gambler who enjoyed a lifestyle beyond the means of the vast majority. Part of that lifestyle could be a house called The Old Vicarage on the outskirts of Woodstock, approximately eight miles northwest of Oxford. Ashton decided he would take a run out to Woodstock and see for himself what the property might be worth. Unfortunately the transport supervisor was unable to oblige him. Every vehicle was already committed and although the Ford Agency would complete a 10,000 mile service on the Granada by 3 p.m., Eric Daniels hadn't come into work and was presumably still at St Ann's General Hospital.

Daniels didn't have to see his reflection in a mirror to know just how rough he obviously looked. The stubble on his face felt like sandpaper when he rubbed his jaw and if soreness was a guide, his eyes must be like two little chips of red-hot coal. He was bone tired, ached in every limb, and couldn't stop yawning, which was only to be expected since he hadn't had a wink of sleep in the last thirty something hours. For all the good he was doing sitting there on an uncomfortable ladder-back chair down the corridor from O'Meara's room in St Ann's General Hospital, he might just as well have gone home and had a good night's rest.

He hadn't been allowed to see O'Meara, and her children had been offended by his presence. Or had it been the armed officer on guard outside her room they'd found unacceptable? No, he was the one they had disliked on sight. Fourteen-year-old Lisette had marched up to him when he'd arrived shortly before midnight on Wednesday and had demanded to know who he was and what right he had to see her mother.

'I'm Eric Daniels, a friend—' he'd begun to explain, and had been silenced by a stream of invective.

He had, it seemed, made O'Meara unhappy and Lisette reckoned her mother had suffered enough heartbreak without him upsetting the family just when things were beginning to get better. And it wasn't as if she cared for him, which was why she hadn't been in touch lately. So why couldn't he take a hint and leave her in peace?

Since the last thing Daniels had wanted was to provoke an unseemly row he had left the intensive care unit with as much dignity as he could muster. All the pubs in the neighbourhood where he could have killed time waiting for Lisette and her brother, Wesley, to go home had closed long before he had arrived at the hospital. In the end he'd taken refuge in his Ford Escort, listening to the car radio until he was certain Lisette and Wesley would have left, when he'd then returned to the intensive care unit. He'd had to go through the same rigmarole yesterday, making himself scarce from three thirty in the afternoon when Lisette came out of school. And like as not, today would see a repeat performance.

He ought to throw his hand in and give the relationship up as a bad job because Lisette and Wesley were never going to accept him. He would go home, have a wash and brush-up, then report for duty, assuming he hadn't been given the sack in his absence. That would be just like Kelso. His eyelids dropped and he floated off as though weightless in space. A muzzy voice a long way off called his name, then a hand clasped his left shoulder and gently shook it. Very reluctantly he opened his eyes and tried to focus them on the white blob in front of him. A woman – fair hair, grey eyes, round face – gentle-looking – some kind of uniform. Had to be a nurse.

'What did you say?' he mumbled.

'Your friend Geraldine,' the nurse said.

'Who?'

'The policewoman . . .'

It had been a long time since anybody called O'Meara by her Christian name.

'She's regained consciousness. Would you like to see her?'

O'Meara no longer in a coma? That had to be good news. 'Of course I would,' Daniels said.

'Only for a few minutes, mind.'

O'Meara was unrecognisable. Her nose was swollen to twice its normal size and was misshapen. Her jaw had been wired up, there were ugly bruises on the cheekbones and both eyes were closed to narrow slits. A metal half-hoop supported the sheet and blankets to keep the weight of the bedclothes off her shattered legs. He could not bring himself to look at the neurosurgeon's handiwork on the skull.

'In all probability Geraldine won't recognise you,' the staff nurse told him in a hushed voice. 'She's been heavily sedated.'

Daniels followed her example and spoke in a murmur. 'Has anybody informed Wesley and Lisette about their mother?' he asked.

'Not yet. We thought you would want to do that.'

'I don't know how to contact them when they're not at home.'

'That's not a problem, Mr Daniels. Sister has the relevant phone numbers in her office.'

'Fine. I'll look in and get them later.'

'Remember what I said – no more than five minutes.'

'I'm not likely to forget, nurse.'

Daniels waited until she left the room, then gently squeezed O'Meara's hand to let her know he was there. Contrary to what he had been led to expect, he was rewarded with a smile of recognition. She also tried to say something but her voice was very low, almost inaudible. When he signalled her not to talk, O'Meara became agitated. To pacify her, he leaned over the bed and put his ear close to her mouth.

'Flynn,' she croaked, 'no good.'

Daniels could not make head nor tail of her message but he nodded sagely as if he understood.

The White House was a six-bedroom property standing in two and a half acres on the fringe of Ashdown Forest a mile north of Duddleswell, a village so small it didn't rate a mention in the *AA Members' Handbook*. The present owners were Keith and Amanda French, who had purchased the property in 1986 for £475,000. The couple also had a flat in the Barbican. There was, of course, no shortage of money in the family.

Keith French was the top negotiator for British Petroleum with special responsibility for offshore drilling rights, an appointment which involved a great deal of travelling in Asia, the Middle East and Southern Africa. Completely in love with his job, it didn't bother him that he was frequently away from home for several weeks at a time. Furthermore, even when he was working in London he often stayed the night at the Frenches' flat, which seemed perverse to those who had met Amanda. Colleagues, friends and casual acquaintances who sought an explanation for his behaviour concluded that the fire in his loins must have gone out.

Amanda, however, was not without her ardent admirers, the latest of whom was Hasan Ünver, Economic and Commercial Counsellor at the Turkish Embassy in Belgrave Square. They had met nine months ago at an official reception for BP executives which she had attended with her husband. While Keith had circulated, talking to everybody in the room, Hasan had danced attendance on Amanda. Before the reception was over, she had given him her telephone number. Two days later he had phoned the house to invite her out to lunch. It was after their second lunch date that Amanda had taken him back to the flat in the Barbican to spend a frantic but highly satisfying afternoon before returning to rural Sussex.

Since that first sexual encounter, they had taken full advantage of Keith's absence whenever he was out of the country. Sometimes they would meet at the flat, more often than not, Hasan would spend the weekend at The White House. When the phone rang shortly before lunch that Friday, Amanda knew who was calling her before she answered it. Nevertheless she waited for Hasan to speak first just in case it was one of her bridge friends.

'Mrs French?' he enquired politely.

'No, it's the French maid,' she said, and laughed throatily.

'This is a joke, yes?'

The trouble with Hasan was that he lacked a sense of humour, or rather he didn't understand English humour. But in view of his other attributes, Amanda was prepared to overlook that particular shortcoming.

'Yes, it's a joke darling,' she said.

'Good. You have heard from Keith, perhaps?'

'Last night. He called from Istanbul.'

'And?'

'You're in an awful hurry, my love.'

'My assistant, Miss Soysal, has been in and out of my office all morning and she already knows too much about us. She could return again at any moment.'

'Let me put you out of your misery then. Keith is staying in Istanbul until next Tuesday.'

'Marvellous.'

'What time can I expect you?'

'Six o'clock.'

'I'll be champing at the bit.'

'We are going riding?'

'You are, my sweet,' Amanda told him, and put the phone down.

So did Hasan Ünver – and Merih Soysal, who had been listening to their conversation on the parallel phone in her office.

When it was safe to do so, she rang Mehmet Ozbek, who lived in the flat above the Kurdish-owned dry goods store on Henning Road in Tottenham. Blessed with a very retentive memory, Merih Soysal repeated everything she had heard.

Ashton was eating the cheese and onion sandwich he'd purchased that morning from a breakfast bar on the way to Vauxhall Cross, when Richard Neagle phoned him. The MI5 man had either been cursed with a voice which, through no fault of his own, grated on people or else he had deliberately cultivated an accent which suggested an innate air of superiority over lesser mortals.

'The Warlock incident,' he said, and sniffed as if he could actually smell the onion on Ashton's breath, 'SOCO and officers of the bomb squad filled half a dozen bin liners with evidence. Of course, it's too early yet for a definitive report but the bomb casing was a ten-gallon steel keg. It's estimated the keg contained four pounds of Semtex and God knows how many metal flanges, nuts and bolts. Considering how close she was to the bomb, you could say O'Meara was lucky to survive the initial explosion. Fortunately for her DC Browne took most of the blast and was literally blown to pieces . . .'

'How was it initiated?'

'By a trip wire linked to a pull switch, according to Bomb Disposal.' Neagle paused, then said, 'I presume that means something to you?'

'I've seen the odd pull switch,' Ashton told him laconically.

A pull switch was slightly longer than a 7.62mm bullet but slimmer. It incorporated a detonator at one end, which was attached to the explosive charge by a length of cortex instantaneous fuse, cut to any size. Around the waist was a metal band with two eyelets, making it possible to pin the switch to a cupboard, door frame, staircase or any wooden surface. The final component was a spring-loaded plunger, which was held in position by a thin metal hasp. A booby trap was rigged by attaching the trip wire to the metal hasp; it was armed by withdrawing the safety pin. The booby-trap bomb went up when someone blundered into the trip wire, which automatically pulled the hasp out of the switch thereby releasing the spring-loaded plunger to strike the rimfire cap and trigger the instantaneous fuse.

'Do they have any idea who made the bomb?' Ashton asked.

'Of course they don't. As I've already told you, it's far too early to expect a definitive report.'

'Can the bomb squad say how this device compares with others they have dealt with over the years?'

'Until the evidence has been thoroughly analysed they are unable to make any comparisons. When they are in a position to do so, I will make it my business to ensure you're brought up to speed.'

'Thanks, I would appreciate that,' Ashton said, and hung up.

'Come back, Clifford Peachey,' he murmured to himself, 'all is forgiven.'

Until Harriet had arrived on the scene, he had always got on reasonably well with the former MI5 officer. Their relationship had soured when Peachey had left the Security Service to become the Deputy Director of the SIS and they had been in daily contact thereafter. The older man had noted Ashton's growing attachment to Harriet with open disapproval and had taken it upon himself to act as her surrogate father.

Peachey's concern for Harriet had started when he had been in charge of K1, the Kremlin watchers, and she had been the bright young officer in K2, the section which kept an eye on potential subversives. He should have let go when they had married but, Ashton supposed, having no children of his own, Peachey had found that impossible. The fact was that co-operation between MI5 and the SIS had never been better than during his tenure as Deputy D, and for all their personal differences Ashton wished he was still in the chair.

Ashton left his office, locked the door behind him and rode one of the lifts down to the Security Vetting and Technical

Services Division. Thomas didn't exactly jump for joy when he tapped on his door and walked into the room.

'What little favour are you asking me to do this time?' he enquired wearily.

'Neagle has just told me what the Bomb Squad and SOCO recovered from the Warlock incident.'

'Don't tell me,' Thomas said, 'I think I can guess the rest. Neagle refused to speculate about the identity of the bomb-maker and now it's my turn.'

Ashton smiled. 'Well, I hope you're not going to refuse?'

'If you want to go up against the politicians on both sides of the Irish Sea, who am I to stand in your way?' Thomas picked up a Biro and ruled a line under the last note he had made on his millboard. 'What trademarks do you have on this bomber?'

'He used a beer keg for the casing and filled it with the usual nuts, bolts and bits of metal to inflict maximum collateral damage to personnel. He used Semtex explosive, not your home-made garden fertiliser variety, and the device was triggered by a pull switch. How's that for a signature?'

'Not bad,' Thomas said, 'not bad at all but don't expect miracles.'

'I won't,' Ashton assured him.

'And don't expect an answer by tomorrow.'

'Tomorrow's Saturday,' Ashton said on the way out.

'That's never stopped you before,' Thomas said, determined to have the last word.

Chapter Eleven

The Ford agency completed the 10,000 mile service and returned the Grenada three-quarters of an hour earlier than the
transport supervisor had anticipated. Some thirty-five minutes
later, Eric Daniels reported for duty, which was fortunate since
Kelso's PA had only just warned the supervisor that the Admin
King was about to make a snap inspection of the transport
section and he had been covering for the ex-RMP sergeant. For
all that the Assistant Director was referred to as the officer in
charge of paper clips behind his back, Kelso was no fool. He had
only to ask Daniels for the latest news on O'Meara and there was
a fifty-fifty chance Kelso would discover where he had been
most of the day. Never a man to take unnecessary risks, the
supervisor decided to send Daniels out on the road and rang
Ashton to say that a vehicle was now available to take him to
Woodstock. He also left Ashton in no doubt that he would be
doing him an enormous favour if he would leave right away. As
a result, and with perfect timing, Daniels and Ashton were
heading up the service road from the basement garage to street
level when Kelso stepped out of the lift. Confident that nothing
could go wrong now, the supervisor went forward to meet
Kelso.

'That was close,' Daniels said.

'You should have asked for more time off. Roy Kelso
wouldn't have objected.'

'Lisette and Wesley were giving me a hard time and I wasn't thinking straight.'

Daniels fell silent for several moments, then began to tell Ashton everything that had happened from the time he had arrived at the hospital on Wednesday night to his departure soon after O'Meara's son and daughter had shown up at the intensive care unit shortly after 10 a.m. Ashton thought that for someone who two days ago had told him he'd no regrets about not seeing O'Meara, Daniels had certainly proved himself to be a devoted friend. All the way across London from Lambeth Bridge to the Bayswater Road and the A40 trunk route he expressed his fears for O'Meara's long-term recovery. No one could say whether she would walk again and nobody at this stage could tell how much damage the blood clot on the brain had done.

'Tell me something,' Ashton said when Daniels finally stopped for breath, 'how much sleep have you had in the last forty-eight hours?'

'Enough.'

'So why do your eyes remind me of a bloodhound's?'

'There's a lot of new building going on at the hospital. Loads of workmen all over the place, dust and grit flying about. I got a few specks in both eyes, when I was walking around, killing time until her kids disappeared.'

'That's an original explanation.'

'You're a regular doubting Thomas, Mr Ashton. Fact is, I catnapped through the early hours of yesterday morning and did the same thing last night. This morning I got home at eleven o'clock, set the alarm for 13.00, kipped soundly for two hours, then stood under the shower before shaving. I tell you I'm as right as ninepence.'

'Not in my book,' Ashton told him. 'Make a left turn and get off the urban throughway. I'm taking over.'

'There's no need for this.'

'No arguments.'

'You're the boss.'

Daniel tripped the indicator and turned left into a residential street with cars parked on both sides. He drove on down to the T-junction without finding a space and turned right. Still out of luck, Daniels made another right to head up to Holland Park Avenue. Just as it was beginning to look as if they would have to find somewhere else to change over, a BMW parked on the right-hand side of the road, pulled away from the kerb and cut in front of them. Daniels braked hard, shifted in reverse and backed the Grenada into the vacant slot before anybody else could pinch it. Then, without a word being said, Ashton got out and went round the back of the vehicle to get in behind the wheel, leaving Daniels to cross in front of the Grenada.

'About O'Meara,' Daniels said when they were back on the urban throughway, 'she recognised me as soon as she came round.'

'I'm pleased for you.'

'The only thing she said was, "Flynn's no good." It was a message O'Meara was desperate to get across to me. I say that because she became very agitated when I tried to stop her talking.' Daniels cupped a hand over his mouth in a vain attempt to stifle a yawn. 'Do you suppose this Flynn was their informer and he double-crossed them?'

'I'd bet on it,' Ashton said. 'But I think Flynn was simply a codename to protect the identity of the source. Five was running the agent in place and the fact is it wasn't necessary for O'Meara and the other foot soldiers of Special Branch to know who he was.'

'It was a set-up, wasn't it?' Daniels said quietly. 'O'Meara and that DC whoever he was . . .'

'Browne with an e,' Ashton said tersely. 'His name was Browne.'

'Yeah. Well, I'm sorry but I didn't know him. Doesn't alter the fact that the Provos lured them into an ambush, does it?'

'No, it doesn't.'

But figuratively speaking the incident had been something of a damp squib and not the spectacular normally associated with the IRA, which was one reason why it hadn't made any sense to Ashton.

'I'd like to meet this Flynn one dark night,' Daniels said grimly.

'It's not a good idea to take it personally. You end up tearing yourself apart.'

The other factor which didn't make sense was Herrara's involvement. There was nothing the Cuban could teach the Provos.

'You're a fine one to talk, Mr Ashton. I've been there when you weren't so cool and detached.'

'Well, you know the old maxim, Eric. Don't do as I do, do as I say.'

The incident only made sense if PIRA, the Provisional IRA, had staged the bombing in order to divert attention away from a bigger and far more important operation. If this assumption was correct, it followed PIRA's participation would be limited to the role of quartermaster to some other terrorist organisation. The rented garage on the Warlock Estate could be likened in military parlance to an ammunition point. Herrara had driven up to it and collected the munitions he needed. In return, the Cuban had armed PIRA's booby trap for them.

'What terrorist organisation, what future operation?' Ashton said, thinking aloud. 'That's the jackpot question.'

Daniels reared back on his seat and shook his head. 'What did you say?' he asked in a voice thick with sleep.

'Nothing of importance,' Ashton told him.

Ashton headed out of London on Western Avenue. Long before he reached junction 1 of the M40 northwest of Uxbridge, Daniels was deep in the land of Nod.

There was no mistaking The Old Vicarage at Woodstock. It had been built in the days when the landed gentry had sent the third son into the Church and everything had been done on the grand scale. Although Ashton only caught a fleeting glance of the house as he drove past, it looked big enough to have at least three reception rooms, six huge bedrooms and there was a fairly large conservatory on the east side of the building. He also thought the grounds were in excess of two acres.

Ashton went on into the village and found somewhere to park the Grenada. Leaving Daniels in the car, he walked into the newsagent's and asked the owner if he could direct him to the local associates of Knight, Frank.

'And who might they be?' the newsagent asked.

'One of the biggest estate agents in London,' Ashton said. 'What's the biggest in Woodstock?'

'You'll be wanting Scoones and Chambers then. Go up the road a piece and it's the second turning on the right. You can't miss it.'

The newsagent was right. A person would have to be myopic to walk past the plush offices of Scoones and Chambers, Estate Agents and Chartered Auctioneers, without noticing the premises. From the receptionist Ashton learned that Mr Chambers was on a skiing holiday in Grindelwald while Mr Scoones was out of the office attending an auction. He was informed that one of the associates, Miss Avril Mars, was, however, available and would be happy to assist him.

Avril Mars was a well-groomed blonde whom Ashton judged to be either in her late thirties or early forties. From the instant she smiled at him as they shook hands, he instinctively knew she was above all else a really nice woman.

'How can I help you, Mr Ashton?' she asked.

'I'm interested in The Old Vicarage,' he said. 'I've been told the Edmundses are putting it on the market and I wondered how much they're asking for it.'

'I didn't know they were thinking of selling. If they are, I'm pretty sure we haven't been asked to act for them. At least, if we have, the partners have failed to pass the word on to me.' She smiled. 'But let me see if we have any details on file.' She turned to face the VDU on her desk, tapped in the entry code and scanned the list of properties on the books of Scoones and Chambers. 'No, I was right, we're not handling the sale.'

'That's odd.' Ashton frowned. 'I mean, you are the biggest estate agents in Woodstock, aren't you?'

'We tend to concentrate on the more . . .'

'Up-market properties?' Ashton suggested.

'That was the word that sprang to mind but the larger and more expensive sounds less offensive.'

'Well, perhaps the Edmundses are only using Knight, Frank, especially if the London firm put them on to The Old Vicarage when they were looking for somewhere to live.'

'Actually they came to us.'

'Really? I don't suppose you have the details on record, number of rooms, acreage – that sort of thing?'

'It should be on the dump file,' Avril Mars said, and tapped in a different entry code.

'I've got a cheek asking this,' Ashton said, 'but it would be handy to know what the Edmundses paid for the house.'

Harriet had observed more than once that, consciously or unconsciously, he had a knack of persuading strangers to do something for him which was not in their own interests. There was nothing devious in the way he went about it; indeed he would cheerfully admit that what he was asking them to do was not strictly kosher. And for Harriet, the truly amazing thing was their willingness to do him a favour even though they had been forewarned of the consequences. So it was with Avril Mars, who produced a copy of the original brochure on the printer.

'When did this house last come on to the market?' Ashton enquired.

'In 1986 and it was snapped up by the Edmundses, who were at home on leave from Hong Kong at the time.'

'I see the asking price was two hundred and forty thousand?'

'Yes, but the owners were happy to accept two hundred and twenty-five for a quick cash sale. The vendors would never have got the asking price anyway; the property needed a lot of renovation.'

Avril Mars knew that for a fact because she had shown two other prospective buyers over The Old Vicarage, both of whom had told her they wouldn't have considered buying the property even had it been on offer for under two hundred thousand. But Martin Edmunds had bought it cash down three years before he had retired from the Hong Kong Police Force in the rank of chief superintendent.

Ashton wondered how Edmunds had put the money together when his terminal grant and pension wouldn't have been available to him. Maybe his wife had money. It seemed unlikely. According to the Foreign Office security file on him, Janet Edmunds had been fresh out of teacher training college when he had met her in 1961, a year before they had married. In those days she had in fact been employed by the Finance Director of Jardines, the biggest import/export trading house in the Far East. It was he who had eventually used his influence in the Crown Colony to secure her a teaching post. Again according to the security file, her father had been a Higher Executive Officer in the civil service, while her mother had been content to be a housewife after the birth of her only child. They were said to be comfortably off but not wealthy.

'Could you put a figure on what The Old Vicarage would be worth today?'

'If they weren't in a hurry to sell, the Edmundses could expect to get in excess of three-quarters of a million.'

Ashton whistled. 'Who said the housing boom was over?'

'Actually they have had a lot done to the property.'

The Edmundses had spent over forty thousand renovating the interior, some eight thousand of which had gone on converting the box room into a bathroom en suite. They had also added a heated swimming pool and a tennis court. They had subsequently turned their attention on the grounds, hiring a firm of landscape gardeners to create a number of water features that would not have looked out of place at the Chelsea Flower Show.

'I've no idea what these improvements must have cost them,' Avril Mars continued. 'However, I do know the full-time gardener-cum-general handyman who was hired to look after

143

the place while they were still in Hong Kong was paid a hundred and fifty pounds a week. Scoones and Chambers were engaged to oversee his work and it was my job to pay his wages. I can't tell you what the partners charged the Edmundses for this service.'

'I can make a pretty shrewd guess,' Ashton said, smiling.

'Well, then, shall I tell Mr Scoones that you are interested, should The Old Vicarage come on to the market?'

'Not at three-quarters of a million or anything like it. To raise even two hundred thousand would be a bit of a struggle for me. I'm only sorry I have taken up so much of your time to so little purpose.'

'There's no need to apologise; it's been my pleasure,' Avril Mars told him, and sounded as if she meant it.

Ashton left the estate agent's and returned to the Ford Grenada to find Daniels still in the land of Nod, his eyes closed, his mouth open. He came to with alacrity, the adrenaline sending his heart into overdrive when Ashton walked round the vehicle and opened the near-side door so that he damned nearly fell out of the car.

'Are you up to driving?' Ashton asked him.

'Always have been.'

'Good, let's drop in on Mr and Mrs Edmunds.'

'Right.'

'I'm a broker with Baldwin Peiper who has heard The Old Vicarage is up for sale and I'm interested in acquiring it. You're my chauffeur.'

'We should have hired a Roller,' Daniels said cheerfully. 'Then they might believe you're in the money.'

'That's not the point, Eric. I want Edmunds to be suspicious. Then with any luck, hopefully I can make him panic so that he does something foolish.'

'OK. Are you going to sit in the back or what?'

'I'm a democratic broker,' Ashton said. 'I'll ride up front with you.'

From the centre of Woodstock to The Old Vicarage on the

outskirts was a three-minute drive. The house had impressed Ashton when he'd caught a brief glimpse of it as they'd swept past on the way into the village; now seeing The Old Vicarage again close to he could see why Avril Mars had put such a high price tag on the property. In the list of improvements she had omitted to mention a double garage. The huge up-and-over door was in the raised position. His and Hers were side by side, a Mercedes SL320 and a Saab 9000. Both cars sported N registrations and were not quite a year old. At a rough guess Ashton reckoned the two vehicles would have set Edmunds back by a cool seventy thousand. There was no way he could afford to splash out like that on a chief superintendent's pension and what he earned as a Queen's Messenger. Either Edmunds was one of the luckiest gamblers alive or else he had found a novel way of printing money.

Aware that somebody was watching them from behind the drawn-back curtain in the downstairs window nearest the porch, Ashton waited for Daniels to open the door for him, then got out of the car and rang the bell. The middle-aged woman who answered the door to him didn't have a trace of grey in her dark brown curly hair. Her bust hadn't dropped, there was no spare tyre around the middle and her hips hadn't spread. Although her youthful figure could be attributed to careful dieting coupled with plenty of exercise, the years had definitely been kind to her features. No lines, no wrinkles and no telltale signs of a face-lift.

'Mrs Edmunds?' Ashton enquired politely, and then introduced himself. 'Your husband and I have a number of mutual acquaintances, the late Adam Zawadzki for one.'

The name provoked little reaction from Janet Edmunds other than an expression of mild curiosity. 'Are you one of Martin's colleagues?' she asked.

'No, I'm not a member of the Queen's Messenger Service. We are, however, members of the same London club.'

'The Portland?'

Mrs Edmunds was not as innocent as she looked. She could think on her feet and was quick-witted. It was a nice try but unfortunately for her, Ashton had a retentive memory and could recall exactly what her husband had declared to the vetting officer during the subject interview.

'No, I mean Pratts.' Ashton smiled. 'Don't tell me he has resigned?'

'I'm sorry, you're absolutely right. What can I have been thinking of?'

'As a matter of fact it was Martin I wanted to see.' Ashton gave her another friendly smile. 'Hopefully he's up and about again after that nasty bout of flu he had ten days ago?'

Ashton stepped back a pace and glanced pointedly in the direction of the double garage to pre-empt any excuse that her husband wasn't at home.

'Why exactly do you want to see Martin, Mr Ashton?'

'I'm a broker with Baldwin Peiper,' he said, and left it at that.

'Oh!'

'I'll wait here, shall I?'

'If you would,' Janet Edmunds said, and closed the door.

Her husband kept Ashton waiting a good three minutes before he deigned to put in an appearance and even then he didn't invite him inside the house. Martin Edmunds was a short, plump, mean-looking man with small deep-set grey eyes and a decidedly unfriendly manner. Ashton suspected this was a facet of his character which he concealed from his peer group.

'My wife tells me you are a broker,' he said belligerently, 'and I'm here to inform you that I don't need any financial advice from your syndicate.'

'I wasn't about to give you any,' Ashton told him brusquely. 'I'm here to make you an offer for The Old Vicarage.'

'You're here to do what?' Edmunds turned a bright shade of red as if afflicted by high blood pressure. If nature had given him a wattle, it would have shook like a turkey's.

'Knight, Frank gave me to understand that you are putting the house on the market. I've got to admit Scoones and Chambers were every bit as surprised as you apparently are.' Ashton took out his wallet and found a calling card which merely gave his name and private phone number. On the back he wrote his office number, before giving the card to Edmunds. 'Give me a ring if you change your mind about selling. My office number is on the reverse side.'

'You'd be the last person I called,' Edmunds spluttered.

Ashton turned away and moved towards the Grenada, then swung about as though some last-minute thought had occurred to him. 'Oh, by the way,' he said, 'didn't our paths cross in Hong Kong when you were a chief superintendent?'

Edmunds didn't say anything, just stood there gawping after him, his mouth open. Ashton got into the car and slammed the door; he was still fastening his seat belt when Daniels fired the engine into life, shifted into gear and moved off down the drive.

'Edmunds is making a note of our registration number,' Daniels said, looking in the rear-view mirror.

'Great. That means he's rattled.' Ashton struck the fascia with a clenched fist. 'He'll be pissing in his pants when all Swansea will tell him is that the car belongs to a government ministry.'

The hatchback which Mehmet had bought from Earl's Motors in Bethnal Green was a cut-and-shut Ford Escort. The front end had been cut from a 1990 model that had been written off in a traffic accident while the back half of the hybrid vehicle had come from a 1987 car which had been sold for scrap. The chassis members had been welded together with metal rods to give them added strength but even so they were unacceptably weak as well as being slightly out of line. The log book submitted to the DVLC Swansea for registration in the name of the new owner originally belonged to the '87 model.

Ozbek had acquired the Escort for a cash payment of two thousand eight hundred on the road. The man who had sold the hatchback to him said afterwards that it had been easier than stealing pennies off a dead man's eyes. As he had cheerfully admitted later, he had never expected to get anything like the asking price and would have been content with two grand.

Ozbek, however, had at least one good reason for behaving the way he had. Haggle with a man, beat him down on the asking price and he was sure to remember your face a lot longer than if you had just paid up. And he didn't want the dealer to remember him because he had given him a false name and address. When the vehicle registration book was returned from Swansea the registered keeper would be shown as Mr Hilak Ersoy, 258 Woodland Park Road, Harringay, and Mr Hilak Ersoy was long gone. If the police should attempt to trace the Ford Escort for any reason, the trail would begin and end with Earl's Motors of Bethnal Green.

Ten minutes after Merih Soysal had phoned him, Mehmet Ozbek left the flat on Henning Road, collected the Ford Escort from the alleyway behind the dry goods store and set off for The White House near Duddleswell. He was accompanied by Kemal Esener, one of the young men who had attended the weapon-training class organised by Colonel Osvaldo Herrara. Esener had the *AA Big Atlas of Britain* open on his lap but he really had no need of it. Both men had been to Ashdown Forest on two previous occasions and could have found their way there blindfolded.

Behind the rear seat and concealed under a blanket were two disruptive-pattern combat suits, army-issue rubber-soled boots and other ancillary items of military equipment purchased at a trendy boutique in Soho. There was also an RPG-7 rocket launcher and two PG-7M high explosive anti-tank rockets. Unbeknown to Ozbek, his companion was carrying a 7.65mm MKE pistol fitted with a noise suppresser.

Chapter Twelve

Ozbek drove through East Grinstead and continued southwards on the A22 trunk route. The traffic on the main arterial was much heavier than he had anticipated but on reflection, he supposed that was only to be expected on a Friday afternoon. Ozbek just hoped it would thin out when they turned off on to one of the unclassified carriageways that ran through Ashdown Forest.

The tripmeter showed they had covered thirty-one miles since leaving Henning Road in Tottenham and they were now approaching Forest Row. The next landmark after that was Wych Cross; thereafter they would see Pippingford Park on their left with part of Ashdown Forest to the right. Kemal Esener was trying to follow their progress on the map but his English was poor and since he couldn't make any sense of the road signs, he had them miles beyond Forest Row.

'You can put that away,' Ozbek said, addressing the younger man. 'I know where we are.'

Esener closed the *AA Big Road Atlas* and tossed it on to the back seat, then opened the glove compartment and took out a glossy booklet on Ashdown Forest. The speedometer was hovering between fifty-five and sixty as it had been ever since the trunk road had crossed the M25 orbital motorway. At that speed, nearly every vehicle on the road was overtaking them, even when it wasn't really safe to do so. Let them, Ozbek thought. With a small arsenal behind the back seat, getting caught up in a traffic accident was the last thing he wanted. Anyway, sixty miles an hour was hardly a snail's pace. Four minutes after leaving Forest Row they had reached Wych Cross and the road they wanted was a little under three miles ahead.

'That's the first,' Kemal Esener suddenly announced.

'First what?'

'Parking area. There are five of them on my side of the road.'

'Did you see any vehicles?'

'A few.'

'Let me know how full the others are.'

Ashdown Forest was a great beauty spot which attracted over a million visitors a year, according to the illustrated guide Ozbek had bought in Crowborough when they had first looked at the area. But most of the visitors came to the forest in summer and, officially, the first day of spring was still nearly a week off. He drew further comfort from the fact that, as far as Kemal Esener could tell, the number of vehicles he saw in each successive parking area could be counted on the fingers of one hand. Things looked even better to Ozbek when he turned off the A22 on to Stone Hill Road and began to climb through the forest. From there on they didn't meet another vehicle.

The higher they climbed, so the heathland, Scots pine and heather gave way to birch, oak and beech which were just coming into leaf. As the road swung north towards Camp Hill, Ozbek slowed right down to under twenty miles an hour to be on the lookout for the bridle path, which led to the hide he and Esener had chosen when reconnoitring the area a fortnight ago. However, since he was approaching the path from a different direction he overshot it and had to back up.

Although the hide they had selected was only a mile from Stone Hill Road, it seemed more like fifty. At every bend in the track Ozbek feared they would encounter somebody on horseback or an elderly couple out walking their dog. If that should happen they would be remembered for weeks, perhaps months afterwards. It wouldn't be a question of simply aborting the operation – they would have to abandon it altogether and find an alternative target. On that particular afternoon, however, luck was still with them as it had been on the previous occasion when they had gone into the forest on foot looking for a suitable hide. They hadn't run into anybody then, nor did they this time around.

The hide was in a small hollow above one of the forest's clear-running brooks which had sufficient undergrowth to conceal the Ford Escort from the bridle path some ten feet away. Ozbek manoeuvred the car into position, shifted the gear stick into neutral and switched off the ignition.

'Not a word from you,' he cautioned Esener. 'Your English is very poor; if we should meet anybody, I will do the talking. Understand?'

'Yes, yes,' Esener said impatiently. 'I am not an idiot, I understood the first time you told me.'

'All right, let's get changed.'

Ozbek got out of the Escort, closed the door quietly, then went to the rear of the vehicle and raised the hatchback. Moving the blanket aside, he handed one of the uniforms to Esener and then stripped off. The chevrons of a sergeant had been sewn on both sleeves of his combat jacket. From a shop specialising in military memorabilia he had purchased two identical cap badges which used to be worn by the officers and men of some British cavalry regiment that had been disbanded nearly forty years ago. Although it wouldn't fool an expert in heraldry, the two-headed eagle displayed against a red and white cloth patch would help to convince most people that he and Esener were Polish soldiers. Poland was now a member of NATO and joint manoeuvres with the British army were becoming commonplace. Ozbek finished changing into uniform, buckled the web belt and water bottle around his waist, then hid his civilian clothes under the blanket.

'How do I look?' Ozbek asked.

'Beautiful,' Esener said, and laughed uproariously until the older man clapped a hand over his mouth.

'Do that again,' Ozbek hissed, 'and I will strangle you.'

There was a lot more Ozbek could have said but it was too late now. Somebody, not very far away, was moving stealthily towards the hide. The intruder must have been walking along the bridle path and had spotted the Ford Escort when he'd turned off the track and headed into the woods.

Ozbek released the younger man and turned his back on him. The intruder was somewhere directly to his front on the bridle path above, and had stopped moving. He could actually hear him breathing.

Esener took the MKE 7.65mm semi-automatic pistol out of his jacket pocket and pulled the slide back to chamber a round. The slide mechanism made two distinctive sounds, a faint click as it cocked the hammer and a definite clunk as it went forward to feed a round from the box magazine into the breech. The noise spooked Ozbek and made him jump; it panicked the intruder into breaking cover, thereby presenting a fleeting target to Esener who took aim only to break into a fit of relieved giggles.

'It's a deer,' he spluttered, 'a deer.'

Ozbek didn't trust himself to speak. There was a tight knot in his stomach and his heart was pounding. Esener was a fool and a dangerous one at that. Had it been a man instead of a deer he would have killed the intruder without a moment's hesitation. Ozbek didn't know where Esener had obtained the pistol and he wasn't about to ask him to hand it over because he was sure the younger man would refuse to do so. He would need to watch him like a hawk because it was also apparent that if they found themselves in trouble Esener would attempt to shoot his way out.

Ozbek went over to the Ford Escort and removed the RPG-7 and both high-explosive anti-tank rockets, then closed the hatchback and locked the car doors.

'I'll carry the launcher,' he told Esener.

'Suits me,' the younger man said.

The White House was roughly six hundred yards south of

their present location. Shouldering the RPG-7, Ozbek led the way to the ambush position he had chosen a fortnight ago.

Amanda French opened the fitted wardrobe and then stepped back from the door to inspect her appearance in the full-length mirror. Her habit consisted of a pair of riding boots, a dark blue silk shirt belonging to husband, Keith, and a black velvet hard hat.

'Not bad,' Amanda said, patting her flat stomach, 'not bad at all for a forty-three-year-old.'

No babies, no stretch marks, that was the secret of her success. There were times when Amanda felt envious of other women when she saw them with their children. However, as she frequently admitted to herself, she wasn't cut out to be a mother and would probably have made a lousy job of it. And Keith had never shown any enthusiasm for fatherhood, doubt-less because he suspected his sperm count was too low to impregnate her. What was indisputable in Amanda's eyes was the fact that Keith was definitely under-sexed and showed no interest in women in general, his wife in particular.

Where sex was concerned Hasan Ünver, the Turkish bull, was different: he couldn't get enough of it. What was more he liked talking about sex, especially the sex he had with her. She enthralled him, he declared, and he was madly in love with her. It was, Amanda knew, complete nonsense but she still liked hearing it, particularly when he was humping her because, meaningless as they were, those few words made her feel less of a tart. Amanda closed the fitted wardrobe and was about to go downstairs when the extension in the master bedroom rang. She assumed it was Hasan Ünver again. He had already phoned once to let her know he was roughly ten miles from East Grinstead. Ten to one she was about to receive the latest update on his progress, together with a few lurid suggestions as to how they should spend the evening. She had a few ideas on that subject herself but action spoke louder than words. Maybe she would wait for him on the porch in her riding habit and unbutton the shirt in the glare of the headlights on his car as he swept up the drive. On second thoughts the night air at this time of the year was a bit on the chilly side for that sort of caper.

She walked over to the telephone on the bedside table and snatched the receiver from the cradle just as the caller was about to hang up.

'So where are you now?' Amanda asked in a sexy voice.

'About ten minutes from the house. How did you know it was me?'

'Keith?' Amanda sat down on the bed, her legs suddenly weak at the knees.

'Now you sound surprised. What's going on?'

The alarm bells started ringing. Whatever else Keith might be he was no fool and she needed to allay his suspicions before he started to cross-examine her like some Crown prosecutor. Fortunately she had always been pretty nimble on her feet.

'Nothing is going on,' she assured him. 'I had this funny feeling it was you before I answered the phone and then I was surprised when my hunch was true. Delighted too, I might add.'

'Are you?'

'Of course I am. Why shouldn't I be? After you rang yesterday I was resigned to spending another lonely weekend. Now you're home for good.'

'Not really. I'm flying back to Istanbul on Sunday afternoon to finalise matters with the Turkish authorities.'

'Well, anyway, it'll be good to have you to myself for the weekend.'

'Yes. I think there are things we need to discuss.'

The alarm bells were ringing even louder now and they would go right off the decibel range if Keith arrived home to find her like this without a damned thing on under his blue silk shirt.

'Are you driving while you're talking on the phone?' she asked.

'I only need one hand to steer the Jag,' Keith told her.

'That's the most stupid thing I ever heard. And dangerous. What are you trying to do? Kill yourself? I'm going to hang up right now.'

Amanda put the phone down, unbuttoned the shirt and removed it; then tugged off the riding boots. What to wear? Something casual which would tell Keith she hadn't been expecting anyone to call on her. Velvet corduroy trousers, a jumper and low-heeled shoes, that was the answer. She would need to do something about her face too; all that heavy make-up was an absolute giveaway. And there was also the intimate dinner for two which she had prepared. Keith might believe she had rustled up the smoked salmon and popped a bottle of champagne into the fridge in the ten minutes it took him to arrive at the house after calling her, but the rest would have to be hidden away in the deep freeze. Then, if there was time she would have to clear the table that had been laid for two. If there wasn't enough time she would have to come up with a damned good explanation.

Hasan Ünver. In her panic she had forgotten about her lover. He had told her to expect him at six and it was now four minutes to. What the hell was the number of his mobile?

Ozbek raised himself up on one knee in the approved firing position and scanned the target area. The White House was three hundred yards away and although this particular spot hadn't been his first choice or even the second, it did offer him a clear line of sight to the front door. He had selected the other two sites while reconnoitring the area but what had looked a good choice from a distance, had proved next to useless close to. The undulating nature of the heathland below the tree line meant the target could only be engaged by standing bolt upright, and both men had been averse to doing that. So they had crawled on their bellies to the alternative ambush site only to find the same restriction applied. They'd had no option but to crawl around until they found a suitable location.

'Are you satisfied now?' Esener asked in a low voice.

'It's not perfect,' Ozbek told him. 'You can only see part of the drive but it will do.'

'Then let's get ready; we haven't got much time.'

Esener placed the rockets on the ground and screwed the cardboard cylinder containing the propellant into the tail of each rocket. While he was doing this, Ozbek cocked the hammer and replaced the range-finding optical day sight with the image intensifier used at night.

'I think I should handle the launcher,' Esener said.

'Why so?'

'Because you are unfit, and are likely to miss the target.'

'Nonsense . . . I'm as fit . . . as you are.'

'Listen to yourself; you're still out of breath.'

Much as he hated to admit it Ozbek knew the younger man was right. 'Take the damned launcher then,' he said gruffly.

Esener inserted the rocket grenade into the muzzle of the launcher and ensured the small projection on the tail mated with the notch inside the muzzle so that the propellant was in line with the percussion hammer. He then removed the nose cap on the rocket grenade and withdrew the safety pin.

Hasan Ünver had opted to take the longer route to The White House. Instead of cutting through Ashdown Forest on one of the unclassified roads, he had stayed on the A22 trunk as far as the junction with the B2026 above Maresfield and had then headed north to Duddleswell. He had told Amanda French to expect him at six, and now there was every prospect of arriving ten minutes early, which was clearly undesirable. The English woman clearly believed she had only to snap her fingers and he would come running, and it was essential to disabuse her of the notion.

He liked his women to be compliant, to know their place as his wife most certainly did. Elçin never questioned anything he told her; she accepted that he would be away all weekend discussing oil exploration rights in the Sea of Marmara with executives of British Petroleum. But the English woman mocked him. All that nonsense about the 'French maid' when he had phoned the house this morning and 'champing at the bit', making him feel a fool with her teasing. What she needed was a good beating like he gave Elçin from time to time. Maybe he would give Amanda a taste of the strap? The thought excited him and he pictured her squirming on the bed, begging him to stop but not really meaning it.

A horn blared a warning and frightened the life out of him. Heart pounding, he swerved towards the grass verge. As he did so a dark green Jaguar swept past and cut in front of him.

French had met some lunatics on the road in his time but the cretin in the series 3 BMW had to be the prize booby of the year. Of course he was free to do as he liked on the highway, and commit any traffic offence in the book secure in the knowledge that the CD plates on the car guaranteed he wouldn't be prosecuted. He wondered in passing which embassy the man belonged to, wondered also what he was doing in this part of Sussex on a Friday evening. Could it be this unseen diplomat was on his way to see Amanda? French glanced into the rear-view mirror. All he could see of the BMW were two small pinpoints of light which suggested the driver had slowed down since Keith had overtaken him.

He toyed with the idea of pulling off the road somewhere and confronting the embassy man when the bastard caught up with him, then rejected the notion. While in Istanbul, he had received a cable from Head Office hinting that Amanda was having an affair with one of the diplomats at the Turkish Embassy in London. Reading between the lines, it was apparent to him that he was expected to do something about it. He hadn't got to where he was today through being indecisive and he had got himself on the first available flight to England.

Although it would give him enormous pleasure to hammer

the diplomat, French knew it would affect the corporation adversely and prejudice the outcome of the offshore oil exploration rights. In any case his real quarrel was with Amanda. The Turkish diplomat was merely the latest in a procession of lovers on whom he'd always turned a blind eye. But not any more; this time he was going to have it out with Amanda and lay down some ground rules for her future behaviour. Tripping the indicator to show he was turning left, French swept into the drive leading to his house.

The waiting was over. While all Esener could see of the target was the twin beams lighting up the drive, the vehicle was in the right place at the right time which was good enough for him. He picked up the car in the image intensifier and tracked it towards the front door, the safety off, his index finger curled round the trigger. To make absolutely sure of a first-round hit, he wouldn't engage the target until it was stationary.

'Hold your fire,' Ozbek said urgently. 'It's not Hasan Ünver.'

Esener didn't see how Ozbek could possibly know that. As he watched, the car automatically triggered a powerful security light above the front door. In that same instant he recalled the Cuban telling them about the degrading effect white light had on an image intensifier and how it was next to useless for approximately fifteen minutes after exposure. Ozbek was saying it was the wrong car but Kemal was having a bad case of the jitters and he ignored him.

Esener squeezed the trigger, releasing the hammer, which detonated the propellant. The muzzle velocity of the high-explosive anti-tank missile as it left the launcher was four hundred feet per second. It immediately accelerated to nine hundred and seventy feet per second when the rocket motor kicked in after the missile had travelled ten yards. These facts were known to Esener; however, nothing the Cuban had said had prepared him for the ear-splitting crack of the propellant or the deafening whoosh from the rocket on ignition.

The distance from the firing point to the stationary vehicle was some three hundred yards; the missile covered it in less than a second. Esener thought he heard a metallic clang as the projectile struck the vehicle; a moment later the warhead exploded and blew the car apart, turning it into a funeral pyre. A ball of fire rose in a mushroom cloud above the roof line and globules of blazing fuel struck the house.

'You idiot,' Ozbek screamed, 'you've killed the wrong man.'

Esener didn't bother to answer him back; shouldering the launcher he started running towards the hide where they had left the Ford Escort. Ozbek was a lot slower off the mark but he soon made up for it, chasing after the younger man as fast as his lungs would allow.

Hasan Ünver had parked the BMW on the grass verge a few yards from the entrance to The White House. Using his side-lights only, he had discreetly tailed the Jaguar from the moment it had overtaken him. According to Amanda, Keith French was staying on in Istanbul until Tuesday, and Ünver had got out of the car and walked forward, hoping to catch a glimpse of the visitor. If the driver of the Jaguar who had been in such a tearing hurry was Keith French, then he was in deep trouble. For Amanda's husband to return home four days earlier than expected could only mean he had learned of their affair and intended to do something about it.

The sudden appearance of a low-level rocket streaking towards the house from somewhere over to his left startled Hasan Ünver; the subsequent destruction of the Jaguar in a fireball completely unnerved him. Much of the blast had dissipated before it reached the end of the drive but even so he felt as if somebody had barged into him. For some moments he stood rooted to the spot, then recovering his wits he ran back to the car and tumbled into it. His one thought was to put as many miles on the clock as he could before the police and other emergency services arrived on the scene.

*   *   *

It was Ozbek who heard the voices first and stopped to listen intently. Esener halted a few yards further up the hill, then turned about and walked back towards him, a puzzled expression on his face as if to say where are they? In answer to his unspoken question, Ozbek pointed straight ahead but that was purely a guess. Although the interlopers were too far away for him to hear what they were saying to one another, he could tell by their voices that one of them was a woman. Signalling Esener to follow him, he moved off to his right, hoping to outflank the couple. Given time he would have preferred to go to ground and wait for the danger to pass but time was one thing they didn't have. Behind them, The White House was now also on fire.

As they circled towards the hide the voices became louder and for Ozbek it was possible to hear and understand what they were saying.

'Hector,' the man shouted. 'Hector, come here, boy.'

The woman said much the same thing but in a thinner voice.

A married couple looking for their dog? Whatever they were doing, Ozbek wished they would go away. He was almost within touching distance of the Ford Escort and beyond the car on the footpath above it, he could see a flashlight swinging from side to side like a pendulum. He froze, uncertain what to do, then the flashlight beam dipped into the hollow and illuminated the Ford hatchback.

The man said, 'Hello, what's this car doing here?'

'What car, dear?' the woman asked.

'Oh, for God's sake, Jean, the one in the hollow.'

Ozbek did the only thing he could and moved round the Escort into the beam, determined to bluff his way out of trouble. The flashlight settled on his legs, then moved up to his face.

'Who the devil are you?' the man asked.

Ozbek raised a hand to shield his eyes from the glare. 'I am Polish soldier,' he said and bowed from the waist as he'd heard all Europeans did. 'We are training with British army.'

'Are you indeed? Were you responsible for that loud bang we heard a few minutes ago?'

'That was not us.'

'I think I can see a house on fire,' Jean said. 'Down by the road to Duddleswell. In fact it's The White House, Henry.'

'Then we had better report it.'

Henry tucked the flashlight under one arm and produced a mobile phone from his coat pocket. He had got as far as extending the aerial when Esener appeared on the track and shot him in the head at point-blank range. The woman screamed, then grunted when a 7.65mm bullet struck her in the chest. She went over backwards and lay quite still but that didn't satisfy Esener. He stood over her body and put another three rounds into the chest and stomach, the pistol making a hollow cough each time he squeezed the trigger.

'What are you going to do now?' Ozbek demanded. 'Find their dog and kill that also?'

'We had no choice,' Esener told him, 'you know that as well as I do.'

'I could have talked our way out of it.'

'The hell you could. Try doing something useful instead of bleating and get the car out of the hollow while I collect the rocket launcher.'

Chapter Thirteen

Ozbek drove through Ashdown Forest, taking the same route out as he had on the way in. His every instinct was to put his foot down and eat up the miles to the A22 trunk road but he knew that would be asking for trouble. Anybody who happened to see a vehicle being driven away from a scene of a major incident at speed was bound to be suspicious, and might well inform the police. It wasn't necessary to get the vehicle registration number; a brief description of the car would be enough. Ozbek didn't fancy their chances if every patrol car in Sussex was warned to look out for a white Ford Escort.

'How much further to the main road?' Esener asked in a nervous-sounding voice.

'Five, six minutes.' Ozbek shrugged his shoulders. 'Maybe longer.'

They would make it in less but he wanted Esener to sweat. The younger man was a dangerous hothead and he had been completely out of control this evening. Despite being ordered to hold his fire, he had engaged the wrong target, because whoever had been driving the Jaguar it certainly hadn't been Hasan Ünver. Then, instead of giving him the chance to hoodwink the English couple, Esener had killed them in cold blood without giving it a moment's thought. Now they were running for their lives still dressed as Polish soldiers, an RPG-7 rocket launcher in the back and Esener nursing the murder weapon as though the 7.65mm MKE semi-automatic pistol was the most precious thing on earth. In their haste to get away they had also left a PG-7M high-explosive anti-tank rocket behind in the ambush position, but in truth that was the least of their worries.

'Look out!'

Esener's warning shout was almost too late for Ozbek to avoid a collision with an oncoming juggernaut which would have crushed the Ford Escort like a bug. A savage blast on a klaxon set his heart pounding like a steam hammer, and in a blind panic, he floored the accelerator thinking it was the footbrake. It was the luckiest error Ozbek could have made; had his foot found the right pedal he and Esener would have been reduced to so much offal crushed under the wheels of the 38 ton Volvo rig and trailer.

He missed the juggernaut by a whisker, found himself heading straight for a hedgerow on the opposite side of the road and put the wheel hard over to the right. Tyres screaming, the car mounted the grass verge and gave every sign that it was about to flip over. The gods, however, were in a mood to be kind to him and the Ford Escort tilted back on to all four wheels. There was a sickening crack from the chassis, which suggested something pretty important had been damaged, but Ozbek was too busy trying to regain control of the vehicle to worry about that. The driver of the Volvo rig expressed his anger with one long, deep-throated, ear-splitting blast on the horn. The couple in the Rover 400, who were forced to take avoiding action as Ozbek swung back on to the road, couldn't compete with the truck driver but they did their best. The man held a thumb on the button while the woman snarled at him as though she would like to sink her teeth into his throat. For a moment or so Ozbek thought he was about to find out what it was like to be a victim of road rage but in the end, the driver of the Rover wisely continued on his way.

'You stupid son of a whore,' Esener screamed, 'you nearly got us killed. What the hell were you thinking of?'

Esener didn't expect an answer and Ozbek wasn't about to

164

give him an explanation. The younger man had got him so worked up that he'd no recollection of driving those last few miles through the forest. Worse still, he had failed to notice the warning sign of a major road ahead and had shot straight out on to the A22. Now that the danger had passed he couldn't stop trembling; another humiliating side effect was the discovery that he was unable to control his bladder.

Ozbek drove on, taking deep breaths and slowly exhaling, an exercise intended to steady his nerves. To add to his troubles, the car handled sluggishly as if it had a mind of its own and was determined to resist him. Two miles south of Wych Cross he turned into one of the car parks on the left-hand side of the road. By nature a cautious man, Ozbek checked to make sure no other vehicles were using it before he pulled up near one of the litter bins and switched off the engine and lights.

'Why have we stopped here?' Esener demanded.

'To change our clothes. Now, stop asking stupid questions and get on with it.'

Ozbek got out of the Escort and opened the hatchback. The whole damned country was awash with mobile phones and he thought it likely that either the couple in the Rover 400 or the truck driver had reported him to the police. It was only necessary for one of the parties to infer that he had been drinking and every police car in Sussex would be on the lookout for a white Ford Escort. Their best bet was to leave the A22 as soon as possible, dump the car within walking distance of a railway station and finish the journey by train. Telling Esener to follow his example, Ozbek stuffed the discarded combat jacket and pants together with the rest of the military gear into the litter bin. 'And bring the rocket launcher with you,' he added.

'You're not dumping that as well, are you?'

'Of course I am. Could you explain what it's doing in our possession if we are stopped by the police?'

Esener shook his head. 'Seems a pity, though.'

'There are plenty more where that came from. Same goes for the pistol you are carrying.'

165

'Oh, no, I'm not leaving that in a litter bin.'

'Don't be stupid.'

'Forget it. I'm hanging on to the pistol.'

There was no moving Esener and arguing with him was a waste of time. Ozbek did, however, manage to persuade the younger man to remove the magazine. Unfortunately he still left one round in the breech and that was one round too many. Tight-lipped with anger, Ozbek started up and drove out of the car park.

Edmunds left The Old Vicarage and walked towards the village. What he particularly liked about Janet was the space she gave him. If anybody organised a contest to determine the least inquisitive woman in the country, he reckoned Janet would win it hands down. However, this lack of curiosity was really part of her defence mechanism. So far as Janet was concerned, the less she knew about his business, the safer she felt. So when he had told her this evening that he was going for a short walk to work up an appetite before dinner, she had accepted the excuse without comment.

The public call box was down the road from Scoones and Chambers, Estate Agents and Chartered Auctioneers. Entering it, Edmunds lifted the receiver and fed fifty pence into the meter, then punched out the number of Alistair Downward's luxury flat in St John's Wood. There was no immediate answer and after a while he began to wonder if the Foreign Office legal counsellor was still in his office or had gone out for the evening. Ten minutes to seven was, however, a little early to be attending a dinner party and somewhat late in the day for him to be at his desk. Edmunds was about to hang up and try again later when a breathless Alistair came on the line.

'I'm not disturbing you, am I?' Edmunds asked.

'I was taking a shower.'

'Then I'll be brief. I'm being harassed by a man called Peter Ashton and I want him off my back. He's either with Five or The Firm.'

'Did he say so?'

'Of course he didn't but I spent twenty-five years in the colonial police and, take it from me, you get a feeling for people like him. Besides, he knew too much about my private life.'

'I think you had better start at the beginning,' Downward said.

Edmunds recharged the meter with a handful of coins, then repeated the conversation he had had with Ashton on the doorstep. He related how Ashton had made him an offer for The Old Vicarage, claiming Knight, Frank were handling the sale.

'It was a stupid lie and he must have known I would check with them but Ashton didn't seem to care. He also told me he was a broker with Baldwin Peiper and there wasn't a grain of truth in that either. Finally, he gave me one of his visiting cards and wrote his office number on the back. Naturally I haven't tried it or his home number. As he was leaving, Ashton tried to make out we had met in Hong Kong years ago.'

'Maybe you had and had forgotten about it?'

'Certainly not. I never forget a face.'

'You obviously have a good memory.'

Downward's tone was supercilious and conveyed the impression that he didn't believe it. What angered Edmunds was his innate air of superiority over men who hadn't been to Eton and Magdalen College, Oxford where he had walked away with a double first in Jurisprudence and Economics. The one blemish on his academic record was the fact that he had only come third in the Bar Finals at law school. Downward had never practised at the Bar; from the moment he had gone up to Oxford, the Foreign and Commonwealth Office had had their eyes on him and he had been head hunted by the Diplomatic Service ten weeks after joining chambers to do a year's pupillage.

'This Peter Ashton,' Downward said in a voice totally lacking in interest, 'what else can you tell me about him?'

'What else? Well, the bastard is roughly half an inch under six feet, weighs about a hundred and seventy-five pounds, all of it bone and muscle, has dark hair and eyes that are as grey as slate—'

'That isn't what I meant,' Downward protested.

'I would say he was aged in his middle to late thirties. A lot of women would be attracted to him like bees around a honeypot. I guess he is pretty good-looking and no doubt that whimsical smile of his gets them going.'

'But you didn't warm to him,' Downward said, and laughed.

'Neither would you. In my day, we referred to guys like Ashton as smiling death. He doesn't believe I'm on the side of the angels and he will keep beavering away until he finds something that will stand up in court.'

'If you haven't done anything wrong, Martin, how can he prove you have?'

Edmunds crushed the phone in a grip of iron. Was it possible that Downward was trying to distance himself from the whole damn business?

'We're in this together,' he said angrily. 'If I go down, you are coming with me.'

'That's a matter of opinion.'

'The hell it is. First thing you are going to do is check the registration number of a Ford Grenada—'

'If you want to find out which ministry the car belongs to please go ahead but don't expect me to waste my time.'

'Now you listen to me—'

'Submit an occurrence report,' Downward said, interrupting him. 'Write to your superintendent of the Queen's Messenger Service telling him everything you have just told me but embellish it a little and conclude by saying you assume Peter Ashton, the subject of your complaint, is answerable to the Security Department of the Foreign and Commonwealth Office.'

Downward was making sure his head was well below the parapet before the shit began to fly. That was a little game and Edmunds wasn't going to have it.

'And just how will that stop Ashton?' He snarled.

'Your superintendent will ask the Head of FCO Security what is going on and the inestimable Shirley Isles will take it up with the appropriate under secretary.'

'You hope.'

'You don't understand. Three days ago Mrs Isles was instructed to show your security file and Zawadzki's to an officer of the SIS. In all probability this officer was Peter Ashton. When he had finished reading the files, this man told Shirley Isles that he was happy about you but had some reservations concerning Zawadzki. Provided your occurrence report is worded properly it will appear Ashton has been using confidential information for his own private advantage. If I know Shirley Isles she will raise Cain when she hears that. So relax, Martin, and do try to be a little less paranoid in future.'

Downward hung up before Edmunds had a chance to come back at him. Edmunds did the same, collected a ten-pence coin from the scoop which the meter had returned and left the call box. He didn't know how Downward could be so sure Ashton had read his security file but the man wasn't in the habit of making idle claims. No doubt he also knew who had told Shirley Isles to make the files available.

The car was behaving like a horse that hadn't been broken in. Ozbek had to wrestle with the steering and literally drag the Escort round every bend in the road, the tyres squealing in protest. At forty the steering column juddered in his hands, at fifty it felt as if the chassis was about to break in two. That this might happen didn't worry Kemal Esener, who kept urging him to go faster. The younger man had the *AA Big Road Atlas* open on his lap and was attempting to read it with the aid of the courtesy light in the roof.

Esener claimed he couldn't read the map in the dark but his poor command of English made him a lousy navigator anyway and the courtesy light was therefore an additional hazard for Ozbek to contend with. Since leaving the parking areas south of

Wych Cross, they had travelled in a westerly direction, keeping to the back roads whenever possible. In the process Esener had managed to get them lost somewhere along the way after skirting Horsham. As a result each time they came upon a signpost Ozbek had to take his eyes off the road and glance at the map in order to check the directions Esener had just given him.

Unfortunately, none of the place names meant anything to Ozbek and he became increasingly desperate. Well over an hour had passed since Esener had engaged the wrong target and some forty minutes had elapsed since they had narrowly avoided a major traffic accident. At any moment Ozbek expected to hear the wail of a police siren. His mouth was bone dry as it always was in the grip of nervous tension; then suddenly, as he drove through the outskirts of Hindhead, Ozbek noticed a road sign pointing the way to Guildford and he began to breathe a little easier. Reaching up, he switched off the courtesy light.

'What do you think you are doing?' Esener demanded in a harsh voice. 'I can't see a hand in front of my face.'

'You don't need to,' Ozbek told him. 'I know where I am now.'

At the traffic lights in the centre of town, he made a right turn and started up the hill leading to the Devil's Punch Bowl. The Escort was becoming even more difficult to handle, especially when he dropped down into third gear. The increased torque made the steering wheel vibrate so much his upper arms began to shake almost as violently. Thoroughly alarmed by his inability to control the vehicle, Ozbek changed into top again and gingerly put his foot down on the accelerator just enough to ensure the engine didn't stall on him.

Ozbek glanced into the rear-view, saw the headlights of a vehicle closing rapidly on him and altered the mirror's trim so that he shouldn't be dazzled. The driver of the following vehicle kept his lights on full beam and started honking as he came within nudging distance of the Ford Escort. The man dropped back a few yards, then put his foot down and tail-gated Ozbek as he negotiated the long left bend into the Devil's Punch Bowl.

The Escort slewed towards the centre crash barrier and an oncoming bus blared a warning. Screaming obscenities at the top of his voice, Ozbek yanked the steering wheel hard over to the left and floored the brake pedal. The back end fishtailed in the opposite direction provoking another string of profanities from Ozbek, who swiftly reversed the lock to correct the drift. The speedometer was showing under thirty when he was shunted a second time.

The camber on that section of the road was markedly biased to the left, which drew the car towards the Bowl. Ozbek turned the wheel and steered towards the centre line just as the rogue driver attempted to overtake him on the outside. Forced to brake sharply, the lunatic in the other car cut inside and drew abreast, his window right down so that Ozbek might hear the obscenities he was mouthing at him. Esener lowered his window, snatched the semi-automatic from the waistband of his slacks and slapped the magazine home in the butt. He then aimed the pistol at the driver of the BMW which had drawn alongside them. He had meant to shoot him in his loud mouth but as his finger squeezed the trigger, the driver turned his head away to glance at the road ahead so that the 7.65mm bullet smashed through the lower jaw and blew out the left cheek of his face. Esener knew it was not a fatal wound and fired again, hitting the driver behind and slightly above the right ear. As he slid sideways, the woman next to him grabbed the wheel and tried to keep the vehicle on the road.

Ozbek finally lost control of the Ford Escort when the rear nearside tyre burst like a pricked balloon. The car slammed into the BMW, mounted the bank at the side of the road and bouncing over the top, plunged into the Devil's Punch Bowl. The Escort struck a tree on the way down and broke in two. The windscreen imploded into several thousand tiny fragments, the seat belts were torn from their floor mountings and Esener went out head first over the bonnet. What was left of the vehicle began to somersault. At some stage before it cartwheeled a second time, the door on the driver's side was wrenched off and Ozbek was thrown clear. He landed heavily, dislocated the right elbow as he instinctively put out an arm to break the fall. He also knocked himself out when his head struck a tree stump.

Ozbek could hear voices, two or three near at hand, others further off, all of them somewhere behind and above him on the slope. His head was throbbing and there was a lump the size of an egg near the hairline above the left eye. He was lying on his stomach, his head over to the right, the left cheek pressed against the earth. He was vaguely aware that his right arm was folded back in a curious position at the elbow which felt as if it were on fire. The nature of the injury only became clear when he tried to push himself up on his hands and knees and fell back screaming.

A voice said, 'Hello, we've got a live one somewhere over there, Dave.'

He heard the men moving towards him, their legs brushing against the undergrowth. Presently, two ambulance men appeared on the scene and gently lifted Ozbek on to the stretcher, then carried him up the slope past the crumpled body of a man, who he only later realised had to be Kemal Esener. Beyond the dead man and further down the Devil's Punch Bowl, a fierce blaze was being tackled by a number of firemen.

'What's burning?' he croaked.

'A BMW,' one of the ambulance men told him. 'There were four teenagers in it, three boys and a girl.'

Ozbek wanted to know if they were OK but neither man was prepared to answer his question. Instead they assured him he would be as right as ninepence in no time, whatever the hell that meant. Ozbek recalled what one of the ambulance men had said to his friend Dave when he had cried out in pain and wondered if he was the sole survivor of the accident. It would certainly simplify matters if he was, provided nobody found the semi-automatic, and the driver of the BMW had been reduced to ashes. Too many things depended on chance and he needed to disappear before the police searched both halves of the Ford Escort and perhaps found two empty cartridge cases. That would be enough evidence to convince them they were investigating something more than an ordinary traffic accident.

'Where are you taking me?' Ozbek asked as the two men lifted his stretcher into one of the ambulances.

'Farnham Road Hospital, just outside Guildford,' a paramedic told him. 'We'll be there in no time.'

The driver closed the doors, got into the cab and started the engine. Ozbek estimated they were doing at least fifty within a few seconds of moving off.

'So what's your name?' the paramedic asked.

'Mehmet Ozbek,' he said without thinking.

'OK, Mr Ozbek, how long is it since you had something to eat?'

'What?'

'No doctor will give you an anaesthetic if you've eaten within the last four hours.'

Ozbek frowned. Merih Soysel had rung him from the Turkish Embassy at two fifteen and he'd had to leave the table to answer the phone. 'I've had nothing since lunchtime,' he told the paramedic.

'That's all right then. So who's your next of kin, Mr Ozbek?'

'Why do you want to know that?'

'To inform whoever is closest to you that you've suffered minor injuries following a traffic accident—'

'I'm not married,' Ozbek said, interrupting him.

'A close friend then, somebody who will collect you from the hospital when you're discharged? Casualty is bound to ask who they should contact and it'll save time if you give me the details now.'

'Mr Hilak Ersoy, 258 Woodland Park Road, Harringay. He's my brother-in-law.' Ersoy was back in Ankara and they weren't related.

'Is he on the phone?' the paramedic asked.

'No, he only moved in on Monday.'

'No problem. We'll get the local police to call on your brother-in-law.'

Ozbek hoped Casualty wouldn't be in too much of a hurry to contact the fictitious next of kin because he needed to be long gone before the police discovered that nobody by the name of Hilak Ersoy was living at 258 Woodland Park Road.

The headline story on BBC 1 concerned a terrorist outrage deep in the heart of Sussex which had resulted in at least two deaths, but although Edmunds was watching the news bulletin, he wasn't taking it in. His mind was busy grappling with the question of what he should do about Ashton. He had taken Downward's advice and written to George McCready, the Superintendent of the Queen's Messenger Service, but he wouldn't get his letter until Monday.

The laid back approach favoured by Downward was all very well but it could be overdone. After reading his letter, McCready might get the impression that Edmunds was merely having a quiet niggle and no further action was called for. Besides, he had been placed on standby with effect from 06.00 hours on Monday and could be off to South American the same evening. No, he wanted to make sure before he left the UK that Ashton was going to be strung up by his balls because that man was as harmless as weeping gelignite.

Edmunds looked across the room at his wife, Janet, wedged in one corner of the settee, legs up on a pouffe, busy doing the latest tapestry she had ordered from Ehrman.

'I think I'll ring George McCready,' he said.

'I wonder if you should disturb him at this hour, dear? I mean it is Friday, and it is gone nine o'clock.'

'It's important.'

'If you say so.'

Janet went back to her needlework. There were times when her detachment angered him and this was one such occasion. She knew damned well what was going on but she preferred to feign ignorance because that was her defence should things go wildly wrong — Little Miss Innocent. But, hypocritical bitch that she was, it didn't stop her enjoying the fruits of his labour.

Edmunds stalked out of the room, went into the study and, lifting the receiver, punched out McCready's number.

Chapter Fourteen

The meeting was scheduled for eight forty-five, which Ashton had thought a trifle optimistic when Hazelwood had phoned on Sunday evening to warn him that his presence was required. Morning prayers usually ran to three-quarters of an hour but on that particular day Victor had excelled himself and wrapped up the proceedings in twenty-odd minutes. However, with the exception of Rowan Garfield, Head of the European Department, and Bill Orchard, who was in charge of the Asian land mass, all the other familiar faces were present – Jill Sheridan, Roy Kelso, the Admin King, and Roger Benton whose fiefdom included the Pacific Basin and Rest of the World. The only person Ashton hadn't expected to see when he walked into the conference room was Richard Neagle of MI5.

'Sit down, Peter,' Hazelwood said, and pointed to a vacant chair on Jill's right.

At the end of morning prayers Victor's PA had distributed an agenda for the meeting under the heading of CATO, an abbreviation which apparently stood for Combined Anti-Terrorist Organisation. Glancing at his own copy of the agenda Ashton saw that the MI5 officer was going to open the batting with the latest update on the terrorist threat to mainland Britain. In the event, the whole thrust of Neagle's presentation was that the Security Service was short of manpower and could not afford to take on any further commitments. MI5 already had their hands full keeping track of the various IRA factions operating in the UK; now, following various incidents in Surrey and Sussex on Friday night, there were grounds for believing a Kurdish terrorist group or the militant wing of the Turkish Communist Party were attacking selected targets in the Home Counties.

'What are these grounds?' Hazelwood had asked.

'The victims were Mr and Mrs Keith French—'

'So the *Sunday Times* and every other newspaper reported.'

'And most of them omitted the fact that Keith French was the top negotiator for British Petroleum,' Neagle said, trying not altogether successfully to conceal his annoyance at being interrupted. 'He had special responsibility for offshore drilling rights. Currently BP is interested in exploring the Sea of Marmara, and both terrorist organisations are not averse to damaging the Turkish economy in any way they can. There are, however, much stronger reasons for attributing the terrorist incidents on Friday to either the Kurds or the Turkish Communists.'

With the help of a tracker dog the police had traced the movements of the terrorists from the moment they had left their ambush position after firing an anti-tank rocket at the Jaguar driven by Keith French. The trail had led them straight to the bridle path where the bodies of an elderly couple had been found shortly before daybreak on the Saturday morning. Following an inch-by-inch search of the immediate area, scene of crime officers had subsequently recovered five empty 7.65mm cartridge cases.

'Two more 7.65mm cases were found in what was left of a Ford Escort after it had swerved off the road and plunged into the Devil's Punch Bowl.' Neagle paused, rather like a ham actor preparing his audience for a telling line they had in fact already anticipated, then said, 'Ballistics were able to match these cases with those found in Ashdown Forest.'

Five people had been killed in the accident, four of them teenage joyriders in a BMW 523 they had stolen from a car park adjoining the Spread Eagle Hotel in Midhurst. Several drivers proceeding towards Hindhead had seen the BMW tailgating the

Ford Escort seconds before the accident, and had reported the reckless behaviour of the driver to the police.

'There was a natural inclination to presume all five victims had died as a result of injuries received when both vehicles somersaulted down the hill.' Neagle paused again, this time to consult his notes. 'Subsequently it was ascertained that the driver of the BMW was dead before his vehicle swerved off the road; he had been shot in the face and the head. That's when the police started looking for the murder weapon.'

'Did they find it?' Benton asked.

'Yesterday morning. The weapon has been test fired and the cartridge case was struck in exactly the same place as the other seven.'

A comparison with the bullet which had been removed from the brain of the dead teenager would be made as soon as the pathologist had completed his autopsy.

'There was one survivor,' Neagle continued, 'a man called Mehmet Ozbek, who had a dislocated right elbow. When asked for his next of kin by a paramedic, Ozbek named his brother-in-law, Hilak Ersoy of 258 Woodland Park Road, Harringay.'

Ashton looked up. 'The same man who rented one of the lockups opposite Fabian House on the Warlock Estate?'

'Yes.'

'I bet Special Branch didn't find him at home when they called at 258 Woodland Park Road.'

'That was not the fault of Special Branch or MI5. According to the neighbours Hilak Ersoy left for Ankara a good three weeks before we learned the IRA had established an arms cache in the lockup next to his.'

If looks could kill Ashton reckoned he would be dead by now the way Neagle was glaring at him. In an attempt to defuse the situation, Jill Sheridan only succeeded in making things worse when she observed that it would be interesting to hear what Mehmet Ozbek had to say for himself.

'We'll have to catch up with him first,' Neagle said grimly. 'Less than an hour after his elbow had been reset, Ozbek walked out of the hospital. From the adjoining car park he stole an old banger belonging to one of the nursing staff on night duty and went on his merry way. The car was later abandoned in Clapham Common near the tube station where it was found yesterday afternoon. He has obviously gone to ground amongst the Turkish community but the police have a good description of Ozbek and they will pick him up sooner or later. Anyway, I hope you can appreciate why we are not really in a position to second an officer to CATO.'

Hazelwood began to drum the table with the thumb and four fingers of his right hand as though practising an ascending scale on the piano, a sure sign the cherubic Mr Neagle was beginning to annoy him. The fact that smoking was not allowed in the conference room didn't improve his temper.

'That's a pity,' he growled, 'especially as there is clearly a direct link between Colonel Herrara, the IRA and Mehmet Ozbek. I would have thought it was in Five's interest to ensure the Combined Anti-Terrorist Organisation got off to a good start.'

'And we are determined it should, Director,' Neagle said hastily. 'We've earmarked a very bright young officer whose primary task will be to liaise with the SIS on all matters pertaining to international terrorism. She will, of course, continue to operate from Gower Street because she will still have other responsibilities, our manpower situation being what it is.'

'May we know her name?' Hazelwood asked, his voice still acidic.

Let me guess, Ashton thought. Even money it's Francesca York, and felt no satisfaction at getting it right.

'A very experienced young officer', Neagle was saying. 'Held a short-service commission in the Intelligence Corps before she came to us and was, for a time, second in command of the army's Special Intelligence Team. This was after Fran had done a stint with 10 Company in Northern Ireland. I'm sure she will do you very well.'

'How long has Miss York been with Five?' Hazelwood asked.

'Twenty months.'

'So she is still a probationer then?'

Neagle reluctantly admitted this was the case but hastened to add that the probationary period finished on 11 July.

'Are you happy to have Miss York on your team?'

Technically Jill Sheridan would be in charge of CATO but Hazelwood wasn't looking at her.

'Deliriously so,' Ashton said drily.

'Clerical support?' Hazelwood said, moving to the next item on the agenda.

It was Roy Kelso's moment of glory and he relished it. Whatever his faults – and there were many – he knew every member of the clerical staff, their strengths and weaknesses. An incurably nosy man, he had made it his business to learn all he could about their private lives, knowledge which he was keen to share with his colleagues whenever the opportunity arose. At the end of an overly long dissertation he nominated a girl in Central Registry called Nancy Wilkins, which seemed to amuse Roger Benton. It did not, however, strike a responsive chord with Jill Sheridan.

'Peter will need a reliable pair of hands,' Jill said, glaring at Benton, 'a gofer who will read everything the CIA and other intelligence agencies have on Colonel Herrara and make an intelligent precis of the information. I think you should provide a Grade II Intelligence Officer. I personally would be happy to accept Will Landon.'

'I bet you would; he practically runs the South American continent single-handed.'

Benton turned to Hazelwood and tried to convince him he couldn't manage without Landon but his plea fell on deaf ears. So far as Victor was concerned things were not so hectic in the Pacific Basin and Rest of the World that the South American Desk officers couldn't go direct to their Head of Department.

Hazelwood looked round the table. 'Is there any other business we need to discuss?' he asked.

'There's Colonel Osvald Herrara,' Ashton said.

'What about him?'

'He's a fast mover. The day after murdering Zawadzki he's on a plane to Managua. Forty-eight hours later he is seen at Mexico City International Airport boarding the Air France flight to Paris. Then on Wednesday the thirteenth of March he's on the Warlock Estate collecting munitions from an IRA cache. In the space of seven days he has been in four different countries.'

'Can we get to the point, Peter?'

'The point is I would like to be reasonably sure Osvaldo is still in the UK. And that's a job for Francesca York.'

'What?' Neagle gaped at him. 'Have you any idea how much work that will entail?'

'Yes. You will need to make several hundred copies of the photograph Roger sent you and distribute them to the police, Immigration and security staffs at airports, cross-channel ferries and Eurostar.' Ashton pursed his lips, then said, 'I would have thought MI5 had already put that in motion.'

'Of course we have,' Neagle said, and avoided eye contact with him.

Mullinder entered the call box near the Gresham Hotel on Dublin's Upper O'Connell Street and carefully arranged a pile of loose change on top of the meter. He had seen the biblical quotation from Genesis 1 in Saturday's *Daily Telegraph* and hadn't liked the caveat about checking with Head Office before he multiplied and replenished the earth. Something had obviously gone wrong and he'd spent the whole weekend trying to anticipate just how much bad news he could expect to hear from Charlie Copeland when he rang him at the office on Monday morning.

Office: Mullinder pulled a face, Jesus what a joke! All Copeland had was a poky little shop in Station Road, Wood Green where he sold burglar alarms, smoke detectors and other electrical goods. For someone who called himself a security consultant he had chosen a real backwater in which to ply his trade. It made Mullinder wonder how MI5 or whatever government department it was which had need of his services from time to time had ever found him. No doubt the people who hired Charlie Copeland knew where the former DI lived but he sure as hell didn't.

Nine fifteen: Mullinder assumed Copeland would be in his office by now, especially as he would expect to hear from him after placing the biblical quotation in the personal column of the *Daily Telegraph*. Lifting the receiver, he got through to the Wood Green number, waited for Copeland to answer and then fed the meter with enough coins to keep the line open for at least three minutes.

'It's me,' Mullinder said, 'checking with Head Office like I was told to.'

'Where are you calling from?'

'A pay phone.'

'That isn't what I meant and you know it,' Copeland said.

'You tell me first what's going on.'

'You ought to try reading more than just the sports page. Tracy Beckingham has snuffed it.'

'Who?'

'The young woman who used to clean house for Laura Greenwood. She was an asthmatic, had a panic attack and couldn't breathe.'

'When did this happen?' Mullinder felt compelled to ask even though a child could have put two and two together and come up with the right answer.

'Last Tuesday,' Copeland told him, 'and you left your calling card behind, which was very thoughtful of you.'

'My fingerprints were on that chart,' Mullinder said in a hollow voice.

'Tell me something new.'

'What about your friend George, who provided the white van? It was his chart I borrowed.'

'He's not in the same boat as you; he doesn't have a record.'

'What happened to the girl was an accident.'

'We both know that but take it from me, you'll be done for manslaughter if the police ever catch up with you.'

'When I burgled the house in Putney, I was working for the government. Right?'

'Yes, but they aren't going to admit it if plod feels your collar. So like it or not you can't come home until the situation has been ironed out.'

'And how long will that take?'

'Your guess is as good as mine,' Copeland told him airily.

'You bastard.' It was all very well for Charlie to shrug it off but it wasn't costing him an arm and a leg to keep out of sight. 'You mind telling me what the fuck I'm supposed to do for money?'

'That's been taken care of; all we've got to settle is when and where I hand the cash over.'

'How much are we talking about?'

'Three thousand now, more later if it proves necessary.'

'Pounds?'

'The equivalent in US dollars, traveller's cheques. And before you start asking for the impossible, so far as I'm concerned, the earliest delivery date is Thursday evening.'

The phone started beeping and the meter showed the call would be terminated in less than ten seconds. Mullinder reached for the pile of coins, only to knock most of them on to the floor in his haste. Giving voice to a stream of four-letter words, he shoved a coin into the slot to keep the line open and told Copeland to hang on. Like a chicken pecking for feed in the dirt, he bent down and picked up the coins one by one.

'OK, you can carry on now,' he said breathlessly.

'You're not in Spain, are you?'

'Where else would I be?'

'How about the Republic of Ireland, you grotty little scumbag?'

Mullinder caught his breath, hoped in hell that yesterday's DI hadn't heard him gasp out loud. How did Copeland know? Was it a blind guess?

'You think I can't trace an incoming call quicker than you can blink?' Copeland snarled. 'I didn't finish my service in Special Branch for nothing.'

'Well, there you go, Mr Copeland, you're too clever for me.'

'Give me an address, I'll get a passport to you.'

'I've got my own on me.'

He didn't need Copeland to tell him he was being stupid; Mullinder knew that moments after the words were out of his mouth. Soon as the police knew he had burgled the house at 104 St John's Avenue they would have turned his place over and called on everyone who knew him. Thereafter they would look further afield, which meant that most of his mates in Dublin were on their list of friends. It didn't matter that nobody had asked to see his passport when he'd travelled to Dublin. By now, the Met would have circulated his name and description to Interpol. Whether they had simply requested information concerning his present whereabouts or had issued an arrest warrant was immaterial. The fact was, every police force in Europe would be asked to be on the lookout for Mullinder, Edward also known as Ted Mullinder, born Pentonville, 23 February 1962, et cetera, et cetera. What he needed was a new identity and only Copeland could furnish that.

'I'm staying at the Mannix Hotel,' he said, '285 Harbour Quay Road, Dublin 1.'

'What's the Mannix – a five-star hotel?'

'I should be so lucky.' The hotel was a flea-bitten dosshouse owned by Terry Mannix, a so-called friend who was charging Mullinder seventy-five pounds a night, room only. It was the sort of establishment where the sheets were only changed once a week regardless of how many people had slept between them. 'I'm registered under the name of Williamson,' he added.

'Next time we talk your name will be Arthur Henderson. Phone me as soon as you have received the passport. OK?'

'Yes.' Mullinder toyed with the idea of asking Copeland for part of the three grand up front, but the ex-DI had already hung up on him before he got round to it.

The Grade II Intelligence Officer who practically ran the South American continent single-handed reported to Ashton twenty minutes after the conference had broken up. Will Landon was six three and built like a heavyweight, minus the scar tissue around the eyes normally associated with a prizefighter. He had light brown hair with an auburn tinge in it and plain features which Harriet, had she met him, would have described as homely. He was twenty-nine years old.

'Until now we haven't had much to do with one another,' Ashton said, waving him to a chair. 'So it would be helpful if you told me a little about yourself, where you were born, family, friends, interests – things like that.'

'There's not much to tell,' Landon smiled, 'but OK, I was born in Weston-Super-Mare and have two sisters, one older than me, the other younger by nine years. She's reading Chemistry up at Oxford; Susan, the elder one, is married to an accountant, lives in Chester and has three children, all boys, aged between four and seven.'

'What about you?'

'I'm still fancy-free,' Landon told him.

Four years ago he had been engaged to a newly qualified barrister but she had suddenly got cold feet and broken it off six months before the wedding date. The hurt he'd felt at the time had been assuaged by a posting to the British Embassy in Lima, which had followed shortly afterwards. Since returning to the UK he'd had a number of girlfriends, none of them serious. Currently he was dating a nurse at the Great Ormond Street Hospital for Children.

'I enjoyed my tour in Peru, made all the sweat of learning Spanish and Italian worthwhile.' Landon smiled again. 'I did Modern Languages at Nottingham University.'

'So did I,' Ashton said. 'That's something we have in common besides working for the Firm.'

But not much else. Landon loved flying, had taken lessons at his own expense and was a qualified pilot. He also held a brown belt in judo, another pursuit he had taken up in his spare time.

'How much has Roger told you about CATO?' Ashton asked.

'Not a lot,' Landon said cheerfully. 'I know the Combined Anti-Terrorist Organisation is the brainchild of the Deputy Director, and the Security Service has stumped up a Grade III Intelligence Officer on a part-time basis, who happens to be still on probation.'

'Yeah, CATO is a bit of a ramshackle organisation.'

'I didn't mean to imply that,' Landon said, colouring.

'I know you didn't, and it will eventually amount to something if Jill Sheridan has her way. However, right now we're interested in Colonel Osvaldo Herrara, Fidel Castro's Deputy Chief of Intelligence before he went freelance. I'd like you to go back to your department and see what you can find on him. Don't limit your search to the Cuban and Caribbean desks, look at all the other South American countries that have anything to do with the Castro regime, no matter how remote. I'm thinking of that darling of the Left, Ernesto "Che" Guevara who was captured in Bolivia and subsequently executed.'

'Right. How far back do you want me to go?'

'Herrara is forty-two and a graduate of Havana University so let's start in 1975 when he left college.'

'Jesus.'

'I never said this job wouldn't entail a lot of hard grafting, much of it possibly unproductive. After you have trawled your department, go and tip your hat to Rowan Garfield and tell him you'd like to see everything the Russian Desk had on exchange postings, liaison, and mutual support between the KGB and Cuban Intelligence from the Brezhnev era to Perestroika.'

'Will he let me do that?' Landon asked. 'I've heard he doesn't like people poking their noses into his bailiwick.'

'Don't worry, I'll prepare the ground for you.'

'I'd be grateful if you would.' Landon cleared his throat. 'How long have I got for this task?'

'If you did it in five working days, I'd be amazed. But call me whenever you come across some pertinent fact. Anything else?'

'Well, there's Nancy Wilkins; she's been waiting outside in case you want to brief her.'

Ashton raised his eyebrows. 'What all this time?'

'As far as I know.'

'You'd better send her in then.'

Earlier, as they'd left the conference room and walked towards the lifts, Kelso had given his assessment of Nancy Wilkins, whom he had described as bright, keen, conscientious and cheerful, along with half a dozen similar platitudes. Ashton had also gathered that she had graduated in Media Studies and was twenty-three years old. The girl who walked into his office didn't look a day over fourteen and a young fourteen at that. She was dressed the part too, in trainers, jeans and denim jacket over a dark blue cotton shirt. Ashton was prepared to bet the admin staff of Vauxhall Cross had never seen anyone quite like her.

'Are you sure you're in the right job?' Ashton smiled. 'I'm told you got a First in Media Studies and you've chosen to work for the most secretive corporate body in the country.'

'I wasn't overwhelmed with job offers from the media,' Nancy told him. 'I did do a year on the front desk of a local radio station, answering the phone, making cups of coffee for visiting dignitaries – that sort of thing. In my spare time I learned to take shorthand, touch-type and I'm not terrified by computers. But so far as the station manager was concerned, I was always going to be the airhead on reception.'

There was a lot more Ashton wanted to ask her but the phone rang and Jill Sheridan made it very clear that his presence in her office was required right now. Whenever there was a bout of in fighting between government departments, no one was more adept at bobbing and weaving than Jill. The moment she asked him if he would care to look up the word 'discreet' in the

Concise Oxford Dictionary Ashton knew why she had sent for him.

'This is about Martin Edmunds, isn't it?' he said.

'Of course it is. And I'm sure you won't be surprised to hear that he has submitted an official complaint in writing to his superior. Sometimes I don't understand you, Peter. I get official permission for you to read his security file and then you go and use the information it contains for you own personal advantage.'

'I saw Edmunds late on Friday afternoon and here it is Monday morning and the roof has fallen in—'

'On me,' Jill said angrily. 'There is every chance the Deputy Under Secretary of State will demand an explanation in writing.'

'Who told you that? Robin Urquhart?'

'What business is it of yours if he did?'

'Just ask yourself how Robin became involved this early. A complaint may have been submitted in writing but I guarantee nobody saw it before this morning. On the other hand, news travels fast when you use a telephone.'

Ashton didn't bother to elaborate. The way Jill suddenly snapped her fingers told him she had made the connection.

'You're saying Edmunds rang the Head of the Queen's Messenger Service late on Friday.'

'Because he was rattled.'

'Or maybe he was simply angry.'

Ashton shook his head. 'You haven't seen The Old Vicarage outside Woodstock. I also know he spent a fortune on the place while he was still in the Hong Kong Police. He's got a Merc inside his double garage that must have cost more than twice his yearly net income as well as making a sizeable dent in his pension. Edmunds is living beyond his means and ought to be looked at. That's the point we should make to Urquhart.'

'There's no "we" about it,' Jill snapped. 'I will tell him in my own good time. Meanwhile you are to keep well away from Edmunds. Concentrate on Laura Greenwood instead, ask her what she knows about him.'

'Right.'

'And don't get caught.'

Ashton returned to his office on the fourth floor, phoned the Passport Office in Petty France and asked to speak to Ms Laura Greenwood. After some delay, he was put through to her immediate superior who informed him that she had taken a week's leave and was holidaying in Switzerland. Ashton gathered Laura's boss was a bit miffed about it because she had given him less than forty-eight hours' notice.

Chapter Fifteen

The office reflected Robin Urquhart's status as the senior of four Deputy Under Secretaries at the Foreign and Commonwealth Office. It was located in the southwest corner of the building at the junction of King Charles Street with Horse Guards Road. From a commanding position on the top floor he enjoyed superb views of St James's Park, the Serpentine and Buckingham Palace. To call the room an office was something of a misnomer considering it was furnished on the scale of a grand salon. From its inception, the room had conveyed the pomp and circumstance of a world power and if this was now out of date, visitors were still impressed by the sheer grandeur of the place and some were even intimidated by the ambience.

The ambience had no effect whatever on Jill Sheridan, and it wasn't just good manners on Urquhart's part that made him leave his desk and go forward to meet her when she entered the room. He had begun to take an interest in Jill a little over five years ago when she had been serving in Bahrain. She had been charged with running the Intelligence setup in the United Arab Emirates and had come to his notice when she had asked to be relieved in her appointment. It had, of course, been an admission of failure but in truth she'd never had a chance of making a success of the appointment. On paper Jill had been a natural for the job but she was a woman and in the Arab world her sex was an insuperable handicap. The only way she had been able to function at all was by posing as the secretary to her own Grade III Assistant Intelligence Officer. After twenty-one months of this charade, Jill had had enough.

Urquhart liked to think he had been instrumental in saving her career when she had been assigned to the Persian desk at Century House. He had pointed out to the Permanent Under Secretary of State that if anyone was to blame it was the then Director General of the Secret Intelligence Service and the selection committee for closing their eyes to the difficulties any woman was bound to face in the Persian Gulf. What had pleased him most was the fact that Jill Sheridan had simply been a name on the FO staff list when he'd fought her corner.

They had met for the first time three years ago when she had been promoted to head the Mid East Department. From that moment on, however, he had been completely besotted with Jill. Six months ago they had become lovers. Of a sort, he mentally added on reflection. In fact sharing an intimate evening with Jill only happened now and again, like receiving an invitation to a garden party at Buckingham Palace. This afternoon she had come to see him because she was in trouble once more.

'You're looking a little peaky, my dear,' he said woodenly and pecked her on the cheek.

He had wanted to embrace Jill warmly but he had always been the soul of discretion and, besides, there was no guarantee of privacy despite the presence of his PA in the outer office. He ushered Jill to a Regency chair lavishly covered in silk, then moved round a low rosewood coffee table and sat down facing her.

'Can I get you a cup of coffee?' he asked. 'Or perhaps something stronger? Whisky? Brandy?'

'Later perhaps.'

'Business first, is that it?' he said, smiling.

'I always run to you when I'm in trouble. You must be sick of it, Robin.'

'I'm a friend, am I not? Anyway, we are both in trouble this time. After all I was the one who persuaded Shirley Isles to make Edmund's security file available against her better judgement.'

'I don't believe that was such a terrible mistake.' Jill raised a hand as if to silence him in case he was thinking of interrupting her. 'I'm not here to defend Peter Ashton, but I know him very well, better perhaps than even Harriet, and the claim that he used confidential information for his own ends is preposterous. Ashton is admittedly something of a loose cannon but in the end he usually gets it right.'

'Does he really? The fact is that after reading the security file, he told Shirley Isles that Edmunds came across as whiter than white.'

'Because the man looked good on paper. And let's face it, Robin, we are both aware of instances where the vetting officer wasn't inquisitive enough.'

'Are you saying Ashton was merely being inquisitive?'

'Yes.'

'I admire you for defending him and I can't think of anybody else in your position who would be quite so loyal to one of their subordinates.'

'Don't misunderstand me, this isn't a question of blind loyalty on my part. I sent Ashton to interview Zawadzki's second wife and she told him what her former husband had said about Martin Edmunds. On the strength of what he had heard, Ashton drove out to Woodstock to have a look at The Old Vicarage.'

'Did he tell you what he was going to do?'

'No. Naturally Ashton told me what he had learned from the second Mrs Zawadzki.'

'And you didn't give him tacit approval to investigate Edmunds' finances?'

'Certainly not. I told him to concentrate on Laura Green-wood. I wasn't even aware he'd been to Woodstock until you rang me this morning.'

Urquhart knew instinctively that Jill was not being entirely truthful. She might not have given Ashton the green light but a nod was as good as a wink. However, there was not the slightest doubt in his mind that, had Ashton told her what he proposed to do, Jill would have put a stop to it.

'The point is, Robin, although Ashton went at it like a bull in a china shop, he has raised a number of questions about Edmunds' financial status which need to be addressed.'

That Edmunds should have paid £225,000 for The Old Vicarage back in 1986 was enough to make Urquhart sit up and take notice. The cost of the various improvements to the property and grounds which had subsequently been carried out while he was still a serving police officer was astronomical.

'And you say Ashton obtained all these figures from the estate agents who had acted on behalf of Edmunds?'

'Yes, from Scoones and Chambers in Woodstock.'

Urquhart knew that even his wife, Rosalind, who had a substantial private income of her own, would have blanched at the prohibitive costs of refurbishing The Old Vicarage.

'I will, of course, apologise to Shirley Isles in person,' Jill said.

'Any apology ought to come from the real culprit,' Urquhart told her.

Jill shook her head. 'I'm the Deputy Director, Robin, and since Ashton reports directly to me, I'm ultimately responsible. Having said that, I do think Foreign Office Security should take a good hard look at Martin Edmunds.'

'Quite.'

'I'm not trying to pass the buck, Robin, but I think she will take it better coming from you. And of course it would be more appropriate.'

More appropriate? Urquhart wasn't sure how much to read into that observation. Perhaps Jill was merely pointing out that she had no jurisdiction over the Foreign Office Security Department and any recommendation coming from her might not carry much weight with Shirley Isles. Alternatively, maybe she was reminding him of his own involvement in making the Edmunds file available. Could it be Jill meant him to see it as a chance to square things with the Deputy Permanent Under Secretary of State and get himself off the hook?

'You were right to come to me with this problem and I'm glad you did.' Urquhart cleared his throat. 'Shirley Isles will also be grateful when she learns what a risk we've been running with Edmunds.'

'Thank you, Robin.' Jill stood up and kissed him lightly on the cheek. 'You've always been a good friend to me.'

'Friends should get together more often,' he said, and despised himself for being so crass.

'They certainly should.' Jill gazed at him thoughtfully. 'Are you free on Wednesday evening?' she asked.

It was an oblique reference to Rosalind, housebound in a wheelchair. Why he should have a guilty conscience about her was beyond his understanding and most other people's who knew them both. After sixteen years of married life, Rosalind had suddenly left him and moved in with a junior, but well-heeled, partner in the biggest firm of commercial lawyers in the City.

From childhood Rosalind had ridden to hounds with the Belvoir Hunt in Leicestershire. Thanks to the influence of her lover she had subsequently joined the Witherspoon Hunt. One frosty morning in November 1989 she had put her horse at a six-feet-high hedgerow by a ditch and the animal had balked. Rosalind had been thrown and, landing awkwardly, had broken two vertebrae in her back, leaving her paralysed from the waist down. The lover had disappeared while she was still in Stoke Mandeville Hospital and Urquhart had taken her back.

'Of course I'm free, and I'm going to be even freer in the not-so-distant future.' Urquhart swallowed. 'I'm going to divorce Rosalind,' he added.

'You've made the right decision, Robin. In fact it is something you should have done years ago.' Jill kissed him again, this time on the mouth. 'Wednesday evening then – my place. Come as soon as you can.'

Urquhart walked ahead of Jill and opened the door to the

outer officer for her. Come as soon as you can: such a simple invitation but it held out so much more than the promise of an intimate supper for two.

Francesca York was the last person Ashton expected to see that afternoon. Neagle had made it pretty clear that she had many other responsibilities besides CATO and would therefore operate from Gower Street. Furthermore, considering how Ashton had cut her down to size at the preliminary inquiry into the Warlock Estate bombing, he couldn't envisage any circumstances which would persuade her to meet him voluntarily. But at seven minutes to four, the formidable Enid Sly on reception rang him to say he had a visitor and would he like to come down to the lobby or should she escort Miss York up to his office? Ashton told her to make out a visitor's pass and accompany her up to the fourth floor.

If Francesca York bore him any malice she kept it well hidden. In fact her warm, friendly manner almost made Ashton forget she had inferred that Detective Constable Kenny Browne would probably be alive today if O'Meara hadn't been so impatient.

'Do you see yourself making regular visits to Vauxhall Cross?' Ashton perched himself on the edge of the table, his back shielding the Visual Display Unit from view, then nodded at the one armchair in the office, which was his way of inviting her to sit down. 'I only ask because if this should be the case, we ought to fix you up with a special ID pass.'

'It would be a help.'

'OK. Send us a passport photo of yourself and next time you come over you can pick up the ID from reception.' He smiled. 'Now, can I get you a cup of tea or coffee? There's a vending machine by the lifts.'

'No thanks.'

'You've just made a wise decision,' Ashton said. 'You can't tell them apart.'

'Let's hope that isn't the only thing I get right.'

Eating humble pie didn't suit Francesca York; fortunately it didn't last. She was in fact rather proud of herself because, largely as a result of her initiative, the police now had an accurate likeness of Mehmet Ozbek.

'He helped Osvaldo Herrara load the RPG-7 rocket launch-er and ammunition into the dark blue van. I saw him full frontal after he had closed the garage door and was walking forward to join Herrara in the van.'

As she had done with the Cuban, Francesca York had been able to give the police a detailed description of his companion. In the wake of the terrorist incidents on Friday evening, Special Branch, at her instigation, had urged the Surrey Constabulary to interview the doctor and nursing staff at the Farnham Road Hospital who had treated the only survivor from the traffic accident at the Devil's Punch Bowl.

'The man who had called himself Mehmet Ozbek was identified by a paramedic and the doctor. In other words, they placed him on the Warlock Estate with Colonel Herrara.'

'I'm impressed,' Ashton said. To have observed that it didn't take them very far would have been churlish, even though it happened to be true. 'I don't recall Richard identifying the rocket launcher as an RPG-7 when he briefed us this morning.'

'That's because it was only found towards noon.'

The launcher had been discovered by refuse collectors clearing the litter bins on the parking area two miles north of Wych Cross. It had been buried under two sets of combat uniforms and other military accoutrements.

'From the cap badges, it looks as if they were aiming to pass themselves off as Polish soldiers. Either the ruse didn't work or else one of them panicked.'

'Offhand I can't think of another explanation,' Ashton told her.

'Well, it's possible the root cause of their panic was the realisation they had attacked the wrong target.'

'Oh yes? If it wasn't Keith French, who were they after?'

'We're pretty sure it was Hasan Ünver, the Economic and Commercial Counsellor at the Turkish Embassy. Mrs French was having an affair with him.'

'Where did you hear that?'

'From British Petroleum's head of personnel. BP weren't happy about the situation and feared it could prejudice the negotiations for offshore drilling rights in the Sea of Marmara if the Turkish Government learned of the affair. Head Office cabled French and as near as dammit ordered him to do something about it. Being a good company man, he booked himself on the first available flight to England. We've since learned that shortly after the terrorist attack, a BMW with CD plates was spotted by a patrol car on the B2026 roughly a mile from Chuck Hatch. Unfortunately the officer didn't get the registration number.'

If the BMW driver was Hasan Ünver, as Francesca was suggesting, Ashton reckoned the Turkish diplomat must have seen French turn into the driveway of his house and decided discretion was the better part of valour. Mehmet Ozbek and his companion might have ambushed the wrong man but they had been in the right place at the right time and there was only one conclusion to be drawn from that.

'The terrorists had inside information,' Ashton said. 'Somebody in the embassy tipped them off that Ünver would be visiting his English lover on Friday evening. I wouldn't mind betting his PA is the source.'

'Yes. Well, that's something we'll have to find out if the Turkish Ambassador allows us to question him.'

Ashton doubted if permission would be forthcoming. It was a question of sovereignty and the Ambassador was unlikely to surrender that in a hurry. On the whole, he thought there would be a lot to be gained from letting Turkish security put their own house in order. When it came to interrogating a suspected terrorist they were unlikely to suffer the constraints imposed on their counterparts in Special Branch.

'Who is Flynn?' Ashton demanded, abruptly changing the subject.

Caught off guard, York held her breath in a brave attempt to disguise her surprise. 'Flynn,' she repeated vaguely, her eyebrows knitted together in what passed for a frown. 'No, I'm afraid the name doesn't ring a bell with me.'

'Flynn is the cover name of the source who put you on to the IRA arms cache on the Warlock Estate.'

'That's news to me.'

'In your shoes, I'd want to distance myself from such a cockup too. I mean, let's face it, if the case officer had deliberately set out to disclose the nationality of his source and leave the poor sod naked, he couldn't have done a better job.'

'I'm sorry but I can't help you.'

'Or won't,' Ashton said grimly. 'I think we should take this problem upstairs and let my Director sort it out with yours. The success of CATO depends on the free exchange of information; if we behave like magpies and store it away, the organisation will fail.'

York nibbled at her bottom lip. 'Nobody wants that to happen,' she said, 'least of all me. I could be in serious trouble if word of this gets back to Richard Neagle but the source is Ryan, Michael Ryan. He works for London Electricity, reads the meters in Kilburn and the adjoining Maida Vale area. The job takes him into a lot of Irish households.'

'Is Ryan Irish?'

'No, English. I told Sergeant O'Meara his name was Flynn to satisfy her curiosity.'

'You were his case officer, weren't you?' Ashton said with sudden insight.

'Yes.'

'So what were you doing as a member of the surveillance team?'

'I pleaded my case with Richard Neagle. A number of people didn't believe in Ryan, called him a windbag who'd never produced anything worthwhile and I wanted to prove them wrong.'

'I think you had better give me the whole story – how you

came to meet Ryan, the sort of feedback you were getting from him and so on.'

It turned out she had met Ryan towards the end of her short-service commission when she had been second in command of the army's Special Counter Intelligence Team at the Ministry of Defence. The actual encounter had taken place in a pub off the Kilburn High Road when he had tried to chat her up. A former corporal in the Royal Signals, Ryan claimed to have done some undercover work for Military Intelligence when stationed in Northern Ireland.

'At the time I thought he was just trying to impress me and that his war stories were plain bullshit. Then I did some checking and found there was more than a grain of truth in what Ryan had told me.'

She had returned to the pub the following evening in the hope of meeting him again and in the fullness of time had become one of the regulars. A would be James Bond, Ryan had given her the names of several IRA sympathisers whose houses he had visited and had subsequently volunteered his services on a regular basis.

'My successor didn't want anything to do with Michael, so I took him with me when I joined Five.'

Michael: that sounded a little too friendly for Ashton's liking and it was conceivable that her critical judgement had been impaired as a result. According to Francesca York, Ryan had continued to provide her with the names of the Irish nationalists, though actual IRA sympathisers were few and far between.

'OK, so most of them hadn't got blood on their hands but you knew where their sympathies lay. Every time the Law Lords decided a conviction was unsafe there they were amongst the rent-a-mob yelling blue murder about the iniquity of British justice. Didn't stop them claiming income support and every other benefit they reckoned they were entitled to. And not too many of them are in a hurry to return to the Emerald Isle either. You don't wonder Special Branch are happy to keep an eye on them.'

Get York on her favourite hobbyhorse and it was evident her political views were somewhat to the right of Genghis Khan. Had that undesirable character trait surfaced when she had appeared before the selection board, MI5 wouldn't have touched her with a bargepole. But right now Ashton had more important things on his mind.

'Let's see if I have got this straight,' he said impatiently. 'The only hard intelligence Ryan ever gave you was the location of the arms cache on the Warlock Estate. Correct?'

'Yes.'

'But the Head of the Anti-Terrorist Branch didn't rate him and wasn't prepared to act on his information. So you buttonholed Richard Neagle and talked him into supporting your case for keeping the lock-up garage under surveillance?'

'Richard didn't need much persuading when I told him how Ryan had got his information.'

His source turned out to be a property owner who was suspected of running a number of safe houses for transitory visitors from Belfast who didn't want to check into a hotel or a bed-and-breakfast establishment. The property owner ran his business from a semidetached on Shoot Up Hill in Kilburn, and over a period of eighteen months the two men had gradually become drinking companions. With the benefit of hindsight it was obvious just who had cultivated whom. The facts were the Irishman had consulted Ryan about some tenant he reckoned was bypassing the electricity meter, and had also expressed other doubts about him, which had included his possible association with one of the paramilitary groups in Northern Ireland. The two men had actually visited the property together where, in the course of inspecting the wiring, Ryan had stumbled on a rent book for a lock-up garage on the Warlock Estate. The name on the rent book had been altered somewhat clumsily from Hayes to Brian Ahearne.

'According to Harringay Council, Hayes was still the tenant of the suspect garage.'

Ashton was tempted to ask York if that was all it had taken to

201

convince her Ryan was on to something but in the end she made it easy for him.

'There were other indicators,' York told him.

He listened with half an ear as she proceeded to list them. The date and time of arrival of a car ferry at Holyhead written on the back of a postcard addressed to Brian Ahearne from someone in Belfast called Mairin. Then there was the advert for a used-car auction at Duxford in Cambridgeshire which, as York reminded him, was the sort of anonymous place the IRA was known to favour when they needed to acquire a set of wheels. Whatever Francesca York might think, it seemed to Ashton that Ryan had been spoon-fed the information.

'Where is this Brian Ahearne now?' he asked, interrupting her.

'Special Branch is looking for him; he's not at his usual address.'

'And the property owner?'

'He's still around. After the bombing on the Warlock Estate he was detained for three days under the Prevention of Terrorism Act but we didn't have anything on him which would stand up in court.'

'So he's back on the streets?'

'Yes – under surveillance.'

'And Ryan?'

'He has not been seen since Tuesday, March the twelfth,' York said, and avoided looking at him. 'I think the whole thing was a setup,' she added in a small voice.

'Are you suggesting that Ryan took the money and ran?'

York shook her head. 'Money was never the motivating factor with him.'

Ashton suspected Ryan was one of those romantics who enjoy the reflected glory from their involvement with MI5, no matter how tenuous that might be. In the company of friends and acquaintances, such a man would imply there wasn't much going on in the Intelligence world that he didn't know about. He was in short a bad security risk, the type who could be turned around and used by the opposition without his being aware of it.

He said nothing of this to Francesca York. After escorting her down to the lobby and saying goodbye, he sent for Nancy Wilkins.

'I've got a job for you, and it could be right up your street. I want a list of all the major building sites within the Greater London area – buildings, road improvements, bridges. OK?'

'Yes. Am I allowed to know why you need this information?' she asked.

'I'm looking for a body,' Ashton told her, 'but keep it to yourself.'

Chapter Sixteen

It was called 'The Little Theatre' because it could only seat an audience of a hundred and eighty, sixty of whom were in the dress circle, which sounded a lot better than the gallery or even the circle. The Little Theatre was the end building in Cavendish Close, next to Lord's Cricket Ground, and had been rescued from dereliction by the St John's Wood Amateur Dramatic Society in 1945, with materials which perforce had to be acquired on the black market, because under existing wartime government regulations, The Little Theatre was considered a non essential structure.

It had been completely refurbished during the Coronation year and had had two further facelifts since then, thanks to the fund-raising activities of various treasurers down the years. The current treasurer and one of the leading lights of the amateur dramatic society was Alistair Downward.

When Copeland had met him ten days ago the amateur dramatic society had just rung down the curtain on their final production of the season. According to the posters displayed outside, the theatre would reopen in October and among the forthcoming attractions was Terence Feely's *Who Killed Santa Claus?*, scheduled for late November in the run-up to Christmas. Copeland walked on down the side of the building and entered the theatre by the stage door. A crack of light drew him to the far dressing room where Downward was waiting.

'You're ten minutes late,' Downward said curtly.

'Blame it on the Jubilee Line; trains are few and far between once the evening rush hour is over.' Copeland pointed to a small brown paper bag on the dressing table. 'Is that the money?' he asked.

'Yes. Three thousand in used twenty-pound notes.'

Copeland picked up the bag and emptied the contents on to the table. There were six bundles in all, each one secured with an elastic band. Taking a wad at a time, he rippled through the banknotes to make sure there were no blank sheets cut to size.

'You're pathetic,' Downward told him. 'What do you take me for? A petty crook?'

'Absolutely not,' Copeland said cheerfully. 'Governments and their civil servants are in a different league. When they pull a fast one, the scale of their underhand dealing is breathtaking. That was one of the first lessons I learned on joining the Special Branch.'

'Really? Well, don't pocket the money just yet, I'd like to know where Mullinder is first.'

'He's in Dublin. He phoned me this morning after seeing the biblical quotation in Saturday's *Daily Telegraph*.'

'Are you going to see him?'

'Not in Dublin. I told Mullinder Thursday was the earliest he could expect to see the money and that won't happen unless he sends a Polyfoto of himself in double quick time.'

'You must get your incompetent burglar out of the Republic before the Garda starts looking for him.'

'I intend to,' Copeland said tersely.

'The road to hell is paved with good intentions. Suppose your man is arrested and is extradited by the Home Office? Can you rely on him to keep his mouth shut?'

In Copeland's opinion only someone like Downward, who was out of touch with the real world, could have postulated such a vain hope. Mullinder was loyal to himself and nobody else; once in police custody he would try to make the best deal for himself. He had to make Downward see there was no way Ted Mullinder would do time.

'You're supposed to be a legal counsellor,' Copeland said in a rasping voice, 'so you should know the score already. Mullinder burgled the house, stole three-and-a-half-thousand-pounds worth of jewellery and killed a young woman who happened to be the mother of a two-year-old child. He's got a previous conviction and the fact that our friend didn't mean to harm her will count for nothing. Take it from me, he is looking at ten years. You don't seriously think he is going to do that for a lousy grand, do you?'

'You must feel rather exposed, Charles.' Downward smiled. 'Naturally, I appreciate that I am also vulnerable, though perhaps not quite to the same extent. The question is, how do we deal with this problem?'

Copeland was tempted to point out that Downward was the lawyer and if he couldn't pull a few strings with his connections, who the hell could? He didn't because no Foreign Office mandarin was going to admit that Mullinder had been hired by a government department to break into 104 St John's Avenue.

'Well, Charles, any suggestions?'

'Mullinder is in a hole right now. Let's give him a spade so that he can make it even deeper.'

'I'm sure that's a very apposite allusion but I think you had better explain what you have in mind.'

'Mullinder was instructed to make it look like a run-of-the-mill burglary, so he stole what jewellery there was in the house. That's what he will tell the police; he will also try to convince them his real purpose for burglarising Ms Greenwood was to recover a document from the Investment Trust Bank in Estavayer-le-Lac. But since he never found it—'

'That's a large assumption,' Downward said, interrupting him.

'You're wrong, it's a logical deduction. If Mullinder had found the document he would have let me know soon enough.

207

In his possession it would give him all the leverage he needed. The fact is, he can only describe the logo on the envelope because that's what I told him to look out for. Mullinder will, of course, point an accusing finger at me but it won't get him anywhere. DI Hughes believes I've had it in for Mullinder ever since 1986 when his brief got a charge of breaking and entering quashed on a technicality. He'll think Mullinder is trying to get his own back for all the aggro I've given him in the past.'

'Has anybody seen you together?'

'No,' Copeland said vehemently. 'I'm just as careful about whom I'm seen with as you are.' There was the landlord of the Irish pub off the Kilburn High Road but he would be a fool to disclose that to Alistair Downward. If he did admit to it, that would be the last he saw of the legal counsellor.

'Did you use Mullinder to break into the head office of Universal Services eleven months ago?'

'You know I did and the answer's still the same. I'm always careful, especially when I'm acting as the middle man for you people. I'm very conscious that if something went badly wrong, nobody at the Foreign and Commonwealth Office would lift a finger to help me.'

'I think you are in danger of overdoing it, Charles.'

It was Downward's silky smooth way of making it clear that he didn't believe him. In the circumstances all Copeland could do was call his bluff.

'You're right,' he said, 'I'm a liar. Lots of people have seen me with Ted Mullinder.'

'I didn't imply that—'

'But the longer Mullinder is at large, the better it is for us, the worse it is for him,' Copeland said, talking him down. 'Think about it and you'll know I'm not whistling in the dark.'

He didn't have to elaborate; the smug expression on Downward's face told him the legal counsellor had worked it out for himself. Unless Mullinder surrendered himself voluntarily, his story would lose credibility with every day he was at liberty. If he was arrested, the veracity of his allegations would immediately be open to doubt. That would be especially true if he was apprehended as a result of an international arrest warrant circulated by Interpol.

'There's one other little wrinkle we can try,' Copeland said casually. 'After he has taken delivery of this bundle, we move Ted on to Spain and then gradually cut him off from the money tree.'

'Won't that be counter productive?'

'Not if I am any judge of character.' Copeland paused in the act of stuffing the six packets of banknotes into the pockets of his jacket and raincoat. 'I can virtually guarantee that Mullinder will gravitate towards his own kind on the Costa del Sol. Then with any luck he will end up running drugs into the rest of Europe. When he is subsequently caught red-handed following an anonymous tip-off, his chances of closing a deal with the Met and the Crown Prosecution Service will be zero.'

'You're a clever fellow, Charles.'

Copeland stuffed the remaining packet into his raincoat and started towards the stage door. 'But not as clever as you, Mr Downward.'

'When you were in Special Branch,' Downward said, stopping him in his tracks as he was about to step out into Cavendish Close. 'Did you know an Intelligence Officer called Ashton?'

'Never heard of him.'

'Long may that last,' Downward said quietly.

Spring was officially two days hence. In the principal bedroom of 84 Rylett Close it was still bleak mid-winter. The unseasonable climate had nothing to do with the prevailing weather conditions outside the house at five thirty on that particular Tuesday morning. It stemmed from a disagreement between Peter and Harriet Ashton the night before, except 'disagreement' was a euphemism to end all euphemisms.

The truth was they'd had a blazing row which had been sparked off by Harriet's sudden announcement that she proposed to drive up to Lincoln in order to interview three would-be housekeepers to her father. Ashton had wanted to know why she felt obliged to do this when her brother, Richard, and his wife lived in the same damned city. Frederick Egan, it transpired, had taken a sudden fancy to his daughter-in-law and Lucy objected to having her bottom pinched every time she came near him. For the life of him, Ashton couldn't see why the applicants had to be interviewed at Egan's place in Ferris Drive when Lucy's house in Church Lane was little more than a stone's throw away. Giving voice to that opinion had been his big mistake.

'What are you suggesting?' Harriet had demanded angrily. 'That Daddy should be kept out of sight because he has Alzheimer's disease?'

And Ashton had told her she was being stupid, that his only interest was to make sure Richard and Lucy took some of the burden on their shoulders, which hadn't gone down too well with Harriet. Things had become even more heated when he'd looked into his crystal ball and predicted that the problem of finding a suitable housekeeper would be a recurring one because, sadly, even the ugliest woman was likely to be molested.

Harriet had packed a bag for herself and Edward yesterday evening before he arrived home from the office, which, as he had observed, was one way of precluding any discussion on the subject. Harriet in turn had accused him of never listening to a word she said. Apparently he was so wrapped up in his job he had no time to spare for his family or hers for that matter. She had told him not once but a dozen times she would make it her business to ensure a suitable replacement was engaged to look after her father. By the time they went to bed, they were no longer speaking.

And of course she was right about his blinkered approach. He was too busy trying to make some sense out of Adam Zawadzki's brutal murder and everything connected with it to pay much attention to Harriet. Osvaldo Herrara, Martin Edmunds, Ted Mullinder, Laura Greenwood, Mehmet Ozbek and

Michael Ryan: those were the people whose names went round and round in his head. The former Deputy Chief of Fidel Castro's Intelligence Bureau, the all-too-affluent Queen's Messenger, the burglar, the lowly civil servant in the Passport Office, the Turkish assassin and the frustrated would-be intelligence agent with the Walter Mitty character – the time he had wasted on them looking for a pattern. And even now he was thinking about them, which was ridiculous when, in a few hours' time, Harriet would strap Edward into his special seat in the back of the Ford Mondeo and then set off for Lincoln. In a rare moment of self-pity, Ashton saw himself leaving notes for their daily, Mrs Davies, asking her to get something in from the local supermarket. Seconds later, Ashton upbraided himself for being such a contemptible wimp.

Lying there awake in the dark, Ashton wished he had made it up with Harriet before she'd switched off the light. 'I'm sorry': two little words, that was all he needed to say. But he couldn't bring himself to do it and Harriet hadn't been prepared to make the first move either. She was still lying in the same position, her back towards him, as she had been when he had muttered good night. He listened to Harriet's shallow breathing and assumed she was sleeping peacefully so that he literally flinched when she suddenly asked him if he was awake?

'I'm sorry,' he said, and turned over on his right side to face Harriet and almost clashed heads with her as she moved towards him. 'I didn't mean any of those things I said to you last night.'

'I know that,' she murmured, and embraced him.

'And despite what you may sometimes feel, I really don't take you for granted because I don't know what I would do if anything happened to you.'

There had been two occasions when Ashton had thought he'd lost her. The first had been that time in Berlin before they were married when a Turkish *Gastarbeiter* had fractured her skull with a rock. Harriet had been rushed to St Thomas's Hospital on Müllenhoffstrasse and he would never forget how close to death she had looked lying there in the surgical ward, her face the colour of white marble, the skin tight as a drum, her cheeks sunken. But the sense of impending loss then had been nothing compared with the feeling of being dead inside just over six months ago when a woman who had been shot through the head had been mistakenly identified as Harriet Ashton.

'You're not going to lose me,' Harriet said firmly as if she had been reading his thoughts.

'You think I'm not going to miss you when you're up in Lincoln?'

'I'll be back tomorrow evening and I won't be going up there again in a hurry.'

'You hope.'

'The previous housekeeper lasted six months and I'm not driving to Lincoln and back with a dirty great bulge between me and the steering wheel.'

'What are you saying?'

'I'm pregnant.'

'Well, that's marvellous — is it definite?'

'We can always make sure,' Harriet said, and began to rouse him with a feather-light touch.

Zurich was the place to go if you wanted to know something about secret bank accounts but Laura Greenwood couldn't speak a word of German. On the other hand she did have a smattering of French, which was the reason why she had chosen to spend a few days in Geneva. The short break had been a sudden decision, one that hadn't gone down at all well with her supervisor at Petty France. But she had dilly-dallied for far too long and, having at last made up her mind, she had wanted to get it over and done with as soon as possible.

It had not been that simple. Laura Greenwood had wanted to catch the last flight to Geneva on the Friday evening, which departed from Heathrow at 20.00 hours, but Swissair were fully booked. If that wasn't bad enough, British Airways were unable to offer her anything until 13.15 hours on Monday. She had thought of flying to Zurich or Basle and completing the journey by train. However, according to the travel agent she was using in Putney High Street, flights to these alternative destinations were also fully subscribed over the Saturday and Sunday. It seemed she had left things rather late; furthermore she couldn't have picked a more inconvenient weekend, it being the last one before skiing ended for the season. Consequently she had gone for British Airways flight BA728 which arrived in Geneva at three forty-five in the afternoon.

The only thing to be said in favour of the enforced delay was that it had given the travel agent time to reserve accommodation for her at the Hotel California on the Rue Gevray. On the other hand, by the time she had checked into the hotel and unpacked, it was too late to do anything other than discover the name of the largest bank in Geneva and the address of an English-speaking lawyer from the helpful concierge.

The head office of Credit Suisse, which happened to be the largest bank in the city was located in the Place Bel-Air, due south of the Rhône from the Hotel California. The six-storey concrete-and-glass structure looked indestructible, which made Laura Greenwood wonder if this was the impression the architects had intended to convey. On the roof of the covered entrance, an illuminated sign announced the name of the bank in letters that were at least ten feet high. The same message was conveyed on a more modest scale in French, German and Italian along the fascia.

Heart beating faster than normal, Laura Greenwood walked into the bank. She had mentally rehearsed what she was going to say over and over again, yet when the time came to voice her carefully prepared request for assistance, neither the bank guard nor the teller she was directed to could understand her French. Eventually she produced a lucid version of the request she had attempted to convey and was asked to wait. Some fifteen minutes later she was introduced to the Assistant Director in charge of Personal Banking, who spoke perfect English. The office seemed to her a little on the small side for a man who held such an important position in the bank.

'My name is Laura Greenwood,' she told him as they shook hands.

'It is a pleasure to meet you, Madame,' he said, and invited her to sit down. 'How may I be of assistance?'

'It concerns my late brother, Martin Edmunds. He was killed in a car crash on Tuesday, the sixth of March.'

It was the same day and date that Adam had been murdered in Costa Rica. She had deliberately chosen it not so much in remembrance of him but because, as he had once told her, the most convincing lies invariably contained a grain of truth.

'I'm sorry to hear that, Madame.'

'Yes, it was very sad.' Laura opened the brown leather handbag on her lap, took out her passport and gave it to the Assistant Director. 'In case you want to verify my identity,' she murmured.

'Thank you.'

'And this is what I found amongst his papers.'

The envelope was the equivalent in size of an A3, bluish grey in colour and had been folded in half and half again. Written on the front and signed with a squiggle was a brief message which read 'Laura, please keep this.'

'I've opened the envelope.'

'So I see, Madame.'

'It contains a slip of paper with two sets of numbers.'

'Yes?'

'Well, they don't make any sense to me; neither does that badge which is embossed on the back of the envelope.' Conscious of the nervous tremor in her voice, Laura took a deep breath, then said, 'I wondered if you could help me to understand them?'

'I don't see why not. The badge you referred to is the emblem of the privately owned Investment Trust Bank in Estavayer-le-Lac. The first set of figures refer to a numbered account which I assume belongs to your late brother. The other acknowledges receipt of eighty-five thousand Swiss francs he must have paid into the account at some unspecified

214

date. I presume you wish to lay claim to the numbered account?'

Laura told him it would be a pity to leave all that money lying around and doing nothing and then gave a brittle laugh to show she meant it as a joke. The Assistant Director of Personal Banking did not, however, share the same sense of humour and the way he treated her changed dramatically.

'The first thing the bank will want to see is your brother's death certificate, then you will have to furnish proof that you are related.'

She would also have to provide documentary evidence to show that she was the legal executor of his estate and produce a copy of his last will and testament.

'Furthermore, if your brother died intestate, the Investment Trust Bank will need to be satisfied that there is no one with a prior claim on the estate.'

'He wasn't married.'

'A partner?'

'I have kept house for him ever since my husband died,' Laura said, and couldn't think why she had compounded one lie with an even bigger one.

'Should you wish to establish your claim to the numbered account, you would be well advised to engage a lawyer to represent your interests in this country.'

There was no mistaking the contempt in his voice. As a result of something she had said, he had seen right through her and knew she wasn't entitled to a single penny in the account. Would he detain her and send for the police? Laura didn't wait to find out; retrieving her passport and the statement, she thanked the Assistant Director for sparing the time to see her and fled the bank.

Ashton stepped out of the lift on the top floor, and, turning left, walked down the corridor towards the Deputy Director's office. This would be the second time he had been closeted with Jill

215

Sheridan that morning and once was more than enough. Shortly before Heads of Departments had assembled in the conference room for the usual daily prayer meeting, he had brought her up to date on the hunt for Osvaldo Herrara. All that that had entailed was a recital of the tasks he had given to Will Landon and Nancy Wilkins and the reasoning behind them. Jill had not been very impressed by the little he had to tell her and had spent a lot of time wondering what other avenues they might explore without coming to a conclusion. Now it seemed they were about to start another session.

Jill Sheridan didn't look up from the file she was reading when he tapped on the door and walked into her office. However, a regal wave, which owed a lot to the Queen Mother, graciously pointed him to a chair.

'The Costa Ricans have arrested one of the men who murdered Adam Zawadzki.' Jill initialled the top enclosure and transferred the file to the out-tray, then gave Ashton her full attention. 'Roger Benton received a copy of the signal Paul Younghusband dispatched to the Foreign and Commonwealth on behalf of the Ambassador.'

'What's his name?'

'Luis Garmendia.'

'I'm none the wiser,' Ashton said.

'Nor is anybody on the Central American Desk. According to the Costa Rican authorities Luis is into drugs – buys the hard stuff from the Colombians and sells it on. Unfortunately the police have never been able to pin anything on him.'

'But they have this time?'

'Provided the girlfriend doesn't retract her statement.'

Two days after the discovery of Zawadzki's body in the packing shed of an abandoned banana plantation, Luis had got very drunk and had boasted how he had shot the Englishman in the foot with a .22 calibre pistol. Although the murder had been extensively reported, this was one detail the police hadn't disclosed.

'The girlfriend only came forward when she saw him with another woman.'

'Is he talking?'

Jill shook her head. 'Luis was only picked up during the early hours of yesterday morning.'

'What do you know about his ex-girlfriend?'

'Very little. The police say she is a bar girl but she doesn't have a record.'

'Hardly makes her a stand-up witness, does it?'

'Let's not be negative,' Jill said briskly. 'Paul Younghusband will be liaising on our behalf and I've prepared a whole raft of questions we'd like the police to ask Luis.' Jill picked up her scratchpad and passed it across the desk. 'Run your eye over this lot; maybe there are some I have overlooked.'

Even before he looked at the list, Ashton suspected he would have nothing to add. Jill hadn't got to where she was today simply by cultivating the right people and fluttering her eyelashes at them. She had a good head on her shoulders and no one was more thorough. There were a dozen questions alone on Luis Garmendia's relationship with Herrara. These ranged from the nature of their business and how long he'd known the Cuban to the precise time he had been stood up to meet Adam Zawadzki at the airport.

'I can't think of a thing you haven't already covered,' Ashton said eventually.

'Pity. I was hoping you would have some input.' Jill picked up a pencil and tapped the blunt end against the desk, a habit she had acquired from Victor Hazelwood. 'What about Laura Greenwood?' she asked. 'Any idea when she is returning from Switzerland?'

'I would guess this coming Saturday. She asked for a week's leave.'

'At the drop of a hat?'

'Yes. Her supervisor claimed she had given him less than two days' notice.'

'Why was that I wonder?'

Ashton shrugged. 'Your guess is as good as mine.'

'I'd still like to hear yours.'

'I don't like gazing into a crystal ball.'

'Humour me, Peter.'

'Well, OK. I think that whatever Mullinder was looking for when he broke into her house, he was never going to find it. I believe she was carrying it around in her handbag because Adam Zawadzki had told her not to let the package or whatever out of her sight. After he was murdered, she didn't know what to do. Finally she came to a decision and shot off to Switzerland.'

'Why there?'

'They've got a lot of very discreet banks in Switzerland,' Ashton said.

Chapter Seventeen

Two large cognacs with her coffee at the café Dufore had stiffened Laura Greenwood's resolve and restored her confidence, which had almost disappeared without trace after her encounter with the Assistant Director in charge of Personal Banking at Credit Suisse. She had got her head back on and knew what she was going to say to Maître Gérard de Quillet, the lawyer whom she had arranged to see on the recommendation of the concierge at the Hotel California. She peered at her Omega wristwatch, saw that it was three minutes to one and regretfully came to the conclusion that there wasn't enough time to have one more for the road.

Maître de Quillet's office was situated at 29 Ruelle Gaspard off the Rue Jacques Balmet. A quick glance at the street map of Geneva, which she had picked up from the information desk in the hotel foyer, persuaded her that walking there was out of the question. She was not an unattractive woman and she had made a definite hit with the waiter who had served her; beckoning him over, Laura asked where she could get a taxi. As she had anticipated, the waiter went over to the bar, picked up the phone and rang for one. Ruelle Gaspard was an extremely narrow cobbled alleyway which all motor vehicles were prohibited from using. Laura discovered that number 29 was one of three tenements grouped round a small courtyard. The janitor, who was responsible for looking after all three properties, resided in the ground floor apartment; Maître Gérard de Quillet occupied the one above.

The lawyer was a small, untidy-looking man in his late forties whose dark grey suit, besmirched with food stains on both lapels, had obviously seen better days. His appearance did not fill Laura Greenwood with confidence and she found it hard to believe that de Quillet was one of the foremost advocates in Geneva. Then, after introducing herself, she discovered he was related to the concierge at the Hotel California and everything fell into place. His English was, however, passable and he claimed to be an absolute expert on commercial law and banking regulations.

'That's why I've come to see you,' Laura told him.

'A problem shared is a problem halved.' De Quillet smiled revealing a gold tooth. 'Is that not a saying in your country?'

'Yes, it's one of those old proverbs which contains a grain of truth.'

'And what is your problem, Madame?' de Quillet asked, and produced a legal pad from the top right-hand drawer of the desk.

'It's to do with the estate of my late husband, Adam Zawadzki, and certain monies lodged in the vaults of the Investment Trust Bank which belong to him.'

De Quillet glanced at his appointments diary. 'Pardon me,' he said, 'but I was given to understand that your name was Laura Greenwood?'

'It is. I reverted to my maiden name after his death.'

'Forgive me, please continue.'

'My husband's family were Jews and originally came from Breslau, near the Polish border. His parents were quite wealthy, and shortly after Hitler came to power in 1933 they began to transfer money and valuables to a Swiss bank. This, of course, became increasingly difficult as the Nazis tightened their grip on the country.'

The legend Laura Greenwood had constructed owed a lot to the books she had borrowed from the local library and the Open University course in Modern History she had taken years ago with a view to getting a degree. That ambition had fallen by the wayside but she had a good memory and the time hadn't been wasted. She told de Quillet that the grandparents had left the country in 1934 and settled in the Netherlands, having turned the family business over to their son. He had been convinced things could only get better after Hitler moved against Ernst Roehm and crushed the Brownshirts. That illusion had persisted despite the so-called Nuremberg Laws in 1935 which deprived Jews of their German citizenship, forbade intermarriage, and excluded them from public office, the civil service, and the professions.

'Adam was the determining factor,' Laura continued. 'He was born in 1937; his mother was barred from entering a nursing home and no Ayran doctor or midwife was allowed to attend her confinement. Adam was born at home and was delivered by an elderly Jewish doctor who had officially been struck off the register.'

That had been the beginning of the end for the Zawadzkis. In the face of growing anti-Semitism they had found it almost impossible to purchase even the basic necessities of life. In the windows of groceries, dairies, butchers and bakeries signs appeared proclaiming that Jews were not admitted. Pharmacies in Breslau refused to sell the Zawadzkis drugs or medicines, and the night before they had left Germany for good in January 1939 no hotel would give them a bed for the night.

'What did they do?' de Quillet asked, looking up from his pad.

'They walked the streets until their train was due to depart.'

'That's monstrous.'

'Yes. When he was old enough to understand, Adam's parents told him it was a bitterly cold night. They also told him they were only permitted to leave after they had sold their house and furniture store at a giveaway price to a high-ranking party official.'

'They joined the grandparents in Holland?'

'Only for a few months,' Laura said.

De Quillet made another notation on his pad and looked up. 'Why was that?'

'Adam's father could see the war coming and decided the English Channel was the biggest and most effective anti-tank ditch in the world. Regrettably the grandparents stayed in Holland; they were rounded up in 1943 and sent to Belsen where they died of typhus. As for Adam's parents, they died within a few months of one another in 1983.'

That part at least was true; the rest was pure fabrication. The legend, however, was totally convincing because it was based on the sufferings of real people Laura had read about. It did not trouble her that she was using the victims of the Holocaust to further her own purpose. Adam Zawadzki had been brutally murdered and she was prepared to use any means to discover why he had been put to death.

'My husband was told by his parents that the family had salted away some of their hard-earned money in a Swiss bank before the outbreak of war. However, he'd always assumed that whatever money and valuables had been deposited with the Investment and Trust Bank of Estavayer-le-Lac had been either used by his grandparents before they were arrested or else the SS had forced them to hand the money over to the State. Then a few days ago I received this mysterious communication from the bank.' Laura produced the statement she had previously shown to the Assistant Director of Personal Banking at Credit Suisse but withheld the envelope. 'It was addressed to my husband care of the British Embassy in Berne. It reached me via the Foreign Office.'

'The Foreign Office,' de Quillet repeated, frowning.

'Yes. My late husband was in the Diplomatic Service before he retired.'

'May I see the envelope?'

'I'm afraid I destroyed it.'

'That is a great pity, Madame.'

'So I'm beginning to realise. The fact remains you are looking at a numbered account which is in my possession and I want to know if this forms part of my late husband's estate. If it doesn't, I want to know the name of the present account holder because clearly he has misappropriated the money which my husband's family entrusted to the bank for safekeeping.'

'But you have no proof, Madame . . .'

'Some cashier in that bank made an error and inadvertently compiled the statement in the name of the original account holder. He didn't have an address for the Zawadzkis but he was aware that Adam's father had written to the bank from England immediately after the war. That's why the cashier sent the statement to the British Embassy in Berne.'

'But there is no accumulative total. All this statement shows is that at some unspecified date the sum of eighty-five thousand Swiss francs was deposited with the bank.'

'Precisely. Now you can appreciate why I want a detailed statement from Investment Trust.'

De Quillet sighed. 'I'm afraid you do not understand the confidentiality of the Swiss banking system.'

It was an argument Laura had anticipated. Her anger was genuine but it was born out of frustration rather than outrage.

'Let me tell you about Swiss banking regulations,' she snapped. 'All over Europe, thousands upon thousands of Jewish people entrusted their life's savings to banks like the Investment and Trust of Estavayer-le-Lac. The vast majority of them were subsequently gassed in places like Auschwitz and Treblinka. But some family members survived and tried to claim what was rightfully theirs. Of course they didn't have the requisite papers, and recognition was refused even to those who could quote the account number in question. So the banks refuse to pay up, and sit tight, making a wad a money while they wait for the claimants to die one by one.' Laura leaned forward, her eyes narrowed and as hard as diamonds. 'That's what your banking regulations mean in practice.'

'Are you questioning their integrity?'

'And the lawyers who protect them for one reason or another.' She leaned even closer to de Quillet. 'Why are you so hesitant?' she asked. 'The Investment and Trust is only a little itty-bitty privately owned bank. A lawyer of your calibre has only to raise his voice and they'll answer any question you ask.'

There was a lengthy silence while Gérard de Quillet performed all the facial grimaces of a man wrestling with his conscience. After what seemed an interminably long time he asked Laura if she would mind waiting in the outer office while he made a few enquiries.

The outer office was the domain of a sour-faced woman in black who wore her hair in a bun. She hadn't said two words to Laura when she had arrived for her appointment and it didn't look as though she intended to buck the trend. Although she had little to say for herself, from the way she wrinkled her nose when Laura offered her a cigarette, it was evident she thought smoking was a disgusting habit. So far as Laura was concerned that was too bad. She had just given the performance of her life and needed a cigarette to help her unwind. In fact she was on her second Benson and Hedges Silk Cut when de Quillet called her back into his office.

The bank, he gravely informed her, had been extremely co-operative and in view of the special circumstances had made an exception in her case which was not to be taken as a precedent. The name of the account holder was Osvaldo Herrara, which left her completely taken aback. So did the bill for 450 Swiss francs which de Quillet presented to her as she was about to leave.

The passport was one of a batch Copeland had purloined before retiring from the Met. Over the years he had rubbed the semistiff cover to the point where most of the gold lettering, together with the Lion and Unicorn motif, had all but disappeared, giving it a well-worn appearance. On the penultimate page where the holder was advised to insert particulars of two relatives or friends who could be contacted in the event of an accident, he'd plucked two names from the phone book and inserted area codes that had been applicable in 1991.

But the real masterpiece was the end page. With the aid of his Apple computer, Copeland had created the legend of Arthur Henderson, British Citizen, born on the 23 February 1962 at Southend-on-Sea, Passport Number 005030661. He had then affixed the Polyfoto of Mullinder, which had arrived by first delivery that morning, and had laminated the whole ID to the inside page of the back cover. To account for the worn appearance of the passport, he had stamped a number of pages at random to show Henderson had visited America, Canada, Hong Kong, Singapore and Bangkok.

Copeland wrapped a sheet of paper around the passport so that it shouldn't be seen if the envelope was held up to the light, added three hundred dollars in traveller's cheques, which he had started to purchase the day after Mullinder had burgled the house in St John's Avenue, and sealed down the flap. He then addressed the envelope to Arthur Henderson, Mannix Hotel, 285 Harbour Quay Road, Dublin, Eire. That done, he left his office in Station Road, Wood Green, caught the Piccadilly Line train to Leicester Square and walked down to the main post office in William IV Street. If the letter should be intercepted at least the postmark would not betray him.

There had been a time when Ashton had known there was a valid purpose behind everything he was called on to do but that was back in the days when he had been a Grade II Intelligence Analyst on the Russian Desk and there had been every reason to regard the Soviet Union as a potential enemy. As of now he felt The Firm was simply drifting along waiting for some unspecified threat to materialise which the SIS could really get their teeth into for the foreseeable future.

Ever since 1991, when Victor Hazelwood had first begun to use him as a stalking horse, he had gradually become a catch-all safety net for Heads of Departments. If an Assistant Director was in any way disquieted by signs of possible trouble in his geopolitical region, the relevant intelligence summary, memorandum or incoming signal was marked up for Ashton's information. As a result he spent a lot of time reading and initialling the files and loose-leaf memoranda which continuously filled his in-tray to overflowing. That afternoon the material contained more than the usual amount of dross and it was something of a relief when the phone rang to break the monotony.

'It's me,' Francesca York said after he had given the number of his extension.

'Can we go to secure?'

'Soon as I press the crypto button.'

Unlike the scrambler system with its cumbersome black box which was so large it had to be positioned on the floor, the latest version of the Mozart range was no bigger than a matchbox and formed an integral part of the telephone. There was no degradation of the voice level on secure speech, which was another improvement.

'I'm ready this end,' Ashton told her.

'Good. I thought you would be interested to hear we didn't get to interview Hasan Ünver. We submitted the request through the FCO yesterday morning and we heard the Turkish Ambassador had no objection in principle. Then this morning we learned that Ünver had left the country. It seems his father has been taken seriously ill.'

'Surprise, surprise.'

'Yes, isn't it?' York said, and laughed briefly. 'Anyway, he was on the Turkish Airlines flight to Istanbul at 21.00 hours last night and I doubt we will see him again.'

'It's what you expected, wasn't it?'

'Oh, yes, I said as much to you on Monday.'

'Who else had flown the coop? His PA for instance?'

'The FCO inferred the terrorists must have had inside information and we were told the Ambassador had taken the point. We were also advised the embassy security staff would deal with the matter. I don't imagine you are surprised, Mr Ashton.'

'Not altogether.'

A junior minister carefully briefed by one of the four Deputy Under Secretaries would have an informal meeting with the First Counsellor of the Turkish Embassy. Although Ashton had never served in an embassy he could make a pretty shrewd guess concerning the nature of their discussion. The junior minister would have informed the First Counsellor that Her Majesty's Government knew the terrorists had intended to kill Hasan Ünver. There would have been no gentle inference as Francesca York had intimated. Instead he would have made it absolutely clear HMG believed the terrorists had been acting on information provided by a source within the embassy. While indicating this was a matter for the embassy's security staff to investigate, the First Counsellor would have been left in no doubt that HMG would expect to be apprised of the outcome. There would have been no necessity to explain the reasoning behind this stipulation. It was the responsibility of HMG to deal with any terrorist cell operating in the UK, not the Turkish authorities'. But whatever information MI5 eventually received after the investigation had been completed, the fact was it would have little bearing on the present whereabouts of Osvaldo Herrara.

'Now comes the embarrassing bit,' York said quietly.

'What?'

'When I tell you, please remember I'm only the messenger.'

'Don't worry, Fran, I promise not to shoot you.'

'I hope you mean it because I've got the unenviable task of warning you off Barry Hayes also known as Brian Ahearne.'

'The man whose garage the IRA used to cache firearms and explosives.'

'The same.'

'Amazing. What makes you think I even knew where to find him? Last time we talked, you told me Special Branch was looking for him.'

'This predates our conversation. Somebody plugged into the bomb squad on your behalf and asked a few questions which got back to 10 Int. Company in Northern Ireland. Need I say more?'

'No, you can tell Neagle I've got the message.'

'Thank you for being so understanding,' York said, and put the phone down.

Ashton hung up, switched off the computer and left the office, locking the door behind him. Of the three lifts in the building, one was now displaying an out of order sign, another was stuck on the second floor, and the third ignored the call button and shot past the fourth floor. By the time Ashton had made his way down to the Security Vetting and Technical Services Division he had got things into perspective and knew he had only himself to blame for what had happened.

'I've been expecting you,' Thomas said when Ashton walked into his office. 'And the bollocking I'm about to receive.'

'You won't get one from me, Brian. I just want to hear everything you've learned about Barry Hayes alias Brian Ahearne.'

'OK. Remember those trademarks you gave me based on the forensic evidence SOCO recovered from the Warlock Estate? Well, the bomb-maker was Barry Hayes. Incidentally, that's his real name.'

Brian Ahearne had been the commander of the IRA Flying Column in County Mayo from January 1920 to May 1921, when he had been killed in a fire fight with a platoon of auxiliaries, a paramilitary police force composed of young, unemployed ex-army officers, many of whom had been decorated for bravery during the war. To Barry Hayes, Ahearne had been a life-long hero and he had adopted his name in honour of him when he'd joined the Provisional IRA.

'When things got too hot for him in Northern Ireland, he slipped over the border and the rumour was put about that he had fled to America. Instead he came to this country where he was known by his real name.'

'When did this happen?' Ashton asked.

'In 1989.'

'You mean he has been operating here under cover for the past seven years?' Ashton said incredulously.

'And he still would be if he hadn't been named by a supergrass.'

The supergrass was a former battalion commander in West Belfast who had become sickened by the punishment beatings and kneecapping of petty criminals authorised by the Army Council. The final straw for him had been the abduction, torture and subsequent execution of a mother of six whose only crime had been to be a Protestant married to a Catholic.

'Ahearne had been one of his foot soldiers and he knew his real name. Soon as the Provos learned the commander of their West Belfast battalion had gone across, they got in touch with Hayes and told him to disappear.'

'And?'

'What do you mean – "And?"?'

'There's something you forgot to mention,' Ashton told him.

'You mean the fact that he hails from the Bogside in Londonderry and is believed to be back in Northern Ireland?'

'Try again, Brian.'

'What can I say? After he had named the bomb-maker, my source developed a bad case of cold feet and ran to his superiors. To make things better for himself, he pointed a finger at me and indirectly at you.'

'I've been warned off Hayes.'

'That's MI5 for you. They're staking out their claim.'

'Which is strange,' Ashton continued, 'because I wouldn't recognise the man if I passed him in the street.'

Thomas shrugged. 'Obviously they thought otherwise.'

'So how am I going to find him if Special Branch can't?'

'You are known to be a resourceful man, Peter.'

'I'm flattered but it won't do, Brian. Your source was a lot more forthcoming than you've made out. He told you a close relative of Barry Hayes was still living in England. That's why he suddenly got cold feet.'

'That's some crystal ball you've got.'

'So who's the relative? A brother, brother-in-law or a cousin?'

'You don't want to know.'

'We've been over this ground before,' Ashton said wearily. 'And as I recall, you said that if I wanted to go up against the politicians on both sides of the Irish Sea, who were you to stand in my way?'

'All right, on your head be it. He's got a younger brother called Kevin who came over here in 1984, married an English girl and settled down in Lewisham. I don't have the address because when I asked for it, my source did a wobbler on me. Satisfied?'

'Yes.'

'Good. Now you can do me a favour. Whatever it is you have in mind, talk it over with Harriet first. She's got more sense in her little finger than you have in your whole body.'

'I hear what you say,' Ashton said.

'Yeah, but are you taking it in?' Thomas grunted derisively. 'Still, why should I worry? Your chance of running Kevin Hayes to ground is about zero.'

'Unless I can borrow one of your props.'

'No way.'

'They killed three people in that bombing – a couple who were having it away on the back seat of a Rover 400 and DC Browne. And even if she survives O'Meara is never going to be the same woman again. Are you going to let them get away with that, Brian?'

Thomas consulted his desk diary, then looked up, his face expressionless.

'I see my controlled stores are due a spot check,' he said laconically.

'You want to carry it out?'

'Why not?'

The various items of equipment held by Technical Services were classified under two broad headings – hardware and software, neither of which had anything to do with information technology. Communications, surveillance aids and small arms came under hardware and were stored in separate lockups in the basement. Software included blank passports, visa application forms and identity papers of every description, much of which should have been junked following the demise of the Cold War.

It was no great hardship for Thomas to carry out a spot check. The software was in fact kept in a small strong room just two doors along the corridor from his office.

'So what do you want to look at first?' Thomas asked.

'Let's begin with the ID documents.'

In a space not much larger than a walk-in cupboard, three security cabinets had been arranged in an open square. Approaching the one in the centre which faced the door, Thomas set the Manufoil lock to zero, then went through the sequence of numbers needed to open the cabinet.

'I think that's my phone I can hear,' he said, craning his head on one side. 'You mind carrying on with the spot check while I answer it?'

'That would be only sensible.'

Largely for the sake of form Ashton waited until the older man had left before he helped himself to a fake warrant card that was good enough to fool the Commissioner of the Metropolitan Police.

Chapter Eighteen

The warrant card had been burning a hole in Ashton's pocket ever since he had lifted it yesterday afternoon from the strong room where the controlled stores on charge to the Security Vetting and Technical Services Division were kept. There were several ways of discovering the home address of Kevin Hayes, all of which, with one exception, involved waving the warrant card at the head man. He could go along to St Catherine's House and ask to see the last population census for the Borough of Lewisham. Alternatively, he could try the Revenue Services Division at the local civic centre and get them to run through the council tax records. Finally, he could visit the borough official responsible for maintaining the electoral roll and seek his assistance. All three avenues of inquiry would be time-consuming and decidedly risky.

'Do me a favour,' Thomas had said to him, 'whatever it is you have in mind, talk it over with Harriet first.' The former Detective Chief Superintendent hadn't been thinking of himself when he'd said that, but if Special Branch should learn they were looking for Hayes in spite of being warned off, his neck would also be on the chopping block.

The telephone directory had seemed the only totally discreet means of discovering where Kevin Hayes lived. It was certainly discreet but as Ashton had discovered for himself, wading through the appropriate BT directory had been a mammoth task which had ultimately proved unsuccessful. The residential numbers contained in Volume 620 covered a total of twenty-two London boroughs, north and south of the river. Hayes was also a fairly common name which took up a full page arranged in four columns with a bit over. Since Lewisham was in the postal district SE13, he'd had to go through the entire entry, jotting down every subscriber living in that particular area because there had been no question of restricting the cull to those persons whose first name began with K. What he couldn't ignore was the fact that some people preferred to be known by their favourite forename, regardless of whether or not it was the second or the third one their parents had given them. A full morning's work had left Ashton with a list of eight starters. He was also aware that Kevin Hayes could be ex-directory or possibly not on the phone at all.

Every new organisation had its teething problems; the trouble with CATO was that it hadn't got going yet and was suffering from a deficit of information. Mehmet Ozbek had gone to ground somewhere, and Osvaldo Herrara had apparently disappeared without trace. Will Landon had trawled the Caribbean and South American files without discovering anything of note and was now looking to see what the Russian Desk had on the Cuban. Nancy Wilkins was still in the throes of compiling a list of major construction programmes currently in progress.

That left Laura Greenwood, who was allegedly on holiday somewhere in Switzerland. Ashton had taken the Underground out to East Putney to make sure she hadn't taken off from some other destination. Alighting from the District Line train, he'd made his way along Richmond Road, then turned right and walked down Putney Hill. He had checked out the major travel agencies in the High Street only to learn that none of them had had any dealings with a Laura Greenwood of 104 St John's Avenue. He had gone past the Exchange Shopping Centre and was approaching the bridge when he spotted a small travel bureau in a cul-de-sac on the opposite side of the road.

The sign above the entrance read 'Taylor Made Holidays'; a sticker in the window to the left of the door claimed no travel agency could beat Taylor's for bargain prices. Once inside it was evident the proprietor didn't believe in spending much on furnishings and fittings. The fitted carpet was haircord, there were half a dozen tubular steel chairs for potential clients and a magazine rack stuffed with brochures in case anybody was thinking of taking a package holiday. There was just one desktop computer and a couple of phones on the counter. On the wall behind, timetables of every description as well as hotel listings for both home and abroad filled the available shelf space. There was only one agent on duty and a definite shortage of clients.

The agent, a plump, dark-haired woman in her forties, looked up from the brochure she had been reading and gave him a welcoming smile.

'My name's Gaynor,' she told him. 'How can I help you?'

Ashton produced the fake warrant card and showed it to her. 'Don't be alarmed, Gaynor, it's nothing serious. A trial date has been rescheduled and we need to contact a witness for the prosecution. Her name is Laura Greenwood and we think she may be one of your clients.'

'The name doesn't sound familiar to me.'

'Maybe another member of the staff dealt with her?' Ashton suggested.

'It's possible.'

'Well, could you look at your office records and let me know one way or the other?'

'I'm not sure I can do that,' Gaynor said, her eyes sliding towards the door at the back of the shop. 'At least not without Mr Taylor's permission.'

'Perhaps I should talk to him?'

Gaynor thought this was a good idea. Moving to her right, she tapped on the door and went inside. A few moments later she emerged from the back room with a youngish-looking man casually dressed in whipcord slacks and a dark grey polo-neck sweater.

'This is Mr Taylor,' she said.

'And you are?' Taylor asked.

Ashton produced his warrant card. 'DC Messenger,' he said with consummate ease. 'This won't take more than a few minutes of your time, sir.'

Taylor raised the counter flap and opened the gate. 'You'd better come on through then,' he said.

The small back room was both an office and a repository for Swiss Travel, Thomson, Thomas Cook, Kuoni and Jules Verne travel brochures, stacked in uneven piles on the floor. The rest of the available space was taken up by a desk, two chairs and a three-drawer filing cabinet.

'Gaynor tells me you want to know if we have a Miss or Ms Laura Greenwood on our books?'

'And have you?' Ashton said, refusing to be drawn.

'We have a L. Greenwood. I don't know if she is the lady you're interested in contacting.'

'Laura Greenwood is a civil servant in the Passport Office. Last Thursday she informed her supervisor she was taking a week off and was going to spend it in Switzerland.'

'That's our client.' Taylor went to the filing cabinet, pulled out the centre drawer, and extracted a file. 'She flew to Geneva on Monday; I booked a room for her at the Hotel California and she hasn't gone for a week. I've got her on British Airways Flight BA725 departing Geneva 12.06 local time on Thursday 21 March. Gets into Heathrow at 12.45 GMT.' A self-satisfied smirk appeared on his face. 'Anything else I can tell you, Constable?' he asked.

Ashton thanked him, said how very helpful he and Gaynor had been and left the travel agency. Although Zurich was the great banking centre, he was damned sure Ms Greenwood hadn't gone to Geneva for a three-day 'End of Winter Break'. Supposition was all very well; what he needed was the odd solid fact up his sleeve when the time came to confront Laura Greenwood. There was just a slim chance that Head of Station, Berne, might be able to assist him there but he imagined Rowan Garfield would have plenty to say about that.

Copeland turned into Station Road and walked up to his office-cum-shop, which was squeezed between a greengrocer and a newsagent. A creature of habit, lunch for him on Wednesday was usually a tuna sandwich. On a Monday it was a round of cold roast beef with horseradish sauce, Tuesday was a cheese and onion roll, tomorrow would be ham and English mustard, and on Friday, a hot Cornish pasty. However, today he had lunched with a potential client whose clothing factory had been broken into time and again. After a long, hard sales talk over a £15 per head table d'hôte at Chez Moi, washed down with a good bottle of Merlot, he had won himself a contract with a profit margin of two thousand for three days' work.

The telephone was ringing as he tapped out the entry code to his office. The answer machine was activated after the ninth peal; the fact that the connection was terminated on the seventh told him that Mullinder had just called. It was a procedure he had introduced eleven months ago when he had hired Mullinder to break into the head office of Universal Services. When you did something illegal on behalf of the government it was vital to watch your back and never more so than now. Opening the safe he took out his battery-powered magic wand, which was shaped like a table tennis bat, and swept the office to make sure it was still clean. Mullinder rang again shortly after he had completed the check.

'You're a hard man to get hold of,' Mullinder complained, and laughed nervously. 'This is the fifth time I've tried your office number.'

'I do have other clients.'

'Yeah. Well, the sample arrived OK. Question is when do I get the rest of the order?'

'I think we'd better say Friday.'

'That's a day later than you originally said.'

'No, I said Thursday was the earliest our Paris office could deliver.'

'Paris?' Mullinder echoed.

'Yes, Paris. The Bar Moris in the Place St-Augustin. Be there noon on Friday.'

'Local knowledge?'

'I've visited a couple of times,' Copeland said, and put the phone down.

Of all the SIS establishments, the European Department was easily the most unwieldy. It had come about by the amalgamation of the old Eastern Bloc with the NATO and nonaligned European countries which, until the collapse of the Soviet Union, had been a separate entity. In furtherance of this cost-cutting exercise the number of desk officers had been steadily reduced. This had been achieved by the simple expedient of not replacing normal wastage. Consequently it had been the old Eastern Bloc which had borne the brunt of this because their manning levels had been far higher than the NATO and nonaligned group. The reduction had only been made to work by combining desks – the Polish with the Czech and Slovakian, the Hungarian with the Romanian and Bulgarian.

As a result of this rationalisation Rowan Garfield's fiefdom had doubled in size, whereas the number of men and women in the department had been reduced by forty per cent. Despite this evident overstretch, Victor Hazelwood and others still expected him to provide the same kind of service as he had done at the height of the Cold War. The injustice of it all was enough to try the patience of a saint, a quality which Garfield did not possess. He was three years short of his half-century and disliked being put under pressure. When asked to do something which in his opinion would stretch his limited resources to breaking point, Garfield was likely to blow his top.

Apart from the Director General his other *bête noire* was

Ashton, whom he regarded as the ultimate loose cannon. There was no denying the man got results but only after a lot of blood had been spilt on the carpet. Garfield had been mentally congratulating himself that, at least in the matter of the Adam Zawadzki business, Ashton was primarily Roger Benton's headache when Ashton walked into his office.

'No,' he said, 'absolutely not.'

'I haven't asked you for anything yet,' Ashton observed mildly.

'I'm not listening anyway. Thanks to you and Ms Sheridan I've got Will Landon crawling all over the Russian Desk, interrupting their work. You will get nothing more from me until he is out of my hair.'

'This is really a job for Head of Station, Berne.'

Astounded by his gall Garfield listened to the younger man, his mouth open as though he had difficulty breathing through his nose.

'You've got a nerve,' he said when Ashton had finished telling him what was required. 'Head of Station, Berne has got better things to do than run errands for you.'

'And the Deputy DG.'

'Oh, yes, we mustn't forget Jill – as if one could.'

'Neither of us is suggesting Head of Station should do it himself. As I recall he has two assistants—'

'Of whom one is a cypher clerk.'

'That still leaves him with a Grade III Intelligence Officer,' Ashton said, unperturbed. 'And I think we agreed what I had in mind wouldn't take up much of his time.'

Garfield was loathe to admit it but he had closed his ears to what Ashton had been suggesting earlier. He had already made up his mind that the European Department was so overstretched he couldn't spare a single body. In the last two years, when his establishment was being sliced to the bone, he had been expected to provide Grade A1 Intelligence on the war between the Croats on one side and the Serbs with their allies, the Yugoslav National Army, on the other. And then, while that conflict was still raging, he had been required to cover the ethnic cleansing in Bosnia.

Now things were beginning to boil over in Kosovo with the Albanian majority demanding independence from Belgrade. Before very long they would be at each other's throats, quite literally. Next time the balloon went up, maybe the Government would allow him to send in the SAS to gather information before things really hotted up. In Croatia and Bosnia he'd had to rely on mercenaries hired by a private company, some of whom had ended up fighting on the side of the Muslim population. The Government had been less than happy about that development.

'What about it, Rowan?'

Garfield flinched. He hadn't been listening again but he couldn't ask Ashton to repeat himself a third time.

'Draft a signal,' he said tersely, 'and show it to me for approval and signature.'

'Thanks. Do you mind if I go next door and borrow a keyboard? It'll save a lot of time.'

'Don't let me stop you,' Garfield told him.

In all the years he had been with the SIS he had never known such a ridiculous state of affairs as the one which existed now. Here he was faced with three major flashpoints in the Balkans, and the Whitehall mandarins who controlled the purse strings calmly expected him to keep on top of the situation with just Head of Station, Belgrade, and his small staff. But a stupid pisspot organisation like CATO would lack for nothing. That was the bitter bit.

'Would you like to run your eye over this, Rowan?'

Ashton again. There was no getting rid of the man. Garfield reached for the copy and noted the signal had been accorded the precedence of Op Immediate.

'Precedence is a bit high, isn't it, considering the security classification is only Confidential?'

'I want them to get a move on,' Ashton said.

Garfield saw what Ashton meant when he read the text.

Basically Ashton wanted Head of Station, Berne to ascertain what Laura Greenwood had been doing in Geneva and had declared that an answer by 16.00 hours GMT Thursday 21 March would be much appreciated.

'You don't want much, do you? By the time this signal is encoded they will have less than twenty-four hours to get the job done. It's not on, Peter.'

'Laura Greenwood is on Flight BA725. Departure time is 12.06 local, which means she will check in at least one hour beforehand. She was staying at the California; all I've asked is for your man to have a word with the concierge. I want to know if she sought your advice – the whereabouts of the nearest bank, for instance. Or maybe she asked if he could recommend a good lawyer.'

'You're guessing.'

'Right. And I've been wide of the mark a number of times recently. But in taking off for Geneva at the drop of a hat, Laura Greenwood appears to have behaved out of character and that's something we shouldn't ignore.'

The round trip from Berne to Geneva was a shade under two hundred miles. To undertake this journey on the basis of a whim could well prove a waste of time, but on reflection Garfield decided not to make the point. When all was said and done, it wasn't as if Head of Station was under pressure and didn't know which way to turn. He glanced at his wristwatch, then in the box below the heading of Date/Time Group he wrote 20 March 1630Z and signed the text as the authorising officer.

'I'm afraid you will have to deliver this to the Communication Centre,' he said, and handed all three copies of the message form to Ashton. 'I can't spare anybody.'

'I rather thought that might be the case,' Ashton said drily.

Hazelwood was ready to commit murder. At short notice he had been summoned by the Permanent Under Secretary to attend a conference at the FCO which had lasted over three hours, and now here he was in the middle of the rush hour stuck in a traffic jam on Westminster Bridge thanks to road works. The meeting had been chaired by Robin Urquhart, which was probably why it had overrun. It had been attended by Richard Neagle from MI5, the Head of the Near East Department whose name Hazelwood hadn't caught, and Alistair Downward who, until this meeting, he had known only by reputation. What had angered him more than the protracted length of the conference was the fact that he had been the only one there who hadn't been properly briefed. There was only one person responsible for that omission and he proposed to hang Rowan Garfield out to dry the minute he was back in the office. Damn it, he hadn't even known a conference to discuss the possibility of reaching a political settlement between the Greek and Turkish Cypriots was being mooted, let alone a change of venue was now on the cards.

After the car had crawled along a few yards at a time for several minutes, the traffic lights on the one-way section stayed on green long enough for Hazelwood's driver to pass the road works without further hindrance. Once the roundabout near Waterloo station had been negotiated, he turned into Lambeth Palace Road and put his foot down in an effort to make up some of the lost time. Four minutes later, he turned off the Albert Embankment into the service road leading to the underground garage at Vauxhall Cross.

Hazelwood barely gave the driver time to switch off the engine before he was out of the armour-plated Jaguar and heading towards the lift. Alighting on the top floor, he walked briskly down the corridor and asked Jill to join him as he passed the open doorway of her office. When she did, his first question was to enquire whether Garfield was still on the premises.

'Rowan is waiting in my office,' Jill told him. 'He was about to leave when you rang from FCO.'

'Then it won't do him any harm to wait a little while longer.' Hazelwood opened the cigar box on his desk and took out a Burma cheroot. He hadn't smoked one in over four hours and it was sheer bliss to draw the smoke down and slowly exhale. 'Do you know anything about a top-level conference on the Cyprus issue?' he asked.

'Not officially. I've heard one is in the pipeline from Robin. From what he said to me it sounded like a conference about a conference.'

'There's to be a change of venue.'

'I'm not surprised, Victor. Nowhere in Cyprus was acceptable to both Greeks and Turks. If one lot approved of the venue, the other didn't.'

All the Arab countries had been ruled out, Israel didn't want to host the conference because Mossad had enough security problems to cope with as it was, and Malta had declined the honour for reasons that had something to do with the tourist trade. Brussels has lost out because the Turkish Foreign Minister had objected on the grounds that his country's application to join the European Community had been blocked on spurious economic grounds and it was unlikely they would get a fair hearing.

'That's how London got saddled with hosting the conference,' Jill continued.

'Yes, well, now we are out of favour.' Hazelwood flicked his cigar over the cut-down shell case and missed, spilling ash on the desk. 'Anyway, Washington has stepped into the breach.'

'Do we have a date for the conference?'

'Not yet. The State Department has to persuade the Cypriots plus the mainland Greeks and Turks to participate first; then the interested parties will have to agree on an agenda.'

'I don't believe that will be a problem, Victor. The State Department has the necessary clout to make it happen. We haven't.'

Hazelwood leaned forward, his elbows on the desk, his shoulders hunched. He was a big man and an untidy one. Even these days, when his suits were made to measure by Gieves and Hawkes, they still lost their shape after a few months and looked rumpled.

'Are you sure we didn't receive any official forewarning of this conference?' he asked, breaking off at a tangent.

'Absolutely. Five would have received advance warning when it was to be held at Lancaster House.'

Well, Jill should know, he thought, considering the number of times Robin Urquhart must have shared her bed. Furthermore it would be grossly unfair to blame Garfield for the humiliating experience he had suffered at the FCO.

'I think I should have a quick word with Rowan,' he said. 'Would you mind calling him in, Jill?'

'Not a bit.'

'And please don't go away. I won't be a minute.'

The expression on Garfield's face when he entered the room was a mixture of agitation, surliness and belligerence. Hazelwood suspected that, in conveying the gist of his telephone conversation with her, Jill had left him with the impression he was for the high jump. Invited to sit down, Garfield informed him he preferred to stand.

'I owe you an apology,' Hazelwood told him. 'Like the rest of us, you clearly didn't have any forewarning of the impending discussions on the Cyprus question.'

'That wasn't my interpretation of your message.'

'I jumped to the wrong conclusion, Rowan, and I'm sorry I misjudged you. I should have known you would have kept me fully informed had your department been made aware of this development.'

'Yes, well . . .'

Hazelwood sighed inwardly. Dear God, the man was still resentful. What did he expect him to do? Go down on his knees and beg Garfield to forgive him? Like hell!

'Let's move along, shall we?' he said briskly. 'What I would like from your desk officers is a list of potential troublemakers in Greece, Turkey and Cyprus, people and organisations with a history of violent protest.'

'Right. How urgent is this task, Director?'

Now Garfield was being childish, addressing him formally as Director instead of using his first name.

'End of this week, Monday at the latest.' Hazelwood aimed

his cheroot at the shell case again and this time managed to deposit the ash inside it. 'Perhaps you would tell Jill to pop back on your way out,' he added.

'Would this be a bad moment to discuss the restoration of some of the cuts made to my establishment, Director?'

'It would. Talk to me about it after morning prayers tomorrow.'

'As you wish, Director.'

Garfield stalked out of the office and told Jill she was wanted as he passed her door. Listening to him as he walked on down the corridor, Hazelwood could not recall an occasion when Rowan had sounded quite so heavy-footed.

'I know somebody who's got the hump,' Jill said.

'Yes. I seem to have ruffled his feathers.'

'That's not too difficult, Victor.'

Hazelwood made no comment. Anything you said in front of Jill was liable to be repeated to Robin Urquhart and he had already said too much.

'How well do you know Alistair Downward?' he asked, moving on to a safer topic.

'He's one of the legal counsellors at the FCO and is said to be an expert on international law.' Jill shrugged. 'I only know him by reputation, Victor.'

'As do I. Still, in my case it doesn't matter, but it's different for you.'

'Why is that?'

'You are Head of CATO; if this overseas conference does take place you will be working hand in glove with Downward. That's why you should get really close and find out all you can about him.'

'Will I be safe?' Jill asked with a wicked smile.

'I should think so,' Hazelwood told her. 'Rumour has it he prefers pretty young men to pretty young women.'

Chapter Nineteen

The Assistant Head of Station, Berne, had telephoned Ashton over an unprotected line two minutes before 16.00. From the concierge of the Hotel California he had learned that Laura Greenwood had sought advice from a Maître Gérard de Quillet while staying in Geneva. He had subsequently gone to 29 Ruelle Gaspard and talked to the maître himself, who had been extremely co-operative. So far as de Quillet was concerned, Laura Greenwood had lied to him and had therefore forfeited any right to client confidentiality.

By the time the Intelligence Officer had relayed everything de Quillet had disclosed to him, Ashton had all the facts he needed to confront Laura Greenwood. Unfortunately he had not been able to make use of them there and then. Between 16.15 and 18.00 hours he had telephoned the house in St John's Avenue time and again without getting an answer.

This morning he'd rung Laura Greenwood from the office and had had better luck. As soon as he'd mentioned de Quillet she had accepted that he wanted to see her and had only asked when she might expect him to call at the house.

'Roughly three-quarters of an hour from now,' he'd told her, and had gone straight down to the basement garage and signed out a self-drive Ford Sierra.

Although they had never met, Ashton knew something of Laura Greenwood's background. When checking her current security status he had learned that she had been born in Ludlow, Shropshire, on 21 August 1951. Both her parents had died in 1989, and her next of kin was now her elder brother whose last known address was somewhere in Wolverhampton. The record also showed she had never been married.

The woman who opened the door to him was about five feet six or seven and could still get into a size 12 without looking emaciated. She wore her hair parted in the middle and cut short, the ends just reaching the lower jaw. Maybe the honey-blonde colour wasn't natural but she could carry it off and Ashton thought most women of her age would give their eyeteeth to look as good as she did.

'My name's Ashton,' he said, and produced his identity card for her perusal.

'Yes indeed.' She opened the door wider and stepped aside. 'Won't you please come in? The sitting room is the second on your right.'

The place looked as if it had been in the path of a hurricane when Ashton had seen it a few hours after Mullinder had burgled the house. Now the sitting room was spick and span and smelled of lavender. Ashton was prepared to bet she had used several cans of air freshener to combat the after-death body odour from Tracy Beckingham.

'Do please sit down, Mr Ashton. Can I get you a cup of coffee or something?'

'Thank you, but I won't just now.' He smiled. 'But don't let me stop you.'

'I don't think I will either.' She sat down in an armchair facing him, her posture bolt upright, the knees pressed together, seemingly unable to relax. 'What can I tell you?' she blurted out. 'You already know about the numbered account at the Investment and Trust Bank.'

'We're pretty sure Adam was murdered by Osvaldo Herrara.'

'You mean somebody paid him the equivalent of thirty-six thousand pounds to kill Adam?' she asked, her voice rising.

'No. Herrara is a freelance terrorist, the money is for something else.'

'Where is this creature now?' she said angrily.

'I wish I knew,' Ashton told her candidly. 'If we're to find Herrara we have to know who is financing him, and to discover his identity I need you to tell me exactly what happened from the moment Adam was told he was going to Costa Rica. I understand he received eighteen hours' notice?'

'So Adam told me when I got home from work. He said the Superintendent in charge of the Corps of Queen's Messengers had rung him shortly after noon.'

'That was on Tuesday the fifth?'

'Yes. Adam was pretty angry when he learned he was stepping in for Martin Edmunds.'

'He really disliked him that much?'

'Oh yes, but Adam would have been annoyed no matter who he had been told to stand in for. He was a keen gardener and had asked to be taken off the roster for seven days so that he could dig over the vegetable patch. Tuesday was only his second day off.'

'He'd never done the Central American run before?'

'Not since I've known him. The Mid East was Adam's stamping ground.'

'Did the switch involve any change in the usual routine administrative procedures?'

'It certainly did,' Laura said.

It was always possible to get a British Airways flight to any destination in the Middle East with a departure time no earlier than 12.00 hours. This arrangement allowed Zawadzki and his colleagues to collect the diplomatic bag from the FCO, and then go straight on to Heathrow in one of the Ford Grenadas from the car pool. This procedure hadn't applied to Costa Rica because there was only one British Airways flight per day to Dallas-Fort Worth and it departed from Gatwick at 10.05.

'In accordance with security regulations, Adam was not allowed to collect the bag the day before and keep it overnight in the house. To comply with this restriction the bag is delivered to the house by the Special Dispatch Service.'

'And this is what happened on Wednesday, the sixth of March?'

'Yes, except things didn't go smoothly, which made Adam mad.'

The Ford Grenada which was to convey Zawadzki to Gatwick had arrived on time at six o'clock. The SDS vehicle had turned up five minutes later instead of ten minutes before the hour.

'What difference does a quarter of an hour make?' Ashton said. 'Even if the driver never went above fifty, he would still have had roughly three hours in hand.'

'I know. But to Adam ten minutes to six did not equate to five after. He was funny like that.'

Ashton recalled what Zawadzki's instructors had said of him when he had been a student at the Staff College, Camberley. 'Pedantic', 'Unable to see the wood for the trees' had been two of their observations.

'The thing is, Adam had to check all the documents in the bag and sign a docket acknowledging he had received them.'

'So?'

'Well, he was complaining he didn't have enough time to make a thorough job of it.'

'You were present when this was going on?' Ashton asked.

'Not to begin with. I was still in bed but I could hear Adam clumping about downstairs, getting more and more heated. At one point he swore out loud and said, "What the hell is this blankety-blank thing doing here?" That was when I got up, put on a dressing gown and went downstairs.'

'Who else was there?'

'Nobody. Both drivers were outside; Adam didn't invite them into the house.'

For all the notice Zawadzki had taken of her, she would have been better off staying in bed. He'd stuffed all the documents back into the briefcase, signed the docket, and then left after giving her a perfunctory kiss on the cheek. Zawadzki had been so distracted he had left his travelling bag behind and Laura had had to run to the door with it and call him back.

'He practically snatched the bag out of my hand and ran back to the car without so much as a thank you. I was so angry with Adam I wouldn't have cared if I never saw him again.' Her face crumpled and for a moment Ashton thought she was going to burst into tears, then a wan smile appeared. 'It didn't last. I found myself missing him before his plane took off from Gatwick.'

'What did you do after Adam had left?'

'I went back to bed for another half-hour.'

Laura had got up again at seven fifteen, the usual time for her. Breakfast consisted of a slice of brown toast with a cup of coffee and, as was her usual routine, she had gone into the dining room to open the curtains before the kettle came to the boil.

'When I'd walked into the front room earlier on that morning Adam had been checking the contents of the bag on the dining table. Now that it was daylight the first thing I noticed was this large, brown envelope under the sideboard. There was no file reference on the back flap and it hadn't been addressed to anybody. Adam had evidently slit it open with one of our silver-plated dessert knives which he hadn't bothered to put away. If he had looked inside, he would have seen it contained a much smaller envelope, but of course he was far too het up to think of that.'

'And impatient?' Ashton suggested.

'He was swearing like a trooper.'

Ashton could picture Zawadzki standing there at the dining table, checking the reference numbers in the docket with those on the back flap of each envelope, then coming across one that was completely blank. In his own mind he was already late and now he was confronted with an unidentifiable document. He had sliced the envelope open, taken a cursory look inside and than tossed it away, convinced it was empty.

'What did you do with the brown envelope?' he asked.

'I put it in the rubbish bin. I didn't see any reason to keep it.'

251

'So what made you hang on to the smaller one?'

'The logo in the top left-hand corner, the quality and shape of the blue-grey envelope itself. The paper was very thin and the size was a shade smaller than anything sold in this country. At first, I kept the envelope in the drop-leaf bureau, meaning to give it to Adam when he returned from Costa Rica. Then I learned he had been murdered.'

'When did you hear that?'

'Saturday the ninth of March. The Superintendent in charge of the Queen's Diplomatic Messenger Service rang me at home shortly after the Foreign Office had broken the news to him.'

The date was significant. Zawadzki had been missing for over forty-eight hours before the police had found his body. After his death had been reported to London another three days had elapsed before Mullinder had broken into Laura Greenwood's house. If he had been hired to recover the envelope, Ashton couldn't understand why the man who had needed his services had waited so long before acting.

'Where did you eventually hide the envelope?'

'In my handbag; it seemed the safest place. Don't ask me why, but I was convinced that what I'd found in the envelope was the reason why Adam had been murdered.' Laura frowned. 'I imagine you'll want the envelope and the bank slip it contained?'

'You're right, I do.'

Laura excused herself, went upstairs and returned a few moments later with a brown leather handbag. Opening it, she took out a bluish grey envelope and gave it to Ashton.

' "Laura – please keep this",' Ashton said, reading the message on the envelope.

'Whose signature is that?'

'Mine,' Laura told him calmly. 'And before you ask, I wrote the message as well. I guessed whoever I showed the bank slip to would ask me how it came to be in my possession.'

'I think you're in the wrong job,' Ashton told her.

'There are times when I think so too,' Laura said quietly.

252

All the way back to Vauxhall Cross Ashton kept asking himself why such an attractive and intelligent woman should ever have been drawn to Adam Zawadzki in the first place. He couldn't think of a single reason.

Jill Sheridan lifted the receiver and punched out 0028, then instantly changed her mind and hung up, something she had already done twice before. She had never been afraid to tangle with Ashton on previous occasions and her reluctance to do so now angered her. It wasn't her fault that Harriet was about to be sacked from her ten-thousand-a-year sinecure, but would he see that? Like hell. Ashton would think she had done it out of pure spite.

With the next financial year a mere sixteen days away, the Treasury had arbitrarily imposed a further one per cent cut on the SIS budget, even though the estimates had been agreed back in January. The amount of money involved had been fairly modest and most of the cut could be absorbed by delaying the start of certain works Services so that payment fell into the financial year 97/98. However, even after the housekeeping bill had been trimmed down to the bare essentials, there was still a shortfall of £100, 000 and suddenly Harriet's salary had become a significant percentage.

It had been Roy Kelso who had pointed the gun at Harriet and the case he had presented for dispensing with her services had been unanswerable. Since the end of the Cold War, the SIS had sold off half the housing stock owned by the services and rightly so. Nowadays, defectors were few and far between and The Firm still had more safe houses than they needed. So why employ a reserve housekeeper and how many times had they called on Harriet anyway? Just once in eighteen months. Jill reached for the telephone again, determined not to hang up this time before he had a chance to answer. Her resolve however was not tested; as she lifted the receiver, Ashton tapped on the door and asked if she could spare him a few minutes.

'It's important,' he added.

'Yes, of course.' She put the phone down, wondering how he knew Harriet was about to get the old heave-ho. Kelso could have told him; he would have enjoyed doing that. 'Take a chair.'

Instead of the anticipated blazing row, Jill found herself listening to what he had learned from Laura Greenwood. Before morning prayers Ashton had sought her out and related the conversation he'd had with the Assistant Head of Station, Berne. Consequently she had gone into the daily meeting knowing Osvaldo Herrara had a numbered account which recently had received an injection of 85,000 Swiss francs. The rest, however, was new to her.

'Now we come to the tricky bit,' Ashton continued. 'If Martin Edmunds hadn't been off sick, we have to assume he wouldn't have thrown that large brown envelope away. Agreed?'

'For the time being,' Jill said, reluctant to commit herself to a definite opinion just yet.

'Well, OK, be cautious. The fact is there are two things we need to know before we can take this any further. First of all, what else did the bag contain besides our Top Secret memorandum on the possibility of establishing an operational base for the SAS on the west coast of Costa Rica? Secondly, of those other documents, which was the first to be received for dispatch and who was the originator?'

'Why do you need this information, Peter?'

'I'm a great believer in the foul-up factor,' Ashton told her. 'And sometimes there is nothing you can do about it.'

Adam Zawadzki had received eighteen hours' notice when he was detailed to replace Edmunds on the Costa Rica run. Whoever had put the bank slip in the diplomatic bag would surely have retrieved the envelope had he been aware of this development.

'When did he find out?' Jill asked.

'I'm betting Zawadzki's flight to Dallas had already taken off. In the absence of any information to the contrary he had to assume the envelope was still in the diplomatic bag. So he arranged for a reception committee to meet Adam at Juan Santamaria airport. Costa Rica is six hours behind Greenwich Mean Time, which would have given him an absolute minimum of fourteen hours to set things up and I'm not being generous.'

'Contacting Herrara could have taken a lot of time.'

'I don't think so, Jill. Edmunds would need to know how to get in touch with him after he arrived in San José and there is only one person who could supply him with the necessary information.'

'All right,' Jill said, 'supposing your hypothesis is correct, why did he wait until the following Tuesday before employing Mullinder to break into the house?'

'There was a communication failure between the man and Osvaldo Herrara. The Cuban left San José for Managua the morning after the killing. He is good and mad because there is no blank slip to show he is better off by eighty-five thousand francs.'

'You can't possibly know how he felt,' Jill objected.

'Look what he did to Zawadzki and then tell me I'm wrong. As I see it, this Foreign Office man is aware Zawadzki is missing and he assumes the Cuban has the bank slip in his possession.'

On Saturday, 9 March, three days after the murder, Herrara was spotted at Mexico City's International Airport boarding an Air France plane to Paris. Ashton thought he had contacted the Foreign Office man while he was in Mexico City or on arrival in Paris.

'And then another four days pass before the burglary is committed,' Jill said derisively.

'What choice did he have? Martin Edmunds was his usual courier; he wouldn't have known where Adam Zawadzki lived even if he'd actually heard of him. When he did get the address from Edmunds, he then had to employ a burglar and he wouldn't have gone direct to Mullinder. Add time on to look the street over and discover the household routine and suddenly four days have gone before you can blink an eye.'

What they had to discover was the identity of the official or officials who had submitted papers for inclusion in the diplomatic bag before it was known Martin Edmunds was unfit for duty. In a continuing process of elimination they would then need to ascertain who had subsequently been away from his desk for more than twenty-four hours.

'That's a matter for the FCO to look at.'

'It always has been right from the beginning.' Ashton got to his feet and moved towards the door. 'But somebody has to prod them into action and I reckon you are the only one who has the necessary clout to make it happen.'

Brian Thomas was reading the vetting papers of one of the young hopefuls who would be joining the induction course in September direct from Durham University, when he heard the sound of familiar footsteps in the corridor.

'Come on in, Peter,' he said, and cheerfully laid the papers on one side.

'You must be psychic,' Ashton told him.

'Not really. Apart from Roy Kelso, whom I could do without, you're the only person who visits me. What can I do for you?'

'I came to return this,' Ashton said, and placed the fake warrant card on the desk.

'You've talked it over with Harriet then?'

'Oh, yes. Like you said, she's got more sense in her little finger than I have in my whole body. I also wanted to borrow your *Police and Constabulary Almanac*. Thought I would have a word with DI Hughes.'

'W District,' Thomas said, and handed him the Official Register for 1996. 'Has this got anything to do with Ted Mullinder?' he asked shrewdly.

'Yeah. I'm going to put in a bid to interview Mullinder when they get their hands on him.'

'You told Hughes you weren't interested in Mullinder.'

'I've changed my mind. I'd also like to see that ex-copper who really has it in for him.'

'Charlie Copeland.'

'That's the man. Any idea where he's living these days?'

'I might have,' Thomas said cautiously. 'Especially if I knew what was going on.'

'It's a belt-and-braces job,' Ashton told him. 'I want to find out who is paying Osvaldo Herrara. I've taken it as far as I can and the ball is now in Jill Sheridan's court. But as the paymaster could be in the FCO, there's a chance she might chicken out. So I'm approaching the Cuban's benefactor from a different direction.'

'I doubt if Charlie Copeland will be much help,' Thomas said. 'But for the record he lives in White Hart Lane, Wood Green. He also has an office in Station Road.'

From his window seat in the café-bar, Copeland could see the whole of the Place St-Augustin from the cathedral on the left to the entrance to the Métro station in the Rue St-Lazare to his right. The French officers' club, le Cercle National des Armées, was directly to his front on the far side of the square. Seven floors high and built in the grand classical style of the late nineteenth century, the foundation stone had actually been laid by Marshal Foch in 1921. At either end of le Cercle National des Armées there was a glass-roofed café, which jutted out on to the sidewalk. Neither establishment had anything to do with the French officers' club. The Bar Moris, where Mullinder had been told to meet him at noon, was on the corner of the Rue St-Lazare.

This was going to be a quick in-and-out job. He had caught the 06.19 Eurostar out of Waterloo, which had arrived at the Gare St-Lazare at 10.23. By 19.40 hours at the latest he would be opening the front door to his semidetached in Wood Green and the neighbours would think it had been just a normal working day for him. He'd stopped to buy a Falk's street map of Paris from the kiosk in the concourse; thereafter it had taken him a little over ten minutes to walk from the station to the Place St-Augustin. Copeland had then spent another ten minutes or so walking round the square looking for a vantage point from where he could keep the rv under surveillance. The café-bar at the junction of the Boulevard Malesherbes with the Rue La Boétie had more going for it than any other location he had seen. Mullinder would show up at the RV all right; he had no doubts on that score. But would he come alone? There was an Interpol arrest warrant out for him and if he had been picked up by the Garda in Dublin or some gendarme had felt his collar when he had arrived in Paris yesterday, Mullinder would have cut a deal with the Met. He would have told DI Hughes what he had been briefed to look for when he had burgled Lorna Greenwood's house and then produced the fake passport to back up his story. Copeland could hear him saying, 'If you don't believe me, I'll introduce you to a bent ex-copper in Paris who will be waiting for me in the Bar Moris with the equivalent of twenty-seven hundred pounds in traveller's cheques from American Express.' That was the reason why he had arrived in Paris ninety minutes before he was due to meet Mullinder. If there was a stakeout, Copeland was certain he would spot it.

He signalled the waiter to bring him another coffee and ordered a second cognac to go with it. The pale blue sky and cirrus clouds might be a portent of spring, but it was chilly out there, or so Copeland persuaded himself. And if he needed another reason for having a brandy it was the fact that he had already been nursing the last one for nearly an hour and was getting dirty looks from the proprietor. He turned to face the square again and froze because there was Mullinder large as life standing there, his back almost pressed against the window.

Copeland held his breath. Where the hell had Mullinder come from? According to the diagram on the back of the Falk map, the nearest Métro station excluding St Lazare was Havre-Caumartin on the Boulevard Haussmann. Had Mullinder used the Métro, he would have been in view as he approached the bar, whereas he'd popped out of nowhere on the Rue La Boétie. Maybe he had arrived by taxi or perhaps the police had dropped him off? Copeland just hoped Mullinder wouldn't spot him out of the corner of his eye when he decided to make his way to the Bar Moris. To get there in one piece he would have to use the pedestrian crossings on the Boulevards Malesherbes, Haussmann and the Rue St-Lazare and that meant he would turn to his right.

A few moments later Mullinder walked off without so much as a sideways glance and Copeland resumed his watch on the square. If there was a stakeout the locals were damned good at it. Of course it was possible that the *flics* were already inside the Bar Moris waiting to pounce on him when he joined Mullinder . . . The hell with it, he was worrying unnecessarily.

At four minutes to twelve Copeland left the café–bar and waited for the lights to change before crossing the Boulevard Malesherbes to join the crowd of people on the corner of Boulevard Haussmann. City dwellers always knew ahead of time when it was safe to cross and the Parisiens were no exception. As the crowd surged forward, someone behind Copeland barged into him. He stumbled, lost his balance and would have gone down if the youngish-looking man in front of him hadn't whirled round and caught him. Before he realised what was happening the Good Samaritan had snatched his wallet and was off like a hare.

Copeland went after him shouting at the top of his voice but nobody seemed inclined to stop the pickpocket. It was always going to be a one-sided contest; the thief was a good thirty years younger than himself and much fitter, but his wallet contained all his French francs, the Eurostar rail ticket and most important of all, his damned credit cards.

The pickpocket had already crossed the Rue St-Lazare and would disappear into the back streets behind the railway station if he didn't keep him in his sight.

The accident happened because Copeland looked the wrong way and thought the road was clear. The Renault 19 was doing forty kilometres an hour when it struck him. Smashed off his feet, Copeland was hurled forward and was still in the path of the oncoming Renault. Before the horrified driver could stop, Copeland's head was crushed under the front wheels and then his body was dragged along the road, leaving a bloody smear on the asphalt.

Chapter Twenty

Mullinder had just ordered a Stella Artois when somebody outside the Bar Moris gave a blood-curdling scream, the kind of inhuman wail that raised the hairs on the back of the neck. The nerve-grating shriek was accompanied by a loud bang and was followed by a few seconds of total silence, which preceded a low buzz of voices.

Mullinder left five francs on the table, which he reckoned would cover the beer he hadn't had, and walked out of the bar. He wasn't a ghoul. Naturally, if he was on the road and came across a traffic accident he would steal a sideways glance as he drove past, but he didn't shift into lower gear to have a better look. And he most certainly wasn't one of those morons who, whenever there was a major disaster, would make a special journey to gawp at the carnage.

He walked round the corner into the Rue St-Lazare where a crowd six deep had gathered on the pavement. In the distance but getting closer all the time, Mullinder could hear the repetitive blee-bla of a police car or an ambulance. Turning sideways on, he edged through the crush, steadily working his way towards the front. A few *excusez-mois* and *mon amis* with a lot of sign language persuaded the more reluctant onlookers to make room for him.

Except for the head and one arm the body was still under the car. The victim appeared to have been wearing a dark blue pinstriped jacket similar to the one Mullinder had seen on Charlie Copeland but he couldn't be sure because the sleeve was ripped and covered in dirt. The head was over to one side and although the left side of the face was in full view, the features had been crushed beyond recognition. Mullinder had never seen so much blood; it had formed a pool around the head like a halo from which a broad stream flowed into the gutter before changing direction to disappear into a drain.

The gory scene finally got to him and he could feel the bile rising into his throat. He reached, swallowed the vomit which had partially filled his mouth and then had great difficulty keeping it down. For a man who liked to think he had a strong stomach, Mullinder was showing all the symptoms of being squeamish. He was, however, not the only person to be affected; a few yards away, a smartly dressed woman with greying hair was sitting on the kerbside, her whole body trembling uncontrollably. The man crouching next to the woman had removed his anorak and draped it around her shoulders but the garment didn't appear to be having the desired effect.

A traffic cop on a motorbike beat the ambulance crew to the scene of the accident by a short head. They were followed in turn by a fire truck with lifting gear, a recovery vehicle towing a low loader and a vanload of half a dozen *gendarmes*, four of whom set about the task of untangling the traffic snarl-up. The remaining two officers, with the assistance of the traffic cop, began to disperse the crowd. Before he knew what was happening Mullinder found himself being shoved out of the way by the tallest and easily the most aggressive *gendarme* of the three.

'Watch it, just watch it,' Mullinder shouted, and was shoved even more violently in the chest. 'That's my friend under that bloody vehicle. *Mon ami – comprendez?*'

Uttering those three little words was the biggest mistake he could have made. Suddenly the *gendarme* got the message and hauled him from the crowd of onlookers to join the other witnesses who had been segregated. How could he have been such a fucking idiot? He didn't even know for sure that the dead man under the Renault was Charlie Copeland. The accident had happened a couple of minutes before twelve right outside the Bar Moris and a gut instinct had told him the ex DI had been somehow involved. Soon as he had seen the head a presentiment had automatically become an established fact in his mind without a shred of proof to support it. He should have kept his bloody mouth shut tight.

The fireman had raised the car high enough off the ground for a member of the ambulance crew to pull the victim out from under the vehicle. Mullinder noticed they already had a body bag in position and, as if handling a side of beef, two medics lifted the dead man up and laid him inside it, flat on his back. Then one of the *gendarmes* beckoned him to come over.

The dead man had suffered terrible head injuries and had bled from the nose, mouth and ears. Although the face looked as if it had been crushed in a giant press, Copeland was not so disfigured that Mullinder couldn't recognise him close up. Nevertheless, when he stepped back from the body Mullinder spread both his hands and shrugged his shoulders, hoping the *gendarme* would take it to mean that he wasn't able to identify the victim. The *gendarme* was not so easily convinced and practically ordered him to take another look.

'*Non. Il est non mon ami,*' Mullinder said in his bastardised French.

The *gendarme* finally gave up and sent him back to rejoin the other witnesses whose names and addresses were being recorded by the traffic cop in his notebook. To be included in the list was the last thing Mullinder wanted. Instead of rejoining the others, he walked boldly past them with every intention of slipping away. When the traffic cop spotted him and called out, he played the idiot Englishman who didn't understand foreigners and kept on going.

In every crowd there was always some boy scout eager to do his good deed for the day. In this instance it was the young Frenchman who had removed his anorak and draped it round the shoulders of the woman driver. It was Mullinder's bad luck that, in addition to his overdeveloped sense of civic duty, he also happened to be fluent in English.

'The officer wishes to know your name and address,' he said, catching up with Mullinder and seizing hold of his right elbow.

'Why? I didn't see anything.'

'He appears to believe you did.'

Mullinder supposed he could shake the Frenchman off and start running, but that would only make things worse. Better to give his name and the hotel where he was staying and then do a runner.

'Would you tell the officer I didn't understand what he was saying?'

'But of course.'

The Frenchman appeared to believe in never using one word when it was possible to convey the same thing in ten. At the end of a long-winded explanation he told Mullinder the officer had guessed he couldn't speak French, but still required his personal details and address of his hotel.

'My name is Arthur Henderson,' Mullinder said slowly in a loud voice while pointing to himself. 'I am English and am staying at the Hôtel Crillon, Rue Ordener.'

The traffic cop looked mystified and turned to the boy scout for enlightenment, then nodded sagely after he had repeated everything Mullinder had told him only seconds before.

'*Arrondissement?*' the traffic cop said tersely.

'What?'

'He wants to know which district the hotel is in,' the boy scout said, coming to the rescue again.

'I haven't the faintest idea,' Mullinder told him. 'Does it matter? I've told him what street it is in.'

'There is probably more than one Rue Ordener in Paris and perhaps there is another Hôtel Crillon somewhere in the city.'

'I wouldn't know. This is the first time I've been in Paris and I only arrived yesterday.'

The boy scout said that he would explain that to the traffic cop and did so at great length. Following a protracted conversation between the two men, Mullinder learned the officer wanted to see his identity card.

'I don't have one,' he said.

'You have a passport?'

'In my jacket pocket.'

'Then please give it to him, Mr Henderson.'

'Why?'

'Because all the witnesses have had to do so.'

Mullinder produced his passport and reluctantly gave it to the traffic cop.

'I still don't see why it's necessary,' he grumbled.

'Now we get into the van with the others and go to police headquarters.'

'What?'

'They want to take our statements,' the boy scout said.

The police had Mullinder's passport and knew where he had stayed the night. In short, he had run out of options, not that he had had much choice in the first place. Mullinder climbed into the van without a word of protest. One of the *gendarmes* who had been directing the traffic followed him in and closed the rear doors. Presently the driver started up, shifted into gear and moved off.

When Nancy Wilkins had reported to Ashton on Monday she had been wearing trainers, jeans and a denim jacket over a dark blue cotton shirt. This afternoon when she tapped on the door and walked into his office she appeared in knee-high boots and a brown leather suit that creaked with every step she took. Despite the change of outfit she still looked a young fourteen.

'This is the list of building sites and road works which you asked me to compile,' Nancy said, and placed an A4 ring binder containing twenty pages on his desk. 'I'm afraid there are no major projects in the areas you designated,' she added apologetically.

'That's hardly your fault, Nancy.'

'I know that but would you like me to take in the whole of London? I mean, that was the original intention.'

Ashton smiled. 'And I changed my mind because it was impractical.'

A few years ago Nancy Wilkins could have obtained all the information he'd asked for from one central authority. However, since the Greater London Council no longer existed, she would have had no alternative but to approach every borough in turn, a task that would have taken her months to accomplish.

In view of this, Ashton had decided to concentrate on a much smaller area. On a large-scale Ordnance Survey map he had drawn two overlapping circles centred on Kilburn and Maida Vale where Michael Ryan had been employed by the London Electricity Board. He had then described a third circle based on the location of Ryan's semidetached house in Neasden. The radius of each circle equated to three miles on the ground. This distance had been chosen on the assumption that, if Ryan had been abducted by the IRA, they would have lifted him either from the workplace or from somewhere in and around Neasden.

'I appreciate you didn't tell me to do so, Mr Ashton, but I've also listed condemned housing stock and properties which have been acquired for redevelopment.'

'That's good thinking, Nancy.'

'I don't know about that,' Nancy said cheerfully, 'but it certainly made the list appear a lot fatter.'

'You're being too modest,' Ashton told her as she left the office.

He opened the ring binder and unfolded the map she had included as an appendix. The two overlapping circles embraced Wormwood Scrubs, Golders Green, Church End, Hampstead Heath, Kentish Town, parts of Holloway, Regent's Park, Hyde Park, Bayswater, Notting Hill, Holland Park and Kensington. The third circle included Ravenscourt Park within its circumference. The road works, building sites, condemned housing stock and properties acquired for redevelopment had been grouped under the appropriate borough, numbered consecutively and then annotated on the map for ease of reference. It was, Ashton thought, a work of art. But that was all it would ever be unless he had some idea where to start looking for a grave. He looked up Francesca York's extension at Gower Street in his personal telephone directory and punched out her number.

'It's me – Peter Ashton,' he said when she answered.

'Well, hello, Peter, and how are you today?'

'Fine,' he said brusquely, 'and you?'

'Oh, I'm on good form.'

Try as he might to ignore it, her plummy voice always set his teeth on edge. Why Francesca York pretended to be something she wasn't with him was beyond his comprehension. Whenever she was in trouble her phoney accent immediately disappeared. He had been there when she had dropped the mask.

'What can I do for you, Peter?'

'I think we had better go to secure.'

'Better safe than sorry,' Francesca said and laughed, then added, 'Switching now.'

Ashton did the same, checked to make sure they were both crypto-protected, then reminded her of their conversation a few days ago when she had told him Michael Ryan hadn't been seen since Tuesday, 12 March.

'What about it?' she asked.

'Was he missed in the morning or afternoon?'

'He didn't sign off at the end of the day, just phoned in at five thirty. Apparently he often did this, much to the annoyance of his supervisor, who'd taken him to task more than once about it. I mean, nobody had any idea where he was calling from. For all the supervisor knew he could have been at home with his feet up. Anyway, that's all I can tell you about the day he disappeared. Naturally, the police are still looking for Michael.'

'Are we talking uniform or Special Branch?'

'Well, he is just one more missing person so far as plod is concerned.'

That meant the uniform branch was unaware of Ryan's involvement with MI5.

'That property developer Ryan was cultivating – is he still under surveillance?'

'Yes, but what has this—'

'And how about Kevin Hayes?' Ashton said, talking her down. 'Barry's little brother who's living in Lewisham with his English wife? Is Special Branch keeping an eye on him too?'

'Now look here—' Francesca said heatedly.

'Yes or no?'

'Yes, but not for much longer because Special Branch is overstretched. Besides, whatever older brother might have done, Kevin is a decent, hard-working man. He's never had anything to do with the Provisional IRA or any of its factions.'

'So why are you watching him?'

'It was a routine precaution once we learned Barry Hayes was better known to the Security Forces as Brian Ahearne.'

'Thanks. You've filled in a lot of blank spaces.'

'Don't hang up,' Francesca said sharply, the plummy voice suddenly replaced by a less refined accent which sociologists were apt to describe as Thames Estuary.

'I wasn't about to,' Ashton told her.

'Good. In case you have forgotten, Mr Ashton, let me remind you—'

'You've been warned off Barry Hayes,' Ashton said, finishing the sentence for her. 'And you needn't worry. As I said the last time we had this conversation, I wouldn't even know where to find him. Anyway, it's my job to run down Herrara.'

'He's no longer in this country.'

'When did you hear this?'

'There have been lots of unconfirmed reports,' Francesca said defensively. 'Various Immigration officers, as far apart as Newcastle upon Tyne to Eastleigh Airport near Southampton thought his face looked familiar when shown his photograph, but nobody was prepared to swear they remembered him. Until this morning, that is.'

'Where and when was Herrara spotted?'

'At Immingham the day after the incident on the Warlock Estate. He boarded a ro-ro ferry to Amsterdam as a foot passenger.'

The Immigration officer who had identified him had taken six days off and had flown to St Louis to be the best man at his brother's wedding. He had departed before Herrara had been placed on the wanted list and had only seen the Cuban's photograph when he had returned to duty that morning.

'Well, thanks for telling me, Fran.'

'I was about to ring you.'

'I know you were,' he said, and hung up.

Ashton looked at the map again with a fresh eye. They had lifted Ryan from the workplace and had forced him to phone the office to let the supervisor know he had finished for the day. He didn't have the faintest idea why the IRA should have kidnapped the poor bastard the day before the bombing and he wasn't going to waste his time dreaming up a reason. The fact was, Ryan had been held in one place and executed in another. That was standard operating procedure with the Provisionals and he should know. He had watched it happen from the bedroom of a semidetached in Waverley Crescent on the periphery of Catholic West Belfast.

A black taxi had drawn up opposite the alleyway between his place and the house beyond it. Three men and a woman had got out of the cab; two of the men had been masked, the other had his wrists tied behind his back and had to be supported because his legs kept buckling under him. The woman's hands had also been lashed together behind her back but somehow she had broken free and had run off down the road screaming for help. The taxi driver had leaped out of the cab and had caught up with her in a matter of a few yards. The shithead had dragged her back to the alleyway, kicking and screaming, and Ashton had wanted to go out there and blow them away with his twelve-shot Browning High Power 9mm semiautomatic but Corporal Sally Drew of the army's Special Patrol Unit had stopped him.

She had persuaded him that if he intervened their cover would be blown, and seven months of hard and dangerous graft would go down the drain. So he had radioed for help while the IRA men had hooded their victims and executed them in cold blood. And two months later, when they had finished their tour of duty with the Special Patrol Unit, Ashton had contacted the Royal Ulster Constabulary to find out what he could about the victims. 'A couple of paid informers,' a hard nose in Special Branch had told him. 'And yes, the IRA had given them the electric shock treatment with electrodes shoved into every bodily orifice – ears, nose, mouth, penis, rectum, vagina'. The 10 February 1980, a date which Ashton would never forget. Nobody had been charged with their murder or was ever likely to be apprehended. Well, this time round it was going to be different; this time round somebody would pay for what they had done. He focused on the map and tried to put himself in the shoes of the man who had lifted Michael Ryan.

The interview room was furnished on Spartan lines – one table, two chairs and a tin ashtray. Mullinder had no idea whereabouts in Paris he was being held and nobody had bothered to enlighten him. All he knew was that over an hour had gone by since the van had been driven into a closed courtyard and he had been conducted to this room. He had no complaints about the way he had been treated by the police. With the boy scout acting as an interpreter he had been asked to write his account of the accident on the official form they had provided and had then brought him a cup of coffee. The statement he had printed in block capitals was a model of brevity. It read: 'I WAS DRINKING IN THE BAR MORIS AND DIDN'T SEE THE ACCIDENT. I TOLD ONE OF THE POLICEMAN I THOUGHT THE VICTIM MIGHT BE THE FRIEND I WAS WAITING FOR BUT I DIDN'T RECOGNISE THE DEAD MAN WHEN I WAS SHOWN THE BODY.'

Nobody seemed in a hurry to collect the statement but that

didn't bother Mullinder. The longer they left it, the more time he had to figure out what he was going to do. There had always been little chance the authorities would believe he had been hired to burgle the house in St John's Avenue; with Copeland dead that faint possibility had ceased to exist. He had gone to Dublin with eight hundred pounds and a few pieces of jewellery in his pocket. The rings and emerald brooch had been worth at least three grand but the fence he had done business with had only been prepared to give him twelve hundred for the lot.

Eight nights at the crummy Mannix Hotel on Harbour Quay Road had cost him six hundred quid for room only and he had spent another sixty-odd on food and drink. Deduct the return air fare to Paris, one night at the Hôtel Crillon plus incidentals, and despite the injection of traveller's cheques he'd received from Copeland before leaving Dublin, he was down to under fourteen hundred. How long would that keep a roof over his head and food in his belly? Not long enough was the short answer. Maybe he should take Charlie Copeland's advice and head for Spain? Lots of ex-pats on the Costa del Sol, some of them good old London boys who might cut him in on a piece of the action? It was worth thinking about, especially when the alternative was a seven-to-ten stretch in one of Her Majesty's prisons.

The man who walked into the interview room was no more than five feet seven, had broad shoulders, and weighed between a hundred and eighty and one ninety pounds, all of it muscle. His face was notable for a misshapen nose and a bulging forehead that was made more obvious by a retreating hairline. He was, Mullinder learned, the Precinct Traffic Officer and had recently spent a year with the Met's Stolen Motor Vehicle Investigation branch, which had enabled him to brush up his English.

'Is this your statement, Mr Henderson?' he asked, and turned the form round to read it. 'Very short and sweet, isn't it?'

'Well, I didn't actually see the accident.'

'So you said. What's the name of this friend you were waiting for?'

Mullinder didn't hesitate. If he plucked a name out of the air he would be asked where his friend was staying in Paris. And the Precinct Traffic Officer didn't strike him as the sort of man who would take anything on trust.

'Charlie Copeland,' he said.

The Frenchman took out a passport and folded the back cover to reveal a head-and-shoulders photograph. 'You mean this man?'

'Yes. I didn't recognise him because of the facial injuries.'

'We found four thousand two hundred US dollars in American Express traveller's cheques in his possession. None of them had been signed. I assume they rightly belonged to Mr Copeland?'

'I would think so,' Mullinder said.

'The traveller's cheques were in a white plastic envelope which we found in the right breast pocket of his jacket together with his passport. There was nothing in the other pocket.'

'Is that significant?'

'It is if you are right-handed. Two of the witnesses said he was chasing a man and shouting very loudly.'

'Like, "Stop thief"?' Mullinder suggested.

'Probably. Other than the traveller's cheques and three francs in loose change he didn't have any money on him. No travel documents either. Do you know when he arrived in Paris, Mr Henderson?'

'This morning.'

'And you only arrived yesterday?'

'Yes.' A raised eyebrow told Mullinder some sort of explanation was called for. 'Charlie rang me at home on Monday and we arranged to meet for a drink when he arrived.'

'I understand you told one of the *gendarmes* that this is the first time you have been to Paris?'

He had the bloody boy scout to thank for that. The ever-so-obliging Frog had translated every fucking word he'd said.

'Charlie has been here before,' Mullinder said quickly. 'He told me how to find the Bar Moris.'

'Was your friend married?'

What the hell was going on? The Precinct Traffic Officer was acting like he was in charge of a murder investigation.

'Whoever is the next of kin will be entitled to the traveller's cheques, Mr Henderson.'

'Charlie was divorced,' Mullinder told him truthfully. 'Last I heard of his ex she was living somewhere in Croydon.'

'Did he have a partner?'

'No. Like the saying goes, once bitten twice shy.'

'No matter. It will be up to the British Consular Officer to trace and inform the next of kin. However, he will have to know Mr Copeland's home address before he can do anything.'

The Frenchman was looking at him expectantly and that was the trouble because Mullinder had no idea where Copeland had lived. All he knew was the phone number and address of his poky little shop in Station Road.

'It's 187 Beechwood Avenue, Wood Green, London,' he said.

'And how long will you be staying in Paris? Just in case the British Consular Officer should require more information.'

'Another three or four days,' Mullinder said, and wondered how many more lies he would have to tell before the Frenchman was satisfied.

'In that case, I think I had better give him your home address as well.'

'That's 135 Cromwell Road, Barking,' Mullinder said, having memorised the address in the false passport.

'Thank you, Mr Henderson. You have been most helpful.'

'You mean I'm free to go?'

'But of course.'

'Thanks.'

Mullinder got to his feet and was halfway to the door when the Frenchman called him back.

'You'll need your passport, Mr Henderson.'

'Right.' Mullinder laughed. 'I must be getting absent-minded in my old age.'

His heart did not stop pounding until he was outside on the street and even then Mullinder did not feel safe. It was hard to shake off the feeling that the net was closing in on him. And the longer he was on the run, the worse it would eventually be for him, but what could he do about it? Mullinder suddenly stopped dead. He still had the three traveller's cheques Copeland had sent him and there was a fair chance the serial numbers would link with some of those found on his dead body. He also had the fake passport and the serial number on that might be traceable back to Copeland. They didn't represent the strongest evidence in the world but to a degree they would substantiate his story. All things considered it would do his case no harm if he walked into the British Consulate and gave himself up.

Most people like to clear their desks on a Friday so that they don't return to work on the Monday to be confronted with already overcrowded in and pending trays. Will Landon was no exception; at half-past five he tapped on Ashton's door and asked if he could spare him a few minutes.

'Of course I can, I was about to ring you anyway.' Ashton eyed the file he was carrying, which appeared to be full of newspaper clippings. 'What have you got there?' he asked.

'Some quite interesting stuff on Osvaldo Herrara but it doesn't lead us anywhere.'

'Herrara has left the country, Will.'

'Does that mean we can forget him?'

'No, it just means we have to look further afield. Have you finished with the Russian Desk?'

'Yeah, much to Rowan Garfield's relief.'

'I bet. What are you doing over the weekend?'

'I've got nothing planned,' Landon told him.

'Well, you have now,' Ashton said. 'Leave that file in my in-tray and pull up a chair.'

'Right.'

'I'm looking for a freshly dug grave, Will.'

'Sounds intriguing.'

'I'm glad you think so.' Ashton extracted the large-scale map from the ring binder and unfolded it. 'This was produced by Nancy Wilkins,' he continued. 'It shows the location of road works, building sites, condemned housing stock and empty buildings acquired for redevelopment. I'd like you to take a look at the properties in Kentish Town and on the fringe of Holloway.'

Chapter Twenty-One

The bottle of champagne was something of a compromise. A dozen red roses would have been more appropriate; unfortunately Vauxhall Cross was not awash with florists and the one in King Street had been closed for some time when Ashton alighted from the District Line train at Ravenscourt Park. Had Harriet been fond of chocolate he could have bought her a large box of Terry's Old Gold from the mini market near the station but she was allergic to anything manufactured from cocoa beans. So he had dropped into the off-licence in King Street on his way home and bought a bottle of Moët & Chandon.

'It's not my birthday,' Harriet said, eyeing the bottle of champagne when he walked into the kitchen.

'Right.'

'And it's not our anniversary either.'

'Right again.'

'A peace offering then?'

Ashton could understand why Harriet should think that. In briefing Will Landon he had lost all account of time and had been taken aback when she had telephoned to ask when he was thinking of coming home. She had had a bad day, Edward was sickening for something and had been fractious. Furthermore their GP hadn't helped by telling her she was worrying unnecessarily and wasting everybody's time.

'You're right, I should have brought you a peace offering.'

'So what's the champagne for?'

'To celebrate your homecoming,' he said.

'But that was yesterday.'

'Better late than never.'

Harriet had returned from Lincoln vowing that should the latest housekeeper give in her notice, it would be up to her brother, Richard, to find a replacement. Ashton hoped she meant it but when push came to shove he suspected Harriet would put her father first. And who could blame her if she did? There must have been times when Harriet had felt neglected and thought Ashton put the job before her. Like tonight, for instance, when he hadn't got home until gone eight.

Ashton went upstairs, looked in on his son, who was sleeping fitfully, then stripped off and took a quick shower before changing into something more casual. He needed to put Harriet first for a change. Maybe he had dropped everything and driven her up to Lincoln when her mother had committed suicide but what man would have let his wife deal with that situation on her own? Anyway, he had just reacted to events, he hadn't shaped them. Ashton finished changing, shoved his feet into a pair of slip-on shoes and went downstairs.

'I'm in the sitting room,' Harriet called out when she heard his footsteps in the hall. 'There's a casserole in the oven if you feel like eating.'

'I'll get it later.' Ashton wandered into the sitting room and plonked himself down on the sofa next to Harriet. 'I've been thinking. How do you feel about going away for Easter? Somewhere in the sun: Tunisia, Morocco or Florida? We could do with a break. I mean, we didn't even have a proper honeymoon.'

'Good Friday is only a fortnight away, we could never get a booking.'

'The spring bank holiday then?'

'You shouldn't make promises you won't keep.'

'I'll keep this one.'

'You may say that now but something always crops up. Like that damned telephone.'

'Let it ring,' Ashton told her.

'Don't be silly. Whoever it is will go on calling until they get a reply.'

Harriet lifted the receiver, answered up and then handed over the phone.

'Jill Sheridan for you,' she said.

'Mullinder's in Paris,' Jill told him as soon as he came on the line. 'He surrendered himself to the British Consular Officer this afternoon. There's a flight leaving at 21.00—'

'Forget it, I'm not—'

'A car is on the way to pick you up.'

'Then you had better contact the driver and recall him because I'm not going anywhere tonight.'

While he was pretty good at talking people down when it suited his purpose, Jill was even better at it. She had a dozen reasons why he should drop everything and get himself over to Paris a.s.a.p. and none of them really stood up to examination. Jill even tried to convince him that if Mullinder was left to cool his heels overnight there was every chance he would have second thoughts and go walkabout.

'Oh come on,' Ashton said, you can do better than that, Jill. Face it, the only way Mullinder can escape a long prison sentence is to prove somebody in the FCO employed him to burgle Laura Greenwood's house. Besides, you've just told me the Consular Officer is holding the two passports which Mullinder had in his possession. How far do you think he will get without them?'

'You are refusing to go, is that it?'

Jill's voice was ice cold and threatening. Ashton could picture her, tight-lipped with anger, the knuckles of her right hand turning white as she clenched the phone in a grip of iron. He also fancied he knew what was passing through her mind. She was the Deputy Director General of the SIS, and a Grade I Intelligence Officer was defying her authority.

'You've got it wrong,' he said, 'I'm leaving first thing in the morning.'

'The time is now eight thirty-seven. You've got exactly twenty-three minutes in hand.'

'Well, the driver isn't here yet and even if he was, we would never make it to Heathrow in time. And we know British Airways won't delay their last flight to Paris on your say-so.' Ashton paused, temporarily arrested by the doorbell, then said, 'Seems the driver has arrived, better hang on while I have a word with him.'

He put the phone down, went out into the hall and answered the door. The duty driver was only a touch surprised to learn he was no longer required. A last-minute change of plan was hardly a new experience for somebody who had spent twelve years with The Firm. To have her plans thwarted was, however, a comparatively new experience for Jill Sheridan.

'You may think you've got away with it,' she told him grimly, 'but, believe me, you haven't heard the last of this.'

'Well, if that's the way it's going to be, I hope you're fireproof.'

'Are you threatening me?'

'No, I'm merely wondering if the police are happy with the arrangement.'

'What are you talking about?'

'The police have got an international arrest warrant out for Mullinder. I don't think they will take it kindly if we squirrel him away.'

'We won't be doing anything of the kind. In fact, the Met will have every reason to be grateful. How long do you suppose it would take them to complete the whole extradition process? This way, DI Hughes will be able to question Mullinder to his heart's content within a day or two instead of weeks from now.'

Ashton was about to ask her if Hughes was aware of his good fortune but she had already hung up.

'I hope you know what you're doing,' Harriet said quietly.

'So do I.'

Ashton lifted the receiver, tapped out the number for Vauxhall Cross and asked the switchboard operator to connect him with the duty clerk of central registry. The irrepressible Nancy Wilkins took the call and asked how she could be of assistance.

'Who's with you?' Ashton enquired, aware that she was still a probationer and had had somebody to hold her hand the last time she had been on night duty.

'Nobody,' Nancy assured him. 'The Chief Archivist reckons I'm capable of fouling things up on my own now.'

'Well, let's see what you can do to solve this problem. I need to be in Paris early tomorrow but I don't want to leave before six thirty a.m. Allow for two hours in Paris from time of arrival and then book two seats on the first available flight to Heathrow or Eurostar to Waterloo, whichever is the earlier departure. I also want you to find out the home telephone number of DI Hughes. He's with W District. Have you got all that?'

'Yes, would you like me to read it back?'

'No just ring me if you have any difficulty,' Ashton said, and replaced the phone, then faced Harriet again. 'Tunisia, Morocco or Florida – what's it to be?'

'We can't afford to go away.'

'Nonsense, of course we can.'

Harriet gazed at him blankly. 'You obviously haven't been told.'

'Told what?'

Harriet got to her feet and left the room. A few moments later she returned with an official-looking envelope which she dropped into his lap. The letter it contained had been signed by Victor Hazelwood who regretted to inform Harriet that due to swingeing cuts imposed by the Treasury, it had been necessary to dispense with her services. She was, however, to receive three months' salary in lieu of notice.

'Victor didn't have the courtesy to tell you, did he?'

'I work for Jill Sheridan.'

'Are you trying to shift the blame on to her shoulders?'

'No, but the fact is Victor would have signed whatever was put in front of him.'

'I might have known you would go out of your way to defend him. When are you going to realise that your loyalty is misplaced?'

It was a familiar assertion and one that Ashton was slowly coming to accept.

As the Deputy DG Jill Sheridan was automatically the chairman of the establishments committee. As such, it was her job to implement whatever cuts were imposed by The Treasury. However, her proposals for achieving the necessary reductions would have to be approved by Hazelwood before they could be effected. Considering how close their relationship had been when he had been the number two man on the Russian Desk, he reckoned Victor should have had a quiet word with him.

'Maybe I can get the decision reversed?'

'Don't do it on my account, Peter.' Harriet smiled. 'I've been expecting this to happen for a long time. I mean, let's face it, why should the SIS pay me ten thousand a year for doing nothing? I've always felt guilty about it.'

'I didn't know you felt like that.'

'You never asked.'

'Well, I've got the message now and we can manage without your salary.'

Ashton placed a couple of fingers under her chin and gently raised her mouth to his. 'We can also manage a holiday,' he added, and kissed her.

'In that case maybe we should have a little celebration and open the champagne?'

'Good idea. What have you done with the Moët et Chandon?'

'It's in the fridge,' Harriet told him. 'And let's not waste the casserole.'

'Even money Nancy Wilkins phones me while we're still eating.'

Ashton was wrong about that. As if blessed with extra sensory perception, Nancy waited until they had finished dinner before breaking the news that she had got him a seat on British Airways flight 304 departing Heathrow at 07.15, arriving Paris 09.20 local time. He was travelling first class on the outward journey because business and economy were fully booked. There were business-class seats available on all return flights but nothing else. With one cancellation already on his hands for which there was no rebate, Roy Kelso had put his foot down and refused to sanction the expenditure. He had also refused her permission to use Air France on the grounds that it was government policy to 'fly the flag'. She had therefore reserved two seats on Eurostar and had arranged for a car to pick Ashton up from Waterloo at 18.15. Finally, Nancy gave him both the office and home numbers of DI Hughes.

Ashton thanked her, broke the connection and then rang Jill Sheridan to let her know what had been arranged. It was only then that he learned he was expected to deliver Mullinder to the SIS Training School at Amberley Lodge near Petersfield.

Mehmet Ozbek opened both eyes and lay there in the dark, straining to catch the slightest sound. Maybe it was all in the mind but Ozbek thought he'd heard a vehicle moving slowly along the alleyway behind the dry goods store. The luminous hands on the cheap alarm clock were showing a few minutes after four, which was too early for it to have been a delivery truck.

For a whole week now he hadn't dared to leave the flat and the claustrophobic atmosphere was beginning to get to him. From his front room overlooking Henning Road he had watched a couple of policemen working the street, handing out leaflets. Even before the owner of the dry goods store had shown him a copy, he had guessed they were looking for him. The door-to-door enquiries had been made on Wednesday morning and now, over forty-eight hours later, they still hadn't come for him. Since the leaflet had carried a photograph of him as well as a very accurate sketch, Ozbek thought it was nothing less than miraculous that he was still at liberty.

How much longer that would last depended on how soon a reward was offered for information leading to his arrest. The Kurdish owner of the dry goods store had recognised him as the man on the wanted poster and was currently charging him ten pounds a day for his silence. He would become vocal when the money was right.

Ozbek got out of bed and tiptoed over to the window. He pressed his left cheek against the wall, then slid his right hand between the curtain and the window to create a narrow observation slit. There were no streetlights in the alleyway and the moon had set, which, taken in conjunction, restricted visibility to a mere sixty feet. Within that distance the lane appeared to be deserted. He moved across to the other end of the window and repeated the drill, this time looking to the left. Nothing, absolutely nothing to be seen. It was definitely all in the mind. Suddenly in need of a pee, he went into the bathroom.

Ozbek had heard nothing more from Merih Soysal at the Turkish Embassy since she had phoned a week ago yesterday but that didn't alarm him. She was simply following orders, severing all contact in order to protect herself.

It worked both ways. The Embassy Security Officer was no fool and he would have soon realised that Hasan Ünver had been the intended target. He would also conclude that the terrorists, as the English press had already labelled them, must have had inside information. As Hasan's PA, Merih Soysal would automatically be a prime suspect. Her phone would be tapped, her quarters in the embassy compound would be bugged and she would be followed everywhere. Consequently he was only too happy for Merih Soysal to keep her distance.

Ozbek flushed the toilet, returned to the small back room and crawled into bed. Sleep enveloped him almost immediately. Some time later there was a deafening explosion and suddenly

284

the bedroom was full of armed men, screaming and shouting at him: 'Hands clasped together on top of your head', 'Face the wall', 'Lie down on the floor', 'On your belly', 'Move, move, move'. With four Heckler and Koch sub-machine-guns trained on him, did they really think he was going to defy them?

'Don't shoot. Don't shoot.'

Ozbek scrambled out of bed, turned his back on the armed policemen and sank down on his knees, which was no easy task with both hands clasped on top of his head. Somebody planted a foot between his shoulder blades, and pushed him down face flat on the carpet. While he was still pinned down, a second police officer grabbed his wrists one at a time and handcuffed them behind his back. Then they yanked him up and shoved his feet into a pair of slip-on shoes.

A fifth police officer entered the room and started to go through his clothes that were hanging up in the wardrobe, before searching the chest of drawers. The shouting began again when he turned over the pillow and found a bayonet with a serrated cutting edge.

Ozbek was scared witless and couldn't stop trembling; every infidel had the index finger of the right hand curled round the trigger and he could see himself being shot to pieces if he so much as cleared his throat. The fifth officer threw a blanket over his head and, still in his underpants, he was hustled out of the flat and on down the concrete staircase into the waiting police van.

'Where are you taking me?' he asked in a trembling voice but no one would tell him.

Paddington Green was unique. Built like a fortress, it was quite unlike any other police station in the Metropolitan area. Guarded by heavily armed sentries, it was the place where terrorists of every persuasion were held while under interrogation. Security was tight: although she was expected and could prove her identity, Francesca York was still subjected to routine screening and the usual body search before she was shown into a spare interview room where Richard Neagle was waiting for her.

That Mehmet Ozbek had been arrested some four hours ago was no surprise to either of them. Late yesterday afternoon they had learned from Special Branch that, following the offer of a £5,000 reward from British Petroleum, the Kurdish owner of a dry goods store in Tottenham had positively identified Ozbek. They had also been told exactly when officers of the Anti-terrorist Squad would raid the flat and had subsequently discussed at length how they should conduct their interrogation after the police had finished with Ozbek. However, this didn't stop Neagle from reiterating everything he had said to her yesterday evening.

'Do we know how the interview is going?' Francesca asked when he'd finally run out of things to say.

'Not very well; Ozbek won't even admit to his own name.' Neagle shrugged.

'I can't think why the police don't go ahead and charge him. Why do they need a statement from Ozbek when they've got enough forensic evidence to put him away for a very long time?'

'Perhaps they want to know why he had wanted to kill Hasan Ünver?'

'They should leave such questions to the professionals. After all, that's what we're here for.'

'I assume we still haven't had any feedback from the Turkish authorities.'

'I would have told you if we had.'

Francesca opened her handbag, took out a packet of cigarettes and lit one. For some unknown reason Richard Neagle had obviously got out of bed on the wrong side this morning but he had no cause to bite her head off. It was, after all, a perfectly reasonable question. Ünver's PA, Merih Soysal, had been recalled to Ankara exactly a week ago. She had been booked on Turkish Airlines flight TK982 departing for Istanbul at 22.40 and had been escorted to Heathrow by the Embassy Security Officer and his deputy who was to accompany her all the way to the final destination. On arrival at Terminal 3 Merih Soysal and the Embassy Security Officer had been taken to a detention room which the Immigration Service had set aside for their use. Everything had been going smoothly but as they walked through the concourse, Merih Soysal had created a scene. Rounding on her escort, she had kicked him on the shin and tried to run away. Although she had been quickly recaptured, everybody within the immediate vicinity of the incident had heard her demands for political asylum. The way Francesca interpreted it, Merih Soysal had been scared stiff by the thought of what was likely to happen to her when she finally arrived in Ankara. Either the Turkish authorities were withholding the information they'd got from her or else she had suddenly acquired a backbone of steel.

'I'll find out what is happening,' Neagle said, and left the room. A few minutes later he returned to announce they were on.

Francesca stubbed out her cigarette and followed him down the corridor into another interview room two doors further on. Mehmet Ozbek looked older than she remembered him from her first sighting on the Warlock Estate. He hadn't been allowed to shave and the stubble on his face was more grey than dark. He hadn't washed either and she found the sour smell of his body odour nauseating.

'My name is Neagle,' Richard announced. 'I'm from the Home Office, so is my colleague, Miss York.'

There was no reaction from Ozbek. He merely sat there across the table from them, hands on knees, his eyes dead as if in a trance.

'There are a number of questions we'd like you to answer,' Neagle said in a surprisingly affable voice. 'The first concerns Mr Hasan Ünver, your intended victim. Who decided he had to die? You or Miss Soysal?' Neagle paused and waited expectantly. When Ozbek remained silent, he began to spell out exactly what the future held for the Turkish dissident. 'You've murdered eleven people – Detective Constable Browne and two others on the Warlock Estate, Keith and Amanda French of The White House near Duddleswell, an elderly couple out walking their dog in Ashdown Forest, and four teenagers at the Devil's Punch Bowl. You will be given eleven life sentences and the judge will undoubtedly recommend that in your case, life should definitely mean life. You will not, however, spend the rest of your days in this country. For administrative reasons you will be transferred to your native country where you will find conditions in a Turkish prison vastly different. Of course if you choose to be co-operative, it won't come to that, will it, Miss York?'

'Indeed it won't,' Francesca said, responding to Neagle's obvious cue.

'I'm sure the Home Secretary will decide Mr Ozbek should serve out his sentence in the UK. And who knows, with good behaviour he may be eligible for parole in twenty years' time?'

There was still no reaction, which led Francesca to believe that Ozbek had received special training in resistance to inter-rogation.

'I think we should leave Mr Ozbek in peace for a while,' Neagle observed quietly. 'He needs to consider his position.'

The plane had taken off on time, the French air traffic controllers weren't on strike, the weather was good and no aircraft were stacked up waiting their turn to land at Charles de Gaulle. Consequently British Airways flight 304 arrived five minutes ahead of schedule. On the one previous occasion when Ashton had been to Paris nobody had met him at the airport. This time round Head of Station had sent the junior Intelligence Officer who was shown as a third secretary on the embassy staff list. The junior IO, who invited Ashton to call him Roland, was the proud owner of a year-old Vauxhall Calibra.

'Have you met this Ted Mullinder?' Roland enquired.

'No, that pleasure is to come,' Ashton told him.

'You'll find he's a very dodgy character. Goes around telling all and sundry that he works for the SIS. Head of Station is hopping mad.'

'I bet he is,' Ashton said.

'The Ambassador isn't at all happy either. I mean, until London reacted we all thought Mullinder was a sort of mentally challenged person.' Roland frowned. 'The only reason why the consular officer didn't send him packing was the fact that he had two passports in his possession.'

Once the consular officer had learned that Mullinder had come to the notice of the French authorities, he had passed him on to Head of Station in the blink of an eye. The Ambassador had been equally quick to make it clear that Mullinder would not be welcome at 35 Rue du Faubourg St-Honoré.

'So where is he now?'

'At my apartment,' Roland said, 'and I can tell you my wife is not best pleased. After all, it isn't as if HM is contributing towards the rent.'

Roland would be twenty-four in August and had been recruited direct from Essex University where he had been reading Modern Languages. Paris was his first foreign posting and the fact that he had married a matter of a few weeks before he was due to take up his appointment had not endeared him to either the SIS or the FCO. Mrs Roland was five years older than himself and a freelance PR agent.

'And a highly successful one too,' Roland added.

They came in on the A3 from the airport and entered Paris via the Porte de Bagnolet. Nothing looked familiar to Ashton and he didn't get his bearings until they reached the Place de la Republique where, for some unaccountable reason, he and Jill Sheridan had fetched up when they had been celebrating their engagement.

Roland hadn't been exaggerating when he had claimed his wife, Elaine, was doing extremely well in the PR business. The apartment they were renting was in the Rue de Rivoli opposite the Jardin des Tuileries. It was, Ashton thought, like having a flat in Park Lane.

Before leaving for the airport, Roland had summoned Head of Station's resident clerk to keep an eye on his unwanted guest. It was a sensible precaution. Mrs Roland was the sort of glamorous, sexy-looking woman who would attract men like wasps to a honeypot, and Mullinder struck Ashton as the type to fancy his chances. Ashton disliked him on sight.

'I hear you've got a loose tongue,' he said. 'So now is the chance to get everything off your chest because once we get on the train to London, I want your mouth zipped tight.'

Mullinder didn't need a second invitation.

Chapter Twenty-Two

It didn't take Ashton long to discover that Mullinder's one great passion in life was football. He was an Arsenal fan, as his father had been before him, and he had started going to Highbury on his own at the age of nine when Kennedy, Graham and Charlie George were playing. He talked knowledgeably about the Compton brothers, Dennis on the wing, elder brother Leslie at centre half, in which position some of the sports columnists had described him as a third back. He spoke of Forbes, a fiery wing half and forwards like Logie, Ronnie Rooke, Vallance, Goring and Lewis. Players from the late forties to early fifties long before his time and probably his father's too. He had started the discourse when they had boarded the train at the Gare St-Lazare and he was still holding forth after they had passed through Ashford and were on the last lap.

Ashton had developed listening without actually taking anything in to a fine art. A few appropriate exclamations every now and then kept Her Majesty's burglar happy as Larry. While Mullinder prattled on recalling salad days at Highbury, Ashton's mind was elsewhere, trying to figure out how he could alert DI Hughes without putting his own neck on the chopping block. Had Mullinder been treated like a suspected terrorist, he could have tipped off the DI and told Jill Sheridan he'd simply used his initiative on the assumption that the prisoner would be taken to Paddington Green for questioning. Unfortunately at the last minute, he had been instructed to convey Mullinder to Amberley Lodge. The fact was he would be in trouble whatever he did: with Jill if he tipped off Hughes; with the DI if he followed her instructions to the letter. On the whole he preferred to stay on the right side of the police.

'I won't be a minute,' he told Mullinder. 'Got to see a man about a dog.'

Ashton got up, brushed past the burglar and made his way to the lavatories. Finding one that was vacant, he locked the door, took out his mobile and called Hughes on his home number. The number rang out for some time before a woman answered the phone.

'Mrs Hughes?' he asked.

'Yes, who's calling?'

'My name is Peter Ashton—'

'We've already had double glazing fitted.'

'I'm not selling anything, this is police business. I need to get in touch with your husband.'

'He's not at home; you'd better try the divisional station at Putney. Do you have the number?'

Ashton said he did, apologised for bothering her late on Saturday afternoon and signed off. He tried to get straight through to Hughes but the call was diverted to the CID sergeant.

'Where's your DI?' he asked.

'And your name, sir?'

'Ashton, Peter Ashton.'

'I don't think I know you, sir. How can I be of assistance?'

'You can get in touch with your guvnor and tell him I've got Mullinder in tow. We're on the Eurostar arriving at Waterloo at 18.15 hours.'

'Mullinder,' the duty sergeant repeated in a puzzled tone of voice which suggested he wasn't familiar with the name.

'The son of a bitch who broke into 104 St John's Avenue and killed Tracy Beckingham. Now stop play-acting and get your bloody finger out.'

Ashton broke the connection, telescoped the aerial and returned to his seat. If Hughes didn't make it to the station in time it would be just too bad; he had done the best he could for him.

'Feeling better now?' Mullinder asked him with a smirk.

'I soon will be,' Ashton said, and left him to work that one out for himself.

Another ten minutes, fifteen at the outside, and the train would pull in to Waterloo International. So, OK, he had been instructed to escort Mullinder to the training school but The Firm was sending a car to meet him and nobody had said he had to ride in the back with Mullinder, especially when the vehicle in question would be one of the high-security Ford Granadas. Once the driver tripped the locks, there was no way Mullinder could open either rear door from inside the car.

That meant Ashton could sit up front with the driver where he wouldn't be subjected to lengthy extracts from the *Guinness Book of Records*, most of them concerning football in general and Arsenal in particular. However, as of now, Mullinder wasn't bending his ear. He was suddenly dead to the world, his head lolling forward, spittle dribbling from the left corner of his open mouth while he snored fitfully. He stayed like that until Ashton woke him up after the train had clattered through Vauxhall and was approaching the first signal gantry outside Waterloo. Ashton's mobile rang as the Eurostar slowed down to a crawl and a voice he didn't recognise asked him not to alight until the platform was clear.

'Who are you?' he asked.

'We're anxious to avoid a scene, sir. I'm sure you can appreciate that.'

'Let's put it another way,' Ashton said. 'Who am I talking to?'

'I'm with Detective Inspector Hughes, sir.'

'Well, put him on.'

'I'm afraid he's busy at the moment,' the man said, and switched off.

'What was all that about?' Mullinder asked.

'A bit of last-minute administration. My director wants us to stay on the train until everybody else has got off. He wants to sneak us away in case some nosy journalist has got wind of your homecoming.'

'Sounds fishy to me. I thought you guys could keep a secret? Isn't that what you people do for a living?'

Mullinder was right, something was damned fishy. Hughes had been out somewhere when he'd phoned the divisional station at Putney less than half an hour ago. Even if the CID duty sergeant had contacted him straight away, Hughes would still have been hard-pressed to beat the train into Waterloo. Ashton figured the DI must have received prior warning, and wondered who had tipped him off.

The train drew into the platform and came to a halt. All around them people reached for shopping bags and hand luggage, then filed out of the car. They were in the fourth coach from the end but it seemed to take for ever before the stream of passengers flowing past the window became a trickle and then finally stopped altogether.

'Time to go,' Ashton said.

'I'm ready when you are, squire.'

Mullinder's laid-back attitude vanished the instant he spotted the reception committee waiting by the gate. Even in plain clothes there was no mistaking plod, especially when all four of them were trying to pretend the other three were complete strangers.

'You bastard.' Mullinder turned on him, his face contorted with rage. 'You whore-son bastard.'

It was the start of a tirade which basically consisted of the oldest four-letter word in the English language used as a noun, verb and adjective, much to the amusement of DI Hughes. It only came to an end when Mullinder was bundled into one of the unmarked police cars parked on the service road.

'I'm sorry,' Hughes said, 'there's no room for you in my vehicle, Mr Ashton.'

There was no sign of the car which Nancy Wilkins had laid on to meet him at the station and there was something wrong with the DI's simple arithmetic. Mullinder and two plain-clothes men were in the second vehicle, leaving just Hughes and the remaining officer to travel with the driver in the leading unmarked car.

'What do you mean there's no room for me?' Ashton said angrily.

'I didn't mean in a physical sense.'

'You're determined to exclude me, is that it? Listen, if I hadn't brought Mullinder back you would have been chasing him through the French courts for the next six months.'

'Don't push your luck, Mr Ashton, we could have you for obstruction.'

'Obstruction? You'd better have a word with your wife and the CID duty sergeant at Putney, especially the latter. I'm the man who told him where and when Mullinder would be arriving in London.'

'Some of us would say you were simply trying to cover yourself.' Hughes opened the rear door on his side and got into the Ford Sierra, then lowered the window. 'The fact is we've known when to expect Mullinder since nine thirty this morning,' he said, and signalled the driver to move off.

The second vehicle followed on. The last Ashton saw of Mullinder, Her Majesty's burglar had twisted round to face the kerbside and was mouthing obscenities at him. Ashton returned to the concourse and made his way to the nearest bank of pay phones. Knowing that Nancy Wilkins would have been relieved at 09.00 hours, he rang the MT section to find out what had happened to the driver who had been detailed to meet him at Waterloo station. After the débâcle with Hughes he wasn't surprised when the duty supervisor was unable to tell him who had cancelled the detail.

Ashton hung up, lifted the receiver again and fed the meter with a fifty-pence coin, then rang Victor Hazelwood. The residential number went unanswered for a good minute before Victor came to the phone.

'It's me – Peter,' Ashton said tersely. 'I need to see you urgently.'

'Where are you now?'

'Waterloo station.'

'Why aren't you on the way to Amberley Lodge with our friend?'

'He's been hijacked by the police, that's why I need to see you.'

'All right. When can I expect you?'

'Forty, maybe fifty minutes from now.'

'Try to make it sooner,' Hazelwood said. 'Alice and I are supposed to be attending a dinner party at eight.'

Eleven stops down the Northern Line from Waterloo, Ashton left the Underground at Hampstead and walked towards the Heath. He had thought of taking a cab, then remembered the West End was invariably crowded with theatregoers at this time on a Saturday evening and decided it was probably quicker by tube. It was a lot cheaper, which was a definite consideration. In the present financial climate Roy Kelso would never pass a claim for the taxi fare whereas he might look kindly on one to recover the cost of the Underground ticket. When your joint income had just been reduced by ten thousand pounds per annum it was only prudent to count the pennies.

A quarter of mile down the road from the Underground station he turned right into Willow Walk and made his way to the large Edwardian residence that had been subdivided into three highly desirable properties. The original house had been built in 1900 when things were done on a grand scale. Beneath the slate roof there had been six large bedrooms, a study, library, games room, parlour, dining room, drawing room, conservatory, kitchen and scullery but only one lavatory and two bathrooms.

Built of Mendip stone, the walls were some eight inches thick. The exterior appearance had changed little in the last ninety-five years, except for the Virginia creeper, which had gradually increased its stranglehold on the mortar. The interior, however, had been transformed piecemeal in the 1960s by various builders and architects who between them had skilfully converted the house into three maisonettes, each one having at least three bedrooms including two en suite. However, they had been unable to do anything about the large sashcord windows, and it was still necessary to use a step ladder to remove any cobwebs from the ceiling.

Ashton pushed open the wrought-iron gate set in the tall hedge and followed the footpath round to the front entrance on the left side of the house, known as Willow Dene. One of the new innovations was a powerful security light which illuminated him before he reached the door. In that same instant, the TV camera under the eaves presented his image on the monitor screen in the hall. The resident bodyguard, a former corporal in the SAS, let him into the house before he could try the doorbell.

'The Director's waiting for you in the study, Mr Ashton.'

'Well, there's a surprise,' he said.

The study was the one room in the house where smoking was permitted by Alice. Consequently, the curtains, the furniture and the books on the shelves were all impregnated with the aroma of Burma cheroots. The white paintwork had also become discoloured, turning a dirty yellow. The atmosphere reminded Ashton of a smoke-laden barroom despite the extractor fan which had been installed since the last time he had visited the house. Except for a speck of ash on his trousers, Hazelwood looked immaculate in what appeared to be a brand-new dinner jacket. He was, of course, smoking a cheroot, while nursing a cut-glass tumbler in his free hand.

'Will you join me and have a single malt?' Hazelwood said, and pointed the tumbler at the bottle of Glenlivet on the drinks trolley.

'Well, thank you, I could do with one.'

'Please help yourself, Peter, then tell me what's happened to make you so aerated.'

'That's easy. Last night, the Deputy DG—'

'This isn't a formal Board of Enquiry, Peter, so let's keep it on a first-name basis.'

'Whatever you say, Victor. The fact is Jill told me that Mullinder had surrendered himself to the British Consular Officer in Paris and I was to collect him from our Head of Station. I was later informed on arrival in London I was to escort Mullinder to Amberley Lodge. I didn't like it because I knew the police had circulated an arrest warrant for him through Interpol and we were stealing a march on them. In practice we were deliberately excluding DI Hughes and his team.'

'And what did Jill have to say about that?'

'She thought the police ought to be grateful since we were saving them a lot of work.'

'And?'

'I decided it was a waste of time arguing with her.'

'And went your own sweet way?' Hazelwood suggested.

'More or less. I collected Mullinder and waited until we were back in England before I attempted to alert DI Hughes.'

'With a view to handing Mullinder over to the police.'

There was a note of censure in Hazelwood's voice which annoyed Ashton.

'Times have changed, Victor,' he said icily. 'The Cold War is over and we're no longer a law unto ourselves, or at least we shouldn't be. If we had spirited Mullinder away, there would have been one hell of a stink once the police heard about it. I was hoping to arrive at some sort of compromise with Hughes.'

Hazelwood stubbed out his cheroot in the heavy glass ashtray he kept on his desk.

'Such as?' he asked.

'I would deliver Mullinder to Putney or any designated police station; in return we would have the right to interrogate him on security matters whenever we chose. Unfortunately somebody at Vauxhall Cross got in first and Hughes was waiting for us when our train pulled in to Waterloo. He had known when to expect us since nine thirty this morning, which was before I even arrived in Paris.'

'And you weren't told of this development?'

'Damn right I wasn't.'

'There was obviously a cockup.'

Ashton begged to differ and said so point-blank. His mobile phone had been open all the time had anybody wanted to get in touch. Furthermore, they could have left a message for him with Head of Station, Paris, which suggested he wasn't the only one who had been kept in the dark.

'And let's face it, Jill managed to contact me easily enough on Friday night when it suited her.'

'Are you saying she deliberately failed to inform you?'

'I don't think it was that simple,' Ashton said.

He believed Jill had had second thoughts about the instructions she had given him and had consulted Robin Urquhart. From what Ashton knew of the Senior Deputy Under Secretary, Urquhart would have recognised the damage Mullinder could inflict on the FCO and would have done everything in his power to gag him.

'Remember Piers-Farendon, the chairman of Universal Services who was fined two hundred thousand and sentenced to twelve months' imprisonment last August? The Crown Prosecution had refused to charge him because they said the evidence that he had driven a coach and horses through the arms embargo imposed on Mozambique wouldn't stand up in court. And then suddenly the evidence is to hand and the lawyers representing Piers-Farendon enter a guilty plea.'

'What if they did?'

'Mullinder claims Copeland hired him to break into Head Office of Universal Services and photograph all the sales invoices that had been sent to clients in the financial year ending the fifth of April 1994. He told me Copeland had even supplied him with a set of master keys to unlock their filing cabinets.'

'And you believed him?' Hazelwood shook his head. 'I credited you with more brains than that.'

'Come on, Victor, you know Copeland finished his police service in Special Branch where he did the occasional job for us which wasn't always kosher.'

'I would remind you that Copeland retired in 1993, two years before the chairman of Universal Services was arraigned.'

'Well, somebody in the FCO is still using him. Mullinder was told to take a long holiday in Spain and Copeland was in Paris to give him the necessary wherewithal to do so.'

'According to Mullinder,' Hazelwood said with heavy irony.

'That's right, but we don't have to take his word for it. The French authorities found four thousand two hundred dollars in blank American Express traveller's cheques on Copeland. Mullinder also had three hundred US dollars in American Express TCs, the serial numbers of which were in sequential order with those in Copeland's possession.'

'Copeland wouldn't be the first crooked officer who'd completed his pensionable service in the Metropolitan Police. He could have gone to Paris to give Mullinder his share of the latest scam.'

Hazelwood was either refusing to accept the possibility Mullinder had been indirectly employed by a high-ranking government official or else he was merely playing the role of devil's advocate. Ashton couldn't make up his mind one way or the other and in any case he wasn't inclined to waste time analysing his motives.

'I'm sorry, Victor,' he said, 'but your suggestion is a non-starter. Mullinder told me what he was looking for when he broke into Laura Greenwood's house and his description of the logo denoting the Investment Trust Bank was a hundred per cent accurate.'

It wasn't necessary to remind Hazelwood that the envelope Mullinder had been looking for contained a bank receipt for 85,000 Swiss francs paid into a numbered account belonging to Osvaldo Herrara. Without any prompting from him, Hazelwood conceded they were looking at something more than a simple burglary, and wondered what their next step should be.

'First of all we should do the best we can for Mullinder.'

'Agreed. You'd better have a word with one of our legal advisers and see if he can't pull a few strings.'

'Then we need to find out who Copeland answered to in the Foreign Office, MI5 and our own firm.'

'That's a tall order, Peter.'

Ashton finished his whisky and left the empty tumbler on the drinks trolley.

'It's certainly beyond me.'

'Leave it with me. I'll raise the subject at the next meeting of the JIC.'

'Well, you can't go any higher than that.'

The JIC was the Joint Intelligence Committee, which met every Tuesday morning. It was chaired by the Secretary of the Cabinet and was attended by the Directors General of MI5, the SIS, the Government Communications Headquarters and the Chief of the Defence Intelligence Staff.

'You'll be wanting to get off home,' Hazelwood observed, which was his polite way of saying 'Don't let me keep you.'

'You're right, it's time I was going.'

'By the way, how is Harriet keeping?'

'She's doing OK.'

'I'm really sorry we had to let her go.'

'She was expecting it,' Ashton said, and moved towards the door. 'All the same, I think we should have been warned before your letter arrived on the mat.'

'I was given to understand you had already been informed before I signed the damned thing.'

'Well, it didn't happen, Victor, and there's an end to it.'

'Not until I've said my piece,' Hazelwood growled and for a moment Ashton felt almost sorry for Jill Sheridan.

The duty bodyguard appeared like a genie from Aladdin's lamp when they went out into the hall. He killed the external security light and in addition plunged the hall into Stygian gloom before asking Hazelwood to stand aside while he opened the front door.

'I know somebody who is determined you will live to a ripe old age,' Ashton said as the former SAS NCO eased him out into the night.

They broke Mehmet Ozbek at ten minutes to four on Sunday afternoon. Richard Neagle was honest enough to admit in private that he had no idea how they had done it and Francesca York was equally at a loss to explain the sudden breakthrough. From the moment he had arrived at Paddington Green in the early hours of Saturday morning, Ozbek had maintained a stony silence, refusing even to admit to his name. They had interrogated him turn and turn about with the police for hours at a time and had got precisely nowhere. When asked by officers of the Anti-Terrorist Squad and the Surrey Constabulary if he wished to be legally represented, Ozbek had remained silent. Although he was known to be reasonably fluent in English, the police were in no mood to take any chances and had an interpreter present the whole time they were questioning Ozbek. They had also insisted the duty solicitor should be present.

The police had put Ozbek on a line-up where he had been instantly identified by the two ambulancemen who had rendered first aid at the scene of the accident and the doctor at the Farnham Road Hospital who'd reset his dislocated elbow. They also had all the forensic evidence necessary to secure his conviction on several charges of being an accessory to murder. His fingerprints had been found on the RPG-7 rocket launcher and on a complete set of combat dress that he had dumped in a waste bin. The only thing they didn't have was a motive for the attempted murder of Hasan Ünver, which worried the lawyers of the Crown Prosecution Service who feared the defence would plead guilty on the grounds of diminished responsibility.

Richard Neagle and Francesca York had been equally keen to establish a motive for the attempted murder of the Turkish Economic and Commercial Counsellor. They had told Ozbek over and over again that they could prove he hadn't intended to kill Keith and Amanda French, but had failed to induce the slightest response. They had also informed Ozbek that they had an eye witness who could place him on the Warlock Estate with Osvaldo Herrara, who had armed the bomb which had subsequently killed three people, but this too had failed to move him and they hadn't proceeded with the threat. As Neagle knew full well, MI5 would be reluctant to allow Francesca York to go into the witness box unless she could give her evidence in camera. The fact that the press would have a field day should they learn the Security Service had been watching the lockup for several days before the incident was another consideration.

Then suddenly and for no apparent reason Ozbek had told them why they had decided to assassinate Hasan Ünver.

'He is a man without honour,' Ozbek had said in a harsh voice. 'He wishes to establish friendly relations with Greece and will sacrifice our brothers in Cyprus to achieve his desire. He believes this will enable our country to join the European Union.'

It was a satisfactory beginning, an opening which Neagle intended to exploit. From personal experience he knew that once a man started talking it was extremely difficult for him to stop.

Chapter Twenty-Three

Amongst all the intelligence summaries, threat assessments, and background briefings waiting for Ashton first thing on Monday was a photocopy of a long report from Paul Younghusband, First Secretary at the British Embassy in San José. Graded Secret and given a signal precedence of Priority, the report concerned Luis Garmendia and was a précis of his interrogation by Costa Rican police. Describing himself as a tourist guide at one time employed by Horizantis Sun Tours, Luis had admitted under hostile interrogation to having met Osvaldo Herrara in Managua in the October of 1992. He had escorted a party of Americans who had travelled by road from San José to the Nicaraguan capital and had stopped overnight at the hotel where the Cuban had been staying.

They had got talking in the bar and, according to Luis, the Cuban had offered him a job over breakfast the following morning. Younghusband thought this was unlikely; Osvaldo Herrara was a highly trained Intelligence Officer and someone of his calibre would want to be very sure of his man before he recruited him. From this he concluded the two men had met before 1992 and that Luis Garmendia had performed a number of unspecified but risky errands for Herrara. He had also confessed to going to Paso Canoas on the Panama border roughly once a month to collect a package which he subsequently delivered to Avenida Central 192 first floor, an accommodation address in San José for the Mecado Trading Company and seventeen other firms.

The Costa Rican authorities had told Younghusband that the local chamber of commerce had never heard of the Mecado Trading Company, which hadn't altogether surprised him. The police had visited the premises and had questioned the janitor, who had pointed out the container used exclusively by the Mecado Trading Company. In common with the other seventeen firms it was fitted with a combination lock, the numbered sequence of which was set by the lease holder. When Luis Garmendia had used it last, the combination had been 18–62–43. However, as the police discovered, it had been changed since then and they had been obliged to employ a locksmith to open the container, only to find it was empty. After examining samples of dust taken from inside the container, police laboratory technicians were satisfied that as recently as the end of February it had been used to store cocaine.

Luis Garmendia had denied transporting drugs and had claimed he had no idea what was in any of the packages he'd collected in Paso Canoas. He had also vehemently denied telling his former girlfriend that he had shot Zawadzki in the foot with a .22 calibre pistol and had challenged the police to prove he had been waiting for him at Juan Santamaria International Airport on 6 March. From being an anxious and worried man the day he had been arrested, Garmendia had become cocky and arrogant within the space of forty-eight hours. The police attributed this transformation to the fact that his ex-girlfriend had disappeared without trace around the same time.

Younghusband was firmly of the opinion that even if the police did succeed in finding the woman, which they admitted was extremely unlikely, she would refuse to testify against Garmendia. Furthermore the plainclothes security officer on duty in the arrival/departure hall, who had recalled seeing a man resembling Zawadzki's description approach a Costa Rican displaying a notice, had failed to pick Garmendia out at an identity parade. Without any forensic evidence to support their case against Luis Garmendia, it could only be a matter of twenty-four hours before the police were obliged to let him go.

Ashton initialled the signal to show he'd read it, and penned a note to Nancy Wilkins asking her to put it on the Herrara file before transferring the flimsy to the out-tray. Top of the pile still awaiting his attention was a file belonging to the Pacific Basin and Rest of the World Department. The latest enclosure on it carried an information only tag, while the file cover showed that it had been marked up for the Deputy DG to see before it had come to him. The folio in question was the original signal from Younghusband. On it Jill Sheridan had written a note to Ashton: 'Please see, then speak to me.' Lifting the phone he rang Jill's PA to enquire if morning prayers had finished.

'They were cancelled, Mr Ashton. The Director, Miss Sheridan and Mr Benton are attending a conference at the Foreign and Commonwealth Office which was arranged at short notice.'

'Any idea what it's about?'

'I'm afraid not. I'm only the PA; nobody tells me anything.'

'I know how you feel,' Ashton murmured to himself, after he had thanked her and put the phone down.

A feeling that he was being deliberately excluded was heightened when he rang Francesca York and learned that she and Neagle were spending the day at Paddington Green interrogating Mehmet Ozbek. It was an even bigger surprise to hear this was something they had been doing since his arrest in the early hours of Saturday morning. Ashton hadn't paid much attention to the news on Saturday night but he was damned sure there had been no mention of Ozbek's arrest in the *Sunday Times* or on any of the TV channels. Ashton went through the in-tray looking for any message that might have been originated by MI5 and found it in the duty officer's telephone log maintained by the resident clerk of Central Registry, photocopies of which had been sent to heads of departments and himself.

It had been received approximately twenty-eight hours after

Ozbek had been taken into custody. The text merely indicated when he had been arrested and stated that, in the interests of security, the news was being withheld until Monday, 25 March while the subject was being interrogated. Far from conveying a sense of urgency, the message implied that the SIS was already aware of the situation, which was probably why Nancy Wilkins hadn't drawn Ashton's attention to it. He was about to pick up the phone and call Roger Benton's expert on the South American continent when Landon tapped on the door and walked into his office.

'Good to see you, Will,' Ashton said.

'I'm afraid I don't have anything for you,' Landon told him. 'I took a good look at all the properties Nancy had listed in Kentish Town and on the fringe of Holloway. A couple of places in the latter area were occupied by squatters but otherwise condemned housing stock is boarded up and visited at irregular intervals by security guards to deter anybody with ideas of moving into the property. In short, I didn't see any place where you could hide a body away without the possibility of being caught.'

'I never thought it would be easy, Will.'

'Right.' Landon smiled. 'So where do you want me to look next?'

Ashton went over to the safe, took out Nancy's work of art and, placing the ring binder on the desk, unfolded the map inside the back cover. 'Suppose you give the building sites in Bayswater, Notting Hill, Holland Park and Kensington the once-over while I see what's on offer around King's Cross and St Pancras?'

'That's fine by me. I'll just make a note of the addresses.'

'Why don't you take the ring binder along to your office?'

'OK.'

'Then ring the transport supervisor and tell him we need two self-drives by ten thirty. If all his vehicles are already committed, tell him to go out and hire them.'

'He's going to love that,' Landon said wryly.

'You're wrong, Will, he's a good chap.' Ashton pursed his lips. 'At least he has never been difficult with me,' he added.

'You did say ten thirty for the transport?'

'Yes.' Ashton pointed to the filing trays on the desk. 'I want to clear most of this stuff first.'

'I'll leave you in peace then,' Landon said.

The float file, which contained all the memos written by desk officers and department heads on Thursday, 21 March, had now worked its way to the top of the pile. None of the enclosures on it was classified higher than Confidential; rippling through them, Ashton initialled the docket on the front cover and transferred the float to the out-tray. The folder containing the press cuttings from the Russian Desk, which Landon had left for his perusal on Friday evening, was underneath the Mid East Periodic Intelligence Digest for February 1996.

Landon had said the cuttings folder was interesting but that was an understatement. The clipping had been taken from the edition of *Izvestia* which had appeared on Thursday, 9 April 1981 and featured a very young-looking Osvaldo Herrara. He was described as a member of the Cuban trade delegation visiting Moscow which had just purchased fifteen Tupolev Tu-154M turbofan medium-range airliners. Standing next to the Cuban was a lean aesthetic-looking man whose face Ashton would have recognised anywhere. Described as a senior executive, his name was Pavel Trilisser; six years later, at the age of forty-nine, he had become the youngest Deputy Head of the First Chief Directorate of the KGB, the Foreign Intelligence Service.

It had been the one and only time they had been photographed together. However, Osvaldo Herrara had appeared with other Communist officials. There was a photograph of him seated next to the Minister Counsellor of the Soviet Embassy at some mass gymnastic display in Havana in 1986, and again with a consular officer at a baseball match some five years later. Subsequently both Russians had been identified as the KGB's Head of Station, Cuba. As Ashton saw it, the clippings indicated that the Cuban was in Pavel Trilisser's pocket. He wondered if this was still the case.

Neagle, believing that once a man started talking it was extremely difficult for him to stop, had expounded on this theory yesterday evening when they had finally called it a day after breaking Ozbek's wall of silence. To prove his point he had cited a number of cases where, as a member of the interrogation team, he had been present when this had happened. This morning, however, it was becoming increasingly apparent to Francesca York that Richard had never encountered someone like Mehmet Ozbek before. Instead of answering their questions he acted as if he had become deaf and dumb overnight. Two hours into the interrogation, Neagle suggested they took a break and adjourned to the police canteen.

'I'm going to have a cup of coffee,' he announced. 'What will you have?'

'The same please.'

'With or without?'

'White – no sugar.'

Neagle got to his feet and patted both trouser pockets. The bemused expression on his face told Francesca he'd no loose change, something that was becoming a habit with him. As had happened before, Francesca told him she would get them and went over to the counter. When she returned to their table a few moments later carrying both cups and saucers on a plastic tray, he asked her why she brought him two lumps of sugar when he didn't take it.

'Well, you did yesterday.'

'I've decided to give it up since then.'

'You should have told me, I'm not a mind reader.'

'Pity, you could have told me what Ozbek is thinking, then we might find a way of getting through to him.'

'Is there nothing we can offer him that would help to loosen his tongue again?'

'We can't promise Ozbek a lenient sentence when he helped to murder eleven people, Fran.'

'I agree but we could try threatening him again.'

'With what?'

'First you told Ozbek that for administrative reasons he would spend the rest of his days in a Turkish prison. Then you dangled a carrot in front of his nose and we promised him the Home Secretary would decide he should serve his sentence in this country. We also gave him to understand that with good behaviour he might eventually be eligible for parole. Shortly thereafter he told us why they had decided to assassinate Hasan Ünver—'

'Would you mind getting to the point?' Neagle said testily. 'We are running out of time and we can't afford to waste any.'

He did not have to point out that this was their last opportunity to interrogate Ozbek in private. Tomorrow, after he appeared in the magistrates' court charged with a minimum eight counts of murder, he would be remanded in custody. Visiting him in a prison like Brixton, where their faces were likely to be seen by other inmates, would prejudice their anonymity, something which nobody in the Security Service did lightly.

'I'm suggesting we go back on our word, Richard. In short we tell Ozbek we've changed our minds and will make damned sure he does spend the rest of his life in a Turkish prison.'

'And if that fails to impress him?'

'What have we got to lose? At the moment we are getting nowhere fast.'

'I think I'd like to know the outcome of this conference at the FCO before we do anything rash.'

'What conference?' Francesca asked.

Neagle was annoyed that she was incapable of putting two and two together when she knew that last Wednesday he had attended a meeting chaired by Robin Urquhart to consider a change of venue for the Cyprus issue.

The talks between the Greek and Turkish Cypriots were to

have been held in London at Lancaster House, which meant MI5 would have been responsible for monitoring the activities of known troublemakers amongst the local ethnic community. Move the venue to some as yet unspecified place in America and the nature of the threat also changed.

'What if Ozbek was an illegal immigrant?' Neagle said, voicing his thoughts.

'I'm sorry, I don't follow you.'

'Suppose he came to this country specifically to kill Ünver? Suppose he is a member of some terrorist movement we've never encountered before? Which organisation would you consult?'

'The SIS?' Francesca suggested hesitantly.

'Exactly. I want to know if anything was disclosed at the conference this morning which we could use to coerce Ozbek.' Neagle pushed his chair back and stood up. 'I'll only be a few minutes.'

Neagle tended to communicate with his subordinates in a form of oral shorthand which meant they had to second-guess what he wanted them to do. In this instance Francesca noticed Richard hadn't finished his coffee and assumed he would be returning to the canteen after he had finished talking to whoever it was he was phoning.

Five minutes went by, then another five by which time the untouched cup of coffee looked as if it was congealed. He finally returned just as she was about to go and find him.

'The conference hasn't finished yet,' Neagle said cheerfully, 'but I think we could be in business.'

'We're going to have another session with Ozbek?'

'That's the general idea, Fran.'

Ozbek hadn't moved so much as an inch since they had left him. He was still sitting bolt upright on a ladderback chair, his hands clasped loosely together and resting on the table. He was gazing at the wall directly to his front but his eyes were blank and unfocused, as if he had been hypnotised and was in a deep trance. Francesca thought the Turk had developed resistance to interrogation to a fine art form.

312

'Your landlord is a talkative chap,' Neagle observed casually. 'Doesn't have a good word to say for you, though. Matter of fact we wondered if you'd fallen behind with the rent he bad-mouthed you so much.'

Richard had obviously been talking to Special Branch after he had left Francesca in the canteen and they must have leaned on the owner of the dry goods store in Henning Road. There was, however, no reaction from Ozbek but this didn't seem to bother Neagle.

'It wasn't very bright of you to hold a weapon-training session in the flat above his shop,' Neagle continued. 'Especially on the very day a terrorist bomb claimed the lives of three people on the Warlock Estate. An incident like that jogs a person's memory. The shopkeeper told the police there were five of you in the flat that afternoon. Yourself, of course, and Colonel Osvaldo Herrara, the Cuban Intelligence Officer who was teaching you all how to use and arm the RPG-7 anti-tank rocket launcher. You were his interpreter, translated everything he said into Turkish. English was the common tongue between the pair of you.'

Francesca couldn't see how Special Branch could possibly have discovered that. The shopkeeper might have counted the number of men who had entered Ozbek's rented flat but unless he had been present, he wouldn't have known how the weapon-training session had been conducted. No, Richard was bluffing, using his imagination and powers of deduction to build on what few facts he did have. It was clever stuff, all right, but unfortunately Ozbek was taking it in his stride and didn't appear the least bit rattled.

'There were two men in each weapon team,' Neagle continued. 'How did you like being paired off with Kemal Esener?'

Francesca didn't know who was the more surprised, Ozbek or herself. As late as Sunday night the identity of the dead man who had been thrown out of the Ford Escort had been a mystery. How Special Branch or the Surrey Constabulary had been able to put a name to him since then was equally baffling.

'I've never heard of this Kemal Esener.'

'Then you've got a very short memory. Special Branch retrieved his landing card from Immigration at Heathrow. His entry visa was good for three months and was due to expire on Friday, the tenth of May. The reason Kemal Esener gave for visiting this country was pleasure; he also stated he would be staying with his cousin, Mr Mehmet Ozbek, at 258 Woodland Park Road, Harringay.'

Neagle leaned forward, both forearms resting on the table, his round puckish face suddenly distorted and intimidating. 'Sounds familiar, doesn't it?' he grated.

'I don't believe you,' Ozbek said in a voice which lacked conviction.

'I'll show you the landing card; it should be here soon. Meantime, do yourself a favour and tell me about Osvaldo Herrara and your friends in the IRA.' Neagle smiled. 'Unless of course you would prefer to keep a date with the hangman in Ankara.'

King's Cross and St Pancras was not the most idyllic part of London. There were no buildings of architectural merit in the area, though some train buffs would claim the two railway stations had a lot going for them, but their view was somewhat subjective. While steam had been dead for over thirty years, the soot from good Welsh coal had not entirely disappeared from the façades of those buildings nearest the railways. It was not a safe neighbourhood after dark, especially in the back streets off the Caledonian Road and down by the Grand Union Canal. The chances of being mugged in this part of London were higher than elsewhere in the capital due, some people said, to the number of drug addicts who had been drawn to the area in search of easy pickings to feed their habit.

The Great Northern was the only hotel in the neighbour-

314

hood to appear in the *Michelin Guide*; there were, however, a fair number of bed-and-breakfast establishments whose managers were prepared to turn a blind eye on the streetwalkers and their clients.

By twelve noon Ashton had checked the sites Nancy Wilkins had listed between Pancras Road and Eversholt Street and had found nothing suspicious. He had visited the construction site of what was to be the new British Library near St Pancras station and had talked to the civil engineer in charge and the chief security officer. Both men were aware the British Library was the sort of prestige target that was bound to attract the Provisional IRA and security was tight, twenty-four hours a day round the clock. Bombing the place would be a hazardous operation, using it as a burial place was an even riskier proposition.

The self-drive Ford Sierra was proving more trouble than it was worth. Leaving the British Library site, Ashton drove past King's Cross station, turned left into York Way, and was lucky enough to find a parking space in New Wharf Road. Of the developments Nancy Wilkins had suggested were worth a look, two lay within half a mile of his present location. The first site was in Steam Lane which linked New Wharf Road with York Way. However, no work was in progress, there were no skips, no dumper trucks, no stacks of building materials, no site office and no Elsan latrines. All the terraced houses appeared to have been given a recent facelift, which had included the replacement of the old sash-cord windows with double glazing. Just going by the number of cars parked on the street it was apparent that every house was occupied, which meant the information Nancy Wilkins had been given was out of date.

After checking the map to see which was the shortest route to the next place north of the Grand Union Canal, Ashton walked on through to York Way and turned right. The site was in Nash Court off Copenhagen Street but a newly painted signboards caught his eye and diverted him into Depot Close. Arranged in a narrow horseshoe were ten semidetached houses built around the turn of the century, all of which were partially boarded up while awaiting demolition. The signboard outside the two semis at the bottom of the close contradicted this assumption. It read: 'Keep Out – Acquired by T.J. Craftsman & Son for renovation.' Ashton thought they had a long way to go; in common with every other property all the windows upstairs had been shattered, leaving just shards of glass in the frames. At one time each two-up, two-down semidetached had had a small front garden partly screened from view by a privet hedge planted behind a waist-high stonewall. Ashton presumed the same vandals who had broken the windows had probably knocked down all the stone walls.

The only work which T. J. Craftsman & Son appeared to have done was to rip out part of the hedgerow in front of number 5 Depot Close. A set of tyre tracks on what had once passed for a lawn were clearly visible and looked recent. Although the lock was missing, the front door wouldn't budge when Ashton put his shoulder to it and he assumed it had been nailed to the jamb on the inside. He tried the back door on the left side of the house and found it too had been secured in a similar fashion.

If the builders were serious about renovating the property, Ashton reckoned there had to be another way in. He went round to the back and glanced up at the bedroom window. Although it had been smashed, there were no shards of glass left in the frame, which suggested somebody had carefully removed all the fragments. The wooden extending ladder which he eventually found concealed under the bushes at the bottom of the garden was in good condition and had obviously not been there very long. Ashton carried the ladder over to the house, extended it high enough to reach the window ledge, then climbed up and entered the small back room.

The place was unfit for human habitation. The bare floorboards were infested with dry rot to such an extent that the fungus was now attacking the dividing wall. Some of the slates on the roof were missing and rainwater over a prolonged period of time had brought part of the ceiling down.

He opened the bedroom door, moved along the landing and went into the front room overlooking the street. Of the two bedrooms, this one was in slightly better condition. It was also furnished with an old free-standing wardrobe secured by a padlock and hasp that had clearly been fitted only recently. Raising the right leg, Ashton smashed his foot against the panelling and kept on doing it until the wood splintered, and he was able to wrench off the padlock and hasp. When he opened the doors, a log wrapped in canvas and wearing a pair of shoes fell out of the wardrobe.

Chapter Twenty-Four

Ashton untied the ropes which had held the canvas in place and then unwrapped the body as best he could. The victim had been hooded and shot through the back of the skull, the bullet exiting through the forehead and removing a sizeable piece of bone in the process. The blood and brain matter had set like glue so that the woollen Balaclava had stuck to the head as had part of the canvas wrapping.

Although he had never seen a photograph of the man, Ashton was pretty sure the victim who had been executed in cold blood was Michael Ryan, the former corporal in the Royal Signals and self-appointed undercover agent for MI5. Ryan hadn't been seen since Tuesday, 12 March, almost a fortnight ago, which, if the ripe smell was anything to go by, was roughly how long the corpse at Ashton's feet had been dead.

He heard a vehicle approaching and moved quickly to position himself by the window, his back to the wall to minimise the chances of being seen from the ground. Ashton had often thought vans came in two colours only – blue and white. The Transit which the driver parked directly below the window was one of the exceptions: it was pale grey and beginning to rust. The man who got out of the Ford Transit and moved round to the back of the vehicle, had curly black hair, was about two inches under six feet and looked physically fit. He was, Ashton thought, in his late twenties to early thirties.

The driver opened the rear doors, then, for no apparent reason, he stepped back from the van and looked up at the window as if aware he was being watched. Ashton side-stepped along the wall, distancing himself from the window, and switched off his mobile phone. The last thing he needed right now was a call from Will Landon or somebody in the office. The neighbourhood was quiet and the slightest sound would carry to the van driver. As soon as the man started to move round to the back of the house Ashton would switch the phone on and call the police. What the van driver's reaction would be when he saw the extending ladder leaning against the window ledge was anybody's guess but chances were he would cut and run. But not before he had removed the ladder.

Ashton heard the driver close the rear doors and resisted the urge to take a quick peep. There had been something almost deliberate about the noise he had made as though he was trying to spook him into making a mistake.

The fact there was a significant pause before he moved away from the Ford Transit seemed to confirm his hunch. His back still pressed against the wall, Ashton edged towards the window and caught a brief glimpse of the man just before he disappeared round the corner carrying two large vats.

Ashton switched on the Cellnet, turned the volume down low and tapped out 999. A woman operator answered up in less than five seconds and asked him which service he required.

'Police,' he told her in a voice only marginally louder than a whisper.

The police operator was equally quick off the mark and asked how he could be of assistance.

'I want to report a murder,' Ashton told him, still keeping his voice low.

'Can I have your name, present location and phone number, sir?'

'I'm calling from 5 Depot Close, he said and gave his mobile number. ''There's a dead man lying on the bare floor directly in

320

front of me. The victim was shot through the head and died approximately fourteen days ago.'

'And you've just found the body, Mr No Name?'

The police operator managed to sound arch, sarcastic and downright sceptical at one and the same time.

'This is not a hoax,' Ashton said icily. 'Number 5 Depot Close is a derelict building near King's Cross station and I'm talking about PIRA involvement.'

'The Provisional IRA?'

'The same. And it looks as if one of their shooters has returned so an armed response vehicle would come in handy.'

Ashton switched off his Cellnet for the second time, moved towards the bedroom door and closed it, then positioned himself to the right of the doorway with his back to the wall. When the van driver saw the ladder he would be faced with two options. He could quietly remove the ladder and get the hell out of it, knowing that whoever was still in the house would be unable to follow him. Alternatively, he could decide to go after the intruder. His choice would be governed by which course of action he considered presented the lesser risk to himself, and that was something Ashton couldn't begin to second-guess. What-ever he was fixing to do, the driver was taking his time. Either that or he was damned light on his feet.

Ashton didn't hear a thing until the driver put his shoulder to the door and burst into the room. Had he been standing with his left side nearest the door, he would have been hit as it swung back on its hinges. With no time to push the cadaver back inside the wardrobe, the body on the floor was the first thing the van driver saw. He was a fairly tall man, dressed like a painter and decorator in white overalls over a check shirt.

As he spun round, Ashton went for him, intent on grabbing the long barrel .22 calibre target pistol the van driver was holding in his right hand. Seizing hold of his wrist, he raised his arm aloft a split second before the man squeezed the trigger. Even though the door to the landing was wide open and there was no glass in the window to keep the sound bottled up in the room, the .22 pistol still made a noise like a cannon.

Ashton laid into the gunman and delivered two short-arm jabs into the belly in an effort to wind him but he looked under thirty and had obviously kept himself in good shape. Instead of the expected hollow gasp to catch his breath, he absorbed both body punches with barely a grunt, then head-butted Ashton above the right eyebrow. Blood flowed from a two-inch slit and ran down his face, half blinding him. Ashton tried kneeing him in the groin and hacked at his shins but there wasn't much the gunman didn't know about street fighting and his nimble footwork kept him out of trouble. The fight was going badly for Ashton. Unable to see out of one eye, he was forced to use his right arm in a purely defensive mode to prevent the gunman from breaking his neck with a rabbit punch. But each scything blow he took on the forearm gradually weakened and deadened the limb and he knew it was no longer a question of simply disarming the gunman. The struggle had moved up a notch and it was now a case of kill or be killed.

Reaching up, Ashton grabbed hold of the gun barrel with his right hand, reversed the grip with the left to an underarm hold and then began to rotate as if he was throwing the hammer. Except he didn't have to worry about stepping outside the circle and he rotated just one and a half times before suddenly releasing the gunman. The ledge was only kneecap high so when he cannoned into it, the gunman instinctively reached out for the window frame with both hands. He was in fact leaning forward and the momentum plus his own upper body weight took him headfirst out of the window. A high-pitched scream ended fourteen feet below when he crunched into the roof of the Ford Transit. Ashton moved up to the window, peered at the crumpled figure below with his one good eye and knew the man was dead. Somewhere in the direction of the Caledonian Road he could hear the driver of a police car using the siren to clear a path through the heavy traffic and reckoned it could be the armed response vehicle he had called for. Knowing that any time now he could be facing a barrage of questions, Ashton went in search of some of the possible answers. He found the answer to one that had been puzzling him down in the hall under the staircase where the floorboards had been lifted and stacked in the kitchen, along with the displaced earth. The grave that had been dug between the joists was roughly three feet deep and just about wide enough to accommodate a corpse laid on its side. Although the earth would be piled in a mound over the body, it wouldn't stay like that for long. Ashton was prepared to bet that the two large vats the gunman had been carrying when he'd walked round the back of the house, had contained concentrated sulphuric acid.

The police arrived in force before he could check out the rest of the ground floor. Any thought they might have entertained about responding to a hoax call disappeared when they saw the crumpled body lying on top of the Ford Transit. Suddenly everything went quiet and he pictured the officers communicating among themselves with hand signals as they deployed to cover the front and back of the house.

Given the circumstances, Ashton presumed they would call for a backup and a tense situation would then become even more fraught. The bigger the number of armed officers on the scene, the greater the risk of a lethal incident. It was, Ashton decided, time he showed himself in the window upstairs.

In the event his sudden appearance in the window only raised the temperature. One of the armed police officers told him in no uncertain terms to clasp his hands together and keep them in sight on top of his head. He did just that and stood there in full view, the blood still running into his right eye and then on down his face to drip on to the shirt front and stain the lapel of his charcoal-grey jacket.

An inspector was already on the scene; when two more armed response teams arrived plus a covey of uniformed police officers in a Transit, the Inspector was reduced to playing second fiddle to a superintendent. There was no question of anybody entering the house via the extending ladder at the back; the Met was coming through the front door and they had the necessary equipment to effect an entrance. Two sledgehammers reduced the door to matchwood in a matter of seconds; the first armed response team were also equally quick to get Ashton out into the street, wrists handcuffed behind his back. There were a score of questions they wanted to ask but the Superintendent in charge decided the answers were likely to be a lot more reliable after his damaged eye had been seen to.

Ashton was therefore taken to 76 King's Cross Road, one of the Divisional Stations in N District, where he tried to persuade the police doctor that all he needed was a Band-Aid to hold the slit together and nature would do the rest. The police doctor was, however, having none of that nonsense, and promptly put a dozen stitches into the wound.

Until three o'clock that afternoon Francesca York had never been asked to identify a dead body. She had been spared the ordeal after the Warlock incident because DC Browne had been literally blown to pieces and she had only caught a brief glimpse of the couple in the Rover 400. Now, thanks to Ashton, she had been required to identify two bodies lying in the mortuary of the Royal Free Hospital on Gray's Inn Road.

Special Branch had contacted her at Paddington Green where she and Richard Neagle were still interrogating Mehmet Ozbek. Despite the fact that they hadn't finished with him by a long chalk, Neagle had decided he could spare her, much to Francesca's annoyance. Ashton had told the officers of N District that he believed the first victim to be Michael Ryan, while the other man was possibly Kevin Hayes. He had, of course, informed them that Francesca York would be able to identify both of the deceased and had suggested Special Branch would know where to find her . . .

Francesca wondered if the sight of Michael Ryan's putrescent body had turned Ashton's stomach. It had certainly made her retch and even now, while nursing a strong cup of tea laced with whisky in the Superintendent's office at the Divisional Police Station on King's Cross Road, she continued to feel queasy.

'I've seen a few bodies in my time,' the Superintendent said quietly, 'but nothing to compare with Ryan. I imagine you must have found it very upsetting.'

'I did,' Francesca admitted.

'Mr Ashton has told us that Kevin Hayes was a member of the Provisional IRA.'

'He's probably right. Kevin's elder brother, Barry, is one of the most ruthless killers the IRA has. He was the man who constructed the bomb which killed three people on the Warlock Estate. In Northern Ireland he operated under the alias of Brian Ahearne. We didn't know his real name until the commanding officer of the West Belfast battalion defected to us shortly before the bombing. By then, Barry Hayes had dropped out of sight again.'

'What about the younger brother?'

'He had never come to our notice until we learned that Barry Hayes and Brian Ahearne were one and the same man.'

'So Mr Ashton said. I assume you are colleagues?'

'In a manner of speaking,' Francesca told him.

'Do you find him a difficult man, Miss York?'

'He likes to have his own way.'

'It didn't take us long to find that out,' the Superintendent said with feeling.

After the police doctor had looked at his eye, Ashton had refused to make a full statement until he had taken legal advice. His own mobile phone had been damaged beyond repair in the struggle with Kevin Hayes and he'd had to use a police line. But nobody had the faintest idea whom Ashton had spoken to because he had insisted nobody else should be present when he placed the call.

'Reminded us of the Official Secrets Acts,' the Superintendent continued. 'He didn't need to raise his voice. Matter of fact your Mr Ashton was very polite but you just knew you were walking on thin ice if you didn't do as he asked.'

After he had finished with the phone, Ashton had waived his right to have a solicitor present while he was being interviewed. He had then given the interviewing officers a very full statement but had refused point-blank to answer any of their questions.

'He merely advised them to get in touch with you, Miss York.'

'Where is he now?' Francesca asked.

'Cooling his heels in one of the interview rooms.'

'May I have a word with him in private?'

'I don't see why not.'

Francesca left the mug of tea on the window ledge behind the Superintendent's desk and followed him out of the office. The interview rooms were on the ground floor on both sides of the corridor to the left of the entrance hall. Ashton was in the first one on the right.

'A colleague to see you,' the Superintendent announced, and ushered her inside.

'What happened to your eye?' she asked when they were alone.

'I guess Hayes thought he could improve my face with his head. What did Special Branch tell you?'

'Only the bare bones. How did you know Hayes was using that derelict house in Depot Close as a burial ground for Ryan?'

The short answer was that he hadn't. Ashton had had a list made of possible burial sites and had been in the process of checking them out when he'd spotted a newly painted signpost outside number 5 Depot Close. It hadn't looked right to him and he had decided to take a quick look at the derelict property.

'And the rest was just pure luck?' Francesca suggested.

'Can you give me an instance in our line of business when luck didn't play a part? When did Special Branch cease to keep brother Kevin under surveillance? Friday?'

'Yes. At the risk of repeating myself, how did you know?'

'You as good as told me that same day when you said Special Branch was overstretched and would have to be withdrawn.' Ashton smiled. 'Of course I'm only guessing again but I reckon

326

number 5 Depot Close was being prepared as a burial ground by the Provos before they actually lifted Ryan. They put up that signboard in case anybody wondered what they were doing in the close. Then everything went pear-shaped and younger brother, Kevin, didn't dare to go near the place until he was sure he was no longer being watched.'

'Are you saying Kevin was a sleeper?'

'He is now,' Ashton said grimly.

'His death leaves an awful lot of loose ends.'

'Well, you know what to do if you want to tidy things up.'

Francesca thought that was pretty rich. Thanks to Ashton there wasn't much MI5 could do. The follow-up was entirely in the hands of the officers of N District, the London Borough of Islington, who at some stage would definitely interview Kevin's widow. No doubt they would also make house-to-house calls in the neighbourhood of Depot Close to see if any of the residents in the nearby streets recalled seeing anybody working at number 5. There remained the property dealer in Kilburn who was unlikely to be of immediate interest to the detectives of N District. Francesca supposed Special Branch could always detain him for seventy-two hours under the Prevention of Terrorism Act but he had already spent so much time in Paddington Green it was almost like a second home to him. She personally wouldn't have him arrested until they had some evidence which would hold up in court. Thankfully their next move was up to Richard Neagle, not her.

'Tell me something,' Ashton said. 'What have you learned from Ozbek about the IRA involvement and how he linked up with Osvaldo Herrara?'

'Quite a lot but I'm not sure everything he told us is reliable. We thought we had made a breakthrough on Sunday afternoon, only to meet with a wall of silence again first thing this morning. Then after a short break, Richard hit him with the name of his dead companion, which Special Branch had unearthed, and his whole attitude changed yet again.'

Suddenly eager to please them, Ozbek had answered all their

questions and had volunteered additional information. According to his account, he had arrived in England in the middle of January on a visa good for three months. He had in fact arrived a day ahead of Kemal Esener. The other two guerrilla fighters who had attended the weapon-training class conducted by Osvaldo Herrara had arrived on separate flights during the first ten days of February.

'Ozbek claims that before leaving Ankara his mission was defined by a lieutenant-colonel on the general staff. He was told where to stay in London and how to contact his local control.'

'Who was Merih Soysal,' Ashton said, rounding it off for her.

'Yes. He's adamant she told him where and when to meet Herrara and how he would recognise the Cuban.'

'Would this also include the arms dump on the Warlock Estate?'

'No, he got that information from Herrara. The Cuban told him the arms dump belonged to an IRA active service unit which was being disbanded. Setting a booby trap for the security forces was the price they had to pay for the RPG-7 and anti-tank rockets.'

'Who actually armed the bomb?'

'Ozbek claims Herrara did.'

'Well he would.'

'You don't believe Ozbek?'

'I've never met him,' Ashton reminded her. 'The question is, do you?'

'I'm not sure. There were moments when I thought he was a little too co-operative; you know, as if he was determined to please us. All the same, a lot of what he said rang true.'

'Yeah, I can believe the Provisional IRA would demand a price for their munitions. But I bet you Ozbek and Herrara were under the impression that the security forces would be lured to the lockup after they had collected the rocket launchers. I can't see a terrorist going to an arms dump knowing the location was under surveillance.'

She thought Ashton was right and wondered why the

328

possibility hadn't occurred to her. And maybe there was another quid pro quo which she hadn't considered before.

'A penny for them,' Ashton said.

'I was thinking about the Kurds.'

'You've just lost me.'

'Ozbek was the only Turk amongst the four. According to him the other three members of the assassination team belonged to the Separatist Kurdistan Workers Party. Trouble is, he can't or won't say what promises were made to the Kurds to secure their participation.'

'Don't worry about it. Soon as I'm out of here I'll see if our Mid East Department has any ideas.'

'That could be some time if you won't answer any of the questions put to you.'

It transpired Ashton had phoned Vauxhall Cross and asked the Admin Wing to rustle up one of the tame lawyers in Middle Temple who had been cleared by Positive Vetting. The snag was his request had to be approved by the Deputy Director General.

'Then you'd better reconcile yourself to a long wait,' Francesca told him. 'The conference she is attending at the FCO was still going strong when I left Paddington Green.'

Alistair Downward never used the Underground if he could help it. He felt claustrophobic in the bowels of the earth and couldn't stand being hemmed in with the rest of humanity as though they were a flock of sheep on the way to a market place. It was therefore his habit to travel to and from the FCO by taxi and tonight was no exception. After paying off the cab, he walked into the luxury block of flats in St John's Wood and took the lift up to his apartment on the sixth floor.

There were two messages waiting for him on the answer phone. One was from the service manager of the dealership where he had purchased his Mercedes who wished to remind him the car was due for a service. The other was from Rauf Kaymak, who had just returned from Cyprus and would love to hear from him. Removing his raincoat, Downward hung it up on the hatstand in the hall, then lifted the receiver and rang Rauf.

'It's me – Alistair,' he said when Rauf answered the phone. 'How were things in Nicosia?'

'The same as they always are in a divided city. The family is doing well, though,' Rauf laughed. 'Taking lots of money off the tourists.'

'I'm pleased for you.'

'And how are things with you?'

'I've had an awful day.'

'Don't tell me the former Mrs Downward has been digging her claws into you yet again?'

'Melissa isn't the problem this time, Jill Sheridan is. Damned woman thinks she is the greatest living expert on the Cyprus issue. She even had the nerve to give me a lecture on the Zurich and London Agreements of 1959 as though I'd never heard of them.'

'Poor old you.'

'I tell you, Rauf, the thought of working hand in glove with that woman over the next few weeks appals me.'

'Well, so long as it's only your hand she will be holding,' Rauf said, and sniggered.

Eight hours in the company of Jill Sheridan was more than enough for any man. Even over lunch there had been no respite for him. The meeting had been chaired jointly by Robin Urquhart and Hazelwood, both of whom had withdrawn after an hour, leaving just Roger Benton to dilute the ever-so-clever Ms Sheridan. And she had shown an uncommon interest in Melissa, Downward's former wife. Some of her questions over lunch suggested that somebody had been dishing the dirt on him. Then, as if he didn't have enough worries as it was, Robin Urquhart had buttonholed him just as he was about to go home. The Senior Deputy Under Secretary had asked a number of penetrating questions about the legal advice Downward had tendered to Her Majesty's Ambassador to Costa Rica concerning the proposed SAS base in the area of Punta Banco on the west coast. Specifically, Urquhart had wanted to know exactly when the document had been placed in the diplomatic bag.

'Are you still there?' Rauf asked.

'Yes, I'm just a little distracted.'

'By the clever Ms Sheridan?'

'In part.'

'I knew she had been holding something more than your hand.'

'No, that's your privilege,' Downward told him and caught his breath, horrified by what he had said.

'Shall I come round?'

'You can't stay the night, Rauf.'

'You want to see me, don't you?'

'Just for a little while.'

'I'll be with you in no time.'

Downward hung up. He felt almost sick with excitement, something that always happened when he was being reckless.

Chapter Twenty-Five

On the eve of Good Friday, some ten days after Hayes had butted him in the face, Ashton's GP had removed the stitches above his right eyebrow. By then the pigeon's egg on his forehead had disappeared and the bruise on the cheekbone had gone from deep purple through banana yellow to a respectable shade of near white. By that time the way the Combined Anti-Terrorist Organisation functioned had undergone a subtle but far-reaching change where Ashton was concerned. From being actively involved in the search for Michael Ryan, he had in effect been sidelined from the moment the police had descended on number 5 Depot Close.

Ashton's terms of reference had been amended the day after he had been discharged from hospital where he had been kept under observation for twenty-four hours with suspected concussion. Instead of taking an active part in gathering intelligence his role had been downgraded to analysing the data gathered by other agencies. Within the United Kingdom, MI5 in conjunction with Special Branch were responsible for countering the threat posed by the Provisional IRA and, as had always been the case, they were also charged with monitoring the activities of Islamic fundamentalists who, while enjoying refugee status, were trying to undermine the regime in their native country.

There was nothing new in the concept of MI5 being the home team while the SIS covered the rest of the world; it was just the way Ashton's revised charter had been written which had made it seem different. The truth was MI5 had their own analysts and didn't need his assistance. However, the Security Service had indicated they would keep him fully informed of developments in their bailiwick which he regarded as little more than a bromide. In evaluating the external threat to the United Kingdom and UK nationals from terrorist organisations Ashton was entirely dependent on intelligence provided by heads of stations around the globe whose reports would go direct to their respective departments. By the time he received a copy, the relevant assistant director would have already given his interpretation of the data at morning prayers.

By the end of the week Ashton had lost the services of both Will Landon, and Nancy Wilkins, who had reverted to being just another clerical officer in central registry. Despite the downsizing of his job, the paperwork had continued to flow across Ashton's desk and he had begun to see himself as an overpaid refuse collector. The one concrete thing he had done before Easter was to initiate a follow-up on Osvaldo Herrara. As there had been no further sighting of the Cuban since he had left Immingham on a ro-ro ferry bound for Amsterdam, Ashton had persuaded Rowan Garfield to signal Head of Station, Moscow, asking him to make enquiries concerning his whereabouts. His request had been based solely on the press clippings from *Isvestia* Will Landon had unearthed, which had shown the Cuban keeping company with Pavel Trilisser, the then rising star on the KGB's First Chief Directorate. Before authorising the signal to Moscow, Garfield had wondered out loud if being head-butted hadn't dislodged a few marbles.

Head of Station, Moscow had been equally scathing but in a more subtle manner. He had begun his reply by reminding London that Pavel Trilisser had left the Kremlin three months ago under a cloud, having been required to resign his appointment as Special Advisor on Foreign Affairs to President Yeltsin. At the time rumour had it that his advice on how to secure an injection of fifty billion dollars from the International Monetary

Fund without suffering any financial constraints had proved disastrously wrong. Now it transpired he had been misappropriating government funds to speculate on the US futures market and was currently under house arrest pending further investigation. In the circumstances, Head of Station doubted if anyone in their right mind would want to be seen in Trilisser's company.

Some good had come from this latest setback: it had prompted Ashton to tack on an extra day to the normal Easter break. He had also made full use of the services provided by the travel agency Kelso dealt with. As a result, and much to Harriet's surprise, he had whistled her off to Southampton early on Good Friday to spend five days in St Malo. The weather had been nothing to write home about but that hadn't mattered; they had both needed a break and some time with one another.

Before going away he had thought of tendering his resignation. When he returned to the office on the Wednesday after Easter the idea was still there in the back of his mind but he was in no hurry to act on it until he had something else lined up. There was, Ashton decided, nothing like a second honeymoon to make you feel on top of the world. The feel-good factor stayed with him even when he walked into Vauxhall Cross and the ever-vigilant Enid Sly on the reception desk informed him his presence was required forthwith by Ms Sheridan.

In all the time he had known Jill, Ashton couldn't recall an occasion when she hadn't looked immaculate, in or out of bed. Even before she had taken Henry Clayborn, her husband, to the cleaners when they had divorced, she had always spent a small fortune on clothes. Fortunately, Daddy, who was on the board of the Qatar Oil Corporation, had regularly settled her account with Harrods, not to mention sundry other bills which he had picked up from time to time. But if Jill was fastidious about her appearance the same criterion applied to her office. To her way of thinking an untidy desk was indicative of a disorganised mind. However, this morning standards had slipped for once and her desk was cluttered with three cardboard boxes which were too large to fit into the in, pending and out-trays.

'I know what you're thinking but these are for you,' Jill said, and pointed to the boxes.

'I'm intrigued. What's inside them?'

'Aerial photographs but there are a couple of points which need to be addressed before we deal with them.'

Jill waved a hand at one of the armchairs which was the closest she got to inviting him to sit down. The gesture also warned Ashton he could be in for a lengthy session.

'Martin Edmunds,' she continued. 'You'll be interested to hear that he has been interviewed in depth about his finances. When he bought The Old Vicarage in 1986 for two hundred and twenty-five thousand, he had already served over twenty years in the Hong Kong Police, during which time he had saved close on twenty thousand from his salary. He also cashed in two life insurance policies to raise a further thirty-eight thousand. His wife, Janet, was able to contribute a like sum because they had never touched a penny of her salary as a teacher.'

Furthermore, following her retirement from the profession in 1985, Janet Edmunds had been allowed to commute up to seventy per cent of her pension. The rest of the purchase price had been made up by her parents who had mortgaged their own house to raise the money.

'How very generous of them,' Ashton observed drily. 'Did Edmunds produce any documentary evidence to support his story?'

'Oh, come on, Peter, all this happened ten years ago. Nobody keeps a bank statement that long or any other document for that matter.'

'What about all the improvements he made to The Old Vicarage?'

'The money came from his terminal grant and Janet's inheritance. Both her parents died in 1988 and, of course, they were quite well off.'

'That's got to be wrong. Her father had been a higher

336

executive officer in the civil service and her mother had been content to be a housewife after Janet was born. And don't forget the parents had already mortgaged their property if Edmunds is to be believed. There couldn't have been much left over after they had been repaid.'

'You're clutching at straws to make a case against Edmunds,' Jill told him contemptuously. 'For your information, the parents owned a four-bedroom house on an acre plot just outside Woking in the heart of the commuter belt. And in case you have forgotten, the first housing boom occurred in 1972 and was followed by another eight years later.'

'I still don't buy it,' Ashton said.

'Well, that's just too bad. Robin Urquhart is satisfied with the explanation and from what I hear, so is Shirley Isles, who happens to be Head of the Foreign Office Security Department. Besides, Martin Edmunds is retiring at the end of the month.'

'Nothing like sweeping the mess under the carpet.'

'He is sixty-two years old,' Jill said with slow deliberation, 'and he is tired of living out of a suitcase. Now let's leave it and move on.'

'Whatever you say.'

'I've been making some enquiries about the diplomatic bag which was entrusted to Zawadzki. Apart from our Top Secret memorandum on the feasibility of establishing a base for the SAS on the west coast of Costa Rica, the bag also contained a paper on the legal implications written by Alistair Downward. In addition there were a number of letters pertaining to trade and cultural relations which Zawadzki was to have delivered to the embassies in Nicaragua, Panama, and El Salvador.'

Ashton frowned; he couldn't help feeling Jill was holding something back. When he had suggested they should discover the identity of the official or officials who had submitted papers for inclusion in the bag before it was known Martin Edmunds was unfit for duty, she had demurred and said that was a matter for the FCO to look at.

'So when did Downward submit his paper for inclusion?'

'Monday afternoon, the fourth of March,' Jill told him reluctantly.

'And where was he the following day when Edmunds phoned in sick?'

'In Brussels on European Union business.'

'So when did he return?'

'The conference didn't end until nine o'clock that night.'

'And?' Sometimes extracting information from Jill was like pulling teeth.

'Downward and the Minister for Trade and Industry returned to London by Eurostar. On arrival at Waterloo they were met by an official car and, after the minister had been delivered to his house in Chelsea, Downward was dropped off at his flat in St John's Wood. He did not go anywhere near the FCO. Any more questions?'

'Not at the moment.'

Jill consulted her millboard, then said, 'Finally, Victor asked me to tell you that when DI Copeland was in Special Branch, he dealt with the Head of the Kremlin watchers in MI5, our own Roy Kelso, and Downward's predecessor at the FCO.'

'But not Downward himself?'

'Alistair was introduced to Copeland in 1991, eighteen months before the DI retired on grounds of ill health. After the fall of the Berlin Wall the politicians told the FCO to clean up their act. There were to be no more dirty tricks, which is why Downward never had anything to do with him.'

'Says who?'

'At your request Victor raised the question at the Joint Intelligence Committee a fortnight ago; that's the answer he got from the Secretary of the Cabinet at the JIC meeting yesterday morning.'

Jill appeared to think that such an assurance coming from one of the highest-ranking civil servants in the land should be more than good enough for a Grade I Intelligence Officer, especially when the great man had the ear of the Prime Minister. And of course she was right in the sense that the Cabinet Secretary would have made far-reaching enquiries. But when you were practically sitting on top of the pyramid it wasn't easy to discover exactly what had been going on lower down.

'These aerial photographs have been supplied by the United States Air Force and National Security Agency,' Jill said, tapping the cardboard boxes with a pencil. 'They show Denver, Colorado, and the Chesapeake Bay area, the latter being the final location of the conference provided the talks on the Cyprus issue look as if they will lead to a successful resolution.'

'Why Denver?' Ashton asked.

'Because it's a long way from Washington and the White House should the talks break down.'

'That sounds as good a reason as any.'

'Well, we're all hoping things go smoothly. That's why I want you to study the photos in detail and pinpoint any potential trouble spots.'

'We're talking possible ambush sites?'

'Yes.'

'And you want me to do this?'

'Why not?' Jill said sharply. 'You're a trained photo interpreter, aren't you?'

Trained was stretching it a bit. Only two days had been devoted to the subject on the SIS induction course which Ashton had attended back in September 1982.

'Won't security be the responsibility of the FBI and US Secret Service?'

'Of course it will be and it's not my intention to tell them how to do their job. I just don't want to appear stupid if I'm asked to comment on the arrangements. OK?'

Ashton nodded. 'How long have I got?' he asked.

'I'm flying out to Washington on Sunday afternoon.'

'Close of play on Friday then?'

'Better make it lunchtime, Peter.'

'You've got it.'

'And you'd better warn Harriet that you might be coming with me.'

'I'm sure she will be thrilled.'

Ashton stacked the cardboard boxes one on top of the other, then picked them up and went on down to his office on the fourth floor.

In the opinion of Brian Thomas the average security file was a better read than most novels and a lot more honest than nine out of ten biographies. Before departing to preside over a selection board, the DG had summoned him to his office and handed over three security files belonging to the FCO.

'Run your eye over these,' Hazelwood had told him, 'and let me know what you think. We're looking for a new Head of Station, Beirut.'

From this Thomas deduced the present incumbent was going to be the next Assistant Director in charge of the Mid East Department, which meant Jill Sheridan was about to be confirmed in post. He also thought it fair to assume the high-priced help considered none of the Grade I Intelligence Officers in the department was good enough to be appointed Head of Station. He couldn't think why else Hazelwood would have gone to the FCO for a replacement.

Thomas plucked the third and last security dossier out of the in-tray and found it contained an earlier file within the covers. The candidate was a man called Joseph Fawkes who had joined the Foreign and Commonwealth Office at the age of twenty-nine, having previously served in the regular army, where he had risen to the rank of captain in the Intelligence Corps. This meant he'd had to be cleared by positive vetting before passing out of Sandhurst in order to be commissioned into what was known as a 'closed corps'. This file, which had been maintained by the army's Security Vetting Unit at Woolwich, had automatically been transferred to the Foreign Office when he had resigned his commission to join the Diplomatic.

Thomas began with the initial clearance Fawkes had been given while in the army, then moved on to the quinquennial review. During the intervening five years from 1972 to 1977 he had attended the Middle East College of Arabic Studies and had qualified as a first-class interpreter. His mother had died of breast cancer in 1975, some fifteen months before his younger sister, Melissa, had announced her engagement.

'Could I interrupt you for a moment, Brian?'

Thomas frowned and looked up quickly to see Ashton standing in the doorway.

'I didn't hear you coming,' he muttered.

'Must be a good read,' Ashton said, pointing to the open file on his desk.

'What can I do for you, Peter?' he asked, and pointedly closed the dossier on Joseph Fawkes.

'I've got a pile of aerial photos to study and I need a stereoscope. Unfortunately I can't find the tech storeman.'

'He's tacked on an extra week to the Easter break and gone to Rhodes. I'll get it for you.'

Ushering Ashton out of the office, he locked the door and walked him down the corridor to the stores section. There were eight stereoscopes on charge, each packed separately in a metal container not unlike a child's paintbox.

'I'll need your signature,' Thomas said.

'Be only too happy,' Ashton said cheerfully and waited, Biro in hand, for him to make out a docket.

'Anything else while I'm at it, Peter?'

'Well, I hesitate to ask but—'

'Wait a minute. Are you going to ask me to call in yet another marker? Because if that's what is involved you can forget it. Thanks to you I've just about exhausted my credit with the Met. You think that nonsense with Mullinder did me a power of good? Never mind what you did to Kevin Hayes.'

'This is different, Brian—'

'I don't want to hear it.'

But hear it he did because, as Thomas had learned many times, there was no stopping Ashton once he got the bit between his teeth. It was, apparently, merely a question of contacting the Chief Security Officer of British Telecom and persuading him to disclose the identity of the person Mr Martin Edmunds of The Old Vicarage, Woodstock, had telephoned some time on Tuesday, 5 March. Ashton was betting the unknown man was Alistair Downward, who had a flat somewhere in St John's Wood. He was, of course, unable to supply Downward's home number and, having checked the appropriate phone book for the area, it was evident the Foreign Office man was ex-directory. Finally Ashton thought both men would probably have mobiles of one sort or another but airily dismissed that as hardly a problem for British Telecom.

'And what if Edmunds used a pay phone to call Downward at home?' Thomas asked in spite of himself.

'He won't have,' Ashton told him. 'Edmunds was in bed with flu.'

'Listen, Peter, if you think it's as easy as you make out, why don't you have a word with this security officer?'

'You've had more to do with him than I have.'

'What does Ms Sheridan have to say about all this?'

'Jill will be working with Downward on the Cyprus issue; consequently she doesn't want to know.'

'You should take a leaf out of her book.'

'You want to tell me why?'

'Because you are in deep shit, Peter. The people on the top floor are getting ready to dump you.'

It had started when Ashton had been instructed to collect Mullinder from Paris. You didn't need a Mensa-qualifying IQ to guess who had blown the whistle on him. Jill had had second thoughts and could see the Permanent Under Secretary of State at the FCO refusing to confirm her in the appointment of Deputy DG. But it was the business at 5 Depot Close when he'd killed Hayes in self-defence which would really stitch him up. Although Ashton hadn't given his name when he'd made the 999 call, the police had found his plastic ID card and chain in his jacket pocket. And once they'd learned the police had established his identity, the people on the top floor had scarcely been in a hurry to bail him out.

'How long did you languish in the interview room before the tame lawyer from Middle Temple arrived?'

Ashton shrugged. 'A few hours. Victor Hazelwood and Jill were attending a conference at the FCO and it overran.'

'Seems to me your legal rep did nothing to preserve your anonymity, and without it you are not much use to the SIS.'

'It's early days yet, Brian.'

'You'd better start looking out for yourself. A couple of months from now there will be a coroner's inquest and some scumbag lawyer representing the Hayes family will be grilling you for hours on end. He won't be interested in discovering the truth; the family will have retained him solely for the purpose of finding out all they can about you. And one day when you're no longer with The Firm and the Special Branch officers have been withdrawn because it has been decided there is no threat to your person, some IRA splinter group will come after you and yours.'

'Thanks for the tip.'

'So what are you going to do?' Thomas demanded.

'Well, in between looking at enough aerial photographs to paper the walls of my office, I'll have a go at the Chief Security Officer at British Telecom.'

'Aw the hell with you.'

Thomas returned to his office, reopened the file on Joseph Fawkes and went through the folios until he found the enclosure he had been reading when Ashton had interrupted him. Fawkes, he learned, had disliked his sister's fiancé on sight. Interviewed again in 1981 at the ten-year point, he had seen no reason to change his opinion after his sister had married the man and much later in another interview had expressed no surprise when she had divorced her husband for cruelty in 1993. The world was said to be a small place and that was certainly true of The Firm. The man whom Melissa Fawkes had married in 1978 was Alistair Downward. Lifting the receiver Thomas punched out 0028.

'It's me – Brian,' he said when Ashton picked up the phone.

'I've changed my mind. I'll get the information you asked for from British Telecom.'

Osvaldo Herrara didn't know whether his name appeared on the FBI's most wanted list or not. However, since the CIA had been keeping tabs on him before he even became Fidel Castro's Deputy Chief of Intelligence he assumed the bureau was at least aware of his existence. The trick of staying one jump ahead of intelligence and law enforcement agencies lay in knowing instinctively where it was safe to linger, when to change your identity, and how long you could afford to stay in a hostile environment.

Matias Inciarte had ceased to exist the instant he had disembarked at Amsterdam where he had assumed the identity of Anthony Perez, a citizen of the United Kingdom born of Spanish parents. In this guise he had made a brief diversion to Cyprus and back before going on to Frankfurt, the penultimate stage of his journey to Toronto and the house he'd been renting on Packmore Avenue in the name of Simon Escobar for the past six months.

He had now been home, as he called it, for exactly a fortnight and Rauf Kaymak would be expecting to hear from him again. In Toronto it was 6 p.m., in London it was five hours later, and Rauf would be sitting by the phone waiting for it to ring. Lifting the receiver, he tapped out Kaymak's number. The phone rang out just twice, proof that his assumption had been correct.

'Hello, Rauf,' he said. 'It's me, Simon Escobar. How's business?'

'Picking up,' Kaymak told him. 'My partner is flying to Washington on Sunday to get a feel for things.'

'So what have you got for me?'

'The preliminary sales promotion will be held in Denver commencing Tuesday, April the sixteenth. Company reps arrive the night before and will be accommodated at the Burnsley on

Grant Street and the Cambridge at 1560 Sherman Street. Have you got all that or am I going too fast for you?'

'This isn't a race,' Herrara told him. 'Take it a little slower.'

'Sorry about that. You want me to repeat anything?'

'No. I'll tell you if I miss anything.'

'OK. My partner and the hosts will be staying at the Brown Palace Hotel; the conference itself takes place in the Civic Centre.'

'And when will you arrive in Denver?'

'Saturday, three days from now. You can get me at the Comfort Inn downtown.'

'Good. I'll be in touch,' Herrara said, and put the phone down.

There was a tight knot in his stomach and his mouth was dry. In going to Denver he would be lucky to stay one jump ahead of the law enforcement agencies and would be operating in a hostile environment longer than he cared to think about.

Chapter Twenty-Six

The mosaics consisted of aerial photographs mounted on stiff cardboard measuring two feet by eighteen inches. There were six in all, four of which covered parts of Annapolis, Alexandria and Washington while the other two showed the downtown area of Denver and the route from the international airport to the Civic Centre. The six were merely a representative sample of the scores of mosaics which Ashton had put together with the assistance of Nancy Wilkins. Since the safe in his office wasn't nearly big enough to accommodate the surplus, Ashton had been forced to lean them against the walls, facing inwards to hide them from prying eyes. It was his earnest hope that after briefing Jill Sheridan he would be able to consign the whole lot to the secret waste destructor.

'So what do we have to look out for?' Jill asked as soon as he walked into her office.

'A madman,' Ashton told her, 'somebody who is willing to sacrifice their own life in order to kill the designated target. I'm thinking of Prime Minister Rajiv Gandhi who was blown to pieces when a Tamil woman detonated the bomb she was carrying just as he was about to shake hands with her. There's no way you can protect anyone from a fanatic like that.'

'And are we likely to encounter a suicidal fanatic in Denver?'

'I don't know, you'll have to ask the FBI and the Denver Police Department.'

Ashton laid the mosaics on the spare chair, found the one he wanted, and placed it in front of Jill the right way up, then walked round the desk and stood beside her.

'This is downtown Denver,' he continued. 'All the hotels where the delegates will be staying are near the Civic Centre. The Burnsley is the furthest away and that's only just half a mile. Even so, I'm assuming the delegates will be transported to and from the Civic Centre, which will reduce the risk of somebody being picked off by a lone sniper. It looks a good location for the conference, it's compact and can be made secure without too much disruption.'

'What measures would you take, Peter?'

It was Jill's way of saying, what should I look out for? It was also symptomatic of her determination to appear with it should she be asked for her opinion.

'It would vary according to the nature of the threat,' Ashton said.

'Give me the worst case.'

'You take the normal routine measures and build on them. Basically this means you start with the conference building, which should be searched from top to bottom twenty-four hours before the delegates assemble for the first session. Thereafter it should be guarded round the clock, and first thing every morning sniffer dogs should give the place the once-over. Ideally, no one who isn't attending the conference should be allowed inside the building but I imagine this isn't possible. So you want X-ray machines and electronic metal detectors because nobody should be allowed to enter the building without being searched. No maintenance should be done on the building for the duration of the conference but if this isn't acceptable, workmen must have an escort at all times.'

The routes from the Brown Palace Hotel, the Burnsley and the Cambridge to the Civic Centre would have to be checked out at daybreak on the Tuesday morning. In practical terms this entailed lifting all manhole covers to make sure no explosive device had been left in the cavity below which could be detonated by remote control. No on-street parking was to be permitted on the designated routes, all litter bins were to be removed and mail drops sealed. Surveillance teams should be established on the tallest buildings, supplemented by a minimum of two police helicopters. These could be stood down after the delegates had arrived at the Civic Centre but would need to be reactivated when they returned to their respective hotels. All limousines put at the disposal of representatives attending the conference needed to be kept in secure compounds when not in use. Regardless of this precaution vehicles were to be inspected before every journey to make sure nothing had been attached to the chassis.

'Now we come to personal security measures,' Ashton continued. 'Hotels should be instructed to accommodate delegates on the same floor, preferably in adjoining rooms, which will make it that much easier to protect them during silent hours.'

'What do we do about the man who likes to smoke?' Jill asked.

'Treat him like everybody else and tell the hotel staff to fumigate his room after he has departed. You haven't said how long these talks in Denver may last?'

'That's because I have no idea,' Jill said.

'Well, I take it the delegates will be discouraged from going out on the town at night but that will be difficult to enforce should the proceedings drag on. If they do go out, you will need extra manpower for escort duties.'

'Is there anything else I should look out for?' Jill asked.

'Yes, the delegate who's got the hots for young women in short skirts. He's likely to give room service a whole new meaning. In other words the security men on hotel duty should turn away any woman who tries to visit a delegate in his room. Doesn't matter if the lady claims to be his fiancée, you don't want some hooker blowing him away. Same goes for any boyfriends.'

'That's only sensible,' Jill said. 'However, it occurs to me that the Greek and Turkish delegates will be at risk before they reach Denver.'

'You're right.' Ashton picked up the aerial mosaic of downtown Denver and replaced it with one that covered the area to the northeast. 'The international airport is twenty-four miles from downtown Denver. They will leave the airport by Pena Boulevard which links up with the I–70 after ten straight miles.'

Ashton didn't need to elaborate. Jill was quite capable of getting a feel for the landscape from the aerial photographs. Maybe the open, rolling countryside didn't offer much scope for a sniper but the numerous culverts and storm drains were a bomber's dream. Pack a hundred pounds of Semtex into a culvert, prime it with an electronically activated detonator and you could blow a busload of politicians into the next county while drinking a cup of coffee in one of the airport cafeterias. Of course you might dismember a few innocent men, women and children in the process but hell, what dedicated, self-respecting professional bomber would give a shit about that?

'We will have to adopt some of the security measures you've already indicated,' Jill said. 'Like checking the route into town and patrolling it regularly on the ground and in the air.'

'Right. Things get a little more tricky when we look at Washington and Chesapeake Bay—'

'Forget Chesapeake Bay.'

'What?'

'There will be plenty of time to look at the security implications in that locale.'

'I must be missing something,' Ashton said.

'It's very simple,' Jill told him. 'Should the two sides reach an agreement, they will wish to consult their respective Governments before signing a concord. That will take the best part of a week.'

'Inside information?' he asked.

Jill nodded. 'From Robin Urquhart,' she said, and handed him the mosaic. 'I'm surprised you bothered to enquire. By the

350

way, you will be accompanying me to Washington on Sunday. I hope you remembered to warn Harriet.'

'There's something you should know—' Ashton began.

'Don't tell me she has put her foot down?'

'This concerns Edmunds.'

'Not that man again—'

'He telephoned Alistair Downward on Tuesday, the fifth of March,' Ashton said, talking her down. 'The first time was at five to eight in the morning when Downward must have already left his apartment to meet the Minister of Trade and Industry. He then rang again at seven thirty that night.'

'When Alistair Downward was still in Brussels,' Jill said.

'I would be amazed if he didn't have an answering machine.'

'What is it with you, Peter? Why are you pursuing this vendetta against the man? Edmunds has already made one official complaint about your conduct and I had to do some pretty fancy footwork in order to save your neck.'

Ashton listened in silence as she reminded him that, as a result of her intervention, Edmunds had been grilled about his financial affairs by the security department of the FCO. Their subsequent report had given him a clean bill of health which had satisfied everybody else.

'With the exception of me?' Ashton suggested when Jill suddenly broke off for no apparent reason.

'I presume you got this information from British Telecom?' Jill said presently.

'Yes.'

'In writing?'

'No, and before you ask, I didn't record my telephone conversation either.'

The Chief Security Officer at BT had in fact rung Brian Thomas but Ashton wasn't about to repay a favour by dragging him into it.

'Any message which Edmunds may have left on Downward's answer phone will have been wiped from the tape long ago,' Jill mused.

351

'If we want to confront Edmunds I could always obtain a printout of his telephone bill to date. Downward is ex-directory and it might be interesting to hear him explain why he should know his home number.'

They could go one step further and pull Downward's phone bill but he doubted if Jill was prepared to go that far. For that matter her continuing silence implied she wasn't ready to tackle Edmunds either.

'Should I leave the aerial photos of Denver with you?' Ashton asked.

'No, that won't be necessary.'

Jill hadn't made a single note of anything he had told her but Ashton didn't find that surprising. She was blessed with a phenomenally retentive memory and could ingest facts like a computer. He picked up the mosaics he had left on the chair and started towards the door.

'About Edmunds,' she said, calling him back. 'Would you let me have a report in writing, please?'

'Surely.'

'By close of play today?'

'You've got it,' Ashton told her.

It was the first time Francesca York had had to go to Vauxhall Cross since Ashton arranged for the Admin Wing to issue her with a special ID card. Waving the piece of plastic at the harridan on the reception desk she sailed on towards the bank of lifts and was a little put out when Enid Sly called her back to examine it in detail. What annoyed Francesca more than anything else was the fact that the wretched woman had not only recognised her but had also known who she was.

'You'll be wanting to see Mr Ashton then,' Enid Sly observed after studying the distinctly unflattering head and shoulders photograph on the card.

'Yes. As it happens, he's expecting me.'

'All the same, I'll let him know you're on the way up.'

'By all means,' Francesca said with a glacial smile.

From the day they had first met, Francesca doubted if she and Enid Sly had exchanged more than a dozen words or so but that hadn't stopped them grating on each other like squeaky chalk on a blackboard. However, by the time she alighted at the fourth floor the scratchiness had disappeared. She felt even better when Ashton said it was good to see her again and actually sounded as if he meant it.

'What can I get you?' he asked. 'Tea or coffee?'

She recalled him warning her that it was difficult to tell the difference and politely declined the offer.

'So who is this Rauf Kaymak you mentioned on the phone?'

'I was hoping you could tell me,' Francesca said. 'All we know is that he is a Turkish Cypriot whose family owns the biggest hotel in Keryneia as well as a couple of high-class restaurants in Nicosia and Famagusta. The family sent him over here to keep an eye on their business interests in this country.'

'Well, how did he come to your notice?' Ashton asked.

'Yesterday morning he called on our friend the Irish property owner.'

'The man who runs his business from a semidetached house on Shoot Up Hill in Kilburn when he isn't providing a safe house for transitory visitors from Belfast?'

'Yes.'

'You mean he's still at large?'

'Yes, but now he's working for us.'

'How come, Fran?'

'We detained him again after you found Michael Ryan's body. This time he saw the light and decided to co-operate with us rather than face a long prison sentence.'

Paddington Green had almost become a second home for the IRA man and being detained yet again under the Prevention of Terrorism Act had not fazed him one bit at first. But some time during those seventy-two hours when he had been locked up, Richard Neagle had got to him. Fran had no idea how he had done it because she hadn't been present during some of the sessions. Privately, she believed Neagle and the Special Branch officer who had sat in when she had been absent, had threatened to stitch him up.

'Anyway, while he was inside, our technicians went over his office and private accommodation, bugging every room. We also managed to rent a flat across the road from his place so that we could keep an eye on him.'

'Do you know why this Rauf Kaymak called at his office yesterday?'

'Apparently Kaymak wanted to know if he had any properties to rent for a maximum of three months. We're missing two of the terrorists from Ozbek's cell and it's possible Kaymak has been moving them from one hiding place to another.'

'Have you got him under surveillance?'

'Round the clock for the next three days. After that, we may have to scale it down if there are no developments.'

Rauf Kaymak followed the A30 into Stockbridge, then turned left on to an unclassified road beyond the bridge over the stream. Shifting into third, he slowed down and kept a sharp lookout for the muddy lane on the right which led to Willow Cottage. Kaymak couldn't see how the cottage had got its name when there wasn't a single willow tree within half a mile of the place, neither could Alistair Downward. He simply referred to it as his weekend country retreat, a haven of peace and quiet he could escape to whenever he could get away from London. According to Alistair he had bought the place for a song fifteen years ago when the cottage had been in a dilapidated condition. Since then he had spent a small fortune on renovating the place from top to bottom. In part the work had been financed by leasing the fishing rights on the trout stream which was included in the deeds to the property. Somehow Alistair had managed to persuade Melissa to agree that, in assessing the terms of the divorce settlement, Willow Cottage would be valued at the original price. He had also contrived to hang on to the villa in Keryneia without paying through the nose for the privilege.

Even though this was far from being the first time Kaymak had been to the cottage, he still contrived to overshoot the lane. Braking to a halt, he selected reverse and started to back up. Moments later he nearly had a heart attack when the driver of a Ford Escort blasted an angry warning because Kaymak had forced him to overtake on what was virtually a blind bend. There were two men in the car and he wondered if this was the same vehicle he had spotted in his rear-view mirror some ten miles back. Heart still pounding, Kaymak tripped the indicator and turned right into the lane. The heavy rain which had started shortly after six thirty had made the lane treacherous and the Volkswagen Passat fishtailed a couple of times when he struck a particularly muddy patch. Fortunately Willow Cottage was only a hundred yards from the road.

Alistair was already there, his Mercedes E220 parked in the gravel drive near the kitchen window. Kaymak pulled in behind it, switched off the engine and, alighting from the Volkswagen, ran for cover under the porch. Alistair met him at the back door before he could ring the bell. In the drawing room at the back of the cottage, a compact disc of *Sinatra's Greatest Hits* was playing.

'I must say you have brought some terrible weather with you,' Downward observed cheerfully, as he stepped aside to let him into the hall. 'I expect you could do with a stiff drink.'

'I would appreciate one of your single malts with a touch of water.'

'I think I'll join you,' Downward said, and closed the door, then led the way into the drawing room and switched off the music centre.

The drawing room was full of photographs in silver frames, all of them featuring Alistair. Some had been taken years ago when he had been at Eton and later up at Oxford; others had probably been hidden away while he was married to Melissa. One of them was so suggestive that even someone as naïve as his cleaning lady could hardly fail to miss the homosexual overtones. Kaymak wondered if the photographs had simply been put on display for his benefit.

'Admiring your own artistry, Rauf?' Downward enquired lightly.

Kaymak took the glass of whisky from his outstretched hand. 'Not especially,' he said.

The photograph in question had been taken on the balcony of Alistair's villa on the hillside above Keryneia. Downward had posed for him leaning forward, his stomach resting on the balustrade, the linen slacks he was wearing stretched skin tight against his upraised buttocks. He was glancing over his right shoulder and smiling lasciviously into the camera.

'I haven't worn too badly, have I, Rauf?'

The photograph had been taken in 1984 on one of the many visits he had made to the Turkish Republic of Northern Cyprus without Melissa. Then aged thirty-six, Alistair had looked much younger thanks to his blond hair, slim figure, and pretty boyish face. Anyone seeing them together could be forgiven for thinking they were the same age, whereas Kaymak had been only twenty-one when they had first met. Now, twelve years on, Alistair still didn't look his age though he was much fuller in the face and his waistline had thickened.

'From your silence it's apparent you don't agree with me,' Downward said, obviously piqued.

'Nonsense, you're a very handsome man and always will be.'

'Please don't be cross with me, Rauf.'

It never ceased to amaze Kaymak that he could exercise such power over a man like Downward who had been born into a wealthy family, had gone to the most famous public school in all England and had it within him to become a Permanent Under Secretary of State if he so chose. But he had this unaccountable urge to behave dangerously even though he appeared to realise that one day his sexual proclivities would destroy him.

'I'm off to Denver tomorrow,' Kaymak said. 'Have there been any developments I should know about before I leave?'

'One,' Downward said briskly. 'I had a phone call from Ms Sheridan late this afternoon informing me that Mr Peter Ashton will be joining the team.'

'An Intelligence Officer?'

'Very much so.'

'Is he any good?' Kaymak asked.

'Ashton made a name for himself when he was an analyst on the Russian Desk; then he became what you might call a field agent, except he's based in London. Some of his colleagues regard him as a loose cannon but there's no denying he does get results. However, at the moment Ashton is in trouble with the hierarchy and we can rely on Ms Sheridan to keep him on a tight leash. She is not going to allow him to damage her career.'

This, Kaymak realised, was the public face of Alistair Downward – confident, incisive, fearing no one and in control of whatever situation he was faced with. Strange then that he had this need to be physically dominated.

'Will Ashton be staying at the Brown Palace Hotel?' Kaymak asked.

'He may be told to go home after we have finished our business in Washington. If Ashton does go on to Denver, he will be a last-minute addition and may have to be accommodated in another hotel.'

Whatever happened, Downward wanted it clearly understood that Ashton was to be left alone. He was not a threat and there had been too many unnecessary deaths already. The National Guard, which claimed to be the will of all Turkish Cypriots, should have left it to him to achieve their aims by diplomacy. He had the ear of the Deputy to the Permanent Under Secretary of State and could have persuaded him that Ankara's desire to join the European Union should not be conditional upon the betrayal of the Turkish Cypriots.

'It's no good regretting what might have been, Alistair. Neither of us had any choice but to follow orders since the nature of our relationship was known to Intelligence.'

'You make it sound so damned inevitable,' Downward complained.

'It was after those photographs fell into their hands. If they should be released, your career will be finished and I will go to prison because what we did to each other is considered a crime in Turkey.'

'This is never going to end, is it, Rauf? No matter if we are successful in Denver, I will always be at the beck and call of the men in Ankara.'

'You're wrong, Alistair.' Kaymak reached inside the breast pocket of his jacket and took out a sealed envelope. 'This is a sign of their honourable intentions.'

'Photographs?' Downward asked, fingering the envelope.

'And the negatives.' Kaymak finished the single malt and left the empty glass on the mantelpiece next to a picture of Downward taken outside the Sheldonian when attending a degree ceremony, then went out into the hall and opened the front door. 'I think you'll find the snapshots are the ones which were stolen from your villa in Keryneia. I advise you to burn them before they fall into wrong hands again.'

'What about the video?'

'All in good time, Alistair.'

Kaymak left the house, got into the Volkswagen Passat and drove off. All the way back to London he kept looking in his rear-view mirror to see if he was being followed by the Ford Escort he had encountered earlier in the evening.

Osvaldo Herrara arrived in Denver on United Airways flight UA285 from Chicago at 13.37 hours local time. Before leaving the airport, he bought a copy of Georgia and Hilary Garnsey's *City Smart Guidebook* from one of the bookshops in the terminal building. He then spent fifteen minutes nursing a cup of coffee while browsing through the publication. To learn that the Hispanic community represented twelve per cent of the population and was the largest minority group in Metro Denver was particularly comforting since this demographic factor was to his advantage and would enable him to merge into the background much more easily. Noting that a large proportion of the Hispanic population lived in West and Northwest Denver, he turned to Section 3 of the guide where the hotels, bed-and-breakfast and motels were listed by areas. Luck was definitely on his side; the very first hotel he called from a pay phone was able to offer him a suite.

The Table Mountain Inn on Washington Avenue in Golden, West Denver, was an all-suite hotel. Nestled between North and South Table Mountains and the Rocky Mountains Front, it was also, according to the guidebook, in the heart of Golden's downtown historic district. Herrara registered as Simon Escobar, the alias he had been using for the past six months in Toronto, and presented an American Express card in the same name. He told the desk clerk he was taking a short vacation in Denver with a view to adding another Spanish restaurant to the chain he already owned and would be seeking the advice of the Hispanic Chamber of Commerce. From the gift shop he purchased copies of *El Seminario* and *El Sol* Spanish newspapers, then went up to his suite on the second floor and unpacked. Ten minutes later he rang the concierge and ordered a cab to take him to the Daniels and Fisher Tower in downtown Denver.

After paying off the cab at the tower, Osvaldo Herrara walked to Tabor Center where he boarded the 16th Street Mall Bus to the Civic Center station at Broadway. Thereafter he walked the routes from the hotels where the Turkish and Greek delegates would be staying to the conference building in the Civic Center.

The ideal ambush position was one that offered an unrestricted field of fire, was unlikely to be discovered before and after the hit, and enabled the sniper to withdraw from his position unseen.

Chapter Twenty-Seven

Ashton joined the other nationals line, passport, visa application and customs declaration form in one hand, executive briefcase and plastic bag containing a bottle of duty-free Scotch in the other. In a last-minute change of plan he had been routed to Denver via Chicago O'Hare instead of Dulles International, Washington. Furthermore he was travelling alone, sans Jill Sheridan, sans Alistair Downward, the man who had caused it.

The whole business had started at nine o'clock on Saturday morning when Francesca York had telephoned him at home with the news that Special Branch officers had followed Rauf Kaymak to a cottage midway between Stockbridge and the village of Houghton. Kaymak had arrived at eight twenty-five and departed just under an hour later. Although neither Special Branch officer had seen the owner of Willow Cottage, subsequent enquiries had revealed that the Mercedes E220 parked in the drive belonged to Alistair Downward.

Ashton had immediately passed the information on to Jill but she hadn't viewed it in quite the same light. As he saw it, Downward had already been involved with too many questionable people like Martin Edmunds, and Charlie Copeland before he was killed; now there was Rauf Kaymak, the Turkish Cypriot who appeared to be on at least nodding terms with the IRA. In the eyes of the Foreign and Commonwealth Office Downward was the greatest living authority on the Cyprus problem but there were three better reasons why he should be excluded from the forthcoming talks in Denver.

Jill had disagreed with Ashton when he had made this point to her. And she had continued to do so even though Francesca York had called him at midday to report that Kaymak had been observed boarding a United Airlines flight to Washington and Denver.

'What evidence do you have of any wrongdoing?' Jill had demanded. 'And don't quote Mullinder at me because he's up for manslaughter and would say anything to get himself off the hook.'

She had wanted to know what possible motive Alistair could have for sabotaging the talks and had told him he was clutching at straws when he had suggested that perhaps Downward was being blackmailed. Their difference of opinion had led to him being sent to Denver, ostensibly to liaise with the FBI, while she and Downward hobnobbed with officials of the State Department.

The line moved slowly forward; eventually Ashton reached the head of it and handed his passport, visa application and customs declaration form to an officer of the Immigration and Naturalisation Service. Ten minutes later, having passed through Customs, Ashton returned to the departure hall, his passport stamped with a visa good for nine days. The onward journey to Denver was by American Airways flight 1181 departing from Gate 55 at 18.45 hours.

The stranger joined him shortly after he had checked in with the airline desk.

'The name is Carl Volkman,' he said, and plumped himself down in the adjoining seat. 'That's Carl with a C and Volkman with just one N. We're on the same flight to Denver.'

'Well, this is Gate 55,' Ashton said, not unreasonably.

'Matter of fact we're staying at the same hotel.'

Mr Volkman was beginning to annoy Ashton. He hadn't asked for his company and didn't want it. 'And which hotel is that?' he asked.

'Why, the Brown Palace Hotel, Mr Ashton. Where else?'

'How did you know my name when we've never met before?'

'I'm FBI,' Volkman said, and produced his badge cupped in the palm of the right hand. 'I'm what you Brits call a minder.'

Volkman looked the part even sitting down. Ashton estimated he was at least six feet two and weighed over two hundred pounds. It was hard to judge Volkman's age; his short black hair was flecked with grey but that was an unreliable yardstick. Ashton had known some men who had turned grey before they were thirty.

'You're going to take care of me?' Ashton queried.

'On instructions from Director Louis Freeh. See, you are what we call a frequent visitor to the US of A and ordinarily that would be fine by us but trouble seems to follow you around. Up at Lake Arrowhead you ran a man down with a Ford Thunderbird; in St Louis there was a small problem with a 130 mm nuclear shell. On Nine Mile Drive outside of Richmond, Virginia, you torched a two-million-dollar property and destroyed three automobiles, one of which belonged to a finance company, and the staff at St Clare's Hospital on New York City's West 51st Street will not forget you in a hurry. Now you're on the way to Denver and we'd kind of like the mile-high city to stay the way it is and not go into orbit.'

'You needn't worry,' Ashton told him, 'I'm only there as an observer.'

'Well, we're going to have a fun time together because there's plenty to see in and around Denver. So, OK we'll go through the motions of earning our pay cheques, look at the measures we're taking and maybe compare lists of the bad guys, but that's as far as it goes. You catch my drift, Peter?'

'I think I'm way ahead of you,' Ashton said.

Volkman left him when one of the girls of the American Airlines desk announced that flight 1181 would now commence boarding starting with first class. Ashton's fun time began with the discovery that, as a johnnie come lately, he had been

363

allocated a seat at the back of the McDonnell-Douglas MD80 nearest the toilets and with the least amount of leg room in the entire cabin.

Herrara parked the Ford Contour he'd hired from Budget outside the Comfort Inn on 17th Street and went inside. In his experience hotels were invariably busy no matter what day of the week or what time of day it was and the Comfort Inn was no exception on that Sunday evening. Every clerk on the reception counter was busy dealing with guests who wanted to register and he had to stand in line for a good ten minutes before anybody was free to deal with him. Smiling warmly at the girl on the desk, he told her a Mr Rauf Kaymak was staying at the hotel and asked if she would call his room number and inform him that Mr Simon Escobar was waiting in the lobby.

'He arrived yesterday,' he added in case there was any doubt in her mind.

When Kaymak appeared in the lobby, they made a show of embracing one another for the benefit of anyone who might be watching them, then moved out into the street. As they approached the Ford Contour, Herrara took out the remote control, deactivated the alarm and released the central locking.

'We'll cruise around, talk things over and then have a bite to eat some place.'

'That's fine by me.'

Herrara grunted. He wasn't looking for Kaymak's approval and didn't need it. Starting the engine, he shifted into drive and continued on down 17th Street past the Brown Palace Hotel to make a left into Broadway.

'Tell me about the four men I trained in London?' he said abruptly. 'One is dead, another under arrest. Correct?'

'Yes.'

'Then where are the other two?'

'They are still in hiding.'

'In London?'

'Yes. They have been moved from place to place.'

Kaymak should have sent the pair of them back home soon after they had set foot in the country when it became apparent that neither one could speak a word of English. They were a total liability. Sooner or later they would be picked up and he wouldn't trust them to keep silent.

'Do they know you?' he asked Kaymak.

'They've seen me.'

'That isn't what I asked.'

'They don't know who I am or where I live in London.'

Herrara didn't believe him. He was also quite certain that if Kaymak was ever apprehended the Turkish Cypriot would not hesitate to divulge everything he had learned about him. Simon Escobar would disappear without trace in Denver; the man who set off on the first leg of the long journey to Naples would be Anthony Perez, UK citizen born of Spanish parents. The problem was that this was an alias he had used before when he'd flown to Cyprus to meet Kaymak but there was nothing he could do about that. Although a new identity was waiting for him in Naples he had run out of legends on this side of the Atlantic. What had seemed a justifiable risk while he was still in Toronto had suddenly become a suicidally rash decision.

'Who else knows you are staying at the Comfort Inn?' Herrara asked.

'No one.'

'What about Downward?'

'He hasn't asked and I haven't told him.'

'I don't want you to see that man while we are in Denver. Don't telephone him and don't leave any telephone messages at his hotel. Understood?'

'Yes. Alistair is very discreet anyway. He makes sure we are never seen together in public.'

Herrara figured he had been travelling north for long enough. At the intersection of Broadway and 23rd Street, he made a left and headed in the direction of the Front Range, having read in the guidebook that the mountains were always to the west, if ever you weren't too sure of your bearings.

'There is something you should know,' Kaymak continued. 'A man called Ashton has been added to the British team. He is an Intelligence Officer and is said to be dangerous.'

'It's the Americans who are in charge of security from the moment the delegates arrive to the time of departure. I know them very well; they will only pay lip service to any advice he may offer.' Herrara pressed the cigar lighter in the dashboard, took out a packet of Marlboro and lit a cigarette. 'Now let's forget Ashton,' he said, and drew the smoke down on to his lungs. 'What I want to hear about is the gear you are supposed to have acquired for me and where it's hidden.'

During the five days he'd spent in Denver in the last week of March, Kaymak had purchased a roll of adhesive tape some three inches wide and a pair of scissors from a hardware store in Aurora. The M72s, both handguns and two battery-powered, hand-held synthesised radios had been supplied by the Iron Mountain militiamen of Wyoming, a right-wing organisation dedicated to preserving the pioneer spirit of the Old West.

'I packed everything into a wooden crate along with some makeweight and left it in a depository on York Street.' Kaymak cleared his throat. 'I paid three months' rent in advance effective from Friday, March twenty-ninth,' he added.

'How many rocket launchers did you buy?'

'Two, like you said.'

The militiaman whom Herrara had put him in touch with lived twenty-four miles north of Laramie in a small community called Bosler where he owned a sporting goods shop. After Kaymak had introduced himself, he had closed the store, loaded a sealed container into his 4-wheel drive and whisked him off to what he called his test firing area at Morton's Pass in the Iron Mountain.

'I personally opened the sealed container and selected one of the M72 rocket launchers which he then fired.'

'And you had the pick of the remainder?' Herrara said.

'Yes. They may have come from an obsolescent lot and batch number but I can guarantee there won't be any misfires.'

'And the handguns?'

'They're 9 mm Smith and Wesson model 469. We didn't test fire them on the range but I stripped both of them and they are in perfect working order.'

'I guess that's it for this evening. Tomorrow morning at ten thirty sharp we'll meet in the lobby of the Comfort Inn and go down to the Civic Center.'

Herrara picked up Interstate 25 and headed south to cross South Platte River for the second time. 'Then I'll go over your role in the operation.'

'My role?'

'I need to create a diversion,' Herrara said cryptically. 'You're going to provide it.'

The guided tour of Denver started for Ashton at seven thirty in the morning with Volkman whistling him down to the Civic Center. Standing in the middle of the plaza, the FBI agent pointed out the Capitol Building clearly visible beyond the Bronco Buster Statue and the Denver Public Library on West 14th Avenue Parkway which dominated the Greek Theatre on the south side of the square. As Volkman described the security measures which had already been taken, it rapidly became evident to Ashton that he had nothing to contribute in that area.

'You've thought of everything, Carl.'

'I like to think so.'

'Just one question, though. Who have your people been told to look out for?'

'You mean the bad guys? Well, that's everybody practically whose name appears on the list your Deputy Director General sent us.'

Not for the first time Ashton couldn't think why Jill had decided that his presence was necessary on this side of the Atlantic. When forwarding a list of suspected terrorists to

Washington she must have known she was pre-empting what little information he could have imparted.

'We had to prune her list,' Volkman continued. 'The more faces you give a man to remember, the more likely he is to overlook that one that counts.' A faint smile appeared at the corners of his mouth. 'The list wasn't entirely accurate anyway. Three of the names on it are out of circulation, all of them Islamic fundamentalists. Two are in jail in Saudi Arabia, the third was killed in a traffic accident in Beirut last December. Fact is, your Ms Sheridan covered every base ten times over.'

Quantity rather than quality? That didn't sound like Jill, but she was still running the Mid East Department while holding down the appointment of Deputy DG and maybe something had had to give. One thing was certain, all three errors were attributable to her former department and someone's head was going to roll for that. All the same, Jill had never submitted a sloppy piece of work in her life.

'Do you think we could compare notes somewhere?' Ashton asked.

'Sure, why not? Let's use the City and County Building. It'll give me a chance to show you our command centre.'

The City and County Building was in Bannock Street on the west side of the plaza. Somebody's office on the 4th floor had been commandeered and turned into a command post which, amongst other things, had led to the installation of additional telephone lines and a Data Reception Unit linked to the FBI Building in Washington. A dozen monitor screens displayed images captured by the remote-controlled TV cameras mounted in the plaza as well as those in 17th Street, Broadway, Grant Street, and Sherman Street which covered the routes from the Brown Palace Hotel, the Burnsley, and the Cambridge to the Civic Center. There was also a transmitter/receiver which provided one-to-one communication with all mobiles. Ashton didn't understand half the technical details Volkman threw at him and he had a sneaking suspicion the FBI agent didn't either.

368

'Although the Greek and Turkish delegates don't arrive until late this afternoon, the system is already up and running.'

'I'm impressed,' Ashton told him.

'Yeah, we like to think we are on top of the situation,' Volkman said, and opened the communicating door to the adjoining room which it seemed had also been commandeered. 'It's quieter in here,' he said.

'Right.'

'You got your list handy?'

Ashton reached inside the breast pocket of his anorak and produced three sheets of A4 stapled together which had been folded in half lengthways. Originally classified as Secret, he had topped and tailed all three sheets thereby removing the over-inflated security grading. From the expression on Volkman's face Ashton got the impression this didn't meet with his approval.

'Before we get into this thing, Peter, what the hell is EOKA-B?'

'The short answer is that it's the son of EOKA, the National Organisation of Cypriot Combatants, the extremists who wanted Enosis, meaning Union with Greece, which the Turkish element of the population wouldn't have. EOKA waged guerrilla warfare against us from 1955 to 1958 but they didn't get what they had wanted.'

Instead Cyprus became an Independent Republic with a Greek Cypriot president and a Turkish Cypriot as vice president. It hadn't worked; by 1964 there was a state of civil war between the Greek and Turkish Cypriot communities. Efforts were made to settle the dispute peacefully but the Greek population was split between those who supported President Makarios and those who still found the idea of Enosis attractive.

'Things went from bad to worse. General Grivas, the man who'd founded EOKA, returned to the island, contacted his old supporters and put them back into the field as EOKA-B, this time attacking the Makarios Government. Eventually there's a military coup staged by the Cypriot National Guard, apparently with the support of Athens, and the Turkish army moves in. End of story.'

369

'So what do I read into all that?' Volkman demanded. 'That we can forget EOKA-B?'

'I wouldn't go that far but if you're looking at winners and losers, I think the Greek Cypriots have the most to gain from a settlement.'

'If you say so.' Volkman produced a fountain pen from his top pocket and uncapped it. 'Now let's see what we can do about this list of yours,' he said.

Ashton watched him go down the list column by column, page by page to put a line through four names before taking out a whole section with a diagonal cross.

'We don't regard the IRA as a threat,' Volkman said, referring to the major deletion.

'We do.'

'That's not the issue here. The IRA is smart. They know if they put a foot wrong in this country no more funds from Noraid will reach them, and it will be a hell of a lot easier for your people to extradite any gunman who takes refuge in America.'

The three Islamic Fundamentalists had, of course, been deleted but there was a fourth man whose name stopped Ashton in his tracks.

'You've ruled out Osvaldo Herrara,' he said incredulously.

'So?'

'Well, he's the man who armed the IRA boobytrap on the Warlock Estate.'

'Yeah?'

Ashton had never heard so much doubt expressed in a single word. 'For God's sake, he was identified by Francesca York, an officer in MI5.'

'OK, you've got an eye witness . . .'

'We've got a second witness,' Ashton said, interrupting him. 'An Immigration officer at Immingham saw him board a ro-ro ferry to Amsterdam.'

'Listen to me, the CIA has been tracking Osvaldo Herrara since the day he first came to notice. This was way back in 1981

370

when he was supposed to be a member of the Cuban Trade Mission visiting Moscow. Right now they have him placed in Tehran where he has been languishing for the past four weeks.'

'How good is their information?'

'Better than yours,' Volkman said. 'Now why don't we take a run out to the airport and look at the security measures we have taken on Interstate 70 East and Pena Boulevard? Then we'll get up in the air and view the city from above.'

And after that, Volkman would probably show him the Botanical Gardens, the City Park and Denver Zoo, anything in fact which kept him on the sidelines.

Kaymak was waiting in the lobby of the Comfort Inn when Herrara arrived exactly at ten thirty just as the Cuban had said he would. For the sake of appearances they shook hands in a perfunctory manner but nobody in the busy foyer paid any attention to them. With a light touch on his elbow Herrara steered him out into the street.

Last night the temperature had fallen to a low of 27 Fahrenheit and Kaymak had woken up to find the street below his bedroom window was carpeted with a thick frost. Since then the thermometer had risen to a touch under 60 and the frost had disappeared, yet despite the sweater he was wearing under a tweed jacket, Kaymak felt chilled to the bone. It was, he knew, symptomatic of the fear that had gripped him ever since Herrara had let it be known he was to take an active part in the operation. Together yet apart the two men walked down 17th Street. As they passed the Brown Palace Hotel Kaymak was conscious of being watched by the external TV cameras on the tenth floor of the Republic Building across the street. At the intersection of 17th with Broadway, they turned right and walked three blocks south to the Civic Center. The building Herrara was interested in stood on the corner of Lincoln Street and 14th Avenue and was one of the original office blocks in Downtown Denver.

'See that place over there?' Herrara said with an almost imperceptible nod. 'That's the Westgate Building. The first floor is the head office of a software company, the next three are occupied by White Star Insurance, the fifth is leased to a firm of brokers and at the top we have Nixon, Lowenstein Willowby, Attorneys at Law. Tomorrow afternoon at four o'clock we've got an appointment with one of their associates.'

'Which one?'

'Whoever occupies the corner office,' Herrara said.

Chapter Twenty-Eight

Downward woke up sweating, breathless, his heart pounding. The nightmare was still so fresh in his mind that for some moments he believed the bedroom was on the second floor of the Hotel Kobatas overlooking the Bosphorous. In the recurring dream, which happened to be true, the police had unlocked the door with a master key supplied by the night manager and had caught Rauf in bed with him. They had not been allowed to dress. After handcuffing them, the intruders had covered their nakedness with the sheets off the bed before they were taken downstairs and bundled into a closed van. Rauf had seemed as terrified as he had been, though for different reasons. Homosexual practices were not unknown in Turkey, especially Istanbul, but officially there was no such thing as sodomy between consenting adults. In truth Rauf had been looking at a minimum sentence of five years' imprisonment. As for himself, Downward had feared word of his arrest for an act of gross indecency would reach the British Embassy in Ankara, which of course would have meant the end of his career. The fact that what they had done in private was perfectly legal in England would have been irrelevant. The Permanent Under Secretary of State would have claimed that Downward had brought the Diplomatic Service into disrepute and would have demanded his resignation.

He had expected to be taken to the nearest police station and charged. Instead he had ended up in an army barracks being interrogated by a major in the Intelligence Branch. The interrogation had taken a novel form, the major dealing him one obscene photograph after another. All of them had been taken at his villa in Keryneia over a period of at least eighteen months and at first he'd assumed Rauf had been a willing accomplice. Only much later had he allowed himself to believe this had not been the case.

The proposition which the major had put to him had seemed harmless enough. No charge would be laid against Rauf Kaymak and the British Embassy would never learn of his disgraceful conduct. For this to happen, he was required to use whatever influence he had to secure recognition of the Turkish Republic of Northern Cyprus.

It had taken Downward only a few minutes to weigh the alternative and decide which option he preferred. They had been arrested at eight minutes past one in the morning; three and a half hours later they were safely back in their adjoining rooms at the Hotel Kobatas. The night manager had been conspicuous by his absence.

Rauf Kaymak had readily confessed to his involvement with the Turkish Military and had begged to be forgiven. He had claimed that their intimate relationship had become known to the Assistant Garrison Commander of Keryneia, who had threatened to send him back to the mainland for trial by court martial. This he could easily have done since Kaymak had been a part-time soldier in the Turkish National Guard. On orders of the Assistant Garrison Commander, Rauf had persuaded Downward to spend a weekend in Istanbul in September '93 when he customarily spent three weeks at his villa in Keryneia.

He had accepted Rauf's explanation and they had resumed their relationship. The truth was that, like an addict dependent on heroin, he could only come to life when the younger man indulged his sensual proclivities towards domination and bondage. So he had quietly promoted the Turkish Cypriot case for a separate state without being too obvious about it. Then the whole damned political situation had turned around and the

374

Turkish Government appeared ready to modify their position on the Northern Republic if this would facilitate their admission to the European Union. The policy change had sparked a violent reaction from a clique of middle-ranking Turkish army officers and suddenly Downward had found himself drawn into their conspiracy.

He had become their paymaster, juggling the money allocated to him from the secret fund to open a numbered account for Osvaldo Herrara with the Investment Trust Bank at Estavayer-le-Lac. To replace the money he had to do business with Martin Edmunds who, in his capacity as a Queen's Messenger, had been smuggling drugs into the UK for years. In the beginning he had derived enormous satisfaction from his ability to stay one jump ahead of his superiors in the FCO. Then Edmunds had succumbed to a bout of flu and thereafter everything had started to unravel. And whenever he had tried to draw back, Rauf Kaymak had appeared with another batch of photographs.

The phone rang, causing his heart to beat even faster. Turning over on to his left side, Downward reached out and lifted the receiver off the cradle in time to hear the hotel operator inform him it was his wake-up call for seven o'clock.

'Thank you,' he croaked.

'You're welcome,' the girl said. 'Have a nice day.'

Downward kicked the sheet and blankets off and got out of bed. In two hours' time the first session of what promised to be a difficult round of talks would begin.

Ashton followed his 'minder' into the City and County Building on Bannock Street and went on up to the fourth floor. Without Carl Volkman in attendance there was no way he would have been admitted to the Command Centre which, if ever Ashton had needed it, was another reminder of just how superfluous he was. Last night he had spent an hour with Jill Sheridan trying to make her see that his continued presence in Denver was simply a waste of the taxpayers' money. Apart from his arguments falling on deaf ears, Jill had suggested that, if he felt so badly about staying at the Brown Palace Hotel, no doubt arrangements could be made to move him into a bed-and-breakfast establishment.

Ashton could think of only one reason why Jill should want to keep him tied to her apron strings. Either on her own initiative or after consulting Robin Urquhart, which seemed the more likely, she had failed to inform Victor Hazelwood of Downward's association with Rauf Kaymak. He imagined Urquhart must have been pretty short with her and she had been reluctant to tackle him again after he had passed on the news that Special Branch officers had observed Kaymak boarding a United Airlines flight to Denver. Knowing Jill as he did, Ashton reckoned she was frightened he would brief Victor Hazelwood if she allowed him to return to London ahead of her.

'The show'll be on the road any moment now,' Volkman said, and pointed to the monitor screens.

Parked outside the Burnsley on Grant Street was a white stretch limousine displaying a miniature Greek flag from a chrome nine-inch mast screwed into the hood near the radiator. A similar limo was outside the Cambridge at 1560 Sherman Street, but this one happened to display the Turkish flag, comprising a white crescent and star on a red background.

'I can't tell you what problems we had with those limos.'

'Problems?' Ashton said bemused.

'You bet your sweet ass,' Volkman grated. 'You can't have one delegation riding around in a black car while the other crowd has a white one. It wouldn't be politically correct. Took for ever to find another hire company which could supply the same colour.'

Presently the two delegations appeared on the sidewalk at exactly the same time and got into the limousines. As both vehicles moved off, two hitherto blank screens came to life to give an aerial view of their progress from the police helicopters above.

★   ★   ★

Until he had reconnoitred the downtown area and picked out a suitable ambush position Osvaldo Herrara had been unable to determine precisely what ancillary equipment he would need. Once he had settled on the law offices of Nixon, Lowenstein, Willowby a suitable glass cutter had become his number-one priority. From a hardware store in the Aurora shopping mall in East Denver he had purchased two suction cups and an electrically powered cutter. He then bought an executive briefcase from a leather goods shop which was large enough to accommodate these purchases. Dumping everything into the boot, he got into the Ford Contour and drove off.

From the shopping mall on Almeda Avenue, Herrara continued in an easterly direction to connect with Interstate 225. The clock in the dashboard was showing 11.15; by now Kaymak would have collected the wooden crate from the depository on York Street and would be making his way to the rendezvous outside Sedalia in the pick-up he'd rented yesterday afternoon. Herrara had picked Sedalia off the Colorado Utah road map. What he had been looking for was somewhere fairly isolated yet reasonably close to Denver and the place he had finally chosen was roughly twenty-six miles from the city and appeared to meet the criteria.

It was a fine bright morning; no clouds in the sky, the temperature up on yesterday's and expected to reach 64 Fahrenheit at noon. At least that had been the forecast he had caught on Channel 2 before leaving the Table Mountain Inn. He'd also hung on long enough to watch the Greek and Turkish delegations arrive at the Civic Center. A voiceover had informed him the preliminary session was scheduled to finish at 5 p.m. It would, he thought, be a hell of a thing if the conference broke up in the early afternoon without him being aware of it; switching on the car radio, Herrara selected Station KO AM85, which was dedicated to news and sports.

Herrara left the interstate at exit 183 to head west to Sedalia on State route 67. Twelve minutes later he came upon Kaymak parked off the road in the pick-up and signalled him to follow on. According to the road map the population of Sedalia was under five hundred but that was still four hundred odd too many for his liking and he turned off on to a dirt road going south. The grassland on either side of the track looked more dead than alive and had yet to green up after the winter snows. After covering approximately four miles without coming across a house or passing another vehicle, Herrara pulled off the dirt road on to a flat piece of ground that hadn't been wired off.

It was only after Kaymak had drawn up alongside him that he noticed the signboard planted amongst a straggly group of saplings.

Herrara got out of the car, walked over to the saplings to have a look at the signboard and learned that the golf course in the shallow valley below was the private property of Hiram J. Zinfaldon III. Nobody was playing on the course and there wasn't a house to be seen for miles.

'Any problems?' Kaymak asked on joining him.

'None,' Herrara said.

'Likewise.'

'How long had you been waiting for me back there?'

'No more than fifteen minutes, time enough for half a dozen vehicles to pass, all but two heading towards the Interstate highway. Nobody stopped to ask me what I was doing there.'

'Good. Where did you leave the pick-up last night?'

'In the light rail parking lot at Interstate 25 and nobody gave me any trouble there either.'

'OK, let's get on with it.'

Herrara returned to the Ford, opened the trunk and packed the electrical glass cutter and extension lead into the briefcase and placed it on the back seat. By that time Kaymak had cut the bonding tape the depository had wrapped around the crate and had drawn a couple of nails with a claw. It then took him another eight minutes to draw the remainder and remove the lid.

The makeweight inside consisted of an assortment of old tyre levers, car jacks, links of rusted chain and a sledgehammer. The military equipment was protected by wads of foam rubber.

Herrara removed the two battery-powered, hand-held, synthesised radios and placed them on the ground. The hand-guns were the Armament Systems and Procedures Version of the 9 mm Smith and Wesson M39 which Herrara had seen and used before. The pistol had been developed for men in the US Government Service or Law Enforcement who had need of a well-concealed weapon of high reliability and good first-shot accuracy. It was seven and a half inches long, had a seven-round magazine and weighed exactly one and a half pounds when fully loaded.

There were two shoulder holsters for the pistols and a carton containing twenty-four rounds of 9 mm. Herrara broke the seal, plucked a handful of rounds from the carton and deftly loaded the magazine, then inserted it into the pistol grip, pulled the slide back to chamber a round and applied the safety. For a man who had served in the National Guard and pronounced both weapons serviceable after allegedly stripping them, Kaymak was all fingers and thumbs. In the short time he had known him, Herrara had come to regard the Turkish Cypriot as a blowhard. Kaymak liked to pretend that he had been a founder member of the movement whereas he had been recruited under duress and was merely a means of applying pressure on Downward to keep the Englishman on board. Snatching the magazine from him, Herrara finished loading it, chambered a round into the breech and then walked off towards the saplings carrying both semi-automatics.

'Where are you going?' Kaymak asked in a hoarse voice.

'To test these weapons.'

The golf course was still deserted, as was the surrounding area. After releasing the safety catch on his pistol, Herrara fired a round into the earth, then did the same with the other weapon.

'You're mad,' Kaymak told him when he returned to the vehicles, 'completely mad.'

Herrara was tempted to inform the Turkish Cypriot that he

would be mad to trust him but the fact was he needed Kaymak. Instead of bawling him out, he simply tossed the semiautomatic at Kaymak, pointed to the shoulder holster and told him to put it on. For a while Herrara thought he would have to do it for him but eventually Kaymak got the hang of it so that the pistol and holster fitted snugly under his left arm and there were no telltale bulges in his jacket.

The 66 mm M72 rocket launcher was approximately twenty-six inches long in the retracted mode and weighed a fraction over five pounds. Herrara placed the rocket launchers on top of one another and got Kaymak to hold them in place while he used a roll of black adhesive tape to bind them together. He also taped up the canvas sling attached to the launcher so that it resembled a leather handle. Although larger and much heavier than a normal briefcase, he reckoned it was good enough to deceive the casual eye. Leaving Kaymak to dump the crate among the saplings, Herrara picked up the rocket launchers, scissors and roll of adhesive tape and transferred them to his car. Subsequently it only took him a few minutes to set both synthesised radios to the same channel and check they were in working order.

'I'll give you ten minutes' head start,' Herrara said, and handed Kaymak one of the radios. 'Soon as you've parked your vehicle come up on the air using call sign one five, give your location and I'll come and pick you up. OK?'

Kaymak said he didn't see any problems with that arrangement. A mere three minutes after he'd left the area, the first car from either direction drove slowly past. Herrara smiled, tipped a salute to the driver and received the same in return.

By three o'clock Ashton was going bug-eyed from watching the TV monitors. Nothing was happening and while Denver undoubtedly had a lot going for it, looking at the same scenery for hours on end tended to dampen one's enthusiasm for the architecture that had made the city. The truth was he had nothing to do and all day to do it in. If the talks dragged on for any length of time and every day was like the one before he was going to end up like a bear with a sore head. Carl Volkman might not be in charge of the security operation but he appeared to know all the agents from the local office and they involved him in all their deliberations.

The hotel staff had provided Ashton with a copy of *USA Today*, which he had read over breakfast. In between gazing at the monitor screens he had also read the *Rocky Mountain News* from front page to back that one of the FBI agents had left in a wastebin after he'd finished with it. What he needed right now was a breath of fresh air.

'I think I'll take a stroll,' Ashton announced to no one in particular, 'maybe take in the State Capitol.'

'If you like to hang on for thirty minutes I'll come with you.'

The way Volkman said it Ashton got the impression he didn't have any choice.

Guided tours of the State Capitol were offered every forty-five minutes from 9.30 a.m. to 2.45 p.m. on weekdays from Monday to Friday inclusive. Herrara and Kaymak were not dressed like the average visitor but nobody took any notice when Herrara parked the Ford Contour in a vacant slot on the west side of the building. So far things were going better than Herrara had dared to hope; communications had functioned without a hitch, Kaymak had left the pick-up in the parking lot adjacent to the Denver Performing Arts Complex and he had collected him from there within minutes of learning his location.

His only cause for concern was Kaymak. Glancing at him as they walked down 14th Avenue towards Lincoln Street, Herrara could tell he was tighter than a spring that had been overwound. Maybe it was due to the fact that he couldn't bring himself to believe the rocket launchers he was carrying could be mistaken for a briefcase? He should have swapped briefcases with him before they alighted from the car but it was too late for regrets now. Herrara thought Kaymak looked a shade better when they turned the corner and entered the Westgate Building.

As they walked down the hall, the attendant on the information desk greeted them with a quizzical expression.

'We have an appointment with Nixon, Lowenstein, Willowby,' Herrara told him and continued on towards the elevators at the far end.

Of the three elevators, one was stuck at the fourth floor, another was on the way up while the third had just passed the second floor on the way down. Drawing Kaymak with him, Herrara stepped to one side and faced the information desk. Four people alighted from the elevator, none spared them so much as a passing glance. As soon as the car had emptied, Herrara stepped inside with Kaymak and pressed the button for the sixth floor. After what seemed an interminable delay the doors finally closed and the car began to ascend before anybody could join them.

Herrara had no idea what to expect when they stepped out on the sixth floor but he knew the corner room overlooking the 14th Avenue and Lincoln Street had to be to the right. He supposed he might have guessed Nixon, Lowenstein, Willowby would employ a receptionist to intercept visitors; fortunately she happened to be on the phone, her back to the elevators and they swept right past her.

The corner office was occupied by Anthony J. Franco, attorney at law. Finding the door locked, Herrara opened the one next to it and walked in on his secretary. The woman looked to be in her early forties, had light brown hair cut in a pageboy style and was a little on the plump side. A Dymo tag pinned to her black jacket identified her as Belinda McKendrew. Herrara drew the semiautomatic from his shoulder holster and pointed it straight at her face.

'Don't say a goddamned word,' he told her in a quiet voice.

'Please don't shoot me.'

'I promise you I won't do that. Now be a good girl and open the door to Mr Franco's office.'

382

'It's not locked.'

'Then lead the way.'

Belinda McKendrew stood up and walked over to the communicating door mewling softly to herself. Signalling Kaymak to lock the other door, Herrara followed the secretary into Franco's empty office, and told her to get down on the floor.

'Please don't hurt me.' Her voice trembled and sounded like a child on the brink of tears.

'I won't if you just do as you're told.'

Herrara placed his briefcase on Franco's desk, took out the roll of adhesive tape and told Kaymak to gag and tie her up. Before the day was out he would have to kill her but that was something he would keep from Kaymak until the very last minute. Meantime he needed to cut a large aperture in the window.

Volkman's half-hour turned out to be nearer fifty minutes and even then he tried to persuade Asthon there was no point in going to the State Capitol.

'I've just remembered the last guided tour went through at two forty-five,' he said.

'I'm happy to see it from the outside.' Ashton smiled. 'Anyway, all I want to do is stretch my legs.'

'Listen, in less than an hour the delegates will be leaving the Civic Center and I intend to be here when they do.'

'You don't have to come with me, Carl.'

'You can't be serious,' Volkman told him.

At ten minutes past four they left the City and County Building on Bannock Street and made their way through the plaza.

The glass was a lot tougher than Herrara had bargained for and the grating noise which the electrical cutter made set his teeth on edge. To cover the whole frontage of the Civic Center he needed to cut an aperture some twelve inches long by nine high, a task that was being hampered by Kaymak. Afraid somebody would come to investigate the noise, he had positioned himself by the door to listen for the sound of footsteps in the corridor. Although it made sense, Kaymak's imagination was working overtime and he kept signalling Herrara to stop work, often for several minutes at a time. The frequent delays angered Herrara and stretched his nerves to breaking point. For quite illogical reasons he cursed Fidel Castro who had stripped him of his army rank because he had made the mistake of seducing the wife of the President's closest friend. He raged at the Colombian drug barons whose money he had taken and who would therefore never let him go. But as of now his number-one hate was Pavel Trilisser, Special Adviser on Foreign Affairs to President Yeltsin, whose freelance agent he'd been and who had then sold him on to those crackpot colonels in Ankara.

Their plan for preserving the Turkish Republic of Northern Cyprus had been complicated, overambitious and impracticable given the bunch of incompetents they had recruited. Assassinate one of the leading Turkish diplomats in favour of a settlement and sabotage any possibility of a successful outcome. Crap, total crap.

Half an inch to go; Herrara checked to make sure the suction pads were in the right position to hold the glass in place, then cut through the last sliver. As he straightened up after laying the cutter on the floor, he saw the stretch limousines enter the plaza and realised the first day of talks was finishing earlier than had been anticipated. He grabbed the wooden handles of the suction pads and transferred them one at a time to the section he intended to remove. He gave a sharp tug to pull the twelve-by-nine-inch piece of glass into the office but it refused to budge. He tugged even harder with the result that one of the suction pads came off and suddenly there was no holding the glass. It struck a ledge on the floor below and bounced clear of the building to shatter into a thousand fragments on the sidewalk.

★   ★   ★

The pedestrian lights had just changed to 'Walk' and Ashton was about to cross from Broadway and 14th Avenue to Lincoln Street when he heard a loud bang followed by a high-pitched scream. At the same time Volkman started yelling at him to turn back. The conference was breaking up and he was needed in the Command Centre.

Ashton ignored him and kept on going. Diagonally across the street from him shreds of glass littered the sidewalk and at least two people were down, one of whom appeared to be unconscious. The sun was in the west playing on the corner building and, looking upwards at each floor in turn, Ashton spotted a black looking square in the corner window on the top floor. He looked back over his shoulder and in an instant realised a sniper up there would have a clear field of fire at the Civic Center.

'Sniper,' he roared at Volkman and pointed upwards, then started to run.

He ran diagonally across the traffic on 14th Avenue which now had a green light and was moving east closing on him from behind. Every driver pressed the horn at the same time creating a deafening cacophony of noise, underscored with a screech of tyres and the occasional crump of metal-to-metal contact between vehicles. A policewoman who'd been attending to the injured, tried to apprehend Ashton but he grabbed her right wrist and hauled her round the corner and into the Westgate Building.

Ashton had no doubt that had she been left-handed and wearing the pistol on the other hip, she would have taken it out and shot him. Kicking and punching, he dragged her past the information desk, elbowed his way to the front of a group of people waiting by the lifts and bundled her into the first available car before it had emptied. Nobody wanted to join them which was hardly surprising since both seemed to have an inexhaustible vocabulary of four-letter words.

*　　*　　*

385

Osvaldo picked up the nearest 66mm launcher and extended the inner tube, which automatically cocked the weapon, then pushed forward the trigger safety handle and erected the front and rear sights with his thumb. The maximum effective range against a stationary target was 300 metres. The distance to the Civic Center was 400 but that didn't worry him. In theory the missile could reach out to 1000 metres and he had every confidence in his marksmanship. He positioned the weapon on his right shoulder at the point of balance and pressed the firing bar on the top of the tube. The high-explosive antitank rocket had just left the launch tube and was beginning to accelerate when the Greek delegation moved off in their limo.

Although Herrara knew the missile was going to miss the target, he watched in total fascination as it hit the steps in front of the building and exploded. The Turkish delegation was somewhere inside the building and he had no idea who the dead man lying at the foot of the steps with his left arm blown off at the shoulder could be. Still dazed, Herrara discarded the empty tube and reached out for the second launcher.

'You're mad,' Kaymak screamed.

Herrara turned to face him. 'Kill the woman,' he said in a dangerously soft voice.

'What?'

'I said kill the woman.'

'The hell with you, I'm getting out of here.'

Kaymak wasted precious seconds before it dawned on him that the door to Franco's office was still locked and there was no key on the inside. In a blind panic he half ran, half stumbled towards Belinda McKendrew's room. Snatching the Smith and Wesson from his shoulder holster, Herrara fired twice. The first round caught Kaymak in the right side, the second hit him just above the ear and blew his head apart.

By the time Herrara picked up the launcher and made it ready to fire, the limousine carrying the Greek delegation was no longer in sight. 'Time to go,' he said, and pointed the semiautomatic pistol at Belinda McKendrew, then changed his mind about killing her.

Volkman entered the Westgate Building and ran towards the knot of people clustered round the elevators at the far end of the hall. Holding his badge aloft, he shouted he was FBI and told them to move out of the way. Several tried to let him know what they had seen but he could put two and two together for himself. The only thing that puzzled him as he pushed the button and began to ascend was why the other car had stopped at the fifth.

Ashton had never met such a tiger. The policewoman might be just five feet six and under a hundred pounds but she could punch, kick, scratch, knee and bite with the best of them. And somehow, while they had been flailing away at each other, she had managed to press the stop button, halting the car at the fifth floor.

'Now listen to me,' Ashton shouted in her face. 'There's a sniper on the top floor and we've got to deal with him.'

She took a bit of convincing but finally she stopped kicking him in the shins and he released her grip on her wrist and pressed the button to send the car on up to the sixth floor. Ashton thought he had drilled it into her that she would cover him while he moved a few paces ahead to scout for the sniper. That all went by the board when they bumped to a stop at the top floor. As the doors opened, a bunch of frightened people surged into the car, momentarily separating Ashton from the police-woman. By the time he had fought his way out of the lift she was twenty-odd feet ahead of him and about to turn into the lateral corridor. He yelled at her to wait for him but she was in no mood to listen.

He heard the loud crack of a pistol fired in a confined space somewhere round the corner to his right. In such a situation nine people out of ten would have stopped dead in their tracks but not her: she stepped out into the corridor, shouting, 'Police. Freeze.'

Ashton ran after the policewoman, saw her go down wounded in the thigh after the gunman fired again and threw himself on top of her. She had dropped her firearm and he scrabbled after it while still trying to shield her body. He managed to get a finger inside the trigger guard and drew the revolver towards him. Folding his palm around the pistol grip, he looked up to Herrara running straight at him, his right arm extended to take aim at his head. Ashton squeezed the trigger and kept on squeezing until all six chambers were empty. Someone standing behind him was also shooting at the Cuban. Empty cases continued to rain down on Ashton long after Herrara had stopped moving. Rolling over on to his back, he found himself looking up at Volkman.

'Welcome to the party,' Ashton said. 'Think you could get an ambulance for the lady?'

In Ashton's experience there was never an abrupt and tidy ending. Officers of the Denver Police Department took a long and very detailed statement from him and afterwards the District Attorney in charge of the case had asked some pretty searching questions. He had particularly wanted to know why Ashton hadn't given the officer a chance for a back-up and he had told the DA he'd thought it more important to deal with the sniper before he blew up the Greek delegation. In any case she had been the only police officer in the vicinity. The DA had then implied that he had failed to use minimum force which Ashton had thought was pretty rich considering how many times Volkman had shot the Cuban. However the DA did have one bit of good news to impart: the bullet which had struck the woman police officer in the thigh had gone straight through the leg missing the bone and there would be no long-term effects.

388

It was gone ten o'clock when Ashton returned to the Brown Palace Hotel. The staff had turned down the bedspread and left a mint chocolate on his pillow. The winking red light on the telephone indicated that someone had left a message for him. The someone was Jill Sheridan, who asked somewhat meekly if he would spare her a few minutes, late as it was.

Ashton collected the bottle of Scotch and walked it down to her room and tapped on the door. When Jill opened it, he noticed her feet were bare and she was wearing just a dark blue slip. As she turned away from him and returned to her armchair, she looked a little unsteady. He didn't have to look very far for the reason; the mini bar was open and there were half a dozen empty miniatures lined up on the table.

'Alistair Downward is dead,' she said in a slurred voice. 'His arm was blown off right in front of me. It was terrible.'

'Yes, it must have been,' Ashton murmured, and felt inadequate because he couldn't think of anything else to say.

'The Greeks have walked out, they're going home tomorrow.'

'That's hardly your fault.'

Jill appeared not to hear him. 'There have been so many mistakes – Edmunds, Downward, Kaymak, Mullinder.'

It was the closest Jill would ever come to admitting that she had made a mistake but she hadn't been the only one who'd fumbled it. With the benefit of hindsight, Ashton knew he should have gone after Downward and leaned on him the moment he'd learned Edmunds had warned the Foreign Office man that Adam Zawadzki would be taking his place on the Costa Rica run. Christ, Brian Thomas had told him what Downward's ex-wife had said of him and even before the Turkish boyfriend came to light, he should have acted on his presentiment that the man was open to blackmail.

If he'd got BT to produce a record of the phone calls Downward had made in March, a Costa Rican number would have shown up. Armed with that information, they could have taken him out of the game, which would have cut Osvaldo

Herrara off from the one person who was in a position to supply him with up-to-the-minute Intelligence. So, OK, Jill had made it abundantly clear that he was to leave Edmunds and Downward well alone, but he could have gone over her head and persuaded Victor to do something.

But what the hell; life was full of ifs and buts. Until today he hadn't really known what Herrara had been paid to do. The rigorous application of routine security measures had done for the Cuban, plus a large slice of luck when part of a window had shattered on the sidewalk.

'What will you tell Victor?'

It was, Ashton thought, typical of Jill that at a time like this she should be concerned about her career. She knew they would have to face a Board of Inquiry on their return and feared his statement would damn her. 'I'll tell him he can stop worrying about Osvaldo Herrara.'

What else was there to say? The Greek delegation had walked out and were threatening to go home, which in the short term would be a victory for the men who'd employed the Cuban. But tomorrow was another day and sooner rather than later, the talks would be resumed.

'Thank you, Peter.'

'That's OK.'

'You don't have to leave. Harriet will never know.'

Same old Jill. His word wasn't good enough for her, she had to have some hold over him to ensure he danced to her tune.

'Sorry, but I'm not tempted. There's been one honey trap too many already.'

'What?'

'Downward and Kaymak,' he said, and walked out on her.